TWIN
DAGGERS

TWIN DAGGERS

NEW YORK TIMES BESTSELLING AUTHOR

MARCYKATE CONNOLLY

BLINK

BLINK

Twin Daggers
Copyright © 2020 by MarcyKate Connolly

Requests for information should be addressed to:
Blink, 3900 Sparks Dr. SE, Grand Rapids, Michigan 49546

Hardcover ISBN 978-0-310-76814-2

Ebook ISBN 978-0-310-76816-6

Cover direction: Ron Huizenga
Interior design: Denise Froehlich

Printed in the United States of America

20 21 22 23 24 / LSC / 10 9 8 7 6 5 4 3 2 1

MY LIFE IS A CAREFULLY CONSTRUCTED LIE.

Even now as my sister and I prepare to slip into the darkness of the tunnel network that runs beneath our city, each movement we make must remain cloaked by magic. Everything we say, everything we do, is designed to mislead and persuade that we're exactly like the people we live amongst.

If we're found out, we'll be executed.

The lid of the drainage tunnel—far too heavy for us to lift by hand—rises into the still night air. Zandria continues to weave her hands in quick, furtive motions, moving the cover with her magic, while my own incantation stirs the air fast enough to make us imperceptible in the darkness of the alley. Zandria nods at me to go first and I climb down the grimy ladder into the black, never dropping my spell.

I hit the floor as she's halfway down the ladder, and the lid clicks back into place. The city of Palinor sleeps above us while we creep along its filthy underbelly. This is our nightly ritual. When the sun sets, we head for the tunnels and hunt for what our people have lost.

We are Magi, a once powerful people decimated by the Techno-Magi wars one hundred years ago. The Technocrats bombed our schools and hospitals, did everything they could to destroy our children and future. For centuries we ruled these lands; now we are just beginning to rebuild our numbers. Our hatred of the Technocrats fuels us as we strive to recover what they stole.

The mere fact we exist is dangerous. Palinor isn't a country that looks fondly on magic. They fear and loathe it. The Technocrats believe they all but eradicated us in the wars. Their leaders have lied to them, relegating us to the status of mere specters in the dark.

They're wrong.

We have adapted.

My twin sister and I are living proof. All Magi can use magic on organic matter, but our powers are different. We can cast spells on anything, including the machines. It is our greatest secret, one we must hide from everyone but our parents. Our legends speak of a Magi sect that once tried to manipulate inanimate matter. They were cast out as tainted, their work destroyed, and their bloodlines removed from our histories. Simply being Magi is the least of our worries.

"This place is nastier than usual," Zandria complains as she bumps her hip into mine. I cling to the rim of the ceiling and scowl at her. One false move and I'll be swimming with the rats.

"And you're just as foolish," I say, taking the lead again. "Now hush."

"You hush," she says. I don't have to turn around to know she smirks at the back of my head.

But she's right—the last few days have been warm and rainless, and it smells fouler than ever down here. The ointment we painted under our noses hardly dims the stench when it's this bad. We creep along the stone walkway in single file. I drop the concealing spell and instead whisper the one that makes our steps soundless.

Guards are usually stationed above, near the entrances, and rarely down in the tunnels. But if there ever are any, we're prepared.

"Aissa, how much longer do you think we'll have to keep this up before Mama and Papa let us do something more interesting? Mapping these tunnels is getting old."

I stifle a snort. Nothing is ever exciting enough for my twin.

Our parents began the mapping project last year, then handed it off when we turned sixteen last month, but we've only scratched the surface of the tunnel network in our nightly missions. This is our first excursion in this sector. The mapping is tedious, but important. It is said that somewhere down here lies the remnants of the Magi's library. All those spells we lost, crushed by the Technocrats and buried under their shiny metal Palace.

"It's necessary. Besides, we haven't been doing this for long at all. We have to prove ourselves before the Armory will move us up the ranks. We can't expect to be at Mama and Papa's level until we've done our share of grunt work."

"But what fun will that be?" she whines.

"Keep your voice down. Do you want to get caught?"

"We haven't encountered a soul yet. I could scream and no one would bat an eye."

"Except for me," I say.

She smirks again. "Yes, except for you."

This may not be the most glamorous task, as my sister reminds me every night, but it is important. Mama and Papa—and our leaders in the Armory—entrusted us with this mission. If we fail, we'll lose our parents' trust and the respect of our fellow Magi. Maybe even our lives if we get caught. Failure isn't an option. Which means we have to work hard and stick this out until the Armory sees fit to promote us.

And ensure they never find out what our magic can do to the machines.

As we walk through the tunnels, we reach out with our magic, probing the walls for hollow spaces behind them. The Armory had hoped that if the Technocrats built their Palace on top of the ruins of our Magi city, exploring these tunnels would uncover sections that survived. In fact, we already have found evidence; the first time we ventured beneath the city, Zandria and I ferreted out a hidden passage beyond the tunnel wall that was clearly much older than what the Technos had plastered over it. Any doubts our parents may have had about giving us this assignment were laid to rest that very night. But not every tunnel has secrets. The sector we spent the last week exploring had none, much to our disappointment.

After one hundred feet, we reach what appears to be a curve in the tunnels. But my magic immediately discerns the gap behind it.

"Here," I whisper to my sister. We exchange a quick grin, then get to work.

Zandria watches our backs and I hum at the wall. We're alike in so many ways—twin features and bright red hair, even matching black tunics and pants on our nightly outings. But when it comes to magic, my sister prefers handspells while I'm partial to incantations. Singing isn't necessary for magic, but it helps me focus. The words and magic and music combine in my head and let the power flow through me in a rush of heat.

Pity we Magi have lost so many of our spells.

Pity the Technocrats who stole them from us.

The wall moves apart, each brick carefully placing itself on the ground at my command, creating two new, shorter walls on either side of the walkway.

A shadowed doorway now stands in its place, tempting us onward. The tunnels run beneath the entire city, but now this section belongs to us.

"*Fiero*," Zandria whispers, and a white light dances in her palm. She holds it aloft and takes the lead while I hum a silencing spell and pull out my paper and graphite to note our path.

We barely take a half dozen steps before I halt in my tracks and whirl around. I swear I heard something thump behind us.

I peer into the darkness. Nothing.

Then the sound comes again.

A trickle of ice slithers down my spine.

"Zandy!" I hiss. "Wait!" I rush back to the doorway and crouch down to the bricks to hum a new spell, willing them to hurry and move back into their proper places. In less than a minute, it's like we never passed. Zandria stands wide-eyed behind me, not daring to speak a word. My heart pounds in my throat and I press my ear to the wall.

"Human or machine?" Zandria whispers. Her hand twines with mine, something we've done since we were little and afraid of the dark.

I shake my head. "Can't tell."

She weaves her free hand and murmurs. The brick near eye level slowly slides toward us. I flinch when it scrapes against the one beside it.

"What are you doing?" I should've cast the silencing spell again. I do it now hurriedly, before whoever is out there gets any closer.

"We need to know who followed us." She squeezes my hand. Above all else, we must protect each other.

"At least put out your light." She extinguishes it, and we're engulfed in shadows. Something runs over my foot and I tighten my grip on her hand. Stupid rats. They'll be the death of me.

The sound is distinctive, a double thump and a pause, which repeats. Over and over.

Just when I decide it's only a patrolling automaton we could easily disable with our magic, a tall boy comes into view around the corner, his form lit by the lantern swaying in front of him. I attempt to clamp a hand over Zandria's mouth before she can gasp, but she ducks and elbows me in the ribs, then settles back so we can both keep watching.

His pale hair curls at the ends against his neck, and his nose is long and straight. When the light catches his eyes, they remind me of pools of moonlight. Pale blue and cold. His pants and tunic are a light gray, not the usual steel-gray uniforms the guards wear.

But he isn't making that strange noise. The small machine next to him is.

Its two legs whir and hit the ground at alternate times, propelling the odd thing forward. It seems to be following the boy.

When he begins to mutter, Zandria and I hold our breath.

Does he know this tunnel exists? The only entrance we've found is through a door of our own creation.

"Where could it be?" He pauses a few feet before our hidden tunnel and presses his palms to the wall.

Oh no. If he does that here, he'll notice the missing brick for certain.

I drag Zandria down to the floor. "I'll put it back as quietly as possible," she says before I can speak.

She repeats her weaving and the brick rises from the floor, moving agonizingly slow into the brick wall. I bite my tongue when it slides into place.

"What was that?" We can just hear the muffled words of the boy.

I clutch my sister and we flatten ourselves against the tunnel wall. Then I hum, ever so softly, moving the air around us to obscure our figures should he find a way through the wall. I should've kept it up after we left the alley and let Zandria handle the silencing spell.

The sound of hands moving along rough stone comes from the wall. Seeking, scraping . . . hunting.

Who is this boy? What could he be looking for so secretively, if not this tunnel? But how would he even know it's here? The only reason we found it is because bricks and metal respond to us. Anyone else would need a door or a map. When Mama and Papa were mapping, the guards patrolled the drainage and sewer tunnels from time to time, but as far as my parents could tell it was just a routine.

There is absolutely no good reason for him to be here.

The scrabbling grows louder and the brick shifts slightly. I freeze. Just the thought of getting caught down here, what that would mean . . .

Zandria pulls me to my feet and shoves me down the stone corridor. We have to escape before he finds us.

"*Fiero,*" Zandria whispers again. The soft light hovers over her hand, once more lighting our steps as we hurry into the maw of the abandoned labyrinth.

We stumble and pause at the sound of a falling brick.

Another brick hits the stone floor. We run down the corridor, the stonework archways flying by us. A sharp clatter and a grunt echo toward us.

"Hello? Who's there?"

"*Rapide,*" I whisper. We won't be able to keep this pace for long, but at least it will put some distance between us and him. Whoever he may be.

We tear through tunnel after tunnel, turn after turn. Though we're in new territory, I lead the way. Something tugs me forward, a sixth sense of which direction to choose. When we slow, the walls have taken on a darker color and glossy sheen.

"*Aissa,*" Zandria says. "This section . . . it's not like the rest of the tunnels."

She's right. The passages we've mapped until now have all been brick or steel or stone. And most in some form of disrepair. Here, the arches are higher and multicolored marble panels are built into them. The black walls have a luminescent gleam, giving off a light of their own.

"It's lovely. Strange though. It doesn't look like something the Technocrats would build." I stand on my tiptoes and run my hand along the crux of the arch with my eyes closed. Tingling magic reaches into my fingertips. The flush of discovery creeps up my neck and cheeks.

"The Technos definitely didn't build this section."

She repeats my action and grins. "You know what this means?"

"Magi," we say together, breathless.

"That boy may still be following, so we must be quiet. No one else can know about this," I say. Zandria sobers. We walk slower down the corridor this time, studying it now that we aren't being chased. The presence of magic is tangible. Whatever hides behind these walls must be powerful enough to allow the magic to seep into the marble.

And it's ours.

My entire body feels like it's vibrating. This is what drew me here, nudging me as we ran. Fear and adrenaline must have opened my senses to it. Questions fill me, but no one is here to answer.

"I can feel it in my toes. It tickles," Zandria says with a soft giggle. But when we turn the corner at the end of the hallway, we're both struck mute.

A door. A perfect, black, glossy door, oozing magic and secrets.

And nothing else. It's a dead end. The door is the only way to move forward.

My pulse begins to race and Zandy lets out a laugh. I'm too excited to bother to shush her this time. We've found something important. Very important, by the looks of it. This find will make our parents proud, and the Armory too. Maybe we'll get promoted sooner than I thought.

My thoughts darken momentarily. That boy was looking for something. What if it was this door? But what would a Technocrat want with something the Magi made?

Zandria grabs the knob, but it doesn't give the slightest twist.

"It's locked. Incredibly well locked."

"Let me try." I hum, then sing, "*Apere.*" But when I try to open it, again the door doesn't budge. I pinch my lips together, frustration brewing in my chest. We've never encountered this problem before.

"Forges!" Zandria grumbles, placing her hands on her hips.

"Were you expecting a welcome mat?" I ask.

"From the Magi? Absolutely." She scowls.

"Maybe this isn't theirs," I wonder.

"Who else would have a magic doorway under Palinor? The stories all claim the Technos built their Palace on the ruins of the Magi library. This fits."

"I wouldn't object to you being right," I say, grinning so wide my teeth tingle from the excess magic in the air.

"Let me try again," she says.

We take turns, vainly attempting every spell we know to force the door to open. The lightness that filled me only a few minutes ago begins to fade.

While it wouldn't be surprising for most Magi, this is the first inanimate thing that hasn't responded to my sister and me. Yet it's clearly of magical origin.

With a heavy heart, I put a hand on Zandria's shoulder after her tenth try. "I've had enough. Haven't you?"

She whirls, throwing her hands up. "I'm dying to know what's inside."

I snort. "Me too, but I don't think we're getting in there tonight. We have to tell Mama and Papa. They might know why we can't get past this door." I frown. "And we need to tell them about the boy."

Hopefully he's gone by now and we can safely exit these blasted tunnels. What was he seeking? Could it really be this door and what hides behind it? It's the only thing of real interest we've seen in this section.

"No," she objects. "Not yet! They'll be so disappointed we were followed."

"We can't endanger the Armory's entire mission just because we're embarrassed we almost got caught. They'll understand. We haven't been at this for long."

She pouts. "I know, but I'd hoped we'd find this library quickly and get promoted out of the drains." She shudders, and I can't help following suit. I'd love to get out of the drainage tunnels too, but the mission is more important than our personal ambitions.

It's more important than all of us.

Finding our way out of the tunnels is more difficult than usual. I didn't have time to map our path when we fled the boy. Now we retrace our steps while jumping at every noise we encounter.

That Techno and his mechanical creature could be anywhere.

The distraction doesn't help. We get lost several times and turn down wrong paths and dead ends. Zandria glowers and barely says two words to me the whole way. She isn't happy I want to tell Mama and Papa about both the boy and our failure to get past the mysterious door. She's never one to play by the rules. If she knows she can get away with something, she'll do it simply because she can.

I, on the other hand, refuse to do anything that might endanger our people, our cause, or our mission. My loyalty is unwavering. That's the problem with my sister; she lives for the moment, one day to the next. But I can't help thinking of the big picture. Everything I do, every step I take, has ripples. That's also what I love about being a spy. Each action, each bit of information I glean, furthers our cause. Brings us closer to defeating our enemy.

Every Magi spy is a weapon, waiting to strike. That's why our elite underground network is called the Armory.

We've seen no sign of the boy and Zandria grows bolder every second. We should reach the hidden entrance any minute. Zandria finally thaws and jostles into me as she dances down the passage, her red hair flaming behind her.

"Zandy, stop being so careless. He could still be here!" I whisper, then hurry her around the last corner.

She laughs. "He could be, but he isn't."

I freeze, staring past my sister. The amusement on her face melts. She turns to see what has me transfixed.

Our hidden entrance is no longer hidden. It's completely destroyed.

The boy managed to take down the entire section of wall. Our nightly missions are no longer secret. And if the Technocrats discover we're Magi, all is lost. The entire hope of our people rests on the tiny web of spies planted in Palinor. While the inhabitants of this city sleep in comfort, believing the war to be long over, for us, it is just beginning.

"Still amused?" I ask my sister. "The Technos will investigate this. We'll be lucky if we can even get into the tunnels from now on."

Zandria pouts. "Stupid Techno boy. What could he be doing down here? As far as they know, there's nothing but rats. Besides, the tunnels are probably much easier to access from inside the Palace."

"Who knows?"

"Could he know about the Magi library?" Zandria asks.

I frown. "I've been wondering that too, but what good would it do the Technos? It's not like they can use our spells. It doesn't make sense."

These troubling thoughts follow me as we creep out of the

drainage tunnels. One hundred years ago, the Technocrats did everything they could to eradicate the Magi and every hint of magic they could find. I can't imagine what a Technocrat boy could possibly want with the remnants of our lost library. And if it's not the library he seeks, what else is down here with us?

THE MAGI COUNCIL STATIONED OUR PARENTS

in Palinor when we were ten years old. Every spy who ventures out of the Chambers—the Magi's hidden underground lair—must have their tailored family history and cover story documented and memorized. Their cover was, and still is, that they were well-to-do traders who had made their way by dealing in fine jewelry and antiquities. They decided to settle in the capital city so their twin daughters could have the best education and position in Technocrat society.

The brilliance of this ruse is that Mama and Papa can have any number of curiosities in their possession without raising the slightest suspicions from our Technocrat peers. Anything new that gets discovered is often brought to us for authentication—by both other Magi in hiding and idle Technocrats hoping for a good conversation piece over their afternoon tea—which means Zandria and I get to study them. Most of the surviving spell books are primers; the more advanced ones were lost. We may have left the Chambers and the rest of the Magi children behind, but we have continued our magical education. In fact, I suspect our knowledge may exceed theirs.

Tonight, when we finally slip through the door to our home, Mama and Papa are on their feet to greet us.

"Where have you been?" Mama says. She hugs me close, her auburn hair tickling my nose. "We were afraid you got caught."

Zandria hugs her next and laughs. "We're fine, Mama."

"Mostly fine," I correct.

Papa puts a firm hand on each of our shoulders and guides us to the kitchen table. "Come sit, tell us what happened."

Zandria sighs but obeys. The warm fire crackles in the hearth, painting shadows on the walls. Bread and cheese and a savory-smelling soup wait for us on the worn wooden table, making my mouth water. I hadn't realized how hungry I was until now. But I must speak first—the knots forming in my stomach will allow no other course.

"We were followed."

Mama sharply sucks in her breath and Papa pats my hand, leaning in closer as his brow furrows. "Did anyone see you?" he asks. If it weren't for the orders from the Armory, my sister and I probably wouldn't even be mapping the tunnels yet. While I want to be honest with my parents, I don't want them to get alarmed.

I frown. "No, I don't think so. It was just one boy and a pet machine. We were inside the walls and I'd already put the bricks back in place. But"—I pause when Zandria kicks me under the table—"he figured out there was a tunnel behind the wall. I think he might have heard us, though he never saw us. He pulled down the whole wall while we ran deeper into the tunnels."

Our parents share our least favorite look—the meaningful one that's never followed by anything we like. I plow onward to delay their response.

"I know that sounds bad, but we found something tonight too. That's why it took us so long to get home—we were investigating."

Papa raises an eyebrow. "What did you find?"

"A hallway," Zandria says. "And a door that refused to open to us. It was dripping with magic."

"It looked very different from the other hidden tunnels we've found so far. It was more polished, almost new, which makes no sense. I believe the walls were made of some sort of marble," I say.

Papa strokes the short, clipped scruff on his chin. "How did you find it?"

Zandria leaves the answer to me. "Honestly? I'm not entirely sure. When we ran, I felt pulled toward certain turns. I can't explain it fully, but I believe it had something to do with our magic." My hands twist in my lap. "I don't know how it's possible, but I think . . ." I swallow hard, wary of what I'm about to say. "I think this door wanted us to find it."

Mama and Papa exchange yet another of those looks we don't like.

"This door, you say, did not react to your magic at all?" Papa says.

"Not a whit," I say. "It was most unusual."

"Could it be a hidden part of the library, Papa?" Zandria says. "A part the Technocrats couldn't destroy even with their bombs?"

"Perhaps," he says slowly, "but let's not get too hasty. We're not even fully certain the library is under the Palace; it's just one of the few remaining places where it's rumored to be that hasn't been ruled out yet."

"What else could it be?" My words hang in the air for a moment while we all consider this question.

"What else indeed? Especially if your magic couldn't move it." Papa strokes his chin again. Until tonight, our unique magic has affected everything we've come into contact with—we of all Magi shouldn't have had any trouble opening the door. Though we're still testing our limits, slowly and under our parents' strict supervision, so the full extent of our power is an unknown quantity. This door is the biggest challenge we've faced so far—perhaps one we could still overcome.

I know how seriously my parents take the fact we were followed, but we must go back. Zandria squeezes my hand under the table, and I know she feels the same. We can't simply let this mystery go.

"Please, don't make us do something else. We're so close," I say.

"We have to find a way through that door," Zandria says.

Mama leans back in her chair and folds her arms over her chest. "This task was supposed to be simple and safe," she murmurs.

"It is," Zandria says. "No one saw us. And they never will."

"This is getting dangerous, girls," Mama says, watching us to see if we show any signs of cracking. Zandria and I straighten up. We want to do this job. We want to be the heroes who find the library and return the rest of our spells to our people. The ones who give the Magi the means to retake their rightful place. "Are you sure you're equal to it? You know our history—what we fight for, what's at stake. If the Technocrats follow you and find a way through that door first, they will destroy everything. Our spells will be lost forever. Do you understand that? The Magi would never rise again. We'd always be on the run, always in hiding."

Chills sweep over me.

Papa nods. "There is much more at stake here than your ambitions, girls."

"We will find out why the boy was down there," I say. Zandria squeezes my hand in agreement.

"And we'll be even more cautious than before," she promises. I resist the urge to snort. My sister, cautious? I plan to hold her to it.

"All right," Mama says. Papa nods. "You can return to the tunnels tomorrow night, but you must give us a full report every evening. If there is even a hint the Technos will find the door and get through it, we'll inform the Armory we're pulling you off the mission."

The years of playing spy have hardened even my dear Mama. In so many ways she and Papa are soft toward us—but when it comes to our missions, they're both tougher than diamonds. For years, they've trained us physically and mentally for the pursuit of our cause. And about the dangers of revealing the secret of our magic. Any normal Magi would be revolted, at best, by what we can do. The wars have tainted the way the Magi see the world.

Once, between the first and second Techno-Magi wars, our people reached a tentative peace, or so the Magi thought. Our emissaries traveled to the far north of the country where the Technocrat king resided to sign an official treaty. But when they arrived, they were tricked—literally walked into a trap. Under the guise of showing off the wonder of Technocrat ingenuity, the king sent them into a room for a display. Then the doors locked behind them and the walls began to close in. Only a couple of servants escaped to share the terrible news: the Technocrat castle was stained with Magi blood. Within days the Second Techno-Magi War began. The moral of the tale, our parents would remind us, is to never trust a Technocrat and never, ever underestimate a machine.

Anything remotely technological is seen as disgusting. Sympathy for or even appreciation of the mechanical is seen as treasonous. We're only supposed to use technology when sent out into the world to spy like our family has been. Mama and Papa have relentlessly drilled these facts into our heads.

"We won't fail you," I say, meaning it with every ounce of power running through my veins. The stakes are too high to fail. Success is the only option.

LONG BEFORE WE CAME TO PALINOR, MAMA

and Papa were our teachers. As a team, they're known in the Armory by their combined code name: Poison Arrow. Mama—the Poison half of the pair—helped us understand the natural world. She showed us how to grow herbs—some dangerous and some delicious—and how to tell them apart. Even now, she keeps a small garden hidden behind our house. Papa—Arrow—showed us how to fight, and how to pick off our opponent from afar. I have fond memories of running through the forest in the farthest reaches of the country, holding a bow taut and doing my best to keep my aim true. Then when we got home, Mama showed us what to do if we were ever poisoned by our enemies and how to transfer the poison from one object into another. In our case, with a special twist: we infused the toxins Mama kept in her vials into Papa's arrows, making them even deadlier. But they made us swear to keep what we did a secret from everyone without exception to ensure Isaiah, the head of the Armory, never discovered what we could do.

When we moved to the city, we enrolled in the Technocrats' schools, though our parents continued our training at home. To hide our contempt for all things Techno, we must fake our enthusiasm, especially in class. It's all about keeping our cover.

Zandria is particularly good at this.

She can smile at the other students in our schoolhouse, then hours later daydream about testing the full limits of our magic and tearing Palinor down brick by brick. I can only reconcile it by reminding myself that every kind thing I say to a schoolmate is a lie. If I believed I meant the friendships I fake, I fear it would tear me apart.

Today Zandria charms our fellow students and the history teacher with her spirited rendition of the Techno-Magi wars. The hundredth anniversary of the final battle is this year, and the celebration starts with tonight's parade and ends several weeks from now with a masquerade ball. "The evil Magi would murder us all in our beds if not for the brave Technocrat, King Melsun, who had the inspiration to hit them at their heart." She makes explosion noises, spurring giggles in Vivienne, the dark-haired girl sitting next to her. "The source of their power was burned to ash, and all the Magi with it."

"Yes, something like that," says Administrator Timothy, our teacher. His wiry dark hair is unruly—much like his classes. "Though perhaps with a bit more strategy and a little less drama."

Zandria grins, and he clears his throat. He's our youngest teacher, and the most affected by Zandria's flirtations. The other teachers find her amusing but aren't as easily distracted.

Sometimes my sister's boldness scares me, but times like this, it fuels me. Her energy lends me the strength to pretend to adore the people I hate. The people who hate me, fear me, even if they don't know it now.

Thankfully today is the last day of our education in Palinor. The last day we will have to suffer through sitting in the schoolhouse and learning their twisted history of lies. People say history is written by the victors—I say it's entirely fabricated by them to suit their own ends.

Despite what our textbooks say, there is nothing noble about the Technocrats. The great-grandparents of the students who sit around us, who share with us their hopes and dreams, did everything they could to wipe out our entire faction.

A tiny part of me smiles inside, alight with the knowledge they failed.

"I know this is your last class, but please try to pay attention long enough to look at your final scores," Administrator Timothy says. The room quiets, and everyone sits up a little straighter. You could hear a pin drop on the steel floor. He isn't just giving our grade for this class—the final overall scores are always handed out in the last session before the summer months when the younger classes of students get a break. These determine our future in Palinor, and for older students like me and Zandria our assignments at tomorrow's Apprenticing Ceremony. The better your score, the higher your rank in Technocrat society. Usefulness is a highly prized trait. For most, it means the difference between a life of leisure and a life of servitude. For my sister and me, it could mean reevaluating our strategy.

Zandria sighs happily when Timothy hands her the sheet of paper. Must be good news.

Vivienne lets out a squeal at hers, echoed by several others around the room, though soon the air is punctuated by groans. Eugene and Melly, two of our other friends, seem none too pleased. Administrator Timothy slides the paper with my scores into my hands and I finally exhale.

Ninety-nine percent. I'm willing to bet Zandria scored the same. We aren't above using our magic to further our goals. Besides, we only learn two things here: lies and machines. The first is infuriating, but the knowledge of machines has proved quite useful and gotten us out of more than one sticky situation. In fact, glancing over the transcript, my scores in the mechanical-focused courses are one hundred percent down the line.

Yes, our magic has indeed served us well.

"How did you do?" Vivienne startles me with her upbeat tone. "I can't believe I got eighty-nine percent. My parents are going to be so proud."

Zandria and I exchange a look. "About the same," I lie. "I fully expect an excellent apprenticeship."

"As you should. You deserve it." She grins, and a tiny spot of guilt pinches my gut. The class has erupted with chatter now, but Melly and Eugene haven't budged. They talk softly, heads bent close together. Melly's face grows redder every second.

Zandria is on her feet before I finish my own thought. She takes the seat next to Melly and squeezes her shoulders, while I settle next to Eugene. He gives me a brave smile.

"Don't worry," Zandria says, "it's just a number. Your parents are rich. Your place is secured regardless. It's those of us who come from the trade ranks who need to score high to advance."

"You really think so?" Melly sniffles and fusses with her sleeves shot through with thin strips of decorative metal, like so many of our other classmates from the higher classes. Zandria and I usually wear tunics and pants, and the occasional dress. Only our finest clothing bears the metal adornments that Melly wears daily.

Curious, I steal a glance at the paper slack in her hands and have to stifle a snort. She got sixty percent. She definitely won't be getting a good apprenticeship, no matter what lies Zandy tries to spin.

"Absolutely," Zandria says, giving her another squeeze for good measure. "Forget about it for now. We have the parade to look forward to."

Melly's eyes light up. Everyone loves the parade. Zandria continues to whisper encouraging, kind words to Melly and Eugene, and I play my part as well. But tonight when we go home, we'll talk about how, one day, we'll destroy everything they hold dear.

Mercifully, the bell rings early. Administrator Timothy shouts above the din, "Good luck to you all. Enjoy the parade!"

Our class runs out of the schoolhouse toward the burgeoning streets lined with anyone who can spare the afternoon from work. Zandria leads the pack, weaving and giggling as she tugs me along. She pulls me to a spot away from our schoolmates, down near the front so we can watch the parade go by from the best vantage point. However horrid the Technocrats may be, they do put on a fine show. The glittering lights can crack even my critical grimace into a smile. The restless crowd murmurs, wondering what fantastic things they'll have in store for us this year.

The annual Royal Victory Parade is meant to celebrate the Technocrats' triumph over the Magi and also usher graduating students into the world. Tomorrow is Apprenticing Day. We have no choice but to join in the festivities. This situation has chafed at me for years, a pebble stuck beneath my skin that cannot be dug out. But we have grown adept at pretending. So today, we'll rejoice at the slaughter of our own people.

When we were little, our parents would travel all the way from the Chambers to bring us to the parade, and we'd sit on their shoulders so we could see the strange mechanical display snaking like some giant beast through the city. Back then, pretending to enjoy it was easier. But as we grew older, our parents schooled us on how to temper our growing rage at the reason for the gaudy show. How to use our disgust to drive us to succeed in our studies. To be the perfect picture of a good Technocrat.

Our success is also theirs.

Vivienne spots us and waves excitedly from where she stands with Melly and Eugene. Zandria elbows me in the ribs and we wave back, all smiles.

Sometimes, I wish our friendship with them could be real. We've shared so much—classes, laughter, and the trials of staying awake through lectures. Everything I do must be a deception, but despite my best efforts, I've grown fond of them. So has my sister. It's a sad thing to admit you care for people who despise everything you are.

The crowd swells and we can hear music in the distance. Zandria wriggles. "Come on, I see a place we can sit higher and have a better view."

We climb to the top of the low wall framing the roadways. We have a clear view of the winding path the procession will take. The brightly colored machines sparkle in the distance and heat. The pounding of drums reverberates through the earth, pulsing into my legs where we sit. The crowd presses closer.

"What do you think they'll do this year?" Zandria asks.

"If they intend to show up last year's parade, they'll have to blow up the square at least." Last time, one of the machines carrying fireworks caught fire early and they all went off at once. The effect was terrifying, loud, and strangely beautiful. It was days before anyone in the city could hear normally again.

Zandria says something else, but I don't catch it over the crowd. The noise is near deafening now. "What?"

Someone rams into my legs and I tumble from my perch on the wall, jostling several people on the way.

"Aissa!" my sister cries and leaps down. Before she can reach me, a strong hand appears to help me up. I take it and stare into the face of the person it belongs to, every nerve in my body thrumming. His fingers whisper across mine like a soft kiss.

There is something familiar about his blond hair and pale blue eyes.

"I'm sorry," he says. "I didn't see you."

I release his hand, my face growing warm. "You didn't see me? How could you not?" I tug a lock of my red hair. The color sticks out like a flame in the crowd. "My sister and I are hard to miss." I gesture to Zandria.

His face falls. "Are you hurt?" He holds my shoulders at arm's length as if to examine my state of wellness. There is something almost intimate about the gesture that makes me flush and squirm at the same time. I clench my fists to resist slapping his hands away.

"I'm fine."

He lets go, just as Zandria squeezes my other hand. She tilts her head toward the boy's feet.

A small machine, with two legs that alternate to propel it forward, whirs beside the boy. The hair, the eyes, the angular nose. My breath catches in my throat.

It's him.

But he doesn't recognize us. The concern in his eyes confirms that.

"Are you sure? You seem upset," he says.

"You just pushed me off a wall. Did you expect me to be happy?" I wrench my fingers out of my sister's hand and cross my arms over my chest. Days like this always set me on edge. Running into the boy who followed us last night pushes me right over it. I sigh, swallowing as much of my irritation as I can manage. If he is the boy from the tunnels, it is in our best interest to get to know him better. Being rude won't help. "Why are you racing around when the parade is about to start?" I put on my most winning smile. "Were you looking for a good seat? Now that you're here, you're welcome to sit with us if you like."

He glances past us, running long, thin fingers through his pale curls. Almost like he's nervous.

"I'm sorry, but I'm afraid I must go."

I narrow my eyes. What could this boy be nervous about? Especially on parade day.

"But you'll miss the procession!" Zandria says, with a smile I recognize. It's the one she always uses when she's flirting to win people over. She's better at it than I am. I'm already kicking myself for not immediately taking full advantage of this opportunity to practice.

He smiles back at her. "That was kind of the point. I don't need to see the parade."

Zandria gasps. "What? And miss the finest show the third Technocrat dynasty has ever put on? Sacrilege."

He laughs. "It is a fine show indeed. Which I have seen many, many times."

Something cold and metallic taps my foot and I yelp.

"Sparky, no. Sorry, sometimes I swear that thing has a mind of its own," the boy says. It whirs and spins and taps Zandria's foot too. "Sparky, no! Not polite!" The machine finally whirs to a stop. "I'm sorry, I haven't even introduced myself. My name is Aro— please forgive my pet's rudeness, and my own." He holds out his hand and the twin moons of his eyes pull me in like a gravitational force. If I really were a Techno, I'd be falling over myself for him. But as a Magi, it would put my heart in debt to my greatest foe. I shake his hand and formally introduce us. "I'm Aissa. This is my sister, Zandria."

"Pleasure to meet you," Zandria says, shaking his hand too.

"Likewise." He clears his throat and glances down the road again as the noise escalates. The parade must be close. "I should go." He flashes me a lopsided grin. "I hope to run into you again, though perhaps not quite so literally next time." With that he bows and vanishes into the crowds.

"I think someone has a crush," Zandria says. Her eyes sparkle with mischief. "Perhaps we can use this to our advantage?"

"I hope we never see that boy again. Not here or in the tunnels." I shiver. "Something about him is off."

"Still, if you do run into him, you should use it. Not enjoying the parade as a proper citizen could mean philosophical disagreements with the crown. Perhaps he is ripe for the picking."

Of course, she's right. That's the best tactical move. Despite the fact he unsettles me, I must keep our mission foremost in my mind. Always.

"You two always find the best spots," Vivienne says behind me, making me jump out of my skin. "Who were you were talking to?"

"Some jerk who knocked me off my seat," I say.

She laughs.

"He did help you up," Zandria says.

Vivienne raises an eyebrow. "You've got to love a little chivalry."

"It wouldn't have been necessary if he'd been watching where he was going," I say, feeling more surly than usual after my failed attempt at flirting. I climb back up to where we'd been sitting before.

The sun sets in the western edge of the city, leaving our section dusky—perfect for the Technocrat parade. The drumbeats pound over our bodies so hard I can feel it in my chest. The rolling wheeled carriages carry the imperial procession of royals, ambassadors, and anyone else who can pay a large enough bribe to secure a spot. King Damon and Queen Cyrene won't appear until the very end, so the first few carriages, all metal and glittering light, are only of cursory interest.

The machines interspersed with them, however, are very intriguing. Most are only used for this, then broken down and scrapped for parts to build more useful machines. Huge metal creatures amble down the streets, their steps shaking the ground in time with the music cascading through the air. Golden lions, silver elephants, and bronze horses with ruby and sapphire eyes—all a tremendous waste of precious metal—prance down the street, a stinging reminder of the real creatures decimated by the Technocrats. They destroyed their habitats in the wars, then hunted them for sport, and now they honor them like this.

Melly squeals and strains to see the gold lions as they parade by with their manes sparkling. The elephants and horses are as tall as a two-story building, massive and strangely beautiful. Their cold, glittering eyes scan the crowd while their moving metal parts undulate and propel them forward.

If I wanted to, I could stop one of the closer mechanimals in its tracks right here and now by seizing up its parts. Magic itches in my veins, but I don't make a move. It would expose us to the Technocrats, and worse, to the other Magi. Our family would be forever stained.

No, we will stay secret and silent, and wait until the time is right.

The spectacle continues with more fabricated animals, then jugglers in metallic suits that shimmer in the torchlights. Fire breathers hold out sparklers that burst forth in spurts with every breath they blow over them. Riders on contraptions I can't make heads or tails of zoom up and down alongside the procession of vehicles, each one more gaudy and colorful than the last, like gobs of colored hard candies.

Then the royal carriage rolls into view. There's no question who sits inside it, not from the jewel-encrusted platinum exterior nor the sparking lights that cascade from the top of the carriage. King Damon and Queen Cyrene and their most trusted guards. This is the only time of year the royals travel through the streets of their own city. Rumor has it that both of them have been augmented, that the queen has bones of steel and the king has eyes that can see for miles. But they are so rarely seen outside the Palace, we hardly know if that's true.

What we do know is that anyone who has ever dared to oppose them publicly has disappeared. Their cruelty is legendary.

My fists tighten and I consciously pull back my magic, the tingling heat of it moving up through my arms and chest and settling at its source—my heart. Zandria is as cool as always, cheering and waving just like Vivienne and Melly and the rest of the Technocrats.

Yes, we bide our time to strike back. For me, that time cannot come soon enough.

THE FESTIVITIES DIED DOWN HOURS AGO,

but Zandria and I are still awake in our room,
whispering in the dark. Lights from revelers
wandering home dance by our window, even at this
late hour.

"I want to be an apprentice lady's maid. Then I could
get into the castle and gossip all day. Subvert and be merry at the
same time," Zandria says, twirling the ends of her long red hair
around her fingers. We're both thrilled to be done with schooling
at last and eager to move on to our apprenticeships. The better the
placement, the easier it will be for us to fulfill our duties to the
Armory. Whatever our differences, we are united in that. Loyalty
to our people always comes first.

I snort. "A lady's maid? You don't mean that. What do you think
they'd call you? The Seam Ripper? The Hat Pin?" Each person in
the Armory has a code name. Most are hidden except to those who
need know about them in order to do their jobs, but others are
more widely recognized among the Magi, like our leader Isaiah,
the Lance. Some are legendary, like the Hidden Knife. Rumored to
be the most loyal spy in history, they've spent most of their life in
deep cover with the Technocrats. Tales of their exploits have made
them more myth than Magi. Only a handful of people know the
Hidden Knife's real identity. We are certainly not among them.

Zandria laughs. "I prefer the Scissors."

I shake my head at her. "You'd be bored to tears in half
an hour."

She props herself up on one arm and giggles across the gap
between our beds. "I wouldn't be bored at all. There are plenty of
handsome men."

I shake my head, but she ignores it. "Just don't get attached, Zandy. You know what they'd do to us. It's dangerous to get involved with Techno boys." A love like that, between a Magi and a Technocrat, would be death-marked. Pale eyes and pale hair flash across my mind. Despite my best efforts, I haven't quite been able to get that boy, Aro, out of my head.

She laughs into her pillow. "That's the attraction. Making them fall for me is part of the fun, and I have no intention of falling for them. Besides, they're cuter than the Magi boys we've met in the Chambers."

I roll my eyes. She hasn't seen a Magi boy for at least two years. The last one must have been our friend Remy, the Magi leader's son. We used to travel to the Chambers once a year under the pretense of visiting relatives on that side of the country, but haven't recently. All Magi call the Chambers—the secret, idyllic underground caverns—their true home, but those who are on extended missions like us may not see the inside of it for years.

The world suddenly goes dark, startling me to my feet. Zandria is right beside me. I crouch near my bed, one hand on the bag of necessities hidden beneath it.

A shadow blotted out the moonbeams glancing through our window, which can only mean one thing: a visitor.

We don't have visitors often. And never at night.

Zandria tiptoes to the bedroom door and places her ear against it.

The shadow's footsteps approach the front of our house. A knock. Then another.

Followed by Mama and Papa's worried murmurings.

The creak of the front door sends my pounding heart into high gear.

Voices waft under our bedroom door and I hold my breath, staring at my sister the entire time. She clings to the doorframe.

But the voices aren't angry. Surprised, yes, but with a tinge of happiness. Zandria leaps back into bed as footsteps approach. I barely manage to scramble under the covers before Papa opens the door.

"Girls? We have an important visitor. Get dressed and come into the kitchen, please."

Papa's face is serious, yet the trace of surprise still lingers. Zandria and I throw on the nicest clean clothes within reach. If the visitor is important, they won't be inclined to wait for us.

Zandria smooths her skirt while I fix a lock of her hair that became mussed when she pulled the dress over her head. She straightens the sleeves of my tunic in return.

"Who do you think it is?" she whispers as we hurry down the hall.

"I'm as baffled as you are," I say.

"Maybe it's Aro, come to declare his undying love for you already. I told you he was smitten," Zandria says with a wicked grin.

I laugh. "I doubt Papa would have even let him through the door if he did."

When we arrive in the kitchen, a tall man with keen, narrowed eyes, olive skin, and chin-length hair sits at our table with his hands tented before him. He brightens visibly at our entrance and my heart nearly stops.

The head of the Armory is sitting in our kitchen.

"Aissa, Zandria, so good to see you again. It has been too long." He rises from the table to greet us.

We have met Isaiah Gaville many times before as we were close friends with his son Remy. Since the end of the Techno-Magi wars, Isaiah's bloodline has held the position of leadership on the Magi Council that oversees the Armory from its base within the Chambers. Seeing Isaiah almost makes me miss our childhood home.

"Sir." I clasp his hand in greeting. He looks very much the same, except for the graying hair that now creeps into the shocking black.

"How is your family, sir?" Zandria asks.

"They're very well. I can see you two are as good as ever. Just as I had hoped."

I'm not sure I like the glint in Isaiah's eyes when he says this.

"Girls, why don't you sit?" Mama's suggestion is more of a command than usual. We both obey.

Isaiah stands for a moment too long, staring not quite at us, instead almost beyond us. Something about it makes me shudder. And yet this is who we work for—have worked for and will work for—all our lives.

Tonight, I get the distinct feeling Isaiah is not here for social reasons. He's here for us. And that makes me nervous. Magic is supposed to be pure and life-giving; machines are soulless. But with what we can do, we may as well be part machine. Mama and Papa have been very clear that Isaiah, Remy, and all the other Magi must never find out what we can do, as our very existence could be deemed an act of treason. Isaiah wouldn't hesitate to cast us out of Magi society as tainted abominations. He might even kill us to hide what we've become.

He sits at the head of the table, hands back in the tent formation.

I hardly dare to breathe while we wait for him to speak. He regards us intensely while his fingers tap the bottom of his chin, and it feels like an eternity.

"I understand you ran into a bit of trouble the other night during your investigations in the tunnels below the Palace," he finally says.

Zandria's hand grips mine under the table. I know she's thinking the same thing: could he have already found out we were followed by that boy? Isaiah's eyes pierce my brain as though he wants to uncover all my secrets.

"You found a door made of darkness. This may be what we seek."

"It wasn't made of darkness," Zandria says. "It was made of marble."

He frowns. "That is impossible. Magic draws on life; it can't mix with marble. You are mistaken." He waves a hand dismissively. "The Council will decide what to do with it next. Above all, we don't want to attract attention. If the Technocrats get wind of the door, they will do their best to destroy it."

Disappointment stews in my chest. He is right, of course, but I already know what is coming next.

"We won't be sending you into the tunnels anymore. We have a different use for both of you. It's time for your apprenticing, and I've made arrangements to place you in key positions to gather intelligence for us."

Zandria breathes in sharply. We're out of the tunnels but at exactly the wrong time. Things were just getting interesting. He's wrong about the door, and he also has no idea how perfect we are for that task. We can't just abandon the assignment; there must be a way we can get back to the tunnels. With a little more time I'm certain we could figure out how to open the door, just like we figured out how to manipulate every machine that has crossed our path. And what is a door but a simple sort of machine?

"Aissa, I understand you have developed an affinity for the machines."

Sometimes, I fear he can truly read minds. "Yes, sir. I excelled at building and deconstruction in our classes." I omit the fact that my "skill" was due to my magic.

"Excellent. There is an opening for an apprentice to the city's Master Mechanic, which we have secured for you. He's a prickly man, but with the access this will allow you to the Palace, you will be in a prime position for your new mission."

"Thank you, sir," I say, my curiosity about the nature of this new mission going into overdrive. Why would they need me in the Palace? The possibility of spying underneath the noses of the king and queen is both thrilling and terrifying.

"Zandria, I'm told you are the fastest runner in your class."

"Yes, sir," she says, unable to keep the disappointment out of her voice. "I win every race."

"That makes you a perfect fit for the messenger apprenticeship we've arranged. You will carry messages all over the city." He leans forward with a wicked smile. "Feel free to read as many of them as you like."

Zandria attempts a grin but falls short.

"I can see you're disappointed, girls," Isaiah says. "But don't worry, this mission is more important than your previous one."

We squeeze each other's hands tightly. A promotion is certainly something we've both desired. But that door . . .

"What would you have us do, sir?" Zandria asks.

"We aim to hit the Technocracy where they hurt, where they're the most sore and vulnerable." He stands and paces in front of the table with his hands behind his back. "Most people assume the queen is barren, but we have known for some time that the king and queen have a child. Our intelligence suggests the child is a girl younger than you two—perhaps ten or eleven. They have kept her a secret, and now we know why. She is rumored to be one of the Heartless."

I stop breathing as Zandria's nails dig into my palm. If that's true, it's no wonder they've hidden her. It's a blight on their family tree. The taint could threaten their stranglehold on power.

The Heartless have a deformity that appears rarely in Technocrats born after the wars. The Technocrat histories say it's the result of lingering curse magic our Magi leaders turned on them after they destroyed our schools. And our legends say we lost our most powerful elder Magi in the wars when they sacrificed every ounce of their strength to craft that curse and ensure it would continue for generations.

Those afflicted are born without beating hearts.

"The girl must be sickly and well-guarded then," I say, and Isaiah nods. Most of these children die the moment they're out of the womb, but the dubiously lucky ones (in other words, the ones who have money) are fitted with clockwork hearts made of steel that pump blood through their veins instead. But even the most well-crafted hearts for the richest Heartless last a year or two at best before needing to be replaced. The surgery is dangerous and the survival rate abysmal.

"You just want us to find her?" I have no doubt Isaiah is not telling us everything.

"For now. Once we confirm she does indeed exist, we will decide on our next move."

"Surely you expect us to do something with her when we find her?" Zandria says.

"We'll tell you what to do once you need to know." Isaiah leans closer and rests his hands, palms down, on the table. "You two are said to be the best at maneuvering into places other spies cannot reach . . . which is why I am separating you."

I suck in my breath so sharply my chest hurts. My sister and I are a team. A well-oiled machine. It's one of our strengths. Alone, we might be at a disadvantage we're not prepared for.

"Zandria, you will carry messages to and from the Palace and across the city. This gives you an advantage and puts you in a position to screen their communications. Aissa, your affinity for machines"—I swear I detect the slightest hint of a frown—"gives you the perfect cover as the Master Mechanic's apprentice. This position will come with opportunities to visit the Palace and learn exactly where she is hidden. The girl may not be at the Palace at all. She might be in a remote region of the country. But you, my twin daggers, will root that out. Then we'll strike the Technocrats in their very hearts."

APPRENTICING DAY IS STIFLING HOT. A
terrible day to wear the long cloaks required
for the ceremony.

"Do you think Isaiah got us the positions he
claims? Are there really Magi spies high enough to influence that?" I say to Zandria as she dangles off the edge of her
bed while fanning herself. She groans in response.

"Of course he did. I hear the Hidden Knife is a close friend of
his and is highly placed in Palinor. Besides, the Apprenticing Board
is not above taking bribes."

I tug at the sleeves of my finest tunic—deep blue with a tiny
bit of steel filigree around the edges—pulling them over my
elbows. I can't think of Isaiah without thinking of his son. Perhaps
Remy is still training in the Chambers.

"Though I'm secretly hoping he didn't," Zandria says. "I'm still
holding on to my dream of being a lady's maid."

I roll my eyes, but I can't help a small smile. While I may not
always agree with my sister's methods, I know we both share the
same dream: to be able to walk above ground—live our lives—
without fear. Without lying about what we really are. We're
prepared to do anything to make that dream a reality.

"Girls!" Mama calls. "Time to go!"

Zandria sighs and rolls off the bed. "Can't I just lie here on the
floor? It's so much cooler."

I laugh, pulling my sister to her feet. "No, you can't. We must
do our duty. You know that."

"You sound just like him."

"Who?"

"Isaiah."

"I'll take that as a compliment. He's only the most powerful person we know." I brush past her into the hallway, not willing to admit how much her remark bothers me. There is something so . . . cold about Isaiah that never fails to disturb me.

I'm not nearly so cold. Am I?

The crowd swells by the time we arrive just before noon. The smell of roasting meat, nuts, and breads from the food vendors mingles with sweat and sunshine. Mama and Papa kiss our cheeks then head for the side of the city square where the parents wait to watch the apprenticing assignments. We have only been here a few minutes, and already I'm dying to peel off this horrid cloak.

"I'm starving," Zandria says as we pass a vendor hawking pastries. "And that's one of the few things that's not too hot to eat."

"What about that one?" I point to another cart fitted with a freezing engine—its contents are bound to be soothing and delicious.

"Perfect!"

We purchase two small metal bowls of iced fruit, watching as the machine in the cart grinds the ingredients together into a sweet slush. We may be here to undermine the Technocracy, but I wouldn't mind keeping some of their inventions.

We pay the vendor a copper each and head for the center of the square. Others our age from all over the city and countryside gather here. A large tent is set up for the ceremony, and we find the seats with our names then sit down to wait.

The others wander and laugh, eager to find out what trades they'll be assigned. They have such hope. Hardly a care in the world.

Whereas we have a heavier weight on our shoulders. Starting today, our efforts to infiltrate must succeed so that our people can use their magic again without fear of repercussions. Without fear of certain death.

Vivienne catches sight of us and runs over.

And success might mean hurting the Technocrats who have been kind to us. Like Vivienne. And many other schoolmates.

I remind myself that this girl, who moments before was flirting with the baker's son at his cart, would turn us in without hesitation if she thought for a moment we might be Magi. Liking her is impossible. If the Magi in the Armory ever suspected we felt anything like real friendship with her, we'd surely be punished. It's a treasonous offense.

"Aren't you excited?" Vivienne bubbles. "What do you think you'll get assigned? I hope I get to be a lady's maid."

I can't stifle my laugh. Zandria gives me a withering look. "You know, Zandy was just saying the same thing this morning, Viv. Maybe you two will get assigned to the same place."

I lean to the side, out of the range of my sister's elbow. "You want to flirt with the courtiers too?" Zandria asks.

Vivienne steals a glance back at the baker's son. "A little. Mostly, I want to see the clothes. The court ladies always look so fine. Perhaps I'll be a seamstress. I was always good at that."

"Good luck," Zandy says, waving as Vivienne moves a couple rows down to take her place. "Did you have to tell her that?" she hisses.

I snort. "Yes. Yes, I did."

The rest of our peers file in and take their seats. I'm almost disappointed to see no sign of Remy. I thought Isaiah's appearance yesterday just before the Apprenticing Ceremony might mean he was finally allowing his son to venture out of the safety of the Chambers and positioning him in Palinor too. Remy is a couple years older and always protected me and Zandy when we were kids, before we came into our magic and moved to the city.

When all the seats are filled under the canopy and the sun has reached the optimal point to melt us all, the city officials file onto the raised platform.

The king and queen are nowhere in sight. They remain safely ensconced in their palatial estate, holding court while the Apprenticing Board takes the lead. Better to remain aloof and adored than sweaty and real like the rest of us. The officials must be sweltering in their violet-and-gold robes. Many of them are quite red in the face.

Good; they'll be as anxious as we are to get this over with. Perhaps they'll keep it short.

When the head official, a ruddy man with graying hair sticking out of his head at odd angles, steps forward, we all fall silent. He clears his throat and wipes his brow, holding several sheets of paper in his hand.

"Now that you have reached the age of apprenticing, you will learn your trades so you can be productive members of our society." The papers rustle as he shifts his weight. "Your future careers have been particularly selected for you based on your school performance over the past few years. I shall announce the names by category, and when I'm finished "—his voice cracks as it reaches an abnormally high tone—"you may proceed to the trade tables in the left quadrant of the square to find the details of your assignments." He eyes the crowd for a moment. "Please don't run. And don't leave your seats until all names have been read."

A scattering of titters waves through the crowd. Zandria snorts and rolls her eyes. Rumor has it that one year the new apprentices didn't wait until the end of the ceremony and complete chaos ensued.

"First, the artisans. Leona Appleby, Anya Behrens, Micah Boskoff . . ."

My mind wanders, only waiting to hear the announcement of

my name and Zandria's. My eyes wander too—the sweaty official is not the prettiest sight in the square by far. Pigeons hop along the sides, grouping near vendors. Children play games in the common grassy area far to our right. A slight breeze sways the real trees edging the square, and the sun glints off the ones that are made from metal.

I start and sit up straighter. Creeping through those trees is a familiar face. The one who followed us in the tunnels the other night, and later knocked me over at the parade. Aro. He does look a year or two older than us. He must already have his vocation.

Strange that he isn't working. From the way he slinks along, it's clear he doesn't want to be seen. Suddenly, I'm desperate for this ceremony to be over so I can run off and find out what he is about.

Unfortunately, the official is only on the apprenticeships starting with the letter F. We have a ways to go until mechanics and messengers, and then until D for our last name, Donovan. I lean back in my chair, fold my arms over my chest, and sigh heavily. Zandria looks at me askance, but I shake my head.

Thirteen sheets of shuffled paper later, the official is finally done making his announcements. Row by row, we file toward our assigned booths. Isaiah was right—I will be apprenticed to the Master Mechanic, and Zandria with the Messenger Guild.

The Magi's network indeed runs far deeper than the Technocrats know. It thrills me with hope that we might actually be successful in our endeavors. Zandria, on the other hand, still mourns the loss of our underground investigation. In the wake of the strange magic door, she has forgotten how much she hated the drainage tunnels.

We've already decided we're going back. It doesn't matter whether we have new assignments—the Heartless royal heir surely won't mind if the spies trying to find her also scurry in the tunnels below the Palace. We can do both. Mechanic and messenger by day, tunnel divers by nightfall.

We just have to hope our parents don't catch on.

ZANDRIA AND I SEPARATE AFTER WE
retrieve our assignments. The boy has vanished, and I proceed to my new workshop instead
of chasing my curiosity.

He's up to something; I can feel it in my bones. I'll
puzzle him out sooner or later.

I walk with the steadiest pace I can muster—I need to be in
complete control when I meet the Master Mechanic. One slip and
I could be done for. While I'm flattered Isaiah entrusted me and
my sister with such a high-risk project, a tiny part of me wishes
he hadn't. Mapping the tunnels was so much simpler.

Breathe in and out. Coil the magic inside my chest. This is my
sole focus on the walk toward the mechanic shop. Squash it down,
hide it, lie about it—these are the rules I live by. If only I didn't have
to remind Zandria of them. I worry she'll be found out as a courier.
It's perfect for her, though. She loves seeing new things and sticking
her nose where it doesn't belong. I only hope it doesn't get cut off.

As I walk, the buildings spread out, the houses are finer, and
the lots are more spacious. Shiny metal trees spring up from the
ground more often than real ones. Grand mansions made from
brick and steel with fancy wrought iron porches and fences watch
me walk down the street. Their colorful gardens and dark green
and silver hedges rustle in the slight breeze. Hardly any children
play in the front yards, not like the tradespeople part of the city.
The few shops dotting the corners have fine silks and confections
in their windows. I must be near the Palace.

By the time I reach the shop, I'm soaking with sweat. When I
left the square, I shed my robes but still drag them around. I wish
it would rain and dash this heat.

The sun glints off the metal-trimmed exterior of the building, blinding in the midday blaze. Squinting, I pry open the front door. A bell rings, and I startle, fumbling with my robes.

"Who is it?" calls a gruff voice from the back room.

"Aissa." I pause. Do they even tell the Masters who their apprentices will be? "You must be Leon Salter. I'm your new apprentice."

"They sent me a girl this year?"

My blood boils at his remark, which is followed by a series of grunts, creaks, and muttered swears.

I feel the same way, sir.

I swallow the retort on the tip of my tongue and study Leon as he limps into the main shop. He's an older man, with white, grizzled hair that stands out against his dark skin. His mouth is set in a hard line and his brow appears permanently furrowed in a deep *V*. His steps make an odd sound.

My eyes widen. His left foot is mechanical instead of flesh. He doesn't wear a shoe, so the toes, hinges, and gears are clearly visible. Definitely not the sort of flashy augmentation the nobles like to get.

I try to look at anything else and end up staring at his left hand. Which is also a machine.

A chill slinks down the skin on the back of my neck despite the heat. What happened to make replacing his left hand and foot necessary?

He grunts in my direction, then steps closer. It's not so much a limp as an odd gait from the human and mechanical parts trying to work in tandem.

"Never seen a mech-hand before?" he says, peering down his long, crooked nose at me. His eyes are surprisingly clear for a man his age.

"No, sir, I have not."

"Show me your assignment papers," he says.

I pull the papers the Apprenticing Board gave me out of my satchel and hand them over.

He studies them, then glares at me for a long moment. I can't help feeling as though his eyes peel away the layers of my flesh to see how I work underneath. It's more than unsettling.

I stand up straighter and look directly into his eyes.

He laughs once, sharply, then motions for me to follow him into the back.

"Come on, then, let's see what you can do. If you're no use to me, I'm sending you right back to the Apprenticing Board."

A sick feeling washes over me as I follow him. Can he do that? He is the Master Mechanic. He supplies and fixes the machines for the royal family and the entire court. He may be a more powerful player in Palinor than I realized.

Which is exactly why I must not lose this apprenticeship.

When I cross the threshold into the back room, it hits me how much Isaiah trusts me to do on my own. My sister, my partner, is on the other side of the city and I'm stuck here with a man who's part machine himself and closely allied with the king and queen.

I'm responsible for convincing him I'm just another Technocrat apprentice who loves the machines. The repercussions of being caught are not only on my own head—they'd fall on Zandria too. I'll never let that happen. We look out for each other, always. Even if she is across the city, I must take care nothing I do betrays us both.

The back area is a mishmash of pieces and parts, screws, and nails. Locked metal cabinets line the back wall. I suppress my smile. I shall find out what he keeps in there when he is not present. No lock has ever withstood my magic.

Except that door in the tunnels.

"Well?" Leon looks at me expectantly when he stops at a table in the center of the room covered in odds and ends.

I blink, then realize what he's asking.

This is a test.

"You want me to assemble this?"

"No, I want you to eat the gears for supper." Leon shambles to a chair along the far wall. Near those locked cabinets.

I can already tell he isn't a very trusting person.

"You have one hour. If you can't figure it out by then, you're going back to the Apprenticing Board."

The sick feeling in my gut threatens to reach up and strangle my throat. I can't go back to the Apprenticing Board. Not when Isaiah pulled so many strings to place me here.

But the parts on the table mean nothing to me. I watch Leon carefully as he sits down at his workbench, facing away from me. Plenty of metalwork is strewn about, but no mirrors and nothing polished well enough to see behind him.

To see me.

My pulse begins to race. I've never used magic so blatantly in front of a Techno before. School was one thing. But here, in proximity to the Palace and a man who hated me the second I walked through the door, is another story entirely.

There's a very real chance I'll be caught today.

My chest constricts, but I take deep breaths and sit at the worktable, running my hands over the pieces and shuffling them around. Leon doesn't look up.

Good.

I hum under my breath and continue to move parts aimlessly. Leon grunts this time, giving me a baleful look.

"There is no singing in my shop. Only work." He turns back to his project as my voice chokes out. I swallow the knives lining my throat.

So. Machine noises are fine, human noises are not. Handspells it is.

I close my eyes for a moment, picturing the pieces on the table and trying to fathom their meaning. I'm nearly certain this is not an engine. Or a clock. We experimented with those often in school, and I'd recognize either one. These pieces are strangely articulated and rounded in unexpected places.

It's probably something so simple that I'll feel like an idiot when it's assembled.

With one eye on Leon's back, I move my hands through the motions of the spell under the table. Sparks skitter through my veins as the magic pools in my palms.

I raise them higher, weaving them in just the right way. I will the pieces to move into their proper places.

The first skips along the table and comes together with one of the larger round pieces.

I hold my breath. Leon is still absorbed in cleaning the machine he works on.

My hands move faster, and the pieces answer the magic. Lines of power connect me to the metal parts; I buzz with the sensation. I work quietly and more slowly than I'd like, but bit by bit, piece by piece, the cogs and gears and strange, curved parts begin to take shape.

It resembles a creature. A small creature with flat planes sticking out from its back, a round body, and a hooked nose.

A bird.

He's having me build a tiny mechanical beast.

Leon is a strange employer. I wonder if this is even the shape he wanted and not just some other thing that was once a toy, then repurposed.

The last piece falls into place. I pick the thing up and look closer. The tiny gears and segmented parts make it look like it could actually move if given a power source.

Just like that strange mechpet the boy, Aro, has.

I clear my throat in an effort to get Leon's attention, but he persists in ignoring my existence.

"Sir, I'm finished."

He snorts, then slides off his stool and shuffles over. He moves at a snail's pace, as though I'm not worth using actual speed.

Leon examines the machine on the table, but he doesn't give me the satisfaction of acting surprised. I thought for certain he would be. He picks it up, turns it over several times, poking and prodding the gears to be sure everything fits like it should.

Then he turns the knob in the back of the bird and sets it on the table. The gears click inside it and then music pours out. It sounds like a bird call, but distinctly machine.

Now I'm the one who's surprised.

Leon grunts, then places the bird in a metal cage hanging from the ceiling.

He heads back to his workbench. "You'll do."

THAT EVENING, EXHAUSTED FROM THE
unexpected stress of my apprenticeship, I'm
ready to do anything but train. I decide to swing
by my parents' shop on the way home to put it off
just a little longer.

When I open the door, I'm greeted by the familiar scent
of antiquities: a little musty, a little dusty, with a dash of mystery.
I've loved it since we first came to the city and our parents opened
this shop. The shelves are a hodgepodge of old books and scrolls,
strange metal knickknacks, antique weapons, and relics from the
ancient world, a time before the wars. Some are of Magi origin and
others Technocrat. Anything that might be useful to furthering the
Magi cause comes home with us for deeper investigation before
being set out on these shelves.

Behind the counter is a little door that leads to a back room.
Zandria and I would come here every day after school when we
were younger, and Mama would test us on spells and drill into us
the Magi code language. All to prepare us for what was to come.
For what we need to do.

Both Mama and Papa are in the far corner speaking to a dark-
haired man in a black cloak with a metallic silver accent stripe
along the edge. Their heads are tilted together and they speak in
low voices, though none of them look happy—especially my parents. There are a handful of other people browsing in the shop,
so Mama and Papa haven't noticed me yet, and I walk through the
aisles toward them, curious as to what they speak of so seriously. I
run my fingers over the spines of the old books lining the shelves
on this wall—I've read them all before, so they hold no more mysteries for me but perhaps they will for some other reader.

"I swear to you, we have seen nothing like that," Papa says, taking off his glasses and polishing them on his tunic. "There's no indication that—" He stops short, eyes widening when he sees me. "Aissa, what are you doing here?"

Mama shoots me a look that all but says *Why aren't you at home training with your sister?* She turns to the man. "Please excuse us, Darian."

The man gives me a long look then shrugs. "It seems you don't have a line on what I was hoping to find. Good day, Bridget, Reeve." He curtly nods to my parents then sweeps out of the shop.

"Who was that?" I ask, but Mama folds her arms across her chest.

"Why are you here?"

I frown, a little affronted. They're usually happier to see me when I stop by. "I just came in for a moment. I'm tired and it's on the way."

"You're avoiding your training."

"No, I wanted to see if you had any new additions to your collection that we need to review." And by review, I mean spell books for Zandria and me to use for practice.

"It is more important than ever that you and your sister stay in top form and hone your agility and reflexes," Mama chastises. Since we turned ten years old, our parents have trained us to be strong in body as well as mind and magic. This is why Zandria can claim to be the fastest runner in our class. Magic helps her along, but her solid footing and stamina is due to our training. Kind of like me with the machines.

"Your sister is already at home training," Papa points out, and I sigh.

"Yes, Papa. I'll go right away."

"Wait," he says, finally breaking a smile. "Give your father a hug first, eh? We won't be around forever. We only want to be sure you're prepared for everything."

"I know," I say, hugging Papa and then kissing Mama on the cheek. "Today didn't go as smoothly as I had hoped."

"Then you will just have to do better tomorrow," Mama says, wiping a bit of stray dust from her chin. "Now, since you're here, you can take these home with you." She hands me a couple new books that she pulls out from behind a counter.

When I reach our home, I leave the books on the kitchen table and head for the fireplace in the living room. Behind it hides the entrance to our training room—or the dungeon, as Zandy and I like to call it.

"*Apere*," I whisper, and two rocks depress into the brick-and-steel structure, which swings open, letting me onto the stairway beyond. I can hear Zandria as she grunts through her workout.

The training room is a wide bunker beneath our home, specially constructed by our parents. The steel walls glimmer in the magic light Zandy cast, everywhere except one climbing wall made of bricks. There are no traditional lights down here. Mama and Papa have been very clear we must learn to use our gifts in tandem with our physical strengths. Magic is a wild, living force, and we use it like a muscle. Concentrating on controlling it for a spell while running an obstacle course is no easy task, but it's necessary. If we're searching the tunnels and can't maintain our silencing spell while we're running from Techno guards, our chances of getting away are slim.

One side of the room is devoted to our weapons practice, the other has an obstacle course we've run so many times we could do it blind and in our sleep. In the far corner is a reading nook with a large couch for studying spells. I hear other Magi spies in the city have similar rooms, but we're not initiated deep enough yet to know their identities. For all we know, half our classmates might be Magi too.

What we do know is due to overhearing our parents' whispers when they don't think we're listening. Most Magi can only affect organic materials within a radius of fifty feet. The last time we pushed our boundaries, we reached up to seventy-five, and that range is still growing. Sometimes I think that fact scares our parents. There have been instances where they take the books we borrow from their shop away from us before we can finish, as if they don't want us to have too much power too soon.

"Took you long enough," Zandria says. I take the staff she holds out to me.

"Sounds like you had a good time at your apprenticeship," I say, countering her strike.

"I did."

We spar across the room, neither of us landing a single hit. "I take it you charmed them all?"

"Naturally." She grins. "I completed my first run in less than an hour. They were so impressed, I get to do a run to the north side of town tomorrow."

The north side is where the rich families live. The same side I strolled through earlier today. "Be careful," I say. "You can't use your magic so liberally there."

She shrugs, and I finally score a hit on her elbow. She scowls and fights back harder. "Don't worry, I'm very discreet."

"Just promise me you'll be careful."

"I'm always careful."

I roll my eyes and she laughs.

"How was your apprenticeship? As easy as you expected?"

I duck her strike and groan. "Not at all. Leon Salter hates me. The first thing he said was, 'They sent me a girl?'"

Zandria scoffs. "He's a fool. Besides, he'll learn."

"I hope I learn. I can hardly use my magic there. I need to get good enough that he sends me somewhere else. Somewhere away from his keen eyes."

"I know a place away from all eyes we can escape to," she hints.

"We should go there tonight," I say.

She catches me on the leg and I tumble to the mat. "Absolutely," she says.

We wait until our parents drift off to sleep. Then we slip from our beds and sneak out the window. It's finally raining, which suits our purposes well. Drops hit the steaming pavement and turn into fog, providing a natural cover we can hide behind.

I hum a spell and the fog curls around us, bleeding into the darkness and hiding our passage.

We're soaking wet before we reach the end of our street. Some sacrifices must be made in the name of research.

As we turn down the alley where we usually enter the tunnels, excitement crackles in the air between us, the playful tug of our twin magics bubbling just beneath our skin. We don't need words to express how much we've been dying to return. The irresistible desire to unravel mysteries is a trait we share.

Zandria weaves the spell to lift the manhole cover and let us pass into the dark network. I climb down the ladder and land softly in the muck. The rain will make the tunnels slicker than usual, and I suspect even Zandria will be careful tonight. Coming here is disobeying a direct order, but we both agreed it's a risk more than worth taking.

We need to know more about that door. No matter what Isaiah may think, that door is made of stone infused with magic. In some ways, it's very like us. Something that's supposed to be impossible. Maybe that's why it called me to it the other night.

Isaiah didn't want to believe it was marble. He was so certain we were mistaken since magic and manufactured things should not be able to mix. But we know better; we're living proof. Perhaps if we can prove this door is Magi-made and truly stone, it will pave the way for our acceptance should the true breadth of our talents ever be revealed.

As it is, part of me can't help but wonder whether Isaiah sent us on other missions simply to get us away from the door. Because being proved wrong would challenge everything he stands for.

Zandria's foot slips as she lands. I catch her arm so she doesn't fall into the storm sewer. She steadies herself, then settles the cover back down over our heads.

"I'll feel better when we can use our magic freely."

I squeeze her arm. "That's why we're here."

We head down the tunnel, cautious and watchful. Noises echo throughout, but it's difficult to discern where they originate. Since we started mapping the tunnel network, it has been silent as the grave. The only time we'd heard anything was the night Aro almost caught us.

"*Silencio*," I mutter under my breath. Zandria weaves the spell to make us invisible in the darkness just to be safe. I take the lead, with my sister close at my back. We don't dare raise a light this time.

We creep closer to our once-secret entrance, now visible to all.

"Should we use it tonight?" Zandy whispers.

"I don't know. Perhaps not until we find who—or what—else is here?" I say.

"Or maybe we can find another way in that isn't so exposed."

Our movements slow to a snail's pace. Our breaths are short, but as quiet as we can keep them. In spite of our silencing and cloaking spells, we cling to the damp walls as we creep closer. The warmth of Zandria's body heat directly behind me and the feel of her hand clutching mine are the only sources of comfort in the darkness. The noise grows louder.

Something is wrong.

We've been sneaking around beneath the city for an entire month and the only encounter we've had was with that boy a few nights ago. Now another? This can't be a coincidence.

The blood freezes in my veins. For all we know, he's behind it all.

I may have the mission from the Armory, but now I have another of my own: Figure out who that boy is and why he's so interested in our tunnels.

We reach the last corner before our secret entrance. Light glances toward us from the source of the noise. I peer around the corner.

Frowning, I scan the entire area, certain there must be more than what I'm seeing.

"It's just a few machines that were left to pull down the wall in this area. It looks like they're taking it all apart for the next few spans or so."

"That doesn't make sense. Why would the Technos want to dismantle their own drainage system?" Zandria says.

I consider. "It might make sense if the person behind those machines doesn't have official permission to use them down here."

Zandria's face turns paler in the dim light from the machines. "The only thing I've ever heard rumored to be down here is the Magi library."

"And they'd have a hard time getting permission from the Techno king and queen to dig that up. It was buried quite intentionally."

"We can't let them find it first. We promised Mama and Papa."

A wicked smile crawls over my face. "Oh, we won't."

From our hiding place, we start the spell, just in case the machines have any sort of optical capturing devices. They shouldn't be able to see through magic, but they make me nervous nonetheless. Zandria weaves her hands as I hum the words, a combined force of movement and verse and power. When our hands begin to tingle, we channel the magic toward the machines around the corner, willing them to unmake themselves, piece by piece.

Bolt after bolt hits the floor like falling rain. The clang of a larger section of metal rings out, then another, and another. Steel creaks and moans as it struggles to hold together and fails.

When the machines are fully taken apart, we end the spell, then examine our handiwork.

Only pieces and shells remain. Steel litters the ground, alongside bits of brick the machines removed from the wall before we arrived. It will take forever to put them back together.

"That should slow them down." I grin, but Zandria's face has gone slack. I grab her hand. "What is it?" I whisper.

"Do you hear that?" Fear lingers in her eyes. I listen carefully. Faint but steady footsteps. Mixed with the telltale sound of a small, lumbering machine.

"Aro." He's here again. My heart stutters in my chest. He must have more machines placed farther along this passage. He's probably making the rounds. "We have to get out of here."

We run back down the corridor to our manhole exit. The spell I cast earlier masks the sound of our steps, but our pace is breakneck and heedless. My pulse throbs in my throat. We may be able to conceal ourselves in the darkness, but a manhole cover floating over our heads will give us away.

I hear the sound of steps not far enough behind us in the tunnel. Zandria begins her spell with a wild look in her eyes. There's nowhere for us to hide here. The passage is far too tight to risk our shield spell with someone so close.

The cover rises and Zandria scrambles onto the street. Those steps grow louder. I'm right behind her, the hair on the back of my neck tingling.

As soon as my feet hit the cobblestones, Zandria lowers the cover, but not before we hear a voice ringing out below us.

"Hey! Who's there?" Zandria's hand flies up over her mouth and the cover clanks into place. The steel echo rings in my bones.

"Run." I drag my frozen sister toward home. Once we're out of the alley, she begins to breathe normally. We keep moving quickly through the streets, glancing over our shoulders just in case we were followed. I can't imagine that boy could move the manhole cover on his own, but he may have another entrance we don't know about nearby.

I'm a little concerned about my sister. She's never frozen like that before. But we've never come that close to being found out either. Zandria doesn't say a word until we reach our house, sneak back into our bedroom, and lock the window and door behind us.

"Aissa," she whispers in the darkness, the uneasy trill in her voice hovering in the space between our beds. "We almost got caught."

For once, my sister sounds worried. She's always been so confident and carefree because she's never considered us getting caught to be a real possibility. But now, for the first time, the heavy weight of reality descends on her shoulders too.

I reach across to take her hand. "But we didn't. That's the important thing. Plus, we did do quite a number on that demolition project down there."

"You think it's Aro, don't you? That boy from the parade, the one who followed us that last night we were down there."

I nod at the darkness. "I think so. That machine. I'd recognize its gait anywhere."

"Do you think he saw us?"

"No. He saw the light of the manhole cover going back into place. He'd sooner think it was some unusually strong robber than two girls like us." I lean closer. "We're safe. I promise."

I see the faint outline of her smile, then she squeezes my hand. "Goodnight, sister," she says as she lets go and rolls over.

I turn onto my back and stare at the ceiling. Unlike Zandy, I'm not worried he'll figure out our identities. I'm more concerned about what Aro is doing down there. Could he really be looking for the Magi library?

More importantly, what does he want to do with it when he finds it?

TO MY DISMAY (AND IN MANY WAYS,

relief), no one appears in Leon's shop over the
next few days to have their demolition machines
repaired. Zandria was happy to hear that. She was less
than her usual chipper self the day after our close call, but
when we parted ways this morning she was back to normal.

I miss her every minute.

"If your mind wanders, you will wreck the machines," Leon
growls into my ear. I startle and the piece in my hand clatters to
the worktable.

"I—"

He cuts me off with a wave of his hand and continues. "See?
Wandering mind means broken parts."

He limps back to his seat, muttering under his breath yet again
about the Apprenticing Board sending him a girl. I bristle but remain
silent. Talking back to Leon is exactly what he wants. I won't hand
him an excuse to send me away and tell them I'm useless.

I'm *anything* but useless.

I return to the project Leon gave me with renewed determination. I'll show him I can do this. That I don't deserve his contempt.

Then, someday, when the Magi reclaim their rightful place of
power, he'll regret every unkind word he's said to me.

That thought warms me as I consider my task. I must admit,
I'm not sure what these small machines are intended to do. They're
circular—about the size of my fist—with flat sides and an enclosed
inner chamber for a power source of some kind.

Needless to say, Leon has not let me in on where he keeps that
power source. Yet.

I started this task yesterday, but despite these machines' small size, it's a daunting one. The order is for one thousand of them. It will take weeks without magic. When Leon went to lunch yesterday, I crafted an extra dozen using my magic, all the while keeping a terror-filled eye on the doors and windows. With every one, they got a little easier and a little faster to make. The schematics are etched into my brain now. I kept most of the finished ones hidden in my mechanic's smock. Over the course of the afternoon, I snuck an extra onto the pile here and there.

He might have caught on to the fact something is amiss with his latest apprentice if the pile doubled over his lunch at the tavern.

I retrieve the piece I dropped on the table a moment ago and examine it. A dent mars the right side, and I curse under my breath. Leon pauses in his work, but I pretend I don't notice. When his work resumes, I tuck the piece in my lap and weave my hand over it, silently focusing on the spell that pulls the unaligned section back to its original position.

I let out my breath a little too loud, and Leon glares at me.

"Sorry," I say, smiling weakly.

"There is no need for sighing when it comes to machines."

"Yes, sir. Sorry, sir."

He continues his work and his mutterings.

I clench my hands around the small metal part. How am I ever going to make myself invaluable to this infuriating man? It wouldn't surprise me if he hated every apprentice he's ever had. That would also explain why I'm his only one at the moment. No one else was up to the challenge of Leon Salter.

By the time the morning rush of customers begins to stream into the shop, I'm sweating from trying to up my count from yesterday. Grease coats my fingers and I feel it smudged over my nose where I scratched earlier.

I've made five more little machines than I did yesterday by this time.

Progress, but still disappointing.

Leon grunts as he examines my work. "Where is the part you dropped?"

"I'm not sure," I say, gesturing to the pile of completed machines on the table next to me. "I used it, but I'm not sure which one."

"You used a damaged piece?" Leon's face turns purple. His hands become fists.

"It was fine. I checked," I sputter, baffled by his sudden show of emotion.

He slams his fist on the table. "Look them over again. Every last one. Find that piece!" He pulls his arms in close to his sides, like he's trying to contain himself. Fear runs over my skin like trickling, deadly shadows. "There is no room for error. One mistake, one dent, could be fatal."

Leon stomps out of the room on his metal foot, slamming the door to the workshop.

All my efforts to stay on his good side today have backfired.

Tension strings my muscles across my back as taut as the wires I weave together with my magic.

I know what I must do. Re-dent that one stupid part and take the fall. He doesn't believe it wasn't damaged. He must've seen it and knows I'm lying.

My heart sinks into my shoes. Better he think I'm a liar than a Magi.

Frustration burns in my eyes as I pore over the pieces. Finally I find one with a tiny nick along the bottom. That's the piece I dropped; I can manipulate the tech, but I can't create more of it out of thin air to fill in missing metal. I concentrate, discreetly weaving my hands over it until the dent returns to almost its former shape.

I don't have the heart to admit I damaged it as much as I actually did.

I work furiously to add to my stockpile of finished machinettes, as I've begun to think of them. Curiosity as to their function brews in my brain.

Motors for Technocrat vehicles? For larger machines? Parts for heating units in the farthest reaches of the country? Nothing quite makes sense. Not enough to provoke such a strong reaction from Leon.

By the time Leon returns, I've steeled myself for his rage, and now have several more new machinettes stockpiled in my smock and on the chair beside me.

"Show me," he says, far more quietly than I expect. I obediently hand over the re-dented part. He examines it, pulling out his magnifying glass and squinting at the dent for a long moment. My pulse throbs in my throat. I can't lose this apprenticeship. I must keep it. At any cost.

It would be so easy to put my hand on his arm and let my power flow through him, paralyzing his muscles and convincing his heart to slow until it stops entirely.

I close my fists to stop myself from reaching out. While we have power, using it in that way isn't what the Magi are about. We're not the murderous, evil beasts the Technocrats would make us seem. I'll succeed here, and on my own terms. I will make Mama and Papa proud.

"This is worthless. No mistakes can be allowed to stand with these machines. Learn that. Take pride in your work, girl. My shop doesn't deliver damaged goods. Not ever."

Shame flares on my cheeks. I do take pride in my work. But I have to hide the way I really work.

"What do they do?" I ask.

He doesn't look up, instead simply stares at the damaged part. "That is not important. All that matters is that every one of them is perfect." He tosses the piece into the melting bucket on his way back to his worktable.

"I'm sorry." My voice quivers and I'm surprised to find I mean it. Upsetting Leon is the very opposite of what I want to do. There is something about the way he talks about these machines that feels intensely personal. I may not understand why, but it resonates with me nonetheless.

I do my best to shove away that strange, kind feeling. It is exactly the sort of thing the Armory frowns upon. A slippery slope too dangerous to navigate.

"You must go," Leon says, and my heart nearly stops before he finishes with, "and get a package from the mining company."

Relief floods through me. He's not firing me. Yet. "Of course." I slide off the stool, careful not to jangle the parts in my smock as I remove it and lay it on the seat.

"A pouch of money is in the drawer by the door. You'll need all of it to pay for the package."

"Yes, sir," I say, removing the pouch from its hiding place.

"When I say you need all of it to pay, I mean it. If one cent is missing, the head miner won't part with the package."

"Yes, sir," I say through clenched teeth.

"Be sure to do it right this time. In some things, failure is simply not an option."

I leave the shop, shivering at how closely his words mirror my own thoughts not long before.

The mines are on the other side of Palinor, far to the northeast well beyond the Palace, but the miners have a trade shop set up on the other side of the central city square. It's only a mile away. For once the weather cooperates. A nice breeze winds through the trees, while the sun flickers between the branches and buildings.

I breathe deeply, relishing my freedom from the hot work-shop full of smelting fires and the tangy smell of steel. When I reach the square, I see several people I recognize going about their business on the streets. I smile and wave as expected, though little real cheer fills me. My mind keeps wandering back to the strange devices and Leon's even stranger reaction to them.

What in the flames am I making for him?

"Aissa?" A familiar voice startles me. A tall, muscular boy with dark hair and eyes grins uncertainly at me a few yards away. He is the spitting image of Isaiah, only younger.

"Remy?" I say, surprised. I'd recognize him anywhere.

A smile breaks over his face and he steps toward me. "At your service," he says. "Where are you headed?"

My stomach flips and I hesitate. "I'm going to the miner's shop. You?" My mind reels. Why is Remy here? Why now?

"Nowhere in particular. I'll escort you." He offers me his arm. I stare at it dumbly for a moment before looping mine through it.

"What are you doing here?" I ask as we continue through the square.

"The usual. Wreaking havoc, disappointing my father, and generally causing trouble."

"On a holiday then?" *Holiday* is our code word for mission, in case we're overheard.

"Naturally."

A sour feeling in my gut grows stronger with each passing minute. Remy has always been kept out of Palinor, safely hidden in the Chambers while Isaiah grooms him as his protégé. He's next in line to lead the Magi. If he's here now, something serious is going on.

"And what sights are you seeing on your holiday?" I press.

"I plan to gawk at the Palace for a bit, then I might make my way down to the seaport. Perhaps I will stop by your home for dinner while I'm in town."

His words almost make me trip. The seaport is on the southern coast of our country, miles beyond the city limits. It's also code for delivering a message.

He leans over to whisper into my ear. "We have more intelligence to help you and Zandria in your hunt."

Excitement blushes over me. "Why didn't you say so in the first place?" I grin, and we walk at a faster pace. "I'm sure my parents and sister would love to see you. And I'd love to join you at the seaport."

"You haven't changed a bit, Aissa. Eager as ever."

"More, actually." I lower my voice. "Did your father tell you about the adventure Zandy and I had the other night?"

Remy's face darkens, but he shrugs off the clouds. "He did, but he also mentioned your new apprenticeship, which is much more important."

"Of course," I say, wondering how far up the Armory ranks Remy has risen since I last saw him. I can't say I agree that finding a child sure to die soon anyway is more important than locating the key to our lost magic. But it's exactly the sort of thing Isaiah would say.

We quickly approach the miners' shop. The trees from the square thin and storefronts rise in their stead. Remy faces me.

"I've wanted to holiday in Palinor for some time." He still holds on to my arm, and his grip slips from my elbow to my hand. Remy steps closer; the magic rumbling under his skin calls to me. He's grown powerful.

He again leans close to my ear. "We could do great things together."

Every word I could say floats out of my head. Before I can gather my scattered thoughts to answer, the storefront door next to us bangs open and out struts Aro, dressed in an official-looking gray tunic. He halts and stares at me, blinking as though he's been blinded by the sun.

Remy's hand burns in mine and I drop it. I do my best not to look at Remy's face out of the corner of my eye.

Aro smiles. "Aissa, isn't it? Looks like I almost ran you over again."

"Don't make a habit of it," is all I can think to say. I sound like a fool, but I smile back, hoping he won't notice.

He laughs, and it lights up his face. "I swear I didn't mean to, though I'm glad to see you again."

Remy clears his throat.

"This is Remy," I say. "A friend of my family. He's on holiday."

"Nice to meet you," Aro says, reaching out his hand.

Remy shakes it, eyeing him warily. "Likewise, I'm sure."

Awkwardness pools in the air while I wrack my brain for something to say, stuck between my ally and the foe I must feign interest in. I'd rather melt into the ground. This day has gone from bad to worse.

I curse myself for being stupid enough to let Remy take my hand. I had plans to use Aro if he were as interested in me as Zandria thinks. Now he probably believes I'm spoken for. I'll have to regroup with Zandria and find a way to fix this.

I force a smile. "It was a lovely surprise to run into you both, but I must complete my errand. Excuse me." I hurry to the miner's shop as fast as I can without running. I have just enough time to glimpse both boys' surprised faces.

Fantastic. Confused boys will not make my job easier. Zandria will never let me live this down.

WHEN I RETURN TO THE WORKSHOP LATER

that morning, I immediately sense something
is off.

For starters, Leon is laughing.

Curious, I hang my cloak on the rack out front and
make my way toward the rear of the shop. I crack the door
and nearly slam it shut again.

Aro.

Grumpy Leon is smiling and chatting with Aro as if they're
old friends. Aro holds up a broken piece of machine and my
breath catches. It's from the demolition mechs Zandria and I
took apart.

I was right. They did belong to him.

I push the door open and step into the workshop. "I'm back
with your package, Leon," I call as cheerfully as possible while I
deposit the parcel on a nearby table. He grunts as though it's too
much trouble for me to exist in the same space right now.

"I suppose I must introduce you. Aro, this is my apprentice—"

"Aissa. I know." Aro recovers from his initial shock and his
face returns to its perfect, placid state. "However, I didn't know
she was your apprentice."

"We'll see how long that lasts." Leon turns back to the pieces
on the table. "Now, I think we've agreed upon a price, yes?"

"We have." Aro examines me in a way that makes magic surge
through my veins. It's everything I can do to keep it masked. This
is the second time in one day we've stumbled upon each other,
like some force of fate is pushing us together.

"But," he continues, "not who will do the repairs. I'd like to
have your apprentice help me."

Leon's mouth hangs open. "What?" he sputters. "Aissa? But just this morning she dented an important piece!"

I remain at my worktable, hands clenched in my lap. He can say whatever he wants, as long as I can keep working for him . . .

"So she needs more experience. This would be good experience, wouldn't it?"

"You realize I'm right here, don't you?" I can only hold my tongue for so long.

Aro winks, but Leon ignores me.

"Experience? A whipping would do her more good."

"It'll get her out of your workshop for the next few days."

Leon pauses and scratches his chin. Aro meets my eyes and grins. He knows just how to work Leon's temper to his advantage. Perhaps if I pay attention I can learn his methods.

"Fine. She can help you. I'll make do without her." Leon's eyes narrow. "But don't think I'm going to lower my fee just because you've requested a subpar worker."

Aro's lips twitch as he holds back his smile. "Wouldn't dream of it."

Leon relaxes again. "Good. Aissa, go with Aro and fix his machines. You'd better do a good job of it too." As he returns to his worktable on the other side of the room, he mutters under his breath, "Unlike this morning."

My face reddens, but Aro does his best not to notice. "Let me collect my tools and my cloak."

I turn aside before he can answer. How can I fix his machines when it was me who took them apart piece by piece the other night? He'll use them again, and Zandria and I will have to find a more permanent means of putting a stop to his plans.

I throw my satchel of work tools over my shoulder. Yes, of course I will fix them, and as quickly as I can.

"I'm ready. Where to?"

"Follow me."

I remind myself that I do this for the good of my people. Spending a few hours with this troubling boy will be worth it in the end. I might even find out what he's been doing in the tunnels.

I can't wait to tell Zandria I was right—those machines do belong to Aro.

"He must be fun to work with," Aro says, holding the front door open for me.

"Leon is the most skilled machinist in Palinor," I say, measuring my words. "I'm very fortunate to be apprenticed to him." This boy may speak his thoughts boldly, but I can't afford to do the same.

He laughs. "And you're very fortunate to have a diplomatic disposition. I've known him for years and know full well how grumpy he can be." He gestures to a road that leads away from my normal path through the square. "This way."

"He seems to think well of you." A connection between them is something worth pursuing. If I can get into Aro's good graces, perhaps Leon's won't be too far off.

"Oh, we've had our differences, but in many ways he's like a father to me. He even recommended me for my position. Don't worry, he'll warm up to you eventually."

"I hope you're correct," I say.

"How long have you been working for him?"

I shrug. "About a week?"

"Then you're doing well. Most of Leon's apprentices don't even make it to the end of their first day. If you've lasted this long, you must be very good."

I blush at the unexpected compliment. "I had no idea," I say.

"Was your sister apprenticed elsewhere?" Aro asks.

"Yes—she's very swift, so she's an apprentice at the Messenger Guild." I pause for a beat, then decide to risk it. "Do you have any brothers or sisters?"

An undecipherable expression flashes over Aro's face. "No, I'm an only child. I always wished I wasn't, though."

We march along the outside of the square, not far from where I spied Aro during the Apprenticing Ceremony.

"When do you plan to tell me where we're going?" I ask. My curiosity increases with every step.

"You'll see when we get there." He grins.

I frown but keep pace with him. "What do you need me to fix for you?" The question I really want to ask (What are you doing in my tunnels?) rests on the tip of my tongue, but I bite it back.

"A few machines."

"I'd never have guessed. What kind?"

"Mine." His moonlike eyes radiate mischief.

"Are you completely incapable of giving a straight answer?"

"Probably."

I clench my fists to refrain from punching him. I scowl instead, and he laughs. "Aissa, you'll see when we get there. Patience. Don't worry, we're almost there."

The mechtrees are thicker along this path, enough that the trail is largely obscured. From where it starts, it nearly looks like a dead end. Suddenly the trees break and we're up against a huge wall.

"Ah, we're here," Aro says.

With a start, I realize we've arrived at the back gates of the Palace. The monstrous brick-and-steel wall rises up for nearly twenty feet, completely obscuring the Palace itself. From farther away, one would be able to see the steel-tipped turrets of the towers, but that and these walls are about all any commoner ever gets to see of the palatial estate.

"Why are we going in the back entrance?" I ask.

Aro turns sober. "I hate marching in through the front of the Palace. Too many nosy courtiers. But this project will likely take several days. You can use that entrance next time on your own."

"Why can't you go in the front?"

"It'll take all day to get through that mob of courtiers. They live for gossip. Any hint of new tech is priceless to them." He gestures to his attire. "My uniform marks me as a researcher. If I want to get any work done, I avoid them."

"They'll bleed you dry for information, then?"

"Exactly." He shudders.

"You again?" says a dark-haired guard from the gate tower. He frowns, his eyes running over my unfamiliar form.

"Yes, Caden. Needed help with some broken machines."

"She doesn't look very useful." He laughs, as does a guard behind him, hidden by the tower walls. I bite my tongue. I can't screw this up now.

Besides, being underestimated—however much it burns me—is one of my greatest assets.

"Brains, not brawn, are necessary for the machines. That's why you're still in the guardhouse," Aro says.

Caden's laugh dies and he grunts. I try not to smile.

The gate opens to let us pass, and I hold my breath, unable to help fearing that at any second someone will see me for the Magi I am.

We walk through and the gates close behind us without incident.

The Palace is not as tall as I expected, only two or three stories. It is, however, as grossly ornate as the carriages the royals took through the square during the parade. Steel scrollwork mingles with carved marble and granite. The sunlight bounces off it, making the whole building shine like a sharp, deadly sword.

Aro notices me staring. "Doesn't seem that big, does it?"

"I always thought it would be taller," I say.

"That's where it's deceptive. There are at least a dozen levels below us."

I gulp. If that's true, then this place is massive. And will be all the more difficult to search.

Aro leads me across the lawn and through a back door, directly into the building itself.

We are inside the Palace. Me, a Magi girl, sealed inside the belly of my enemy. The very thought makes me shiver with a bizarre mix of fear and delight. When my sister and I were younger, our parents would walk us by the front of the Palace every week as reminder of what we had to prepare for. *The people inside are evil,* they'd whisper. *Look on it, remember it, and never forget it. Because someday, we'll tear it down from the inside out.* Mama and Papa, even Isaiah, will be very proud. Zandria will seethe with jealousy. We might actually succeed at this.

Provided I can keep my job with Leon.

All around us is a long, polished steel hall. Colorful tapestries line the walls, which are also dotted with paintings and statues. Some of the statues move—machines. The floor and ceiling are jewel-toned metal tiles that remind me of the sea and the sky.

The metal halls are so cold in their beauty. Glittering and gorgeous, but no warmth underneath. Just like the Technocrats themselves.

Aro leads me down the halls and we pass several other people dressed in civilian worker's clothing—black or green, like mine— and researcher garb the same gray as Aro's. He greets a handful, but most don't pay him a whit of attention. We seem to have avoided the courtiers entirely.

Aro stops before one door. It looks just like all the others— tall, sleek, and steel. If I hadn't been counting the number we have passed already—nine—I'd have great difficulty discerning this one from the others.

He takes a slim key from his pocket and unlocks the door, holding it open for me. "After you."

I step into the room. The same steel-gray walls surround us, but here there are a couple of tables with small parts and bolts and screws. Large pieces of the machines' metal shells are piled along one side of the room.

"What is this?" I ask, feigning confusion just like any new apprentice would.

"Your project for the next few days." He gestures to the sheets of paper laid out on one table. "There are your blueprints, if you need them."

"But why are they all in pieces?" I know the answer, but I need to gauge how much he suspects. "This isn't a mere repair situation—these need wholesale rebuilding." I put my hands on my hips.

Aro's face clouds over. "Someone dismantled them while they were being used in a renovation job."

I do my best to look shocked. "Who would do such a thing?"

Aro spreads his palms wide. "I don't know. I left them alone for all of ten minutes, and when I came back, this is how I found them. Whoever did it had to have either been a masterful machinist . . . or a Magi who somehow slowed me down and made me lose more time than I thought." His lips twitch.

"Magi? That's ridiculous. They've all but died out." So say our fearless Technocrat rulers. The royals do not publicly admit Magi still exist because that would mean their victory was not complete. It would mean they failed. Instead they let the commoners believe we're simply nightmares to scare their children into behaving, while the royals are secretly vigilant. But unless we use magic, Technos have no way to tell us apart. What makes us different is in our hearts and in our blood. The magic that lives in our core. And they can't see that unless they open us up.

"Maybe, maybe not. Some believe they still live on. Biding their time to attack and take their revenge." His hands turn into fists and the muscles in his neck constrict. "But their revenge is already quite complete, if you ask me."

"How so?"

He looks at me in surprise.

"Oh," I say, covering my mistake. "Of course, you mean the Heartless."

"Yes. You asked what I do in the Palace. I'm a researcher working toward finding a cure for them, something permanent so they can live longer and lead more normal lives."

"I can see the need for longer life. But are their lives so bad? Don't they get the best of everything?" At every New Year celebration Mama and Papa dutifully donate to the Heartless. Everyone is required to do so.

Aro looks aghast. "Are you joking? Most live in poverty."

"How is that possible? We donate food and toys every year." I'm genuinely confused. I never thought much on the Heartless until recently.

He scoffs. "Do you really think that lasts all year? Or that everyone complies?" His fists clench and unclench as he speaks. "Or that those donations even reach the Heartless?"

"I-I never thought—"

"No, you wouldn't have. Nor would most people. Everyone holds up the existence of the Heartless as proof of our people's virtue, but no one really wants to be near them. Except perhaps the nurses who care for them. Those who suffer are hidden away, but paraded in theory."

Aro's passionate words unsettle me. I've never heard anyone talk of the Heartless in such a manner. His fervor animates his features in a way that steals my breath. He's right; what we learn about them is all theory, and very clinical. I assumed the nature of our education on their condition was informed by the general disposition of the Technocrats, but now I have to wonder. Maybe they're an excuse for an outrage no one really wants to remedy. The Heartless are a curse, but they're also a convenient political tool, a rallying point to remind the royals' supporters that the Magi stole something precious. To remind them that it was the king and queen's bloodline that finally vanquished the Technocrats' foe.

An inkling as to why Zandria and I have been charged with finding the Heartless heir niggles at the back of my brain, then drifts away before I can catch it.

"Anyway, that part doesn't matter. What does matter is that I'm trying to help, and someone is sabotaging my progress."

The look on his face . . . could he know it was me? For one awful moment I think he does. But no, of course not. There's no way he could have any idea.

"Do you know who?" I ask, a little short of breath. I force my hands not to fidget.

He shakes his head. "Not for certain. I have a couple theories. But as long as they try to stop me, I must keep on. The Heartless children may be an embarrassment to our country's pride, but they didn't ask to be born that way."

"How exactly are you helping them?"

Aro considers me for a moment. "You really want to know?"

I take a step toward him, every nerve conscious of the fact that this boy might know something about the heir. At the very least, Isaiah will be keen to know more about this cure Aro is searching for.

"Yes. I've never heard them spoken of as you do. I—" I swallow the lump that has inexplicably formed in my throat. "I feel for them."

He leans closer, his eyes alight with fire. I have to remind myself not to pull back as instinct demands.

"I'm going to find a power source for their mechanical hearts that doesn't kill them."

I gasp.

"Everyone believes they're doomed to die young, but I don't. The mineral we use to power the hearts is the same we use in our vehicles, worker machines, and streetlamps. It was never meant to be put under someone's skin. It releases a gas that slowly infects the bloodstream. It poisons them. That's why they die."

Real pain and desperation swim behind his words and in the depths of his pale eyes.

And here I thought Technocrats couldn't cast spells of their own. I must be careful not to fall under his.

"That's terrible." I say, taking a step closer. "But what could you use instead?"

Aro's face darkens. "A new and different means of harnessing energy may lie beneath Palinor. That's why I need these machines to be functional again. The sooner the better."

His tone tugs at my emotions. I'm infuriated that he's managed to affect me in such a manner, but perhaps indulging them will win over his trust.

"I'll get started on these machines."

"Thank you," he whispers. It feels colder when he straightens his spine and moves back. "Thank you," he says again, but more aloof this time. "I appreciate your help, and your silence. It isn't public knowledge. We don't want to get anyone's hopes up yet."

"Of course." I turn toward the machines, then glance over my shoulder. "The king and queen, are they aware of your project? They must have hired you."

Aro's face blanches. "This isn't the only project I work on. But it's the most important."

"They're not aware of it, then."

He tilts his head. "You'll keep it secret?"

"I just want to be sure I know exactly who I'm keeping it a secret from." I smile and fiddle with the parts on the table.

"Thank you. I'll come back for you at the end of the day. One of the Palace guards will bring you lunch shortly."

I frown. "Am I a prisoner?"

"No, no. But I can't afford you to be slowed down by silly things like hunting for the kitchens."

"Oh. Thank you."

"You're welcome." With that, Aro is out the door. Deep in the pit of my stomach, something strange and uncomfortable blooms. I can't quite put my finger on it, can't pin it down and examine it. But something new is there. And I'm not sure how I feel about it.

I focus on the blueprints. From the looks of it, at least four machines need to be put back together. It could take me all of a few minutes to do with my magic . . .

But it would be foolish to waste a golden opportunity to spend time in the Palace. I can hardly believe I've wheedled my way in here already, in spite of Leon's contempt for me.

Zandria was right; flirting with boys does have its perks.

I must put these machines back together the hard way. I suppose there's something poetic about that. I'll do the work quickly . . . for a Technocrat.

After all the time I spent studying the machines in school, the blueprints are easy to understand. I did take these machines apart, after all. I start with the arms, six on each machine, and screw the hinges back into place so they can bend as they were meant to. The legs come next. They're less adroitly made than the arms. These machines were not designed to run; they're intended to dig, probe, and plunder.

Eventually I'll discover more about this energy source Aro thinks is under Palinor. Perhaps my parents have heard of such a thing. Or Zandria in her travels across the city.

Magi legends say our lost library is buried beneath the city; perhaps the Technos have their own legends about what's really down there too. They must. It's not like they can use magic, after all. I'll have to see if I can get that information from Aro without giving myself away.

I focus on completing the first machine, placing and bolting, hinging and oiling, and by the time the guard arrives with my lunch I'm almost sorry to stop. Seeing the machine come back together is oddly gratifying. In some ways, it's like magic, but much less elegant. And more taxing. If I didn't have magic, perhaps I'd have a real career in this and not just one to use as a cover.

The afternoon passes quickly as the first machine takes shape. My thoughts continually stray back to Aro, no matter how hard I try to avoid it.

His words stick with me too.

He wants to help his people. I've never really considered that there might be dedicated, loyal Technocrats who genuinely wish to help and cure others. I always assumed those who work in the Palace were the sort who want to destroy their perceived enemies and create false histories to justify it.

But Aro seems sincere. Plus, he's hiding his work from the king and queen. He's doing it—whatever it is, exactly—for the Heartless, without being in the spotlight and seeking glory. Of course, he could be biding his time. Technocrats are well-known for their pride and vanity.

Though I don't think that's the case here. Sincerity flowed in every word he said.

His connection to the Heartless must be personal.

A rush of heat floods through me. What if Aro knows the heir? What if she's the *reason* he's hunting for a permanent solution? Every inch of my skin prickles with the possibilities.

By the time the light outside the workroom window begins to wane, I've nearly completed one entire machine. When Aro arrives to walk me out, a grin breaks over his face as he sees my work.

"You're as fast as I'd hoped."

I just smile.

"I'll walk you back to Leon's," he says. "This time we can go through the main gate. The courtiers are all in the dining hall now, vying for King Damon and Queen Cyrene's attention."

"Do they spend the whole day amusing the courtiers?" I laugh. Rumors abound, but no one outside the Palace really knows what the royals do all day. They represent the epitome of Technocrat society: wealth and an ever-expanding arsenal of inventions at their disposal. The people benefit from and adore them for the huge laboratories they fund that are dedicated to crafting better and new machines. But underneath that adoration is a current of fear. It's rarely uttered aloud, but everyone knows the royals are capable of all sorts of atrocities.

Aro shakes his head. "Thankfully not, for both their sakes. When they're here and not at their summer home by the seaport, they hold court most afternoons and confer with their advisers."

I'm almost disappointed. Being royal sounds tedious. No wonder their expressions always looks so dour in official portraits. "Should I wait for you at Leon's again tomorrow?" I gather my things and follow him into the shiny steel corridor.

"You can enter through the servant's entrance, which I'll show you on our way out, and come right here to this room."

My heart inexplicably sinks. What do I care if he meets me at Leon's? Not having to see that crotchety old man first is a blessing. Besides, Aro just handed me the perfect excuse to wander around the Palace. If I get caught, I can invoke his name and claim I'm lost.

I can't wait to return and find out more.

BY THE TIME I ARRIVE HOME, ALL I WANT

to do is collapse onto my bed. And perhaps
unload on Zandria. But Remy already arrived,
and my family awaits me at the table. Zandy beat me
home as usual. There's a reason she's a messenger, and it's
not only because that's where Isaiah wants her. She's fast—
with or without the assistance of magic.

It doesn't matter that Leon was a bear to work with or that
I now have an excuse to explore the Palace or that I'm dying to
know what those small machines are. Nor does it matter that the
last thing I want right now is to see Remy after the awkwardness
earlier in the day. I must do what's necessary and that means listening to what Remy has to say.

I hang my cloak in the hall and take my seat at the table, not
meeting my sister's eyes. I'm brimming over with my news, but
I'm not ready to share it yet. I can sense Zandria's excitement that
Remy is here. He was always our friend and looked out for us like
an older brother. But over the past two years, with little to no
contact with the Chambers, something in me has shifted. He's still
Remy, but different. And he no longer feels like an older brother.

Any Magi girl in her right mind would be over the moon to
have the attention of the Head Councilor's son. And I am glad he's
here. But did Isaiah send him to help us or to report on us?

By the sparkle in Zandria's eye and the way she looks back and
forth between me and Remy, I can tell she is already pairing us off
and thinking of ways to push us together. When we were little,
my sister and I would giggle about what it would be like to find a
boy who loved us so much, he'd risk the wrath of the council to
perform the Binding with us.

Once, long before the Techno-Magi wars, the Binding rite was a common practice, permanently intertwining the lives of couples who married. It was considered the highest declaration of love. Their magic, minds, and hearts tied together always. When one died, the other would too. Or they could help the other stay alive if they were particularly strong. Once our population was decimated, it was outlawed. If they'd continued the Binding, we would have died out twice as fast.

Now that we're older, the romantic idea of the Binding has lost its luster.

I don't need a sentimental fool to bind his life to mine. Love like that is madness and only leads to an early death, unless you're lucky enough to have a partner who is unusually hardy. Allowing yourself to be so vulnerable because of your dependence on another has long seemed foolish to me. Besides, I want more than to be joined to someone. I want to be someone. I want to do something important. So does Zandria. Loyalty is more important than love. Our work— saving our people—is what consumes my thoughts. Not boys like Aro or Remy. While Zandria enjoys them far more than I do, I think, out of anyone, she'd understand how I feel the most. I'll just have to tell her before her imagination gets out of hand.

Right now, she understands something is bubbling inside me. Her cool hand is soothing as she winds her fingers through mine and squeezes. I squeeze back, a silent promise to tell all—later.

Remy smiles at me. "I was afraid you wouldn't make it."

"Sorry. It was a long day at work."

Zandria snorts, then covers her face when Mama gives her a sharp glance.

"Have something to eat, Aissa. You look pale." Mama pushes the pot of chicken stew and a basket of rolls in my direction. My mouth waters. I barely ate a thing all day, except the lunch Aro had the guard bring me hours ago. I grab a roll and ladle the thick, savory stew into a bowl while Remy resumes what he must have been telling them before I arrived.

"As I was saying, the council has obtained more information about your search. You seek the Technocrat heir, and we have managed to narrow a few things down."

My heart stumbles in my chest, unable to keep up with my excitement. The better and more detailed the intelligence, the higher our chances of success. Maybe this time it will come with an explanation as to why the Magi want the heir.

"The Heartless heir is being kept close. She's almost certainly hidden somewhere in the city, possibly even the Palace."

A smile creeps over my lips, but Papa's eyes narrow. "Where did you get this information?"

"From my father."

"We presumed as much," Mama says. "Where did the council obtain it? We know the network; you can tell us."

A quiver of concern flashes over Remy's face. "I'm afraid I can't. All I know is that my father has it on very good authority. It must be one of his most trusted spies, someone who's gotten close to the king and queen. That's why we need Aissa and Zandria. The better the royals know those spies, the more noticeable it is if they venture where they shouldn't. But with the two of you and your vocations, you won't attract much attention."

Mama and Papa exchange a look. Underneath Remy's words is a hidden truth we've always known, but never really considered: we may be strong and valued for our skills, but we're also expendable.

"So we're looking for a little girl without a heart who's strolling around the Palace. That shouldn't be too hard," Zandria says.

"Much harder than you'd think," Remy replies. "I've only been here a few days, but I've been watching the Palace. It is not the sort of building one just walks into without an invitation."

Zandria can't contain her smirk, but it fades at another sharp look from Mama. We must be careful in front of all Magi, even Remy. Perhaps that's why the Binding rite holds no interest for me. I could never fully confide the whole truth about myself to anyone apart from my twin and my parents.

"Actually," I say, "I can." Mama raises her eyebrow, and Zandria swats at my knee under the table. "A researcher from the Palace came to the shop today, and Leon is letting me do the repairs on some machines of his."

Zandria gives me a look that leaves no doubt she's bursting for details. And I'm dying to share them. But only after Remy leaves.

"That's wonderful news, Aissa. My father will be delighted to hear about this development. I'm also being placed at a job in the Palace. Father is arranging it, I'm just waiting for word my holiday is over."

Papa's brow furrows deeper. Mama sits still. Too still. They're worried about something. But it's clear they don't want to talk about it in front of Remy.

Mama locks eyes with Papa. "Perhaps it would be helpful to have someone with a direct connection to the Chambers close by."

"I suppose," I say. "But what I really want to know is, what are we supposed to do with this Heartless girl once we find her? She's going to die anyway. How could she possibly be useful to our cause?"

Remy's face is blank. Practiced. Just like any other spy, who doesn't want to let their features betray them.

Shock trills over me. Remy knows.

And he won't tell us.

"My father hasn't told me. I . . . I need to prove myself first." The crack in his voice almost makes me believe him. It could be the reason behind his masked features. His own pride is hurt at my question. Or he knows and has been instructed not to say. Remy sits up straighter. "And even then I don't expect to be given that information until absolutely necessary. No one but my father and one or two of his highest-tier spies know. Everyone else involved must be kept in the dark for the sake of the mission. You'll just need to trust there is a purpose, and it will be revealed when the time is right."

What worries me is that we may be too low on the ladder to ever really know the master plan. Mama and Papa have long warned us about the necessity of compartmentalizing information in the spy network, but I didn't expect it to chafe so stingingly. The thing is, I can't figure out what they could possibly want us to do. Nothing makes sense. The whole thing doesn't make sense. We would be far more useful figuring out why someone is trying to find the Magi library and then keeping them away from it.

But of course we can't share that information without suffering punishment for breaking a direct order.

We'll have to simply do as the Armory instructs and bide our time until they deem us ready to handle whatever they have in store for the unfortunate Technocrat heir.

"Anyway, I ought to be going. Thank you for sharing your dinner with me." Remy rises from the table. "Aissa, will you see me out?" The soft edge that creeps into his voice surprises me. I set the remains of my supper down.

"Of course." I lead him out of the kitchen, Zandria's eyes burning into my back.

Remy opens the front door then pauses. "I just wanted to say I'm sorry we've spent so much time apart. I hope we get to make up for that. Lost time and all."

I stare blankly, trying to process his words. Remy ducks his head, and the darkness swallows him.

When I close the door and turn back toward the hall, Zandria leans against the kitchen doorframe, chewing on a roll and smirking.

"Don't even say it," I mutter, brushing past her to rejoin our parents and finish my dinner.

"What did Remy say?" Mama asks.

"Yes," Zandria echoes, grinning. "Tell us, what did Remy want?"

"Nothing. Not really. He just wanted to say he's looking forward to working with us."

"Of course he is," Zandria purrs. I throw a pointed look her way.

"I don't think that's important," I say. "What I want to know is what they expect us to do with a young girl. What is the endgame?"

Papa chuckles. "No wonder Remy wants to work with you. He must like your drive." He sets his glass down. "The Armory Council is not in the business of telling all. They only release snippets of information and exactly when it's needed."

"It's rather infuriating of them, don't you think?" I say.

"Why should they tell you more than you need?" Mama says. "If you were to get caught, the Technocrats might force that information out. You can't tell them something you don't know, can you?"

I frown. "Well, no. But we're not getting caught. We can affect organics and machines. We're in little danger."

Papa gives me a stern look and I know the conversation is about to come to a close. "The Armory doesn't know about the extra benefits of your magic. As far as they're concerned, you two are normal Magi. We must keep it that way."

Before I can apologize for upsetting him, Papa leaves the table and retreats to his study. I know better, and I know why he's upset. Our powers could mark us as Technocrat sympathizers no matter how loyal to the Magi we really are. Over the last hundred years, the Magi have stewed in their resentment of what the Technocrats did to them, sharpening their hatred of all things technological to a razor-thin edge. There is no telling what our punishment would be—or how dire.

"Nice, Aissa," Zandria says.

"I didn't mean—"

"He knows," Mama says. "But he worries. We both do. We have to."

"I'm sorry. I just want to do well. I want us all to be free."

Mama takes my hand and Zandria's in hers. "So do we. Just bide your time, and eventually we will."

THE NEXT MORNING I MAKE A POINT OF

arriving at the Palace early. As in two hours
early. Zandria thought I was crazy, but I want to
explore everything while I have the chance. Once I've
finished this project, it's back to Leon's workroom and
those tiny machines. I don't know how many days I can
stretch this assignment out, and I have no guarantee of being
invited back to the Palace in the future. I need to take advantage
of it while I can. And I wouldn't mind spending more time with
Aro and doing my best to win him over.

But when I arrive, the first thing I see is Remy patrolling the
grounds with the guards.

He did mention his father was placing him at the Palace, but
he should have sent us word before starting that it was set, unless
there wasn't time. The last thing we need to do is take each other
by surprise. Any hint that we aren't what we claim will cast suspicion on us all.

He stops me when I try to pass him on the Palace steps. The
stirrings of irritation rumble in my chest, and I squash them down.

"What's your business here?" he says.

I scowl on the inside but smile sweetly as the other guards draw
near. "I'm working on a repair project for Aro. He's a researcher in
the employ of the king and queen. He's expecting me."

The guard behind Remy, the tall fellow from the back gates
yesterday named Caden, grunts. "Ha, you don't want to be late for
Aro. He's terribly impatient."

"Then I'd better be going."

"Perhaps I should go with you, miss, to ensure you get there quickly." Remy puts a hand on my elbow. I wish I could shake him off; instead, I nod curtly for the benefit of the others.

As soon as we're out of the guards' earshot, Remy leans over and whispers, "You're here very early in the day." Curiosity lights his eyes.

We pass a handful of courtiers on the front entryway of the Palace, and before I can answer a sudden hush falls over them and every servant nearby. They all halt what they're doing and stand at attention as a figure in a frosted blue gown with a diamond-studded skirt and a bodice of platinum lace appears. Her long pale hair falls over her shoulders, and her sharp blue eyes take in every face with the speed of a hawk. Every muscle in my body clenches when they graze over me and Remy.

Queen Cyrene.

My heart stutters in my chest, and Remy and I cast our eyes down in respect as quickly as possible, but not before I've marked the unmistakable look on the servants' faces: fear. The official portraits I've seen do not do the queen justice. She is lovely in the same way winter is lovely: sparkling and serene on the outside while only cold and ice lie underneath.

The group of courtiers bow as one and begin simpering as soon as they've straightened their backs. The queen gives them a bored look before snapping her fingers and turning on her heel down a hallway. The courtiers follow her like children, tripping over themselves for attention. She and the king must be holding court today. I file that information away, making a mental note to record what days that occurs.

Once the courtiers and the queen have moved on and the halls only have a few servants scurrying about, I answer Remy. "I wanted to get an early start fixing Aro's machines."

"That boy we ran into the other day?" I nod, and Remy gives me a sidelong look.

I wriggle my arm out of his grasp. If anyone in the Palace gets the wrong idea about me and Remy, it will become rather difficult to encourage a flirtation with Aro. It's a far too important part of my plan.

Remy's face falls and he slows his pace. The anger slips out of me. Hurting him is not my intention.

"Sorry—I wasn't expecting you to be here already. You should warn me if we're going to cross paths like this." I sigh. "Aro mentioned he wants to save the Heartless, and he's working on a cure. Some kind of new power source. He might have useful information. The faster I get into his good graces, the better."

Remy eyes the empty hallway and lowers his voice until it is barely audible. "My father will be very interested to hear that, I'm sure. I think I may have a lead for you. There's a group of children in the Palace, cared for by nannies. They're all Techno royalty—nobles and courtiers' children. If they wanted to hide the heir in plain sight, that would be a logical place."

"I'll keep an eye out for them. We'll talk more later."

I continue down the hall alone, the weight of Remy's gaze on my back. I duck into the workshop I used yesterday. My plans to sneak through the Palace unnoticed are dashed, but I still have the better part of an hour before I expect Aro will arrive.

If I could just be sure Remy is gone.

I know he means well, but if I'm going to sneak around, I'm better off doing it by myself. And to accomplish that, I need to know the hallway is completely clear. I can't remove the door handle or make the metal turn from hard steel to transparent glass here. I may be able to manipulate the machines and metal, but I can't risk half the Palace staff seeing it.

Though I can still amplify sounds.

I kneel close to the door, murmuring the words to the spell. I close my eyes and absorb the patterns of footfalls, paying attention to the direction they fade.

The heavy boots of a guard—Remy, I assume—get softer every second. Good. This morning hasn't been a waste.

But just as I put my hand on the doorknob, another set of steps, more purposeful than the others, approaches my door very quickly.

The steps stop directly outside my workroom, and I leap onto the stool by my table as the door creaks open.

"Oh, good, I was hoping you might be here early," Aro says. When he closes the door behind him, I realize he's holding that little pet machine in his hands.

"Good morning to you too," I say, making sure to smile, despite my racing heart. That was a little too close. It would definitely be bad if Aro caught me skulking around the Palace. I'll have to remember that he likes to begin work early too.

He places the small machine on the table. "Sparky isn't walking anymore. Can you fix him?"

I examine the machine, poking and prodding to see if anything is clearly broken on the outside. When I flick the switch at the bottom, it makes a sad attempt to walk away and turns in a circle instead. One leg isn't moving at all and the other is overcompensating.

I smother my smile, but Aro chuckles. "Depressing little bugger, isn't he?"

"I can fix it by lunchtime." I turn the thing off. Its strange gait is disconcerting.

"Thank you." His pale eyes rove over the machinery waiting to be put back together. "Do you need anything? Tools? More water? Breakfast?"

"I'm fine, thank you."

Aro stands there for a moment too long, hands fumbling at his sides. Something tangible and awkward hangs in the air between us, and it unexpectedly makes my pulse race again.

He clears his throat. "I'll come back at lunch. For Sparky."

I don't look up from the table, pretending to be absorbed in Sparky's leg so Aro won't see the flush creeping up my neck. The door clinks shut and the breeze from the hallway brushes my hair across my cheek. I shiver, but I'm not entirely sure why.

I turn my attention to Sparky for real this time. I can't believe the Technocrats name these things. They're nothing compared to the sweet, cuddly pups we have in the Chambers, or even the rabbits and goats we keep in our yard here in town.

These are cold. They only play at life.

But I suppose they don't have many options. In the Great War, the Technocrats wrought so much destruction on the natural world in and near Palinor that the only animals they have left must be used for food. Or they range much farther afield across the lands. That's why Techno parks have a mix of real trees and metallic ones. They've wholeheartedly embraced their coldness and treat it as if it's just as good as the warmth the Magi have always revered.

I wait another ten minutes to ensure Aro is gone before I begin to weave my magic. I'll get this thing out of the way first, then go back to the other machines.

The threads of my magic pull at the motionless foot, teasing the bits and pieces apart until they lay before me. I inspect them closely for anything that might be rusted or broken. A loose piece that likely belongs deeper in the body of the machine rolls out of the leg and onto the table. It must have slipped into the leg shaft, wreaking havoc.

The rest of the machine unravels at my words and motions, laying itself out neatly on the table. It doesn't take long for me to realize something's wrong with this machine. It's just a pet, a thing to follow and keep company. But it has more parts than a normal machine would inside the body.

I sharply suck in my breath, alarm skittering down my spine.

A device with a cracked reflective surface and wiring rests inside. The extra piece appears to have broken off this device.

It's a listener.

Aro's pet is a trap.

Is Aro spying for someone? Or is someone spying on Aro?

Either way, this listener is broken. I certainly have no intention of fixing it. Cold creeps over me. If that thing had been functional when I used my magic to take it apart, muttering the words of the spell for all to hear . . .

I'd be a dead Magi faster than you can say "put me in irons."

I throw the device onto the floor and stomp on it for good measure. Then down the furnace chute with the vile thing. Hopefully no one will notice. If it is Aro's, I doubt he'll confront me. If it's someone else's . . . well, that's none of my business and I'm probably much safer keeping it that way.

It doesn't take long for me to put Sparky back together. By the time Aro reappears at lunch, it walks perfectly again.

"You're a miracle worker," he says with a lopsided grin that makes my stomach flip while the metal beast thumps around on its feet.

My face heats without my permission. "It just needed some fine-tuning."

"Thank you." Aro takes a step closer. "If you're half as good with the rest of these machines, I'll see to it that you're very well rewarded."

"I appreciate that." My face is now burning hot. The proximity of this Technocrat boy is having the strangest effect on me.

I don't like it one bit.

I fiddle with my tools on the bench to put some distance between us. "I should continue my work."

"Of course." He pauses. "But first, why don't we go to the kitchens and get a bite to eat? I have something I want to show you."

My eyes snap up. "I . . . yes. Are you going to tell me what you wish to show me this time, or will that remain a surprise too?"

Amusement flits across Aro's face. "I do love surprises."

I raise an eyebrow at him and together we leave the room, the newly fixed Sparky happily thumping behind us. I mark the halls we pass through to get to the kitchens and file them away in the back of my brain. I try to steer the conversation toward various people in the Palace, but all Aro wants to speak of are machines. When we reach the kitchens, he charms the cook and she gives us heaping sandwiches and lemonade to drink. Aro thanks her and ushers me up a flight of stairs. I'm struck by how kind he is to her. As a researcher, he's on a higher social level. Most of my old schoolmates barely said two words to the kitchen workers at our school, and never thank you. Something almost like respect begins to brew in my chest.

We walk upward for several minutes. If it wasn't for my training I'd be sorely out of breath by the time we reach a landing and Aro pauses outside the door. He wears a mischievous smile.

"I take it whatever is beyond this door is what you wanted to show me?"

In answer, he opens the door wide. I gasp.

The room before us is a garden. It's stunning, unlike any Techno garden I've ever seen before. Not a single mechanical plant or bug in sight.

We must be near the top of the Palace. The walls of the room are made entirely from glass windows. Along the sides are trees heavy with fragrant fruits, and roses and tulips and sunflowers and more line the curling pathways that all lead to a small fountain in the center of the room. Sparkling sunlight glances off it all.

It's a small speck of life in a dreary maze of boxes.

Aro's eyes are filled with awe as he breathes in the sweet smell of the garden. "It's my favorite place in the Palace. Most people don't know it exists, there are so many halls in this place."

"It's beautiful." It almost reminds me of the Chambers. I never thought I'd see anything so pure and lovely here in this tainted city, let alone be led there by a Technocrat who clearly values it. I swallow the lump in my throat. When the Magi ruled, there were many more gardens like this. Since Zandria and I were ten years old, we've learned all about the origin of the Technocrats, how they rose from the mud and eventually, due to their brilliant minds, gave birth to the machines they rely on. How they finally crushed their Magi oppressors.

But before that we learned how the Magi revered the earth and life, and later from our parents how they tried to stop the destruction wreaked by the Technocrats and were rewarded only with their own. It never occurred to me that a Technocrat might also love something so simple and natural and beautiful as this. I can't help but look at Aro with a new appreciation. I didn't expect we'd have something in common.

Aro grins. "I was hoping you'd like it. Let's sit by the fountain."

We eat our sandwiches to the sound of water gurgling with the warmth of the sun on our skin.

"How did you find this place?" I ask.

"An old friend of mine showed it to me once. I come up here every chance I get. It's peaceful." I can't help but notice how gently he runs one of his long fingers over the petal of a nearby flower.

"Ha! They let you take time from the workday to laze about up here? I had no idea the research division was so lax."

"Hardly. But I may make an excuse or invent an errand once in a while that isn't really as necessary as my superiors believe."

"Is that what you did the day of the parade?"

"Perhaps. But the white lie was worth it." Aro winks.

Heat crawls up my neck as his implication hits home. It was worth it because he met me. A tiny part of me feels the same, but only because he was my way into the Palace so soon.

Sparky thumps past us, the only mechanical thing in the

room, as he does another circuit of the garden. I remember the listener I found this morning. Aro may think no one knows he comes up here, but I bet someone does.

"It's so bright. Even with the mechlights, the rest of the Palace is dark in comparison."

Aro nods.

"I must admit, I'm surprised. Why are there no mechanical plants or mechbees? I don't believe I've ever seen a garden in this city without them."

An expression passes across Aro's face too quickly for me to discern its meaning. "I don't know for certain, but the friend who showed this garden to me said it was made on special request of some royal. Probably to entertain and show off the novelty of it."

"Kind of like you're doing now?"

He laughs. "I suppose so. But it is novel, isn't it? These plants are the perfect machines. And we didn't even have to build them. They were already here. They can heal and replicate all on their own. They work in perfect harmony. It's truly wondrous if you stop and think about it."

I can tell from the light shining in his eyes that he's thought about this often. More and more surprises from this boy.

Our lunch is over too soon, and Aro stands. "We need to get back to work. But thank you for joining me for lunch. Let's keep this place our secret, all right? Don't want too many people crowding it out."

"Of course. Thank you for showing it to me."

I look back wistfully as the door closes on the lovely room. But the warmth I felt there follows me all the way down the stairs.

ON OUR WAY BACK TO THE WORKROOM, WE

pass through a courtyard, only to find Remy
posted across the way. He raises an eyebrow as
he bites into an apple. Just as we take one step into
the otherwise deserted area, loud noises make me freeze.

Boots stomp against concrete and steel in a furious
rhythm. My pulse spikes with every step they take. Have they
found me out? Or Remy?

"Are you all right?" Aro asks.

"I'm fine—I just heard something."

When the owners of those boots round the corner and enter the
courtyard, it's clear neither me nor Remy are the ones in trouble.

It's the baker and his son. The kind man used to give me
and Zandria cinnamon buns when Mama and Papa took too
long chatting at the counter. His son has grown up to be just like
him. They're some of the few Technocrats I like. What could they
have done?

The elite guards drill past us, dragging the two protesting men
with them. The guards' silver-and-black cloaks, woven with metal
fibers, mark them as higher ranking than the regular Palace guards
who wear a steel gray.

I meet Remy's gaze. We're thinking the same thing. *Follow them
and find out more.*

Remy takes off in the other direction.

"Afraid they were coming for you for neglecting your work?"
Aro whispers into my ear.

"That isn't funny." I ball my hands into fists. "Besides, I was
just coming back from lunch. With you. I doubt anyone will hold
that against me."

He leans against the doorway, arms folded, and grins.

"Do you know those two men? What did they do?" I ask.

He tilts his head at me. "Want to find out?"

"Possibly. As long as it doesn't mean I'll suffer their fate. Whatever it is."

"Of course not. No one else could fix Sparky so quickly. I can't do without you."

My cheeks burn, and I silently curse my body for betraying me. "Then by all means, lead the way."

He opens the side door into the Palace, and we take turn after turn until we reach a closet. I eye Aro inquisitively, and he gestures for me to go in first.

"Is this a trick?"

"Aissa, if I wanted to trick you, I'd have done it by now, don't you think?" He shakes his head and enters the closet.

I can't afford to trust anyone in the Palace. But if I want him to trust me, I must appear trusting too, like any normal Technocrat.

I set aside my pride and follow him. Every muscle in my body is wound tight, ready to fight or flee if necessary.

The closet is about ten feet long by six feet wide, and filled with linens and guard uniforms. Aro pushes aside a large standing shelf. Behind it is a strange contraption—part metal and part mirror. It's as though we're looking directly into the throne room. This closet must be right next to it.

"How does it do that?" I whisper. And how did he get it in here without anyone noticing?

"I work in research. I know a few tricks involving smoke and mirrors. And I like to stay informed."

Something bordering on respect trickles over me yet again. If the royals knew a researcher was spying on them like this . . . Aro might be as ripe for the picking as Zandria believes.

"Can they hear us?"

"Only if you scream."

The throne room is a combination of carved red-veined marble and steel, dotted with columns of white at regular intervals. I can't see the thrones, only the guards marching up to where we hide.

"Are the king and queen on the other side of this wall?"

Aro nods, then I fall silent as the baker and his son are forced to kneel. I can't see the monarchs' faces from here, only the prisoners'. They look terrified.

"You conspired against the crown," King Damon says in a booming voice. I imagine his unhappy face, etched with lines. I've seen it enough times, glaring out the fancy carriage windows in the annual parade. "You shall be punished."

The baker's face tightens at this declaration, while his son lets out a sob.

"But we are merciful," Queen Cyrene continues. "The sentence will be life in prison."

The prisoners' faces fall farther at her words, and I swear the temperature drops a few degrees from her cold tone alone. "What's the matter?" I ask Aro. "Why are they disappointed by the queen's mercy?"

"Watch." Aro grimaces, and what I see next shakes me to the core.

Two more guards appear. They carry a hammer, a red-hot poker, and what appear to be steel hoods.

The prisoners thrash and struggle. The baker's son manages to get one hand free but is quickly overpowered again.

"No, please," the baker begs. "Don't do this to my son."

But his cries are ignored. The guards force the hoods over the prisoners' heads. They're secured by chain straps crisscrossing the shoulders and neck, with manacles hanging down for the hands.

Once the hoods are in place, the guards slide a mask plate in front of the eyes. The baker and his son's sobs reverberate strangely behind the metal hoods, punctuated by a locking mechanism that echoes loud enough for us to hear in the closet.

Horror rolls over me, weakening my knees, but somehow I remain standing. The rest of their lives, locked in darkness. I can't even fathom.

But it is not over yet. The guards drag the prisoners to a nearby table and hold their arms down.

"No! No, please. We're innocent!" the baker's son screams.

Blood throbs in my ears and my nails dig into my palms. There is nothing I can do to help them. This feeling of helplessness is suffocating.

One of the guards lifts the hammer and brings it down with sickening force. It's over in seconds—their hands broken beyond repair—but their screams echo between my ears and make my head ache. The guards slide open a panel over the baker's mouth and force the hot poker down on his tongue. I look away, my stomach turning like a rock rolling down a hill and picking up speed. I choke down the bile rising in my throat. I don't need to watch to know they do the same thing to his son, and why. They were Magi all along.

I swallow the sob welling in my chest. This is it. This is why we fight.

Aro takes my shaking hand. "It's all right. They're Magi. It's a precaution to prevent them from casting spells on the guards. With their tongues and hands ruined, it will make casting extremely difficult. And the guards will never risk removing their helmets. They only open that panel over their mouths to pour in soup and water twice a day. They'll put them in cells that have no light or trace of organic matter. Even if they heal, they have nothing to use their magic on. They can't escape and harm us."

My gut turns into a giant block of ice. Heavy, uncomfortable, and cold, cold, *cold*.

If they catch me and my family, this will be our fate. Zandria and I are the only ones who'd have a prayer of getting out of it.

I force my hands to stop shaking and summon the will to talk normally. "I thought all the Magi were extinct."

Aro laughs nervously. "Well, not exactly. Most of them, definitely. But a few stragglers survived. The king and queen won't publicly admit that. I wouldn't even know if I didn't have this setup here." He gestures to his contraption. "You didn't hear it from me, but I have it on good authority that the royals have spies everywhere—every school, every market, every pub. You can't go anywhere in Palinor without being monitored. Hidden listeners are planted everywhere just in case they pick up the mutterings of a spell. They put on a good show for the masses—their rule is founded on their claim to power, after all—but in private they're intensely paranoid. Especially the queen, or so I'm told."

Aro's information isn't as shocking as he thinks it is, but I act appropriately surprised for his benefit. No Magi has taken their safety in Palinor for granted since the Technocrats toppled their regime. Every Magi spy has a meticulously falsified history and family tree just in case they run into trouble. But some, like the baker and his son, still get caught. Usually when they do something careless.

Like Zandria dancing and singing in the tunnels at night, just begging for a guard to hear her. I shudder.

Before I can respond to Aro's words, a commotion breaks out in the throne room. More guards enter, dragging a girl between them. They shove her to the floor in front of the king and queen. I'm stunned to realize I recognize her.

"We found her trying to get into the Palace," one says. "Followed us all the way from their home." He gestures to the baker and his son.

Vivienne leaps to her feet and throws herself on the baker's son. "You can't do this!" she cries. She clutches the boy's arm and his chest rises and falls as though he cries too. If any sounds escape his throat, we can't hear him through his awful helmet. No one will ever hear him again.

"He's kind and good and he loves the empire. Why would you do this?" Her lovely face is red and puffy and marred by black streaks from the kohl lining her eyes. I never suspected this side of Vivienne existed. She was always nice enough, but passionate? Not how I pegged her. I wonder if Zandria had any inkling.

The queen finally responds after a long pause. "You love this boy?" Something in the quiet, calm tone of her voice makes the hair raise on the back of my neck.

"Yes! He wouldn't do anything against the empire—I swear my life on it."

"Do you know what he and his father have been charged with?"

Vivienne's face falters, and she shakes her head. "No, but I'm positive they're innocent."

"Then you're a fool. They're Magi. They would destroy our realm. They cursed so many of our country's children to be born Heartless. They condemned them to die."

Vivienne's demeanor melts into horror at the queen's words. "But—but I thought all that was left of them were myths."

The queen's voice hardens. "There are only a few, but they are devious, evil creatures."

Vivienne stares wide-eyed at the baker's son, but the monarch doesn't stop her tirade.

"We will lock what's left of the Magi away in the dungeon, where they'll remain until they die. They won't plague us much longer."

"They won't?" Vivienne whispers as Queen Cyrene leaves her throne and steps toward her. The blue gown she wears shimmers in the brilliantly lit room, her long pale hair spilling down her back like snow falling in moonlight.

"No." The queen takes Vivienne by the throat and lifts her up. "Nor will anyone who sympathizes with them." I clamp my hands over my mouth as the girl struggles and claws at the queen's hands. The queen's gown and long sleeves are reinforced by steel, and thin metal bars studded with diamonds have been grafted onto her fingers and wrists. No wonder she is so strong.

"Come on," Aro whispers. "I didn't mean to upset you." He tugs at my arm, but I refuse to budge.

"Aissa, you don't need to see this. I shouldn't have brought you here." Something miserable in his voice gives me pause. Vivienne now hangs limply between two guards. The queen choked her until she lost consciousness. Rage burns in my blood and it's all I can do not to let my magic slip out. I want to curse her right now. But I can't risk undermining our mission. I can't endanger my family and risk that fate for them too.

Another guard enters the room with a hood just like the ones on the baker and his son. Anguish fills me with a sudden intensity.

So this is what happens to those who help us, even if they aren't Magi. Torture, imprisonment. Endless night. As they lock the helmet over Vivienne's head, Aro tries to pull me out of the closet once again.

"Let go of me!" I hiss and slap his hands away from my arms. "That girl was in my class. She doesn't deserve to be treated that way."

"I'm sorry," he says, but I refuse to look at him. Instead, I storm out of the closet toward the workroom. I wonder if Remy saw the same scene. I wonder if he was as horrified by it as I am.

I quickly walk back to the workroom, doing my best to tamp down the rage and anguish leaking out of my pores. Hide it, bury it, and use it as fuel instead.

Never let it show.

A fine job I'm doing of that this time. I should be focused on my mission and winning over Aro. I thought I was better trained, better prepared. But nothing could have prepared me for that.

I am just outside the workroom, my pulse nearly returned to normal, when Aro catches up to me.

"Wait, Aissa, please."

I open the door and duck inside, and to my surprise he follows. I whirl on him as the door closes, my best attempt at a smile on my face. I fear it looks more like a grimace. One glance at my expression and Aro's face crumples.

"I'm sorry, Aissa, I—I guess I was just showing off. I had no idea you knew them. It was foolish of me." He places a gentle hand on my arm and a lump suddenly forms in my throat. My cheeks feel like they're flaming. I close my eyes, racking my brain for a convincing lie to explain these emotions I'm failing to control.

A light hand brushes my cheek. Two more tears roll down before I recover enough to open my eyes again.

"I thought she was my friend. I can't believe she's been consorting with Magi." The half-truth burns like ash on my tongue.

Aro's grip on my arm tightens. "It isn't your fault that you were trusting."

"Isn't it though?" I frown. "I should have seen through it."

"No," he says, sliding his hand down my arm. My skin tingles and this time it isn't my magic. "Magi are known for their deceptive ways. Even the best of us could be taken in by one. They are cruel, callous creatures."

I smile weakly, his words jolting through me. Strange emotions war in my chest. Here's a Technocrat attempting to be kind and comforting, yet all he's done is reinforce how much he'd hate me if he knew what I really am.

When he leaves the workroom, the ghostly impression of his compassion quickly fades. The weight of his animosity left behind stings far more than I expected.

BY THE TIME I REACH HOME THAT AFTER-

noon, my blood buzzes in my ears. The poor
baker. His poor son. Poor Vivienne.

The Technocrats must be stopped at all costs. We
have to find that library. Isaiah, the Armory, and their
alternative plan can all jump into the flames. It's too slow.
Those people need help—freedom—right now.

Our parents aren't home yet, so I head straight for the cellar.
As soon as the panel slides back into place, I break into a run on
the obstacle course.

Ducking and weaving, punching and leaping, all while using
my magic to enhance my natural abilities, keeps my focus sharp.
And keeps my mind on something other than the horror I wit-
nessed only a few hours ago.

But it doesn't work long. My hands tremble too hard to hit
the punching bag with the usual force. I stumble over hurdles I
normally clear with ease.

I scale the climbing wall but fall back to the ground hard
enough that the air is forced from my lungs. I stare at the ceiling,
panting, while stars dance in front of my face. I wish I could just
pass out and wake up having forgotten all about this afternoon.

My mind refuses to stop racing. My entire body shakes. Even
the cool floor can't quell the awful burning terror that creeps over
my skin like a slow blaze.

Trapped in permanent darkness. No light. No sound but the
blood ringing in your own ears. The only food what you can
choke down of what's poured into your mouth. No movement.

No magic.

I can't fathom anything worse than the sentence of endless, metallic night.

What troubles me the most is why the royals keep them alive. Is it a warning to other Magi who might try to take the Technocrats down? Or do they so delight in cruelty that they do it for their own amusement?

I roll onto my side and curl my legs up to my chest. My eyes sting, and the sob I've been holding in all afternoon finally breaks free.

The front door slams shut and Zandria's familiar hum resonates through the house. Relief floods over me. I'm not alone anymore.

Her steps ring out and Zandria appears in the training room. I scramble to my feet, but I'm still unsteady.

She takes one look at my face and puts her arms around me.

Now I can't help but cry harder.

"What happened?" she whispers.

"They captured some Magi today. The baker and his son," I say between halting breaths. "Then Vivienne defended the baker's son and they took her too."

Zandria's arm tightens around my shoulders. "Vivienne? But why would they take her? She's a Techno through and through."

"Apparently she's in love with the baker's son, which makes her a sympathizer."

"Did they . . . did they kill them?" Zandria's voice cracks on the last two words.

I shake my head. "Worse. They locked them in steel helmets and bound their hands to their sides, then burned their tongues and broke their fingers. They can't move, see, or do anything on their own. They're trapped in a steel prison."

"That's horrible." Tears form in the corners of her eyes, a mirror of my own. We liked the baker. We liked Vivienne.

We hate the Technocrat king and queen so much it drowns out every other feeling. I wipe the last of the tears from my eyes.

"You know what we need to do?" I ask.

"Resume our search for the library. Even with that boy and his machines down there."

Something sharp twinges in my chest at the mention of Aro. Despite the fact he's a Techno, I didn't mind Aro as much as I first expected. Even though it was his machines in the tunnels. He seemed harmless enough, kind even. That was foolish of me. I know better than to underestimate him. He showed his true colors when he told me how he felt about the Magi.

Cruel, callous creatures.

Maybe he does suspect my involvement in the destruction of his machines and his kindness is a trick to draw me in. I won't let my guard down around him again.

Zandria squeezes my hands. They no longer shake. "We should go tonight. We can take out more machines if we have to, but we need to find another way to that door."

"Agreed. Did you learn anything of interest today?"

Zandria laughs, but her smile doesn't reach her eyes. I'm glad she didn't have to see those awful helmets. I wish I hadn't seen them.

"I think I may have found another Magi here in the city, but my day was not half as exciting as yours."

"That's probably for the best."

She nods absently and considers the obstacle course. "Do you want to practice?" she asks.

I take a deep breath. With my sister here beside me, I feel stronger, and ready to run this circuit. "Yes. We can never be too ready."

———◆·∞·◆———

As soon as our parents fall asleep, my sister and I creep out our bedroom window and slink through the shadows. But something feels different. The back of my neck prickles like we're being watched. Yet an examination of the alleys reveals no one.

"What are you doing?" Zandria whispers impatiently after the third time I stop to stare down a wayward shadow.

"Someone's following us. I can feel it."

"You always feel that way." She turns her back on me and hurries down the alley we just entered.

"Doesn't mean it isn't true," I mutter, taking one last look behind me. I swear something moves, but my eyes don't fix on it and then it's gone. Maybe I am just being paranoid.

After what I saw this afternoon, I am jumpier than usual.

I can't let it happen to anyone else.

With the library lost and our most powerful Magi dead, we've been a people adrift. Hiding in the shadows, hoping for a time to reappear and take back our lives in the sunlight. If we can find the library, we can recover our lost spells. We could crush the Technocrats, raze their Palace to the ground, and free the Magi prisoners.

Completing this mission is the key to making that dream a reality.

At least, I hope it is. It has been so long, we don't even know for certain what type of spells the library might contain. All we know is that the most powerful ones were once housed there for use by the most advanced Magi.

Before the Techno-Magi wars, the Magi were trained in an academy, the best and brightest moving up the ranks and learning the truly formidable spells. Now, the few spell books we've salvaged are safely hidden in the Chambers and used to train all Magi. There are still those who are more gifted than others, of course, but everyone has the same basic education. Except Zandria and me. Our parents' shop gives us an edge, the potential to see and learn spells no other Magi in living memory has seen. That taste of power has only made us even hungrier for what lies waiting in the library. And aware of what that extra knowledge could do.

Fog whispers across the streets, coating the alley in gray, moving almost as if it has a mind of its own. I can't quite tell if it's natural or not. Fog is an excellent cloaking device. But it was raining this evening; it's not surprising such a haze would appear.

Still, even Zandria proceeds more cautiously. By the time we reach the alley containing our entrance, we've slowed to a crawl.

The fog trails us. Something is definitely not right.

Zandria's hand encloses mine and we stand to face the creeping mist. "Who's there?" I say. Brick walls surround us on all but one side now. If someone is coming toward us, we'll have to take him down quickly and quietly.

This is what we've been training for in the cellar. A night just like this.

A shadow in the midst of the fog moves toward us. Zandria and I tense, readying ourselves to attack both physically and magically. The figure moves closer. Zandria's hitching breath is the only noise besides the wind whistling down the alley.

"It's just me," the figure says, materializing before us. Remy grins and I lunge at him.

"You!" I shove him hard in the chest and he stumbles backward. "How dare you sneak up on us like that," I hiss. Zandria pulls me back, but from the look in her eyes she wants to hurt him as much as I do.

Remy laughs and coughs as the fog dissipates. "I didn't mean to scare you. I have news to share and saw you leave your house before I could knock on your door."

"What news?" Zandria says.

"Thanks to Aissa's information that the Technocrats are in

search of a cure, the Armory Council wants you to kidnap the heir once you find her. We cannot allow her to be cured. Their bloodline must die out. And once that happens, feuds between the powerful houses will send the Technocrats into civil war and provide the perfect opportunity for us to reemerge and take back Palinor."

Zandria pales. "But that could take years."

Remy shrugs. "The Armory has been playing the long game for the last hundred years. What's a few more?"

"That's it? What are we supposed to do with the heir once we capture her?" I ask, an unexpected heaviness weighing on my chest.

"Hold her for ransom. Our source close to the royals has confirmed the queen cannot conceive again. The heir is their only hope for their line to continue. We'll use her as a bargaining chip to return the Magi they've taken prisoner." Remy yawns. "Now, where are you two going so late at night?"

I bristle. "None of your business. If we wanted you to know, we would've included you in our plans."

Remy raises a dark eyebrow. "What plans are these?"

My face flames with anger, but Zandria responds before I say something I'll regret. "We're out for a walk. A little exercise before bed helps us sleep." She folds her arms over her chest, daring Remy to call her a liar.

He steps closer. "Is this walk something my father would want to know about?"

My heart sinks into my feet. He wouldn't do that to us, would he? Since coming back into our lives he sometimes seems just like the old Remy I knew so well, but other times I can't decide what to make of him.

"You wouldn't do that," I say. The last thing we need now is Remy reporting to his father that we're pursuing a mission he expressly forbid.

"Not if you include me in your plan." He stretches.

My sister and I exchange a glance, and I understand exactly what she wants to do. We may not fully trust Remy's motives, but if he does report us to Isaiah, it will be better if he's seen the door too and can vouch for the necessity of further investigation. Maybe his father will deem it important enough to put us back on that mission.

We turn to him with the sweetest possible grins.

"Of course. We'd welcome the help."

"Show me the way."

We head back down the alley, Remy between us. When we stop at the sewer grate, he stares at us, puzzled.

"What are we doing here?"

I step toward him. "You want to know where we go? Into the sewers and drainage tunnels. The Technocrats are up to something down there, and we're going to discover what it is."

"The sewers? Really?"

"If you don't want to go in there with us," Zandria sighs, "I suppose we shall have to make do."

I snicker softly. "I know your father told you about the door we found. It's down there, and we must find a way to get through it. And we want to be sure it's safe from the Technocrats."

"I'll go with you." Remy slowly heaves up the grate and rolls it over the edge of the alley. "You two do this on your own?"

We share a smile. "We're stronger than we look."

"I'll say," he mutters.

"You first," I say.

Remy looks at me askance. "No," he says slowly. "I'll follow you."

I shrug. It makes no difference. We know the tunnels well; Remy doesn't know them at all.

Zandria climbs down and I follow right behind her. I mutter

the silencing spell while she holds a light aloft. My hands slip a little on the metal ladder, but I don't fall into the muck below. The stench is lighter today; the rain must be to thank. Still, it might be enough to dissuade Remy from following us again some other night.

Remy casts his fog spell again so no one passing by will see the grate askew. When he reaches the bottom, he wipes his hands on his cloak and coughs. "Is this a joke? You actually still come down here of your own free will?"

"We do," Zandria says, then starts across the slim metal walkway along the wall. Remy looks a bit green, and I can't help feeling smug. We smeared the ointment that keeps the stench at bay beneath our nostrils before we left home.

"You can go back up if you want," I say.

He scowls and picks up his pace.

When we reach the landing and tunnels, Zandria stands still as a statue. I wind my fingers with hers and listen.

"What are—?" Remy begins.

"Shh!" Zandria and I hiss together.

Something small moves farther down the tunnels. The telltale clink of tiny metal legs echoes with a tinny ring. Remy's drawn face looms like a ghost in the darkness.

"What is that?" he whispers.

"Seekers." My heart ricochets against my rib cage. Those horrid creatures have only one purpose—to find anything out of place.

In other words: us.

This is no doubt a result of the two of us destroying their demolition machines. Aro must have brought them down here.

Zandria releases me and weaves her hands, obscuring us with the movement of the air.

"Can we get by them?" Remy's question hangs in the open. The trundling seekers pause, then resume with gusto.

"Maybe if you'd stayed quiet." Fury builds in my chest, but I stamp it down. Now is not the time to be angry. The torn-down wall lies in front of us, and the tunnel with the seekers runs to our right.

Forward it is.

"We'll have to lose them," Zandria says, and I nod in agreement.

We run down the newly exposed tunnel, but Remy lingers. His hands weave and it takes me a moment to realize what he's doing.

Water rolls over the tunnel floors, rising higher every moment. Zandria puts a hand on my arm just as a wave slams down the main tunnel at Remy's direction, washing the seekers back into the network.

Remy joins us. "Have I redeemed myself?"

Zandria grins. "Perhaps a very little."

"Then we better hurry before they recover," he says. We take the lead again. The effect of the Technocrats on the once-hidden tunnel is clear. Walls are destroyed, debris litters the floor, and the tangy scent of steel lingers in the air.

I exchange a worried look with Zandria. We both hope they haven't discovered our door yet. I have no doubt they get closer to it every day.

"This is the area where you found the door you believe is magic?" Remy asks.

"Yes," Zandria says. "We suspect it's connected to the legends of the Technocrat Palace being built on the seat of Magi power. We're hoping it's the library. That's why we come down here. If we stop looking, they might find it first."

"You really believe it's under the Palace?"

We exchange another meaningful glance. "Definitely," I say.

We all know the legends that the Technocrats built their Palace on top of the most revered spot of the Magi. What better way to rub it in? Destroy us, then prevent us from salvaging anything. What else could be behind the door if not our lost library?

We walk at a speedy clip for what feels like miles. The tunnels meander and split so often we can hardly keep track. My map isn't as useful as it has been in the past, since I only found the door the first time by running heedlessly toward it. But tonight I am making notes; even if this is the wrong way, at least we can rule it out next time.

As we get deeper into the tunnels, it doesn't look familiar at all. The walls are gray and drab, brick and steel. A hint of magic called us to the door before, but none remains here.

Only the steel, the bricks, and the faint echo of skittering mechanical feet.

Then we hit a dead end.

We don't realize until we turn a corner after a few hundred feet and discover—dull gray bricks.

Something is odd about them, though. They don't fit with the area.

"I take it we're lost?" Remy says. "Perhaps we should call it a night."

"You're welcome to do so," Zandria says. She turns to face the wall and her hands move. Not enough for Remy to notice, but more than enough for spellcasting.

She senses something is off about the wall too. I'd bet something lies behind it. Perhaps even a way out.

I take Remy's arm and start back the way we came. "You can go back. You've escorted us long enough. We will tell you all about it if we do find something of interest." I smile my sweetest, but it cracks as I hear a terrible sound.

The mechanical skittering echoing down the tunnels is no longer far off.

Remy's face falls. "Is that . . . ?" he mouths. I pull him back toward Zandria.

The wall has swung open like a trapdoor, revealing a long, dark tunnel inside. Zandria must have been practicing her skills with bricks and walls. She never was able to do this before.

"Secret latch," Zandria says.

"Where does this go?" Remy asks.

"Who cares?" Zandria says as she steps through the door. "It's away from here and from them." The rustling is almost upon us. If they turn the corner and catch us on their optical capturing devices, we're done for. We can fool humans with our cloaking spell—one that not many Magi can cast—but we don't know whether the machines can see through it.

We've never tested it, and we don't wish to either.

I shove Remy into the tunnel and leap after him. I speed ahead with Remy as Zandria closes the door with her spell, keeping him none the wiser. The bricks scrape into place and seconds later the metal beasts on the other side clamber all over the wall.

The sound is a piercing, scraping, chilling thing.

The sickening feel of metal slipping over my skin makes me shudder, like those helmets on the baker and his son. I'll have to learn how to incapacitate those seekers. Permanently. Remy's wave slowed them down, but it certainly didn't stop them.

I'm sure this won't be the last time we encounter them.

"*Fiero*," Remy whispers, and light bursts in his palm. This corridor is older than the others. The brick walls crumble, but as we progress we reach a main landing and they're replaced by steel.

"We're getting close to the Palace proper," I say, uneasily.

"And we've been going uphill for some time." Zandria says.

"Not going to visit the library tonight, then?" Remy asks.

"This is better. A secret passage into the Technocrats' stronghold," I say. "All captured here on my map."

The passage turns into a stairway and leads to a panel with a peephole. I put one eye to it and gaze out onto a hall near the kitchens. Not a soul stirs.

We prepare our cloaking and silencing spells and then slide the panel as quietly as we can. When it creaks, we halt and hold our breaths. Relief floods over me as the echo fades to nothing. We slip out one by one and hurry down the hall, cautious not to disturb anyone or anything. At the end of the kitchen area is a door that leads to the back garden and the servants' entrance. Half the guards are in their cups, and the other half are asleep. We keep our spells taut and slip through the gate unnoticed, then race down the street toward home.

Tonight didn't go as we planned, but a new escape route is always good to have. Just in case.

THE NEXT MORNING IT IS IMPOSSIBLE TO

hurry. After our excursion last night, I was
only able to sleep in fits and starts. The memory
of the baker and his son wouldn't allow me to rest.
Even now as I finally slip out of bed, the image of the
steel helmets closing flickers behind my eyes.

The last thing in the world I want to do is go back to the
Palace. Just thinking of returning to that place, of being discovered,
of suffering that fate, is enough to steal the air from my lungs.

But I must.

I am one of the Armory's Twin Daggers. I have a mission to
complete. I don't have the luxury of being terrified.

I have no choice but to be invincible.

Grabbing the nearest clothes, I pull on my tunic one sleeve at
a time. Zandria is already gone, but she left a note by my bedside:
I'm up and ready before you—miracles do occur! —Z

A wry smile flits over my face. Of course Zandy is gloating
over this. Usually I'm the one dragging her out of bed. But the
note from my twin strengthens my resolve. I have to go back and
hunt for the heir. I can't abandon my mission, not when I'm perfectly situated in the Palace and Aro is beginning to regard me as a
friend. Not returning would arouse suspicion, and that would cast
suspicion on Zandria. I cannot allow that to happen.

I swallow my fears and set out for the Palace.

By the time I reach the mirrored steel halls, my hands are clenched
into fists to keep them from quivering. I open the door to my

workroom and quickly slip inside. When I close the door behind me, I gasp. Magic flows to my fingers, but I hold it back.

Aro scrambles to his feet from the chair where he was waiting for me. His face is beet red and his hands are tucked behind his back. Sparky whirs as if in greeting.

"You startled me," I say, feeling oddly out of breath and very annoyed with myself.

"I'm sorry, I didn't even think of that." He grimaces. "Maybe surprising you wasn't the best idea after what happened to your friend yesterday. I just . . . wanted to apologize again and bring you something."

I swallow hard, reminding myself that my mission here is to find the heir, and that means playing along so I can use Aro to reach that goal. I am his enemy. I am everything he hates.

I step closer as Aro brings his hands out from behind his back. He holds a lily, blue as midnight with yellow fronds and tips. I remember seeing them yesterday in the hidden garden. This flower is exquisite, and a sudden stab of homesickness strikes me. I don't think I realized how much I missed real flowers until I saw that garden.

Aro runs his free hand through his hair with a hint of nervousness glinting in his eyes. "This is my favorite flower in the garden. I thought you might like it. At the very least, it would brighten up this room a little."

I smile, casting my eyes down, hoping to appear flattered and grateful. Inside, all I feel is hollow and sad. "Thank you. It's lovely." I take the lily and prop it up in a cylindrical spare part on the table.

He laughs. "Handy and resourceful. I'm so glad I found you." He glances down and clears his throat. "Anyway, I hope you can forgive me for yesterday. I should have known better."

"It wasn't your fault," I say, squeezing his arm in a comforting manner. He smiles; good, let him trust me.

"I'm just glad you came back today. You're a great mechanic, and I'd hate to lose you."

I glance at the lily; its sweet scent has begun to fill the room, but it turns my stomach. "I wouldn't worry about that."

"Good, that's good." He steps toward the door. "I'll stop bothering you." He halts, one hand on the doorknob. "But would you like to join me for lunch again?"

I force a grin. "I'd love to."

He leaves along with his mechpet, and I turn back to the work table, letting out a held breath. Zandria is right; I might be able to make Aro fall for me after all. And it doesn't hurt that he brought me something beautiful to improve the ambiance in this room. No, I will not feel the slightest bit bad about using him as completely as possible. I'll show him exactly how cruel and callous we Magi can be.

For the next hour, I work diligently on the machines, sometimes using my magic, sometimes not. Even though I'm repairing machines I destroyed, I can't help feeling a glimmer of satisfaction at my progress.

But after an hour of work, I am ready to go about my mission again. And this time I know exactly where I want to look. After checking that the hall outside my workroom is empty, I sneak out using the shield spell and make my way down the hall to the closet Aro showed me yesterday. I don't know how often the king and queen hold court, but I can't pass up the opportunity to spy.

I move the shelving aside to reveal Aro's mirrored contraption. Now that I am alone I can examine it more freely and can better see how it works. It's ingenious.

I keep my shield spell up, just in case anyone wanders in, though the closet appears to get little use if the thick layer of dust is any indication. Then I settle on a stool with my eyes glued to the mirror. I can wait here for any hint of them, then return to my workroom in time for lunch with Aro.

I watch the empty throne room for nearly half an hour before anyone appears. My patience is rewarded when Queen Cyrene sweeps in with a figure in a black hooded cloak with a silver stripe along the edge close behind her. I can't see the figure's face, but the queen is clearly angry. She whirls around near the far wall of the throne room.

"Are you sure the signal is gone?" They are on the opposite side of the room, and her voice is softer than when she was sitting on the throne behind the wall but just as icy.

The hooded figure nods. If he speaks, I don't hear it.

The queen's eyes narrow. "We must remedy this. It is for the safety of the kingdom."

"It shall be done," the figure says in a low voice I almost miss. "For the sake of your line."

Prickles run over my skin.

"Good. You know how important it is to me. You are the only one I trust with this."

The hooded figure bows.

Queen Cyrene motions to the red-veined marble wall. "Show me the status of the rest."

The hooded figure presses a section of the marble and a hidden door slides open smoothly. They slip inside the room, and before the panel closes I catch a glimpse of a member of the elite guard, along with wires and some mechanical apparatus contained within.

I recognize it. It's something the Armory warned us about, but I've only seen drawings of one before: a listening receptor.

They're eavesdropping on people in there.

A lot of people, by the looks of it. Maybe this is who put the listening device in Aro's pet. He wasn't lying when he said the royals are intensely suspicious, far more than perhaps even he realized. For all I know, the queen might be listening in on all her employees.

I BRISKLY WALK BACK TO LEON'S WORK-

shop from my morning errand, full of
trepidation that we'll see Aro's machines in
the tunnels once again now that I've fixed them. I
stretched out the task as long as possible but still had to
maintain the illusion I'm a skilled worker. I managed to keep
up the charade for a full week, and now another week has passed
since I finished. During my time in the Palace I made little headway
on finding the heir, though I snuck around at every opportunity.
I identified several tantalizing doors to halls that are off-limits
to all but doctors and nannies, but they were too well-guarded.
However, I did spend time nearly every day watching the throne
room. Queen Cyrene visited the listening room two more times,
and the elite guard inside the room appeared to change shift every
eight hours. It's unlikely I'll be able to access that room unnoticed
in the future, but I kept my eye on it just in case I overheard
anything more. I reported everything to Isaiah, but according to
Remy, he was not surprised. He already knew the king and queen
eavesdropped on their people, though he was pleased I'd gotten
so close that I could monitor the comings and goings.

I must find another excuse to get into the Palace. I had hoped
Leon would be impressed enough by my good work that he would
send me himself. But he remains as surly as I remember, and I
suspect I shall have to devise some other way. He has kept me hard
at work on the machinettes ever since I returned to his workshop,
and I've managed to keep up a good pace. By now I've memorized
the schematics; I could build them in my sleep.

It's a bright, sunny morning, the kind where children play
on the green in the center of the city while the elite parents and

caretakers watch them. The metallic trees chime as the wind rustles through them, interspersed with a handful of pines and one weeping willow. Workers like myself hurry off to jobs and apprenticeships, but the warmth of the rays fills us all. Even that gruff guard from the Palace, Caden, is out, lifting his small, laughing daughter onto his shoulders.

It doesn't touch my heart. That's locked away. Vivienne's sacrifice for the baker's son still troubles me, but I have gotten better at squashing it down over the last few days. I have my sister, my family, and my magic—that is all I need.

I open the door to Leon's workshop and it creaks on its hinges as usual. It's almost a welcome sound now.

"Who is it?" Leon grumbles from the back room. His steel foot thumps on the floor as he walks out front. "Oh," he says when he sees me. "Only you. Get to work. You have more of those machines to build. We should've delivered them last week, but the Palace claimed you." He has greeted me with this same speech every morning since I returned.

He shuffles back to the workroom, muttering about the court and their wanton, wasteful ways. No one ever bats an eye when things that might be considered treasonous come from his mouth. I suppose when your skills are in high demand, you can get away with a lot.

I pad after Leon, opening the door he let slam in my face, and set my things on my workbench. Someone important must have placed a large order for these odd little machines he still has me tinkering with. Leon has yet to explain what they do, and I know better than to ask. I'd like to keep the skin of my nose where it is, thank you very much.

My curiosity simmers beneath the surface as I sit down to my task. Leon already has his back to me, hard at work on a complicated machine. It takes up most of his workbench and several pieces lie beside it. He curses under his breath every few minutes.

Everything is back to normal.

A small part of me misses the Palace and its strange steel walls. Even the cold stares of the other servants and the haughty laughter of the courtiers. Beneath it all is the mystery I must puzzle out, and secrets wait behind every door. I only got one brief glimpse of the children Remy told me about.

Unbidden, Aro's smile framed by the green brightness of the secret Palace garden springs to the front of my brain, startling me. It is quickly chased away by the resounding echo of his words. *Cruel, callous creatures.*

I don't miss Aro a whit.

The morning passes quickly, me at my workbench and Leon at his, steadily progressing while we tinker. I have become such a part of the scenery to him that it has grown easier to hide my magic, but I'm still very cautious. Now that I know the queen has listeners everywhere, it wouldn't surprise me if she has one here in the Master Mechanic's workshop. While I was in the Palace I took to humming as I worked even when I wasn't using magic, just so no one would be suspicious when I did. I weave my hands under the table, the pieces obeying my commands. By force of habit I continue to hide several little machines in my smock, but not as many as I used to. I'm so absorbed in my thoughts and my tasks that Leon surprises me when he leaves for his usual lunch.

He shuffle-steps over to my table and grunts—startling me back to reality—as he examines my work. I swallow hard. My throat feels like it's coated with dust. Have I been working too quickly? What did I do to attract his scrutiny?

"You're doing better than I expected. Keep that up and you might get to stay here." He ambles out of the workroom, leaving me behind with my jaw hanging open.

Did Leon Salter just give me a compliment?

If he's noticing my progress, I mustn't give him anything to be suspicious about. I may need to slow down.

In that case, perhaps I should take a break. He showed me the machinettes' power source the other day—havani, a liquid mineral—that he keeps just above his worktable in a lead-lined reinforced cabinet. I've been dying to get a closer look.

I creep to where Leon usually sits, all the while keeping a close eye on the windows. I watch him enter the tavern at his usual pace, no sign he may have forgotten something and will be coming back soon.

The cabinet doors are locked, naturally. I place my hand over the lock above Leon's bench and hum softly as the magic tickles my fingertips; soon the metal gears inside the mechanism twist and turn in response. A smile lights my face.

Then the door to the shop opens and snaps me back to the here and now.

I quickly relock the cabinets, then scurry to my workbench and hunch over my project. I don't let out a single breath. Someone moves in the shop, but we don't normally take customers while Leon is out. He doesn't trust me with them yet. Perhaps that will change now that I worked in the Palace for a week.

The rustling turns into bumping and a crash directly outside the workroom door. Magic humming on my fingertips, I slide off my seat and tiptoe to the door.

I'm ready to defend myself if necessary and with any means I possess.

"Hello?" calls a familiar voice that makes my heart flail inside my chest. I pull my magic back inside my body.

"Hello? Leon? Aissa? Anyone?" Aro jiggles the doorknob to the back room, and I throw it open.

"If you're looking for Leon, I'm afraid you'll be disappointed. He's at lunch."

Aro's eyes brighten when he sees me. "I wasn't looking for him."

Butterflies inexplicably take up residence in my stomach. "Then what are you doing here?"

He grins sheepishly. I realize he knocked over a machine Leon had set out that, when activated, records conversations, essentially a portable listening device.

Perhaps that was not an accident after all. Could it be one of the queen's? I wonder if he knew about the listener in his pet mech too. Or did he put it there to listen to me while I worked?

This is the trouble with Aro—everything he does brings more questions and no answers at all.

He turns his strange pale-blue gaze back to me. "I was hoping to find you."

"Why?"

"I need help on another project. One that's sensitive and requires discretion."

"Shouldn't you ask Leon for assistance, even if you want to employ me?"

"It's sensitive enough that I'd rather not."

I raise my eyebrows. "I'll have to tell him something. I can't just disappear for days on end, or I'll have no apprenticeship to return to."

"I'll think of something, but I don't want even Leon to know the true nature of your work. Agreed?" He holds his hand out to me with a hopeful look on his face.

"Agreed," I say as I shake his hand. I did my job even better than I thought, if Aro is back here looking for me already. "When do I start?"

"The day after tomorrow."

My smile falters. "Not immediately?"

His face grows serious for a second, then returns to its usual playfulness. "I have some other commitments tomorrow, but the next day we can begin."

"What is it this time? More broken machines?"

He shifts his weight. "Not exactly. You'll see."

I laugh and lean closer to him. "That's not much to look forward to."

"I'll look forward to it nonetheless."

Something in my chest flutters. "As will I."

Yes, I *am* looking forward to it. I didn't think I'd have a chance to continue my hunt for the heir again so soon.

"I take it your other machines work all right now?" I ask.

"They do. You did a fine job. Yet another reason I want your help with this one."

The familiar thud of my employer's false foot removes the smile from my face. While Aro's interruption was a welcome surprise, it means I won't be able to investigate the havani today after all. Seconds later the door of the workshop slams shut behind Leon.

"You again," he says gruffly to Aro. "What do you want now?" He shoots me a suspicious look. I examine my folded hands so I don't have to meet his eyes.

"I want to hire your apprentice again. She is needed at the Palace."

"Needed at the Palace, huh?" He mutters to himself as he heads to his worktable. "Gone for a week and her head is filled with delusions of grandeur."

"Is that a yes?" Aro asks.

Leon waves a hand in response, simultaneously signaling his agreement and that Aro should leave. Unless he's going to buy something.

The edges of Aro's mouth creep up. "I'll be back for her the day after tomorrow."

Leon again waves him off.

"Sorry, I think he's already lost in his work. He gets that way sometimes." I laugh. "All the time, really."

"Until then," Aro says. I smile just as Zandria has schooled me—enough to seem pleased but not overeager. Enough to convince him I'm looking forward to seeing him. I don't like the strange effect Aro has on me, but perhaps it will be easier to flirt and use him if I give into it more often. Maybe I can bend it to my cause.

He heads back out the way he came, adjusting the broken listener as he passes. I watch him and his shadow until Leon's grumbling sends me hurrying back to my worktable.

When I arrive home that evening, Zandria sits at the table removing her courier boots. Couriers have special, custom-made shoes that conform to their feet and legs in a uniform, skin-tight manner. They've always looked terribly uncomfortable to me.

She gives me an exasperated look. "These boots cling to my feet like crazy!"

I hold my hand over it and whisper a release spell. The shoe drops off her foot and clatters on the floor. She pouts. "Aissa, you've ruined them. Now I'll have to get another pair. They might get suspicious since this will be my third request for new boots."

I start, then examine her shoe and see what she means. They've melted in two places. "I'm sorry, I didn't know."

She stands. "That's because you're not a messenger."

It's true. All I know of the inner workings of the courier service is that my sister is apprenticed there and they have odd shoes.

"Why did they melt?"

She winces. "I found out the hard way on my second day. This is a special sort of material, light and durable, but it can't stand the energy from our magic. Burns it right up." She tosses the shoes aside. "I did the same thing the first time." She sighs. "It's a rather bit of a pain, actually."

I settle into the chair next to her. "You won't believe who I saw in the shop again today."

Her eyes spark with mischief. "The boy whose machines we broke? And who brought you that lily?"

"The very one."

"What does he want now?" She leans forward. "Was he so taken with you that he had to see you again?"

I laugh. "Perhaps. He dropped by when Leon was at lunch and he as much as admitted it was intentional."

"Even better. Did he declare his love then and there? Read you an epic love poem?"

"No," I say, rolling my eyes. "But he did enlist my help on a new project. He won't tell me what it is yet. He swore me to secrecy once I agreed to help him, then Leon returned and scared him off."

"Fascinating that he wants you for another project." Her eyes flash. "I'd wager there's no project at all; he just wants to get you back in the Palace to have you all to himself. It's the perfect opportunity to scour the halls for the heir. Keep this up and he'll tell you anything you want, I'm sure."

"If he dared do something so brazen, I'd stop his heart and end his life."

"I know you would. That's why I never worry about you."

"I worry about *you* constantly."

"That's because you're a worrywart."

She takes my hand with cold fingers. I wonder how her apprenticeship has been treating her. She answers before I get a chance to ask.

"It's very chilly sometimes, spending all my time outdoors."

I rub her hands to warm her fingers. "We should get you some gloves."

She puffs out her chest. "No, no, no, absolutely not. Standard-issue gear only. No exceptions."

"Oh dear. You have one of *those* in the courier service."

She grabs a roll from the basket on the table. Crumbs fall from her lips as she takes a bite of the crusty bread. "My superior is exactly as insufferable as he sounds." She winks. "Fortunately, there are other, far more interesting men on my route."

"Oh no," I groan. "Already?"

"I'm only practicing," she says, as she always does. She considers affairs of the heart to be an important part of the spy game.

"With who? Someone you delivered a message to?"

She nods.

My eyes narrow at her. "Have I met him?"

She laughs. "Never."

"Well, who is it? Don't keep me in suspense!"

Her smile falters. "I . . . can't tell you. Not yet. He says we must keep it a secret for now."

I frown. "What? Why?"

She leans forward. "Remember the other day, when I mentioned I suspected I'd found another Magi spy? I was right. He's one of us."

I gasp. "How do you know? Does he know that you are too?" My head reels with the implications of Zandria confiding in the wrong person.

"He gets messages in code from the Magi Council. I read every one I get, then seal it back up." She grins. One thing we've both always loved is languages. The old Magi dialects and our new code language are particular favorites. Growing up, our parents' shop provided the perfect opportunity to learn more about them. We spent a lot of time together poring over tomes before the Armory sent us into the field.

"So he's received letters from Isaiah? What do they say?"

"Well, not Isaiah per se, but I recognize the names and it's in our code. I'd know that anywhere." She stretches. "Nothing interesting yet. Just movements of the king and queen, their plans for balls and vacations, and some of the other nobles too."

I rub my temples. "Please tell me you haven't told this mystery man that you're Magi too."

"Of course not. But he is very handsome, and well-placed in the Technocrat hierarchy. They trust him. He is poised to do so much damage. If I can earn his trust, maybe he can help us with the door in the tunnels."

"Be careful, sister."

She blows a raspberry at me. "Oh please, Aissa, a dalliance won't hurt. If anything, he can help us. If he's high enough up in the Armory, we might even be able to go places." Her expression softens. "Besides, like I said, I've read his messages to the Armory. I . . . admire him, really."

"I'm sure his handsome face doesn't hurt either."

Zandria laughs, and plays with the buckle on her sleeve.

"Can you tell me his name?"

"I don't know it—he's only gotten Magi correspondence so far. But his code name is the Hidden Knife."

My breath hitches in my chest. "The Hidden Knife? You can't be serious. Are you certain it's really him?"

She nods, her eyes glowing. "Oh yes, and I'm beginning to understand why he's become something of a legend."

I shake my head at her, not sure I believe she's correct. It would be just like Zandria to jump to such a fanciful conclusion. "He can't be the Hidden Knife. He's young, isn't he?"

She nods. "Well, he's older than us, but that doesn't mean anything."

"Of course it does. The Hidden Knife must be middle-aged at least. They'd have to be in order to be so legendary."

My sister laughs and shakes her head. "That isn't necessarily true."

"He's making this up, faking the letters somehow, either to impress you or trap you. I'm serious, Zandria." Worry burns in my chest, but she still waves me off.

"Just be cautious, all right?" I decide to humor her, just a little. "Was there anything about the Heartless heir in his letters?"

She shakes her head. "No, though if there ever is you will be the first to know. But enough about me. What will you do about Aro?"

"What do you mean?"

"If he falls in love with you—and if you're being your charming self and not the self-righteous grump you are at home, I dare say he will soon—what are you going to do? Have you considered it?"

"Not seriously, no." I toy with the crust on my roll. "He's aloof enough that I don't think that's a danger. But today . . ." I pause, remembering Aro's face and the listener he knocked over. Not to mention the one in his pet mechanimal. "I'm not so sure. He might be a little infatuated with me. Or he's determined to keep his work secret and goes to great lengths to do so."

"I saw how he looked at you at the parade. He fancies you. No doubt about it."

I brush off Zandria's certainty. "If he does, then he's a great fool." I lean closer to my sister. "I'm much more concerned with discovering why he must be so guarded about this latest project. If he can't tell Leon, I have to wonder if even the king and queen are in the know. If it has something to do with the Heartless, he might let on more than he realizes about the heir."

"Perhaps his work was ordered directly by the king and queen," Zandria says.

My eyes brighten. "Whatever it is, it must be important."

"And he's so smitten with you that he wants nothing less than you by his side while he does this important work for the good of society." Zandria places her hand over her forehead and sighs.

I can't help but laugh. "You're ridiculous."

"I'm right. Soon he'll tell you all his secrets." She pouts. "I'm a little jealous, sister. I was sure I'd be the one to break hearts and get information, but you've beaten me to the punch."

My sister has no qualms about using hearts for her own ends. But doing so myself still makes me uneasy, despite our training. Despite Aro's clear disgust for all things Magi.

I toss my roll at Zandria's head, and she ducks. Seconds later a potato is launched at me. Salad flies through the air and a carrot catches me on the nose. I chuck the remaining basket of rolls across the table in my sister's direction and she yelps.

"What on earth is going on out here?" Mama stands in the doorway of the kitchen, her mouth a harsh line. We crawl out from under the table.

Once there was a time when Mama and Papa were not as stern as they've become. When she'd spend afternoons getting lost in her herbs, and he in books and bows. When they laughed more and danced together in the kitchen while we sang old Magi tunes. The stress of our prolonged mission is wearing on them. And possibly we are too.

"Sorry, Mama. We, uh, made a mess," I say. Neither I nor Zandria can meet her eyes under the irritation we feel burning there.

"You'd better clean it up—and fast. Your father will be home any minute and he'd be none too pleased to see this." She surveys the table with a frown. "I'll have to make him more dinner since you threw his potato on the floor. And wasted all those rolls." She lets out a heavy breath. "Get cleaning, girls."

We scramble to obey. Our mother isn't one to be trifled with. She loves us, she protects us, and fears for us. But she also doesn't tolerate any slack. There's a reason she's a valued spy in the Armory.

As soon as the last of the food is off the floor, Zandria and I dash down the stairs to the hidden cellar room behind the walls. Time to train—we must keep up our strength and agility, and I must focus on staying alert and keen-eyed so I can ferret out what Aro is up to.

I'm certain it's nothing good.

THIS MORNING THE SKY IS OVERCAST, THE gathering clouds hanging over Zandria and me as we head for our apprenticeships. It's already been two weeks, but I still hate being separated from my sister each day. She's reckless enough that I worry she'll get into trouble without me to keep her steady.

Then again, she's probably equally concerned that I'll scowl everyone to death without her to lighten my mood.

But the stakes are higher now. We aren't playing anymore, and Zandy's plan to flirt with potentially dangerous men like the one pretending to be the Hidden Knife disturbs me. Telling her that would only make her more determined, so I stew and fret in silence.

When we reach the city center, bustling with the sounds and smells of the workday, the clouds break and rain barrels down on us. We say a quick goodbye, then rush off to our separate tasks.

It may be wet, but it's warm, and I let the rain soak my skin as I meander to Leon's mechanic shop. I should run, but I'm in no temper to deal with Leon this morning. The rain bothers his knee, and the gruff man is always more surly than usual on days like this. The building comes into view faster than I wish.

The bell rings when I open the door. "Aissa? Are you finally here?" Leon grumbles from the back room.

This ought to be a delightful day.

"Get in here, girl. I need you to deliver something for me."

I hang my cloak on the rack near the door then hurry to the back room, past the army of metal arms, legs, and other spare parts that hang from the walls and languish haphazardly on shelves. I open the door to find Leon struggling with the cart of machinettes we built last week.

"Take these to the hospital. They need them now." He releases the cart and limps over to his worktable. A rusted mechman lies there with both legs stuck in the air. I try not to snort at how ridiculous the thing looks. Zandria wouldn't have been able to control herself.

"They need them right this moment? Or can it wait until the storm passes?"

Leon gazes balefully at me, then turns back to his work.

I sigh. "Which hospital?"

This time he doesn't even look up. "The Heartless one. The directions are on the table next to you."

My breath catches on its way out of my lungs. The Heartless hospital. Could the child of the king and queen be there? With Aro determined to accompany me to lunch every day while I worked at the Palace, I never discovered anything about the heir's whereabouts. It would be good to rule the hospital out. If anyone there is getting special treatment or has overly fine clothing, she might be the one I seek.

I shudder. I've never seen a Heartless before. We only read about them in school and heard whispers on the streets. I stare down at the pieces on the cart. The strange, round clockwork objects suddenly make sense.

"Are these . . . are they hearts? For the Heartless?"

Leon looks at me askance. "What else would they be?"

My hands quiver, the magic whispering to let it break through and make these hearts beat for just one moment. I squash it down. I can't feel sorry for the recipients of these machines. Their punishment is severe, but no less than what the Technocrats did to my people.

"I hadn't realized. But yes, that makes perfect sense."

"Good. You made them well." He grunts, and the approval in his tone surprises me. Perhaps the old man will warm up to me after all. It would certainly make my mission easier.

"Thank you, sir."

"Go on, get out of here."

He doesn't look up again. I grab the directions and roll the cart into the main shop. I pause to put on my cloak, wishing I'd walked faster this morning. The material is soaked and now I'm about to get even wetter. I braid my long hair, then tuck it under the hood. After double-checking that the tarp covering the machine hearts is secure, I wheel the cart into the muddy street.

The hearts in my cart are filled with havani, which Leon warned me never to touch with my bare hands. I would love to get my magic on it, see how it feels to manipulate that substance. Yet even though I now have access to the strange liquid metal fuel, I resist the temptation to pry one of the hearts open. I know havani is a volatile substance. Poisonous, and probably expensive too.

Plus, if I were to accidentally damage one in my curiosity, Leon would inevitably find out. He counted these hearts three times, I'm sure, and a single complaint that there's one less. . . . it would annul all the progress I've made with him. It might even get me fired.

I heave a breath of resignation and push the cart onward. My curiosity will have to wait a little longer.

How must it feel to have these strange contraptions beneath your skin? Many rich Technocrats have their body augmented by reinforcing bones with metal or commissioning more decorative work. Or both, like Queen Cyrene's jeweled steel bands reinforcing her hands and fingers. But those don't need a power source like the hearts do. And I recall what Aro said about how the liquid metal seeps into the body.

I grip the handle of the cart tighter.

I refuse to feel for them. I can't. Sympathy for our enemy is a dangerous thing. Empathy would be worse. This trip to the Heartless ward might supply the information necessary to find the hidden royal child. To give the Magi the edge we need.

Before we came to Palinor, we learned the hazards of trusting a Technocrat. One of our playmates disappeared with her family when she was only seven years old. Her parents were spies stationed in the mining community in the north, who'd been about to turn one of the miners to our side. Money, they thought, was the surest way to his heart. A language the Technocrats would understand. The night they were supposed to bring him into the fold, they vanished and all communications ceased.

Our friend's body was eventually found a mile away down river. Her parents were never heard from again.

The directions take me through the center of the city, then to a rundown section in the outer reaches of Palinor. They really do treat the Heartless like pariahs.

The houses have dull coats of peeling paint, and no shopkeepers wave. More windows are boarded up than open. The rain beats steadily down, a gently thrumming background that makes me feel like I'm the only one left in the world. Me, my cart of clockwork hearts, and the pouring rain.

By the time I reach the hospital, I wish I could use the spell that will dry my clothes and hair, but I refrain. Entering the hospital dry as a bone on a day like this would arouse serious suspicion. I'll have to suffer a while longer.

The front of the large brick building appears empty. That is, until I see the faces peering out of the windows upstairs. Children. Staring at the outside world. Staring at me.

I knock on the front door of the hospital. A frazzled nurse greets me.

"I have a delivery from Master Mechanic Leon."

The relief on her face is palpable. "Oh, thank you. You don't know how much we need these this week. We've had ten more children born Heartless the last few days alone, and several patients who are in desperate need of a transplant. I swear, even more are born each year."

I nod, uncertain how to answer, or if I'm expected to answer at all. The nurse, a slim woman clad in plain gray robes, leads me toward a hallway around the back and a lift that takes us to the second floor. Everything is a sterile gray, and the tang of disease hangs in the air. It's far too quiet for my liking. We pass people in the hall, still and silent as ghosts, like they're afraid to move. This place makes me uneasy. And queasy.

All I want to do is drop these off and leave. Even Leon's shop is more welcoming than this place.

The nurse examines the contents under the tarp as she presses the button on the lift.

"Is it—is it enough?" I ask.

"It'll have to be. I know they say this curse only affects a small percentage of the population, but by my estimate, it's risen steadily over the last few years. Yet our supplies remain the same."

"That's terrible."

"It is. Most are left to die before they even reach our hospitals."

My stomach drops as the lift rises, and I grimace, stifling the gasp that attempts to slip through my teeth. Lifts have always made me nervous. I don't like being in the belly of a machine. Even though no one knows what I am, I can't help but remember that story of the Technocrats' betrayal during a peace treaty. That's what affects me, not the nurse's information. The woman clicks her tongue. "It takes some getting used to."

When it stops, we step onto the second floor and I push my cart forward. Children of all ages lie in sick beds against the wall, huddle by the windows watching the falling rain, or rest in the handful of armchairs that dot the large room. Nurses shuffle between the beds, checking each one. The entire floor is dedicated to these children.

Their sallow faces all wear the same expression. Hopeless.

"This way," the nurse says. I follow her to a smaller room

at the far end of this one. It serves as a supply closet, filled with instruments that do things I never want to know about. She helps me stack the hearts in a cabinet not unlike the one where Leon keeps his havani. When we finish, she makes a point of locking it shut, then ushers me out.

I stumble as we reenter the room. Not far from where I stand is Aro, crouched by the bedside of one of the sickest-looking children. He holds the little girl's hand gently and whispers to her. She smiles, and when she does I realize her skin is not just sallow. There is an odd tint to it. Dark, like a bruise.

Like the liquid metal.

The nurse frowns when she sees me staring. "Yes, that one is very ill. In about an hour we will transplant one of the new hearts you brought us. You may have just saved her life."

I thrust down the emotion that threatens to choke me. "Why is her skin that color?" Now that I look for it, I see she isn't alone. That sickly tint colors other children in various degrees. Others have tendrils of darkness climbing up the exposed skin of their necks and arms.

The nurse shakes her head. "The havani. It's the only power source that will last a full year, but it's poisonous. Leon's clockwork hearts are well-crafted, but not even the best machines can stand up to constant wear and tear with no repairs or regular care. They break down and a poisonous gas seeps out of them. The symptoms start as fine lines, then turn the skin gray as the gas disperses throughout the body." She sighs. "But once we transplant a new heart and flush the poison from their blood, they look good as new. Symptoms don't appear again until at least six months of use. This floor has the sickest children. If you'd seen the third floor, the surgery recovery area, you wouldn't even know they were Heartless."

Something inside me cracks as the little girl with graying skin hugs Aro. The look on his face—intense grief—roots me to the spot. "Will she make it?" It's a struggle to get those words out.

"I don't know." The nurse walks back to the lift. I glance at Aro one more time, grateful he hasn't seen me, then follow her out.

I must know how he's connected to that child. A thrill runs through me. Could she be the royal heir? Would they leave her here in a sick house filled with other hopeless children? I'd believe the king and queen are capable of that level of cruelty after what I've seen, but I find it hard to believe they'd unleash it on their own flesh and blood. Though this place would be perfect to maintain her anonymity.

I'll have to inform the others of this hospital's Palace connection.

As I roll the cart back out into the rain, the vision of Aro holding the girl's hand troubles me. He called the Magi cruel, callous creatures—which is exactly what I've always been taught the Technocrats are. But here he is, comforting the Heartless. I had no idea there were so many, and I only saw one of the floors in the hospital's tall building. We've always been told it's a tiny portion of our population. But the number of children inside felt overwhelming. The nurse said there were more every year, that she feels the percentage of the population afflicted is growing. And Aro's face, filled with regret and kindness . . .

"Aissa!" I whirl at the hissed voice. Remy sidles up to me from a nearby alley. "What are you up to? Deliveries?"

"Something like that. Shouldn't you be working?" I must tell Remy about the Heartless, but I need to think on them more first. I don't understand what the Magi want with one of them. I don't see how we can use even a royal heir to our advantage.

But it's the task Zandria and I have been assigned, and we must carry it out whether we understand it or not. I know Remy—and my parents—would tell me to be patient, that all will be revealed when I need the information. It just chafes that they don't feel I need it now.

Remy shoves his hands into his pockets and walks beside me. "I have the day off from guard duty. Getting to know the city."

The rain doesn't seem to bother him a jot. His hood isn't even up.

"Have you seen the sun today?" he asks in a low voice. Talk of the sun shining is code for *do you have any intelligence to share?*

"Only briefly." *I might have something.*

He laughs. "Do you think I might see it if I wait out the rain?" *Will you tell me?*

"No," I say, glancing at him sideways. "But the clouds should clear enough to see the moon later." *Not now, but later tonight.*

For now, all I want to do is put as much distance between the Heartless hospital and myself as possible. The Technocrat Palace is a far more interesting place to visit. The tang of blood and metal still clings to the inside of my nose.

Remy startles me by squeezing my hand. "Then I look forward to later." His dark hair and warm brown eyes stop me in my tracks. I don't remove my hand from his. After the unsettling experience I just had, I rather like the comfort, the familiarity.

He lets go and continues down the street in the rain, away from the Palace and Leon's shop. I hurriedly wheel my cart back to the mechanic shop, knowing any proper Magi girl would still be thinking of Remy, our leader's son. But instead thoughts of another boy, one with blond hair and pale, sad eyes follow close behind me.

I'VE SPENT HALF THE NEXT MORNING ON
pins and needles in the workshop, building
more clockwork hearts and waiting anxiously for
Aro to claim me for his project. The vision of him
with the little Heartless girl has plagued me since that
moment. It won't let me go. Seeing those children—and Aro
caring so tenderly for them—twisted something inside me.

I shouldn't care about what happens to any Technocrat. But my
better understanding of the plight of the Heartless resists reason.

In school, they were creatures kept at arm's length. Theoretical
people used for political agendas. Not real children wasting away
in hospital beds, desperate to live just one more day.

No mention made of the people desperate to keep them alive
either.

The possibility the girl Aro was visiting might be the heir
makes me hate the Technocrat royals more than I thought was still
possible. I don't want to admire Aro and his kindness—every part
of my brain screams in opposition—but my heart can't help it.

I halt my train of thought and stare at the worktable, gripping
the edges hard enough that they prick into the palms of my hands.
I'm here to use Aro; I can't afford to be swayed by his compassion.
I can't afford to feel anything for him other than hate. He's my
enemy.

And that's what he must remain.

Leon, as usual, ignores me, only grunting on occasion as he
smooths over the rough and tricky parts on his own machine. Today
he's fixing some courtier's pet, a machine in the form of a tiger. He
has yet to give me anything other than the mechanical hearts, but I
understand better why he wants so many of them made.

Leon has a soft spot for the Heartless. I've made other deliveries with strict instructions to collect payment from the noble or merchant, but he didn't have me collect a cent from the hospital. And that's why he was so upset when I dented one of the hearts. If it wasn't perfect, a child could die. He employs me in what seems like busywork, but that busywork is clearly his pet project. Does this mean he trusts me? Or is it a convenient way to keep me out of his hair?

It could easily be either one.

The shop has been busy this morning with all sorts of people shuffling in and out, looking for new generators to light their homes, machines to clean their floors, and other such things. Every time the bell rings, I jump in anticipation. When will Aro come for me?

My distraction is crippling. I fumble with more pieces than usual and retrieve and fix them fully before Leon notices. In short, I'm a mess.

So when the shop bell rings for the umpteenth time, my pulse leaps. This time, when I throw open the door to the front room, Aro stands there, wearing a smile. I can't help but return it.

Behind me, Leon thump-steps into the front room, then halts when he recognizes Aro.

"You again? What now?" He taps his metal foot on the floor.

"I'm here to collect Aissa for my project, remember? She is very talented, and the king and queen were pleased with her work."

"Talented, indeed," mutters Leon. "Just return her in one piece once you're finished with her." He stalks back to the workshop, saying under his breath, "Fat lot of good she does if I always have to do the work around here anyway . . ."

When the door slams behind him and his metal footfalls fade, Aro cracks another smile. "I think he likes you." He opens the door, and I follow him out.

We walk toward the Palace, but this time Aro takes me directly past the guards—including Remy and that guard we met my first day at the Palace, Caden—and we head into the steel-walled halls. The reflections make the halls always appear to be full of people even when only a handful are present. It's a disconcerting effect, and I try not to stare at the images of Aro and myself and the other servants and workers who trundle by.

"I'm glad to have you back here in the Palace," Aro says.

"Have your lunches been lonely?" I joke, but Aro's face is more serious than I expected. I clear my throat. "What am I fixing for you this time?"

A grin tugs at Aro's lips. "It's not fixing so much as testing. Creating, even. It's a project that's very important to me."

My heart skips over itself. A rewarding project that Aro holds dear? I remember what he said to me the first time I came to the Palace. This has something to do with the Heartless.

He forges ahead, passing door after door without giving them a second glance. He turns a corner and starts down a long hallway. I struggle to keep up.

When we reach the fifth landing—I have no idea how far below the earth we are, but it must be almost as deep as the drainage tunnels—Aro turns off the stairs and down a hallway instead. It's a short corridor with only three doors. He opens the one on the right. My pulse suddenly skyrockets. What if he's figured me out? What if he's taking me this far down and away from everyone else to kill me?

I shake off the troubling thoughts. No, this is Aro. The boy who loves the real green of a garden and laughs in the sunshine. The one who comforts a dying child.

Or I'm completely foolish to be trusting any Technocrat—especially one who works for the Palace and considers Magi cruel creatures. I let magic pool in the palms of my hands just in case.

The lights blink on, revealing several tables, one with scopes and other measuring instruments and another with what appears to be raw minerals and vials of liquid. On a third table, I recognize the machines for what they are—the false, deadly hearts for the Heartless.

"What are you doing with clockwork hearts?" I ask, somewhat bewildered.

Aro's head whips around. "How did you know what they are? Most people have no idea what they look like."

"Leon has me working on these. I made a whole slew of them over the last few weeks."

Shock flickers on his face. "Leon lets you make their hearts."

"Of course," I say. "I don't think he's even getting paid for them. He does all the pricey projects."

He goes very still. "Do you understand the importance of those machines, however small they may seem?"

"I do," I say softly. I don't like the insinuation I'd screw them up, but I understand the Heartless children mean something to him. Something I only partially understand.

I swallow hard. The horrors I saw yesterday flood my brain. The graying skin, the dark tendrils roving over their arms and necks. The memory is sickening.

He takes a step closer. "The hearts are both a blessing and a curse." His voice is tinged with strained emotions. "They keep the Heartless children alive, but at such a price that it's hardly a life at all. After only six months of use, they begin to turn on the wearer." He rubs his hand over his face. "The core keeping the heart ticking degrades in that time, but the cost of making them is high and replacing them even higher. Too many surgeries and the child dies. Their bodies can only take so much."

"Isn't it better than never living at all?"

He closes his pale eyes so I can't see the emotion clouding

them over. "Did you know most of the Heartless are given up and placed in a hospital? Parents don't want the world to know their families have been touched by the curse. They go to great pains to hide it. At the expense of their children. For many, death would be better."

I suck my breath in sharply, pretending to be surprised. "They didn't tell us that in school."

"And they're to be pitied, right?" Aro scoffs, then turns his back to me and paces around the room. "You want to know what I do here?"

"Yes," I whisper, stepping closer to him.

"I'm testing new solutions. Something better to power the hearts than the liquid mineral that slowly turns to poison inside their chests." He grips the edges of the nearest table so hard his knuckles turn white. "What they teach you in school is wrong. It may have started as a small percentage of the population, but every year the number increases. The suffering is only going to get worse."

"What would you use instead?"

He turns his eyes back to me and places a hand on my elbow. "That's where you come in. With your finesse with machines, I need you to test some of the possible power sources I've located so far and see if you can get them to work for any length of time."

"Why me? Wouldn't Leon be better suited to this task? He's far better a mechanic than I am." Indeed, I have to wonder if Aro only asked me for the reasons Zandria thinks. But he seems so dedicated to this cause that I can't imagine he wouldn't want to use the best possible person for the task. Which, in fact, is not me.

"I . . . don't trust Leon. Not for this," Aro says. His words cause the blood to drain from my face. "I do trust you."

"Why don't you trust Leon?" He's gruff and abrasive to be sure, but as far as Technocrats go I'd have pegged him as trustworthy.

Besides, he's the main supplier of the hearts, and he clearly has a soft spot for the Heartless too.

Aro grabs my hands so tightly they ache. "I've known him too long, and he's always been kind to me. But first and foremost he works for the king and queen."

I frown, confused. "I don't understand."

"They assigned me to work on a different project. They . . ." Aro swallows and stares at the floor. "They would not be happy if they knew I was distracted by this. That's why I need you."

Aro's eyes shine as he takes my hand and pulls me closer. My skin tingles between our palms, and I wonder for a moment if he might be trying to play with my emotions as well. "If Leon knew, he would be forced to tell them. Even if he believed in the work. It would put him in a bad position. They might try to shut down my research. There might be . . . repercussions."

I shudder. I'd hate to get on King Damon and Queen Cyrene's bad side too.

"They believe I'm working on my official assignment. And I do, in my spare time. But this is the most important contribution I can make."

He's close enough that only an inch of air stands between us. His breath cascades over my face, nudging my red hair out of place. "Aissa," he says. "Will you help me?"

The Anvil save me, but I'm moved. By this strange boy I know better than to trust, better than to like, and certainly better than to admire. I'm here to spy for the Magi, but I want to help Aro too. Is it wrong of me to want to help some children live a little longer?

I swallow the emotion down. They're Technocrats. Helping them live is beside the point. They massacred my people. What are a few hundred or even a thousand Heartless children to me?

The tiny voice inside my head says they are something, worth something, but I shove it aside as best I can.

Emotions are things I can't afford here. I'm only doing this because it will get me that much closer to finding out anything he may know about the heir.

"Yes," I say to Aro. "I will help you."

FINALLY, I HAVE THE OPPORTUNITY TO
experiment with havani. I spend the first part
of the afternoon testing it while Aro fetches the
alternate power options. It is a dark, viscous liquid,
which swirls inside the glass vial. I learned that in order
to use it as a power source, the liquid is poured straight
into the innermost chamber of the machinette hearts. There,
it's contained inside a steel vial that gradually degrades. When it's
similarly used in the engine of a vehicle or mechanimal, it doesn't
matter if the engine needs to be replaced every few months. But
when it's a human body, the difference is immense. It's incredibly
toxic, and the human body can only take so much exposure. Now
that I've seen firsthand what it does to the Heartless, I'm extra
careful.

With Aro out of the room, I can use my magic to help experiment, though I'm careful about that too. I haven't found any
listeners in this workroom, but I'm not about to take too many
risks. The ghostly feel of cold steel whispers over my face and I
shiver.

I know the consequences all too well.

I pull on the leather gloves the researchers use from the box
Aro left for me and get to work. I open the stopper on the vial and
gently pour it into the metal bowl. A coughing fit overtakes me
momentarily, leaving nausea in its wake. The fumes alone are dangerous. With discreet handspells, I probe the substance with my
magic. When I make it swirl, it sparks and snaps. When my magic
tries to hold on to it, I get dangerously close to losing my breakfast.

I have no choice but to stop. This havani is pure poison.

And the options for the Heartless are either to die immediately or use it and live a half life for as long as their bodies can stand it. Most don't make it past twenty years.

I confess, I don't know which of these options I'd choose if I were a parent. They're both equally awful. Which is crueler: to let them die before they have tasted life, or to let them know exactly what they'll be leaving behind in a handful of years?

Aro soon returns with a larger box and Sparky ambling behind him. He sets the items out one at a time, ready for me to attempt various means of connecting them as power sources. His long fingers treat them as delicately as glass, and when he explains each one, his brow furrows just a touch with concentration.

"Try this first." Aro hands me a rock that glows red even under the bright lights of the room. I take it warily.

"What is this?" I ask.

"Gautamite," he says. "It's from a country over the seas. Not easy to obtain, but if it works and doesn't poison the Heartless, it will be worth it."

"You just need to figure out how to harness it?"

"Exactly."

I consider the mineral, wishing Aro would leave me in peace. I might be able to fashion it into something usable with my magic, but not with him watching over my shoulder. I examine the other potential sources on the table. One is an odd, gelatinous substance in a vial—"Don't touch that one with your bare hands," Aro says— and a spiky, dull-looking rock lies next to it. Of the others, some glow, some shimmer, some are small, some are large, and some look as though Aro is reaching to find something, anything, that could be a substitute.

"Can you do it?" he asks.

"Possibly. I don't know what any of these things are, aside from what you've told me," I say. His face falls. "But I'll try. However, I need peace and quiet. I can't work with you hovering like this. I know you want to be informed as soon as possible, but this isn't the way."

Aro runs a hand through his pale hair. "I'm sorry. I know better. This is very important to me."

"You make it sound like this is personal."

His face turns ashen. "I . . . I know some of the Heartless. Their plight means a lot to me."

"More than it does to the king and queen?"

I regret asking as soon as the words are out of my mouth. Aro looks as though he's going to be ill.

"I'm sorry. Did they forbid you from working on this?"

"Not exactly."

"But they expect you to work on a different project, not hover over me?" I smile, trying to lighten the suddenly stifling air.

Aro sighs. "You're right. They have other things to keep me occupied."

"Then go and do those things, and leave this to me. It'll go faster without you here, I promise." I pause and turn back to him. "By the way, if someone does happen to find me working on this, what's my alibi?"

"You can simply tell them you're testing new power sources. The king and queen are always on the lookout for anything to give their technology an edge." Aro sighs again and takes a long look at the hodgepodge of rocks and vials on the table in front of me. "I'll be back in a few hours."

"Excellent," I say. "I should have made some progress by then."

He smiles, full of sadness, then steps out of the room, taking his strange mechpet with him. The locking mechanism in the door clicks into place and I roll my eyes. That won't hold me if I choose to go exploring, but for now working on this project should endear me to Aro enough that he'll be inclined to confide in me.

I'm half convinced that little girl he was so kind to the other day is the Heartless heir. She looks to be the right age, and his devotion to her is suspicious. Of course, she could be only a family member, but even then he still might know the heir.

Yes, ingratiating myself to Aro is the best course for now.

It doesn't hurt that he's rather handsome, in an aloof, Technocrat sort of way. Zandria would encourage me to enjoy it. Perhaps I can keep my heart close, yet stay in the moment . . .

I settle in at the worktable, propping up my tools and pulling out a pair of tweezers to get a better look at the potential sources.

The red ore looks the most promising. I've not informed Aro that we never worked with power sources in school and that Leon won't let me anywhere near that locked cabinet. Though I'm smart, and with my magic I'll figure something out. Or I can lie and tell him none work. He'd take my word for it, I'm sure.

But success would be much more useful.

I lift a tiny piece of red ore up with my tweezers to examine it. Keeping to minimal handspells, I reach for any traces of energy inside the pretty rock. Power flickers in answer to my call. Something is in there after all.

I put the red piece down and turn to one of the mechanical hearts. I pry the power chamber open and reexamine the way the vial of viscous black liquid inside is harnessed. A wire there, a plug here. Taking an unpowered heart, I retrieve the red rock and gently place it in the chamber, connecting wires and plugs to it in a similar fashion.

Nothing happens.

I call to the energy, but it won't exit the rocky exterior.

Power lies within it, but it's not easy to access.

Frustrated, I hum very softly but insistently at the energy in the rock, focusing on drawing it out and into the little clockwork heart. The red ore glows bright.

Before hope can begin to form, the ore explodes, sending pieces of shrapnel all over the room. I throw myself to the floor, arms over my head and magic thick on my tongue.

I sit up and wince. My left hand has a few slivers of metal in the palm, and it stings. But it's better than the clockwork heart; some of the larger pieces are lodged in the wall, making it far beyond repair.

"What in the flames is going on in there?" someone yells from the hall as they bang on the door. Forges. It's only my first try and I'm already attracting the wrong kind of attention.

Shoving my magic back down, I get to my feet unsteadily, then unlock and crack open the door. Caden stands there, red-faced, with his arm raised to knock again.

I smile sweetly. "Sorry for the noise. Just an experiment gone awry." I hold up my hand to show him the slivers. "Luckily, I didn't get the worst of it."

Caden pushes the door open wider, looking past me to see the pieces of metal embedded in the walls. "You *did* luck out. What's Aro got you working on in there?"

"Just testing some power sources. And that one was not stable, unfortunately." My hands sweat and I wipe them on my smock, then wince.

He shakes his head but appears to have calmed down. "That Aro, always chasing something new. Unbelievable. Do you need a medic for your hand?"

"No, thank you. I have some tweezers in here. I'll be all patched up in a moment."

He gives the room one last look, then pauses when he sees the samples spread out on the table. "Wait a minute. Aren't those . . . I swear the Head of Invention threw those out just last week." He places a foot in the door though I've got it half closed.

I shrug. "I'm sorry, I have no idea. I'm new, and I'm only here to work on whatever Aro tells me. I'm sure it's fine."

Caden still frowns.

"I really ought to get back to work, if you don't mind. Thank you for checking on me." I turn up the saccharine in my smile, and Caden finally moves his foot so I can close the door.

"All right. Let me know if you need anything."

"Thanks," I say.

I close the door, swiftly locking it behind me, then take a deep breath.

Interesting that Aro would have me working on sources the head of the division already ruled out. He's more desperate than I thought.

Obviously, there is power in some of these, but harnessing it is the challenge. What I need is something that will transfer power more easily. Or to construct something new to access it. I fear the latter is a bit beyond my skills at present.

I consider the gelatinous substance. Aro warned me not touch it with my hands, so I'll have to either scoop it with a spoon or move it with a spell. Now that Caden is around and likely more vigilant than he was a few minutes ago, any magic I do will have to fall under discreet handspells for now. Just to be safe.

I'll save that one for last. It looks like it could get messy.

I break off a piece of the spiky, dull rock instead. It's very heavy, and grows heavier when I try to activate its power. I frown, unsure what that means, but I hope it's a positive sign. First, I try heating the metal on the burner Aro left for me, but that seems to make its power recede. Instead, I place a spike in a vial of water, connect the plug and tiny wires, then place it inside one of the hearts. I continue to coax with my magic, feeling the fine lines of energy spinning inside the strange metal.

Out, come out, spark . . .

I close the chamber and press the switch to activate the heart, working the spell all the while. Magic streams from my fingertips into the device.

It churns, just for a second. The core in the center makes half a revolution before sputtering out and grinding to a halt.

Close, but not enough to power this for a year or more.

I imagine Aro's goal is to power the hearts for considerably longer than one year. The longer the power source lasts, the fewer times they will have to perform the operation to replace it and the longer the Heartless can live.

I try the next few minerals on the table, but with the same frustrating results. They work fleetingly but aren't strong enough to use even for a single day. I grow more discouraged as the afternoon rolls on, dreading Aro's return. I don't want to tell him I failed.

I try the odd, gelatinous substance last, and while that powers the heart for an entire minute, it's not enough.

I rest my head on top of my folded arms on the table. Aro won't have me come back. He might even complain to Leon. Panic stirs in my chest. If Leon has the slightest excuse to end my apprenticeship, he'll jump at it.

That decides it. I slide off my stool and hook my satchel over my shoulder. If this is my last day in the Palace, I'm going to make it count.

I QUIETLY USE MY MAGIC TO EXPAND THE

reach of my ears, waiting until I am sure the
hallway and those connecting to mine are empty.
All that remains is Caden's soft snore from down the
hall. As long as I'm careful, he shouldn't wake up. And if
he does, I'll simply tell him I'm getting a late lunch.

I open the door and lock it behind me. Once visually con-
firming the hall is indeed empty, I cast the cloaking spell and
hurry toward the part of the castle where Remy told me the children stay most of the day.

When I pass the first servant, I hold my breath even though
I know my spell should hold. The girl rushes by me without a
single glance, believing herself to be alone in the hall. Feeling
bolder, I plunge into one of the main hallways. This is trickier,
because I need to dodge and weave around many people and not
be noticed.

Bumping into something they can't see? That would be
noticeable.

I have one near miss, but otherwise smooth sailing. Then I
see them. A small group of children, ranging in age from toddler
to a few years younger than me, is ushered through a doorway.
I move as fast as I can, but it closes before I can reach it. And it's
guarded. Guards I could manage, but all these people—courtiers
and servants—roaming the hall? Someone would see that door
open by an invisible hand. Someone would know a Magi was here.

I'll have to wait for someone else to enter or exit the door, all
the while hiding here in the busy hallway. It could be minutes or
hours. And I don't have hours.

Five minutes. I'll wait here, safe under my shield but as near to the door as I can get without risking being stepped on. After that, I'll have to try another time.

The minutes tick by, and several times I narrowly dodge a running servant or courtier's metal-hemmed skirts.

I bite down hard on my tongue. I want to scream, but I must remain silent as a grave instead. I am so close to reaching those children—just behind that door—and I can't afford to wait any longer now. If I want to try that door, it will have to be very early morning or later at night . . .

Or perhaps not.

In the hall perpendicular to this one, there are other intersecting hallways. One of them may lead me to the same place, but through a different entrance. I take a left, narrowly avoiding a servant precariously balancing a tray full of tea on his shoulder.

There are only a couple of doors in this hall. One I quickly determine is a water closet and the other has strange sounds behind it. I put my ear to the wall.

It's a girl crying softly.

This could be it. I need to get into that room.

A servant rushes down the hall carrying a steaming iron on a tray of hot coals. She struggles to open the door, and as she stumbles inside I hold it open a tiny crack.

My blood turns cold.

It's a large drawing room, the kind normally used for entertaining. But here the couches and chairs are all pushed aside, the curtains are drawn closed, and what looks like a spurt of blood streaks along the far wall. And in the center of the room a girl is strapped face-down to a table. Tears stream down her cheeks and pool on the metal surface. My teeth clench when I realize it's Vivienne.

Inside the room, the servant sets the tray down on another table nearby. Then she curtsies and scurries to a corner to await further instructions.

"If you tell me what I want to know, you shall be spared," says the voice that gives me nightmares. Queen Cyrene comes into view, resplendent and terrifying in her peacock-blue gown, reinforced by steel sleeves and metal lace that could slice bread like a whisper. She gestures to the serving girl, whose chest hitches as she comes close and picks up the hot iron for her mistress.

My hands ball into fists. I don't want them to hurt Vivienne. But saving her would require exposing myself, and that's too high a price. I may not believe she deserves this, but I can't sacrifice myself—and my sister—for a Technocrat.

"I don't know anything, I swear. I just liked to flirt with Paul."

Paul, the baker's son. Another life I couldn't save. Helplessness worms its way through my belly.

"And he was Magi, and therefore guilty of treason. If he and his father infiltrated our city, there must be others. Tell me his associates. Tell me who they worked for."

For a brief moment, I catch a glimpse of the queen's face. Utter, wicked delight.

Bile rises in my throat. She enjoys this. That's why she's doing the interrogation herself.

"I don't know, I don't know." Vivienne dissolves into sobs. The queen stands beside her, resting one hand on the girl's shoulder.

"Do not fear. We are merciful."

She nods at the serving girl and turns away. The last thing I see before I silently close the door is the hot iron headed for Vivienne's feet and the awful smile on the queen's face.

When I reach my workroom again, I am quivering uncontrollably. Vivienne's screams still ring in my ears.

She's a Technocrat. The queen is a horror, but I can't spare a thought for what she does to her own people. I just need to keep my own out from under her metal-spiked thumb.

I must pull myself together.

Resting my head in my hands, I take deep, calming breaths. It isn't long before the door clicks open. I know it's Aro before I turn to see his hopeful face. It immediately falls.

"No success?" he says.

I shake my head. "Not yet."

He sits next to me on the bench. His disappointment is palpable, weighing down the air.

"This one"—I point to the gelatin in the vial—"was the most promising. It powered the heart for an entire minute." I face Aro, mustering every ounce of sincerity I have. "I'm sorry. I failed you."

To my shock, he laughs. "No, you didn't." He gestures to the power sources on the table. "These are only scratching the surface of potential energy candidates. There are many, many more where they came from. You may be trying them for weeks. Don't worry, I'll take care of Leon. He won't complain as long as he's well compensated."

His smile surprises but pleases me. He's still hopeful, even though this round didn't go well. Better yet, I have an excuse to return to the Palace regularly. I find myself looking forward to that a little too much.

"So I can try again tomorrow?"

"Yes. Go to the old workroom first. I'll meet you there and bring you here each morning. This is a restricted part of the Palace, and the guards wouldn't let you in without me until they get more familiar with you."

"You can depend on me."

"I know. That's why I came to you." He stands, offering me his hand. "Come on, let me walk you out of this sector."

I take his hand—it's softer than I expected. Something almost like magic trickles through my fingers where they touch his. I swallow hard.

I must encourage this. I need information from him. But is it against the rules to enjoy it, just a little?

By the look on his face, Aro feels the same electric charge running between us. Despite his excuse for taking my hand, neither of us makes a move toward the door. My mind races, dying for something to say, but my brain seems to have gone numb. All the training in the world didn't prepare me for the way my heart is flailing in my chest and how thick the air around us suddenly seems to be. Zandria would be so much better suited for this. But even that thought causes my cheeks to flush. I don't at all like the idea of my sister seducing Aro.

I step closer to him and he sucks in his breath between his teeth.

"I really do," he says quietly. "Depend on you, I mean."

A smile flirts over my lips. "I hope I don't disappoint. If I could I'd stay here all night, just to see if I could make more progress." I squeeze his arm, letting my hand linger on his shoulder.

"I wish you could."

"I can tell this is personal for you. We'll find a way, I'm sure of it." I take a deep breath. Our bodies are close enough now that I can lean in to kiss him on the cheek. When I pull back, the fire I saw in Aro's eyes before when he spoke of the Heartless blazes there again—only this time those flames are directed at me.

He puts a hand on the small of my back, his warm fingers burning through the fabric of my tunic. His head begins to tilt toward mine when a sharp knock on the door startles us both back. The door opens and Caden pokes his head in.

"There you are, Aro. The Head of Invention is looking for you. Says he needs to see you right away."

Red heat creeps up Aro's neck, but Caden is oblivious. "Of course. Tell him I'll be there shortly."

Caden nods and ducks out. We both let out a nervous laugh when we realize our hands are still entwined.

"I suppose I really ought to walk you out." He runs his free hand through his pale hair.

"If you must." Disappointment unexpectedly runs over me. Aro was about to kiss me, I'm sure of it.

And I wanted him to. Much, much more than I should.

He leads me back up the stairs and down the steel hallways, never letting go of my hand. When we reach the upper halls, Aro bids me goodbye, pressing my fingers to his lips. I return the gesture, then I rush from the Palace as fast as I can. I don't look for Remy, though I feel his eyes searing into my back as I flee.

An unfamiliar ache throbs in my gut. I don't know how to reconcile it with the cold, calculating self I've trained to become.

I think I'm going to be sick.

On the walk home, I lift my head to the sky, hoping the breeze will cool my skin and bring some sense back to me.

But instead, wild energy courses through my veins. A twisting force I've been shoving down, denying, ignoring for weeks.

I'm falling for Aro. The truth of it is suffocating and liberating at the same time. The need to see him, be near him, fills up my lungs with sweet air while simultaneously ripping apart my insides.

It wasn't supposed to be like this.

I only intended to use him, to pretend. Not be charmed by his resolve and dedication, his kindness and compassion. He isn't what I expected a Palace researcher would be.

I'm a Magi, he's a Technocrat. The divide is too deep. Love, for us, is a mad, brutal thing. It will only lead to destruction. It could even lead to our deaths.

If I don't get this under control, it will definitely compromise my mission.

Centuries ago, some Magi tried to find a way to use magic on more than just the living. Our parents never would tell us exactly what happened, only that the results were disastrous and anyone who had intermarried with Technos was executed for polluting their family lines and committing treason. After the wars, that hatred of anything Technocrat only sharpened. The machines are the one thing the Magi can't control, and it's what they fear and loathe the most. Before we moved here, we were given strict instructions on what was acceptable behavior and the consequences of crossing the line from blending in to actually caring for these people.

I know this, I understand this. I live and breathe this truth every day. But that does nothing to convince my heart to release its hold. It's latched onto Aro in a way that is unshakable.

The sun slinks away, hiding behind the trees and lighting their branches with red and purple fires. The moon peeks out, as though waiting for the sun to vanish offstage before taking its place in the sky.

It only helps the tiniest bit. But by the time I arrive home, I'm ready to face my family, determined to squash down every foolish emotion in my heart.

TODAY LEON SENDS ME ON AN ERRAND TO

the miner's stall I must complete before he'll
let me return to the Palace and my work with
Aro. I grumble as I hurry down the streets, wishing
to get this over and done with as soon as possible.

It has been slow work, earning Aro's trust, but now I
am making excellent progress. Zandria has helped me analyze
his every action and reaction, and after yesterday's almost-kiss she
feels certain he will soon tell me all I need to know.

What I have not told her is the truth about my own traitorous
heart.

It's a lovely summer day—mechbirds chirp in the trees, the
sun coats everything with gold. Despite the butterflies violently
upending my insides, I take a small amount of pleasure in my
walk, though I don't slow at all.

Not until something—or rather someone—stops me clean in
my tracks.

Across the main square, a flash of red hair moves swiftly
down the street.

"Zandy!" I start to call for her, but by the time the words reach
my lips she's already turned down a side street. I keep walking
for a moment, but a thought strikes me. She wasn't carrying her
messenger satchel or wearing her uniform. Every messenger must
wear them when on duty.

If my sister is not on duty, then what is she doing?

A sense of foreboding turns me around. I must know where she's
going. At this time of day she should definitely be on duty. But she
has a nose for trouble, and it always falls to me to keep her out of it.

I reach the street she turned down only to see her standing on the steps of a private home, grinning into an open door. A man's hand pulls her inside, but I'm on the wrong side of the street to see his face. The door shuts hard enough to jolt me.

What is Zandy up to? Could this be the man she claimed is a Magi? The one she seemed a bit too keen on knowing? Fear circles around my neck.

Sometimes Zandria is much too trusting and sure of her own judgment. She may accuse me of being too cynical, but my knack for second-guessing has saved our skins more than once.

Though I can't stand here on the sidewalk all day. That will get me noticed, and that's the last thing we need. I walk nonchalantly down the street, past the brick-and-steel townhouse Zandria entered, noting the address and details. A small but well-manicured front yard. Narrow, newly cobbled walk and steps. A door that is not yet worn from years of use and constant opening and closing. The windows are all shut and the curtains drawn. Given the weather, that strikes me as strange.

I'd bet the person who lives here is often away from home or has not lived here long at all. Or perhaps some combination of the two. The drawn curtains tell me he must be very protective of his privacy. Perhaps Zandria is right; maybe he is hiding something. Maybe he is a Magi. It would fit. I still don't believe he's the Hidden Knife, but the travel, unlived-in home, all sound like a cover any Magi spy would use.

A tiny twinge of jealously darts into my chest. What does Zandria need with another Magi spy? It's been drilled into us since we were young that we should not seek out others like ourselves or it will endanger the cause. The less we know about other spies in Palinor, the safer the network is, and the less information we can spill if we happen to be caught. It's the reason the real purpose of our mission has been kept from us.

I keep walking, then turn onto one street and another and

then another until I'm back on the route I should be for my own errand. All the while, I can't help wondering what Zandria has gotten herself into and, more importantly, how I will get her out of it.

When my errand for Leon is done, I hurry to the Palace, eager to see what Aro has me working on today. But when I arrive at the old workroom, Aro is not there to bring me to the lower levels where my new task awaits. I pace the room, anxious energy coursing through my veins. My mood shifts from fear to anticipation and back again with every beat of my heart.

I rub my arms and force myself to sit. I close my eyes and breathe deeply. What if Aro has found me out? Could Caden have seen me sneaking around after all? Could one of my spells been captured on a listening device? I can't lose my means into the Palace, not now when I am so close to finding the Heartless heir. I must keep my blossoming feelings in check. Stamp them out and focus on the cause. My loyalty to my people must trump every kind feeling I have for Aro. I cannot betray them like that. They are depending on me. I will not fail them. Even though my own heart has failed me.

After nearly half an hour, someone knocks on the door of the workroom, startling me to my feet. My pulse throbs in my throat, spiking when the door opens to reveal Aro. Something like hope sparkles in his eyes, and I can't help but return the look.

"Aissa," Aro says as he crosses the room to me. "I hope you haven't been waiting long."

"Not at all." I smile, even though it felt like an eternity. "Will I be testing more power sources today?"

"Yes." He pauses and shifts his weight from foot to foot, then extends his hand to me. I can tell he is holding his breath, like this is some kind of a test.

When I take his hand, it's clear from his grin that I passed.

We walk back down the halls, our pulses twin beats between our palms. My magic stirs in my chest, but I rein it in. I've never felt this lightheaded before in my life. I find myself sneaking glances at the contours of his face, his neck, his lips . . .

And then when he glances at me, we both blush and look away.

Aro pauses near a junction in the hallways, just before we get to the stairs leading down to the new workroom.

"Aissa, I—"

But before he can speak, the hallway falls silent and the words he meant to say vanish. The only sound is the steady clip of steel heels and boots on the floor. Aro peeks around the corner, then ducks back, pushing me into the nearest closet. It is much smaller than the one where Aro has his contraption set up to spy on the throne room. He holds a finger to his lips.

"Hiding from the queen and her courtiers again?" I whisper.

He lets out a small laugh. "Something like that," he says under his breath.

It's too tight to move around between the mops and cloths stacked against the walls. We are pressed together whether we like it or not, and after a few awkward moments Aro puts his arms around me. Our breath mingles as we wait in the darkness for whoever Aro is hiding from to pass.

I am extremely curious to know why Aro's projects matter so much to the queen, but I have more trouble than usual concentrating on that with my heart pounding in my ears.

Aro places his chin on the top of my head and sighs. A strange, fizzy feeling begins to fill me from the inside out. I need to remember my task—find the heir by any means possible. I must get information out of Aro. And Zandria assures me that kisses always lead to looser lips.

Before I can think better of it, I tilt my head and stand on my tiptoes, but a familiar voice from the hall—too close—stops me. The queen ordering her courtiers to follow her. Their murmurs swell and Aro's arms tighten around me just as I try to move back. We bump into a mop that sends several others tipping over, making us freeze.

When we realize the chatter in the hallway has returned to normal, we begin to laugh. Aro presses his forehead to mine for a moment, then releases me. "I suppose it's safe to move on now," he says. He sounds just as regretful as I feel.

Aro peeks out of the closet, and once the coast is clear we march down the hallway like nothing at all happened. But the sparkle in our eyes betrays the truth.

"The queen certainly keeps you on your toes," I say, clearing my throat.

Aro groans. "The last thing I want to do is face the queen and her courtiers at the same time. My other project should prevent me from wandering the halls with a mechanic. And the queen is not a woman one wants to disappoint. Certainly not in front of her entourage."

I inwardly shiver. How true that is.

It stings a bit that he won't confide in me about the other project, but it is not surprising. I'll have to keep trying. My lips tingle at the thought. I remind myself that this is all for the cause. Even if I am indulging my personal feelings at the same time.

It is a strange thing, these new, uncontrollable emotions. My magic can control so many things, more than your average Magi, but it is powerless in the face of what happens inside me. Those elements are ephemeral and inconstant, impossible to hold on to like earth and steel.

They have rendered me at the mercy of my enemy. And I do not like that one bit.

"DO YOU REALLY THINK THIS WILL WORK?"

I ask Zandria.

It's been two days since I saw her sneaking into that other Magi's house, and she has dodged all my hints and questions. Tonight she brought home a book of spells. She claims her new friend has all sorts of books and ancient Magi artifacts passed down through his family. I can't decide if it's a fake or the real thing. After the wars, families were forbidden from hoarding spell books. Gone were the days of the elite Great Academy. It was imperative the remaining Magi were as well-trained in our magic as possible to ensure our survival. If it is indeed an heirloom, we could get into trouble just for having this and not sharing.

Zandria gives me a withering look from her corner of the sparring room. "Of course it will work. If the Magi used it in their heyday, surely we can now."

"We're due to find our limits any second then." The reach of our magic may be almost double the range of other young Magi, but we're certainly not omnipotent. I sit next to her at the table and pull the book she has been poring over toward me. "When are you going to tell me who your new friend is?"

She grins, catlike and secretive. "Never. I can't betray his identity."

I fold my arms across my chest. "Then I'm never practicing this with you. I won't trust it without knowing the source."

She sighs, exasperated. "Please? Don't you want to try these new spells?" She leans forward on her elbows. "It will be our secret. And you must swear you won't tell Mama and Papa."

Understanding warms my face, but not pleasantly. "They wouldn't approve of this supposed Magi you've been seeing and you know it." I can't say I'd blame them either. I don't approve of Zandria sneaking into his house in broad daylight.

Her eyes glitter. "He's definitely Magi. And he's amazing. The work he does here, it—" She pauses. "But I can't talk about that. He swore me to secrecy."

"I highly doubt that includes your twin."

She smiles slyly. "Lucky for you, he didn't say a thing about twins in regard to this book." Her face clouds over. "About himself and his work, though, he was quite clear."

"You don't think that's strange?"

"Not at all. We're not supposed to know much about the other Magi here in Palinor. It's too dangerous. He took a huge risk confiding in me in the first place."

"Fine. Tell me more about the book." I lean back in my chair, trying to relax, but a river of tension swims up and down my back.

She places her hand on the leather-bound cover, red and cracked from age. The front is embossed with silver lettering and runes snake down the spine. At the very bottom are what looks almost like two *A*'s, perhaps the initials of some famed Magi from long ago. "This book was salvaged from the library. One of the originals. They used it in the ancient academies to teach Magi students advanced spells." Her eyes have a wicked gleam I don't like at all. "I think we're ready."

"How can you be sure he isn't lying to trap you or win you over? Or to get you in trouble with the Council for hoarding spell books?"

"He'd never do that. And besides, it's true! I tried one earlier."

"What did this spell do?"

"It made my hands blue, but only for a moment. I reversed it quickly."

"Show me," I say. I confess I'm intrigued, but I don't see how this can be useful to us. I'd rather hunt for the real library in the tunnels than turn my hands pretty colors.

She opens the book to a page she's marked and waves one hand over the other in intricate movements I don't quite follow. Within a few moments her hands begin to turn blue. First the tips of her fingers and fingernails. The color swiftly creeps along her knuckles and toward the backs of her hands. It darkens, then turns the center of her palms a deep royal shade.

"You can stop gaping any time," she says.

"All right, you have my attention. What spell did you want to try tonight?"

She squeals excitedly and hugs me. "You won't regret it, I promise. I've found a way to search the tunnels completely undetected. Even if someone sees us, no one will know who we are because it provides the perfect disguise."

"Show me," I say.

She flips to another page, then makes hand motions over her face and hair. Each spell in the book is written out in motions and words and tunes, but Zandria always prefers the handspells. It doesn't take long for her hair to change color, the ends lightening to a frosty blond then transforming all the way to the roots. Her eyes shift from their natural green to a piercing blue. Her nose takes on more angles than before. Her ears lengthen and point slightly at the ends. Her jaw widens and her mouth thins. A gasp forms on her new lips. She moans and rests her now unrecognizable head on the table.

I place a hand on her shoulder. "Are you all right? Does it hurt?"

"Only a little," she says. Her strange eyes gaze at me, but the sparkle is unmistakably Zandria. "I need a mirror."

When we leave our house that night, we don't leave as the red-haired twins the city knows. We leave as a blond, tall girl, and a short, dark-haired, dark-eyed pixie. Zandria's spell book may indeed prove useful, even if its origins are suspect.

We could be different people every time we leave the house. Imagine the possibilities! Not even our own parents would know us.

The transformation does hurt. The movement of skin and bones during the process is very uncomfortable. The pain fades quickly, for which I'm grateful, and our spell should hold for a whole day unless we reverse it sooner.

Zandria skips down the street under the full moon's brilliant light. "Be careful!" I hiss, but she pays me no heed. Just because we can change our appearance doesn't mean we're safe.

Nothing I say will change Zandria's attitude. I hope she doesn't draw too much attention tonight. I'm pleased with my disguise; I might like to use it again.

Miraculously, we enter the tunnels unseen and without much fanfare. Zandria skids down the slick walkway and almost falls into the muck before sliding to a stop at the platform and the exposed tunnel we wish to explore more.

Zandria!" I admonish. She smirks but says nothing. I mutter the spell to amplify distant sounds, then listen. Down the main corridor, I hear the steady thrum and bump of machines. But in the one we want to investigate, I hear nothing at all.

"I think it's safe," I say reluctantly. I can't put my finger on it, but something about the tunnels has my nerves on edge tonight.

Whatever it is, I want to proceed with more caution than Zandria is willing to give. We found another spell in her book that might hold the answer to opening the door. It's written in an old dialect, but it appears to be used for opening stubborn objects.

That door should qualify.

Zandria leads the way, while I keep a wary eye on our rear. I can't shake the feeling we're being watched. Yet nothing appears, no flashes or listeners in sight.

We had the presence of mind a few weeks ago, after we had trouble finding the tunnel that night with Remy, to retrace our steps and ensure we recorded how to get back to the correct tunnel. It's tricky and the door is hidden down a corridor that's very easy to miss. That night, the door still refused to open, but the strange magic-infused walls and rock were energizing. Zandria doesn't need any more energy tonight, but I know we both want to feel that rush again.

We look for the subtle change in shadow, and the glimmer of the magic marbled walls that signal we are close. Zandy skips along the way, and in spite of the sound dampening spell I have in place, I cringe at every step.

"Zandria, you're far too reckless tonight."

She giggles and springs farther ahead. It's the excitement of the new spell. She always gets this way when we try something new. Zandria reaches the hidden turn that leads to where the magic walls begin and vanishes inside. I blink, then she's gone. I swallow the panic, knowing it's nothing. She's right behind the wall.

If only my senses would agree with my rationale.

I follow my sister and I'm rewarded with the sight of her form turning the next corner. I shake my head at my own foolishness. I worry more than I should, but I can't help it. I know all too well what's at stake.

Everything.

Maybe I'm just troubled that Zandria's been sneaking out to meet her mysterious boyfriend. And that she refuses to tell me his name. Never before has she kept anything like this from me, and that scares me most of all.

What if she's wrong? What if he isn't a Magi as he claims? What if he betrays us?

Then again, he did have that book—and others, according to Zandria. She claims he even demonstrated some of the spells himself, so he must have magic in him.

But her lack of confidence in me is disturbing.

I push these feelings away and pay attention to the walls instead. They thrum with power. The air in this passage feels different. It feels alive. What still confuses me is that nothing Zandria and I have researched about the library mentions magic-infused walls. Surely the Magi from before the wars would have known. I can only suppose the secrets of our most sacred place were kept confidential, and thus lost along with their keepers.

Zandria reaches the door first—of course—and immediately pulls out the sheet of paper on which we copied the spell. We plan to burn it once we cast it, destroying all evidence.

She holds it out to me so we can share and combine our powers. It's jolting how strange she looks now. I must appear as odd to her as well, but her altered appearance combined with her behavior regarding this new boyfriend make her feel like a complete stranger.

She tilts her head when she sees my hesitation. "What's wrong?"

I laugh at myself. "Nothing, I'm just not accustomed to your new face."

She winks with those strange eyes. "Don't worry, I won't wear it much longer. Promise."

She begins her handspell while I sing the words on the paper. At first nothing happens, but then there is a flash and the doorknob turns a dull black. We exchange an excited look and leap toward the door. Zandria grabs it first and tugs and turns with all her might.

It doesn't budge. Not even when I try for good measure.

We attempt the spell again, but this time there's no spark, no flash, and no dulling of the marble. We try several more times, hoping it might have a cumulative effect, but after an hour it's clearly to no avail. The door won't let us pass tonight.

By the time we head back down the passage, the doorknob has returned to its normal shimmering tone. We've left no mark at all.

Dejected, we trudge back the way we came, out of the magic-lined passage and into the regular tunnels.

I shouldn't have gotten my hopes up about that spell. Maybe we copied it down wrong. Something must be missing from it, as it should have worked. Unless there's more to the door than even we suspect. But what?

My frustrated thoughts buzz around my head like a pack of mechbees, a distraction I can't afford.

We don't hear them until they're upon us.

Zandria, running ahead, is caught in their trap first.

Trip wires.

The machine set to catch us, a nimble spiderlike thing, latches onto her legs and arms and slams her to the floor.

My throat chokes with horror. Wires crawl over her body, fastening her to the ground. She glances back, her dazed face turning an ashen shade.

I run toward her but before I get far, she wrests her hands free of the wires and raises them to perform a spell.

The thunder of Technocrat boots rings in my ears, spurring me forward until a fierce gust of wind blows me back against the far wall and my skull cracks against the stone. The world spins around me as Zandria is fully pinned, the machine's web complete. Her eyes even from this distance plead with me to run as far and fast as I can.

That wind was from her. She was trying to keep me safe.

"No, no, no," I plead with the air, crawling to my feet and lurching toward my sister. Still dazed, my vision swims. Zandria's eyes harden and she twists her hands so that they're firmly on the ground. Her mouth moves rapidly. The walls shake beneath the pressure of her magic. Cracks form, then ripple through the stone and brick. Pieces fall and shatter on the floor just as the first of the Technocrats swarm around her. My knees weaken but I leap in Zandria's direction, only to see her press the magic deeper into the tunnel infrastructure.

The walls explode.

I throw myself away from the collapsing junction. The guards shout, then I hear nothing but sliding rocks and the convulsing of my own heart.

I gasp for breath. The horror of what happened slices through me like an old, jagged knife.

We did the one thing we were never supposed to do: fail.

I find myself on my feet, scrabbling at the rubble. I don't stop until my fingers are bloody and raw. When it finally occurs to me to use my magic, I pull away rubble until I've made a hole big enough to peek through. But they are gone, Zandria is gone, and I have no choice but to admit defeat.

By now, the Technocrats must be bracing her hands with steel gloves and locking her into an awful steel hood. No hearing in front of the king and queen for her. They caught us red-handed.

I have one option for escape, before they sweep these tunnels again and find me too. It means giving up all hope of reaching my sister. The calculating part of my brain insists it's too late, that I don't even know where in the tunnel system they might be by now. But every bit of my being can't bear to face what's happened. The only way for me to run is across the tunnel and up to the drain on the other side of town.

A storm surges in my head and it's all I can do to force my feet to stumble down the long passage.

Keep moving, keep moving.

One foot forward.

Don't stop moving or they'll catch you too.

Bile rises in my throat, threatening to choke off my breath.

I swallow the burning sensation and keep running. This passage feels twice as long as I remember it, but I can't stop. I must not stop. If I do, I'll never be able to get back up again.

Rock shifting and shuddering slaps me with a new wave of fear. My feet move faster than I thought they could. My chest heaves, my spells all but dropped now. My footsteps must give my location away, but I simply don't have the breath to hum nor the strength to cast with my hands while I run.

Faster. I must move faster.

Magic throbs in my veins, panic summoning it to the surface. It aches to be released, set free to destroy the people who took my sister.

I failed her.

My feet catch on a rock and I fall to my hands and knees. It's so dark here I can hardly see the way in front of me, but I know it by heart. I squeeze my eyes shut and gasp in air, then struggle back to my feet.

A steady shuffling and shifting echoes in the corridors connecting to this one, suggesting more machines are down here. It sounds like the seekers that nearly found us once before. I tremble, even as I run. If they catch me I have two choices.

Let them rip me apart limb by limb, or expose the secret of what my magic can really do.

But if I do that, I also expose Zandria. She's caught in their grasp. If they knew, they'd never let her go. They'd kill her on the spot. If she were lucky.

Don't stop moving.

A shaft of moonlight peeks around the corner of the tunnel. The moon is high tonight, and it clearly reveals the drainage grate up ahead. When I reach it, I pause to listen for people on the streets above.

All I can hear is the rushing of the blood in my veins, the

steady, echoing thump-thump-thump of machines down the corridor, and the furious impetus repeating in my head to get out of these suffocating tunnels.

The sound of pursuit grows louder. My throat is rough and dry as I hum the spell to move the grate. My magic, angry at being chained while I ran, pushes up faster than I expect and I almost lose control of it.

The sounds are closer than I'd like as I scramble out into the alleyway. I settle the lid back in place, but it will be too easy for them to tell where I escaped. They can't follow me any farther. Frantically, I search the alley for something to place over the grate.

Panicky pressure builds behind my eyes. Nothing. Nothing here will hide my tracks. No spell comes to my scattered mind that could help. I have to hide, I—

I know exactly what to do.

I hum breathlessly, winded from running, at the bricks in the walls around me. One by one I pull a few out and they float through the air, laying themselves perfectly together over the grate like a brick floor set in the middle of nowhere. Within a minute, no hint of the grate remains, which means the tunnels are dark, leaving no trace of my escape hatch.

Though my legs are rubbery and my lungs and eyes sting, I run from the alley. This time I have the presence of mind to use a handspell to cast the shield. The last thing I need is a zealous Technocrat to report my midnight run as suspicious activity.

Finally I reach the shadows of the huge willow tree in the square—one of the few real trees in the city. Only a few more blocks to my home, but I can't move another muscle. Every part of me is overcome. Overextended. Overwhelmed.

I collapse beneath the swaying boughs—gasping for breath, for sense, for everything to be put right again.

The tears I've held back burst through, here where no one will spy me unless they venture beneath the tree. It's ancient and its branches extend all the way to the ground. The soft breeze sways them, brushing my cheeks as though to comfort me.

The storm in my head descends into my body, wreaking havoc on my insides. I retch and gasp and heave, then crawl over to the base of the tree and curl up in an effort to keep the pieces of myself from falling apart. Every molecule in my body spins in a different direction, desperate to escape the horror that has taken up residence in my gut.

My sister sealed herself in with the Technocrats. Our mortal enemies.

And I couldn't stop her.

I'll do everything in my power to get her back.

By the time I reach our home—my disguise dropped—a light shines in our front window. A visitor at such a late hour.

I open the door with quivering insides and step into the light of my family's kitchen. Remy sits at the table with my parents, all talking in such serious tones that they don't hear my quiet steps until I drop to my knees at their feet, broken and desolate.

"Aissa!" cries Mama. "Thank the gods. Where have you been?"

"We've been searching everywhere for you," Papa adds. He frowns, then his eyes widen. "Aissa," he says with a hoarse voice. "Where is your sister?"

I can't meet their eyes. In a heartbeat, their stares will silently accuse me of my greatest failure.

"They caught her."

"WHAT?" MAMA WHISPERS, HER FINGERS
tightening over my shoulders.

My father's reaction is worse; he doesn't say a
word. Instead he goes strangely still. For a moment, it
feels like the world has stopped, waiting for me to take my
next breath. If I don't say it out loud again, maybe it won't be real.

"She's gone." I choke on the words. "We disobeyed you and
Isaiah. We went back to the tunnels. We've been doing it for weeks.
But this time there were guards and seekers and they trapped her."

My head throbs. I should have noticed them. I should have
been more alert, paying better attention to my instincts. I'm always
so careful and now the one time I wasn't . . .

"How did you get away?" My mother's voice is oddly distant
and echoes inside my head. It feels as though I'm moving through a
thick fog, like everything around me isn't quite clear, isn't quite real.

"Zandria." I sob. "She was running ahead and sprang the trap.
I tried to reach her, but she used a wind spell to throw me back
down the tunnel." I take a deep breath. Remy's here. I have to be
careful what I say next. I've already betrayed my sister more than
I ever imagined possible; I won't betray our secrets too. "I hit the
wall just around the corner and lost consciousness. Thanks to her,
the guards didn't see me when they arrived." I curl my knees to
my chest from my spot on the floor. I'll tell my parents the unvar-
nished truth of it later. They'll understand. "I'm so sorry." I rock
back and forth. "I'm so sorry."

Papa's expression as he rises from his chair is one I have never
seen before. He grabs his coat from the hook on the wall and heads
out the door, still mute.

My heart sinks right through the floor.

Is he so furious that he can't bear to be near me right now? I don't blame him. Everything about me—my voice, my face—is a reminder of my sister. A reminder that she's gone and only I remain. If I could escape myself, I would too.

Mama shakes me, halting my rocking.

"Stop it. You're safe. We will get her back."

"Yes," I say, clinging to her shoulders. A new, sudden energy fills me. "Yes. We must contact the Armory. They must send everyone they can right away. We can't wait to find the heir, we have to attack now—"

"No." Remy who has been silent until now, finally speaks. His hands tremble. "The Armory doesn't have the manpower to launch a full-scale attack on the Palace, and even if we did my father would never authorize such a thing. He won't deviate from his careful plans without very good reason. He will not let us all abandon our mission for the sake of one soldier."

My blood boils and I find myself on my feet. "You don't think Zandria is a good reason?"

Remy flinches. "I do. But I doubt my father would agree."

The fight goes out of me and I slump into the nearest chair. "I have to get her back. I need her."

I lost her. My other half. This is my fault. I know better than to let my guard down. Better than to give in to distractions. Zandria counted on me for it, and I failed her.

Mama puts her arms around me. "You will do nothing. If they have seen her face, they have seen yours. We will not risk you too. No, you will have to go into hiding, maybe—"

"No!" I cry, shaking off my mother's embrace. "I will not. And besides, they didn't see my face or hers." My fingers knot together in my lap. I'm about to be in even more trouble. "Zandria found a spell book on her route. We tried one tonight that let us change our appearance. We were both wearing new faces."

Remy gasps. "You had a spell book and didn't turn it in?"

"You tried spells without coming to us first?" Mama says at the same time. "They could have been dangerous."

"They weren't, I promise. I wanted to tell you. Zandria insisted we try it first." I glance at Remy. "And we were going to turn it over to the Council as soon as we determined the spells were real and not counterfeits. This was our test." The least I can do is cover for Zandy with a little white lie.

"Well, at least we have some time until the spell fades, anyway," Mama says.

"That won't matter." My hands quiver as Aro's words come back to me. "She's sealed up in one of those metal hoods by now. And the guards won't risk taking it off. They'll never connect her to me. I have to rescue her."

Mama pushes a stray lock of my hair behind my ear. "We will find a way, just us. Fewer people involved means less chance of being caught ourselves."

Remy sighs. "You know I'll have to inform my father of any plans we make."

Mama shoots knives at him with her eyes but doesn't respond.

"Remy, you can't. You must help us," I plead.

He runs his hands through his hair. "My father will never forgive me if I don't keep him informed. And who knows? Maybe he'll have an idea we can't see because we're too close to this."

My mother's gaze softens, but the vein pulsing at her temple gives away her true feelings. "That is a fair point," she says tightly, then turns back to me. "Your father is pursuing one avenue for assistance as we speak. I'm sure we can think of other options too."

"I hate to say this, but our best option is already in play," Remy says.

"What are you talking about?" I ask.

"The heir. When you find and kidnap her, we will hold her for ransom and demand they release all Magi prisoners. The sooner we find the heir, the sooner we get Zandria back."

The thought of waiting even another minute to rescue my twin is excruciating. I have to fix this now. "Absolutely not. It will take too long."

Mama doesn't say anything for a long minute. "I don't like that option either. But you may be right."

For the next hour we toss ideas back and forth, all of them far too slow for my taste. I know what the Technocrats do to the captured Magi. I've seen it with my own eyes, and it is terrible. I can't let Zandria waste away inside a metal suit. Just the thought makes me want to crack in two.

But we reach no conclusions, nothing that seems realistic and that won't result in my own capture. Mama is insistent we not risk that.

I should've tried harder to reach her. Should have insisted she not run ahead. There must have been something I could have done. Suffocating guilt refuses to release me. A constant reminder of my separation from my twin. Ripping off my arm would have been kinder.

Despite what my parents say, I'll risk anything to get her back.

When dawn approaches, bathing my lonely bedroom in a faint red hue, I hear our front door open and close. I have not slept all night and Papa's footsteps, quiet as they may be, sound like explosions to my exhausted ears. Mama has not slept either; I know because, despite her best efforts, I've heard her crying in her own room. She's heard my father arrive as well and meets him in the kitchen. I tiptoe to the bedroom door and whisper the spell to amplify sounds. I must know what news Papa brings, where he's been all this time.

The first thing I hear is the sound of a fist slamming into the metal counter. I jump back from the door, frayed nerves flailing.

"He won't help us." Papa's voice trembles with rage. "He's ordered us to wait until we hear from the Council."

"Coward," Mama growls. Then more softly, "Here, give me your hand."

For a moment, all I hear is her murmuring a spell. Probably one to heal Papa's hand. It reminds me of all the scrapes and scratches Zandy and I got when we were little and running free in the Chambers. Mama always used magic then to fix us right up. But ever since we moved to Palinor, we've learned to carry our scars.

"You didn't let on why we need her back, did you? He hasn't guessed?" Mama asks. I'm surprised to hear the fear in her voice. It is not an emotion she shows often.

"No. I gave him no reason to think she's anything other than normal, like we told him years ago. Zandria is safe in that respect at least."

Mama barks a mirthless laugh. "Yes, she is very safe locked up in the Palace." Something clatters in the kitchen. "We should go after her ourselves right now. Before the city is awake."

Papa lets out a quavering breath. "We can't. If we go after her, disobey a direct order, Isaiah will not let it drop until he finds out why. We are trained to compartmentalize our emotions; failure to do so will put both our daughters in even more danger."

"What are you suggesting? That we just leave her there?" This time a tea kettle clangs onto the stove.

"If we deviate from our mission, we leave them exposed. I hate this as much as you do, and we will find a way to get her back. But perhaps we can use the mission to aid us. The plan is to hold the Heartless girl for ransom in exchange for our Magi prisoners. We'll just have to use all our resources to find her faster."

Mama scoffs. "That's just what Remy said. He's becoming a bit too much like his father."

"He's right. More than he realizes."

"Aissa will never agree to this, you know. She'll be livid."

Mama is right. I already am. Part of me wants to tear down the wall that separates us and scream at them for even considering for one second that leaving Zandria where she is right now is the best course of action. But the rest of me hears the pain in every word they speak, and it feels like blades jutting into my skin.

"If she wants Zandria back in one piece, she'll have to agree. We have no choice."

I shudder. I don't know who Papa went to for help, but it's clearly left him hollowed out and resigned. I won't ever give up. But for my parents' sake, I'll try to wait until we find the heir.

And every ounce of energy I have will go into finding her. No matter who I have to use to do it. Zandria was sure I could convince Aro to help me, and it's time I test that theory. The Heartless heir is no longer just my mission; she's the key to my sister's freedom.

THE RISING OF THE SUN DOES NOT DULL THE

pain a whit. If I don't find Zandria soon, I fear
I will explode.

I will get her back. No matter what.

My parents are heartbroken, but they are nothing if
not dedicated to the cause. They informed me this morning that they've begrudgingly decided to go along with Remy's
suggestion of kidnapping and ransoming the Heartless heir, and
all their plans focus on that goal. Based on the conversation I
overheard last night, they believe it's the only way to keep Zandria
and my unusual powers secret too. The Technocrats will have to
free Zandria and all the other Magi prisoners if they want their
precious daughter back. For my parents' sake I promised I will try
to wait. But the fine cracks in my resolve may as well be visible
on the outside of my skin.

My parents already sent a notice to the Messenger Guild excus-
ing Zandria's prolonged absence—she's supposedly out of the city,
tending to a dear, sick aunt. Just the thought of that lie nause-
ates me.

I need to find her now, and I need help. From someone who
is not wrapped up in the plot to kidnap the heir. I've barely slept,
but I leave home earlier than usual and hurry toward the square,
remapping in my head the route I took the day I saw Zandria enter
a stranger's townhouse. It isn't long before my feet lead me back to
that street. I hide behind a fence and ensure no one is in sight, then
cast the shield spell. I circle around to the back of the townhouse.
Unlike my sister, I'm not so brazen—or foolish—to enter by the
front door. I make quick work of the lock on the fence then enter
a small yard adorned with rocky tiles and not much else.

The lock on the back door is no match for me either, and I slip inside the house. If anyone is home, my looks alone—identical to Zandria's—should explain my appearance well enough. In fact, I have half a mind to pretend I'm her just to see how much she told him.

I drop the shield spell and let my eyes adjust to the dim light. I'm in a kitchen. The floor looks newly polished, and the stove and a nearby table are a bit too neat and clean. Only two chairs. I open the pantry and find it empty. An uncomfortable feeling brews in my chest.

I move quickly through the rest of the house. The owner is nowhere in sight. In fact, there is hardly a sign of anyone having lived here. My initial assessment on that day I caught Zandria sneaking in was correct; the owner is not here often. The only rooms that look lived in are at the front of the house: the study and the sitting room. I rest for a moment on the sofa, watching the early morning light sneak in between the cracks in the pulled curtains.

My sister sat here not long ago. She talked to this strange Magi and learned spells from him. She was right here. I bite my lip hard enough that it bleeds.

I miss her so much.

I gulp in a breath and get to my feet to examine the rest of the room. The sitting room has the usual sofa and chairs, but also a harp in one corner. It hides under a drop cloth. Strange; Zandria didn't mention this Magi had an interest in music.

My confusion increases when I enter the adjoining study. There are no books at all here. None, and I've now searched the entire house. But there are shelves. Lots of shelves. Zandria swore he had many books.

Uneasiness swims in my lungs, swelling with every breath. I run my hands over the shelves, hoping to find a hidden panel, but instead I find something else.

A torn piece of very old red leather caught on a nail. Possibly from a book binding.

I tuck it into my pocket and turn my attention to the desk. The drawers are locked, of course, but that doesn't slow me. Only blank papers are in the first several I open, but I use my magic to reveal a false bottom on the lowest drawer. My pulse speeds up.

He's hiding something. I knew it.

I set the false panel aside and frown. There are only a couple items in the drawer: a miniature painting in a gilt frame of a woman playing a harp and a decaying mechanical heart.

My hand freezes as I move the frame aside, mind reeling with the implications.

Underneath is a small object that strongly resembles a key. It's made from the same material as that door we found. Isaiah may have denied the material could be what we suspected, but Zandria's mysterious Magi friend must know something more.

My hand tightens on the key and the magic tickles my skin. I slip it into my pocket and turn my attention to the mechanical heart.

From its blackened state, I can tell the heart is far from new. The havani that once powered it corroded the mechanics from the inside out. I shiver and withdraw my hand.

That is not a thing I want to touch.

I am sure my sister did not discover this. She must have been too blinded by the books that once lined the shelves to search his desk. If she had investigated, I don't think she'd have been half so taken with the man.

I'm willing to bet the woman in the portrait is the owner of the heart. Judging by the state of it, she must be dead. Was this man Zandria encountered really a Magi? She knows enough to be able to discern between Technocrat tricks and real magic. But if he is Magi, what is he doing with this hidden in his desk?

Could this man who claims to be the legendary Hidden Knife actually have fallen in love with a Heartless woman? If not, why keep her picture? Her instrument? Her heart?

The only thing I'm sure of right now is that I won't find the help I need here.

I'm dreading working with Aro today. The mere thought is intolerable, and yet it must be done. I need my place in the Palace now more than ever. But how can I stand to look at him, flirt with him? Not when he's one of them. Not without Zandria to analyze the meaning of every glance and word. I am not a whole person without my sister.

I must stamp out every kind feeling I have for Aro no matter how much my heart objects. Leave it to shrivel in darkness like the wicked thing it is. Loyalty must come before love. Every ounce of affection for him is a betrayal to my sister.

The decayed mechanical heart hidden in the mysterious Magi's home comes to mind. If he loved a Technocrat, it didn't turn out well for him. I should take that as a warning.

But my feet still lead me to the Palace, right through the servants' entrance and into the workroom where Aro awaits. He stands when he sees me, face beaming.

It is torture to smile back.

"I have some sources today that seem very promising," Aro says. "I think we might be close."

"That's wonderful," I reply, playing my role as best I can. Together we walk toward the research sector in the lower levels. Once we hit the stairs, Aro takes my hand.

I flinch, and immediately curse myself as his face falls.

"Sorry," I say with a laugh. "You just startled me, that's all."

Then I swallow my disgust as I put my hand in his. It fits perfectly, and his grip is strong and welcoming. It makes my heart flutter and my stomach roil at the same time.

I cannot allow my cover to slip, not now.

He flashes that lopsided grin I've grown to love. "I suppose I have a terrible habit of doing that, don't I? Even from the day we met."

The day of the parade. When Zandria and I had no idea what was to come next. It feels like a lifetime ago.

"How does your sister fare in her apprenticeship? She's a messenger, isn't she?"

Aro's words slice through me. He is only making small talk, but it is the worst possible subject. "Yes. But she's on holiday right now."

"Without you?" Aro looks surprised.

"She was invited to visit the seaport." We've finally reached the workroom door and I turn my most winning smile on him. "I could have gone too, but I'm needed in the Palace for some important work, am I not?"

Aro runs a thumb across my chin and it makes me shiver. "Yes. Yes, you are."

"Then I should probably get to work."

He sighs. "Of course." He opens the door and I step inside. "I'll see you at lunchtime."

I release his hand and close the door, resisting the urge to slam it shut. I curl inward, gasping.

Half of me misses Aro already and the rest is full of revulsion. The two sides of my heart war with each other, making me feel dizzy and sick.

This is even worse than I expected.

The workday is long over, and I've wandered the streets for hours in the pouring rain, unwilling to go home and face my parents and their assurances we'll do something soon.

Soon isn't good enough for me.

The itch to do something, anything, buzzes between my ears with a ferocity I can't ignore. It is near midnight when I find myself alone in the alley we'd been using to sneak into the tunnels. I weave my hands toward the grate. Every finger aches to tear into the Technos who took my sister. Who are probably torturing her right now.

A couple weeks ago, we found a way into the root cellars of the Palace. I'll dig out the cold steel-loving heart of every Techno I can find within those walls with the dagger at my side. Or turn their machines against them with one deadly whisper.

If Zandria is hurt . . . I will rip the entire Palace apart. I will raze it the ground.

The bricks I laid over the grate two nights ago have just begun to quiver when a hand clamps onto my shoulder. I wheel around, dagger in hand and spell on my lips. I kick the legs out from under my attacker, and he's on his back on the cobblestones, my knee pressed to his chest, before I even glance at his face.

"Aissa!" Remy gasps, holding his palms up in front of him. My raised hand, poised to strike, shakes.

"Are you following me?" I don't lower my arm.

"I'm here to help you." He gives me an exasperated look. "Could you lower that knife, please?"

"I don't feel like it yet."

He sighs and leans his head back on the wet cobblestones. The rain doesn't stop its downpour and the droplets run over his face.

"Why are you here?"

"You've got to be joking. How long have we known each other?"

I hesitate for a moment. I've known him since we were children. But what if he saw me spelling the bricks?

I tilt my head at my knife, now hovering over his throat. "Do I look like I'm joking?"

"Not even a little."

"So," I say, digging my knee deeper into his chest, "what are you doing here?"

"Fine. I was following you." I press my dagger to his neck. He winces.

"Why?" I hiss. Remy's father is the head of the Armory. Who wouldn't hesitate to dispatch his own son to ferret out the truth and punish anyone he feared might endanger the cause. I just don't know whether Remy would actually do it.

"Because we're all upset about Zandria, and I want to help you."

I scoff. "Does it appear I need help?"

He lowers his voice. "Look, I'm worried about you and I don't want you to do anything stupid. And I don't want Zandy to be stuck in that dungeon either."

Something twists inside my chest, but I push it down. I ease up on the knife and stand. "I'm not doing anything stupid. I'm saving my sister. Protecting her is the smart thing to do." I can't think about what the Technos might do if they discovered not only is she Magi, she can manipulate their machines. Though if they've ruined her tongue and smashed her fingers like they did to the baker and his son, they may not discover anything at all.

"Protecting her and saving her are at odds with each other right now, Aissa. It's suicide to sneak into the Palace and carry her out on your back." He gets to his feet, rubbing the sore spot on his chest. The rain recedes to a misting. His damp hair clings to his forehead and cheeks.

The look in his eyes forces me to turn away. That concern, so clear and candid, is the last thing I need. And it's completely undermining my determination to be suspicious of him.

But there's no question the only one I will ever fully trust is Zandria.

I whirl to face him again. "I have a plan. And it doesn't involve you." It does involve me wreaking havoc with the Technos' machines, however, a thing I can't do if Remy is watching.

"We can be a team, you know."

Heat flashes up my neck to my head, making me dizzy and furious at the same time. "I already have a partner. She's in there, somewhere."

He puts a hand on my arm and I clench my teeth.

"If you try to get to her tonight, you'll be sacrificing yourself as well."

I shake uncontrollably, but not from the rain. I stare Remy down, unable to deny he may be right. But I don't care. I want to go out in a blaze right now no matter who I sacrifice—as long as it's not Zandria. She needs to be freed. That's all I can fit in my head at the moment.

Remy is clouding it up.

He reaches out again, very carefully and slowly, placing one hand on my dagger and the other against my cheek. I grip my knife even harder, but the gesture brings tears to my eyes. It's something Zandria would do to comfort me.

"What would you have me do instead?" I say through gritted teeth. "Don't you dare say sit at home and wait. That's not an option."

Remy's dark eyes soften, and he steps closer to me now that I'm not trying to knock him onto the ground or kill him. "Let me help you."

It takes all the strength I have not to slap his hand away from my face, in spite of the comfort it brings. "How can you help me? Zandria and I ran circles around you."

Water droplets drip off his chin. The damp begins to numb me, dulling the sticking point of pain in my gut.

Just not enough.

"You need help, and not only from me," Remy says. My eyes flit back to his. They're deep, warm, and sincere.

I turn away and face the wall, wishing I could tear it apart instead of being trapped here in the alley.

I won't be doing any of that tonight. Tomorrow I can try again. Or see what help Remy has in mind. Perhaps it'll be worth a try.

And if it's not, then I'll be back—and much more secretly.

"What are you suggesting?" I whisper, still not facing him.

"We can go to the Chambers, plead with the Armory Council to send a rescue team."

"I thought you already told them what happened."

Remy shakes his head. "I think a personal appearance would be more effective."

My curiosity flares. "You think they'd help me get Zandria back?"

"It's worth trying before you throw your life away. At the very least, they may have information that can help us get her out ourselves if they can't spare anyone."

I mull it over. The Armory might prove useful. And perhaps it would shed some light on who her mystery love interest really is. He may not be the real Hidden Knife, but if he's as well-placed as she believed, the Council would know. And if he knew what happened to her, maybe he could be persuaded to help.

"All right." Now I turn to Remy, resolve hardening my features. "We will try it your way first. But if that doesn't work, I'm going after her with everything I've got, and neither you nor anyone else can stop me."

"It's a deal," Remy says, then takes my arm. The last of the rain leaves only the damp and cold behind as we silently walk back to my parents' house.

This better work. I failed my sister once. I won't fail her again.

REMY AND I DECIDED TO BRING OUR PLAN TO
my parents as soon as we both secure the
time away from our jobs. Maintaining our covers is a critical sticking point. As much as I wish
to act right this second, I see the value in keeping my
apprenticeship—and access to the Palace. That can only aid
us in saving Zandria.

And I know just how I am going to do it too.

This morning I wait in the workroom, my knee anxiously
bouncing under the table. Aro nearly always arrives at the start
of the day. It has been torture being close to him, but it serves a
purpose.

My purpose.

The door opens and I halt my leg from tapping. Instead I let a
tear squeeze out of my eyes at the same moment Aro lays a hand
on my shoulder. I try not to tremble at the sight of Sparky following its master. It reminds me too much of the little machines that
overwhelmed my sister.

"Good morning, Aissa, I—" He halts midsentence as I turn,
hurriedly wiping the tear off my cheek. I smile weakly at him,
careful that the smile never reaches my eyes. "What's wrong?"

"It's nothing. Nothing at all, I swear." I take a deep breath and
let it out slowly. "What is my assignment today? Do you have new
sources for me to test?" I glance at the box he carries in one hand.

He places it on the table but shakes his head as he sits next to
me. "It isn't nothing. Please, tell me what's wrong. I want to help
if I can."

I glance at the floor, keeping my mask forlorn. But inside I am
pleased with how easily he falls into my trap. "It's—it's my aunt.

She was like an older sister to me growing up. She fell ill a few days ago, and I've just received word this morning that she is even worse." I put a hand over my mouth as if I must physically hold in my sob. It is not a thing I have to fake. Breaking down has never been easier for me nor so convenient.

Aro places a tentative hand on my shoulder. "I'm so sorry. Does she have a good physician? Maybe I can recommend someone."

"That is very thoughtful of you," I say. "But yes, she has a good physician. I just . . ."

"What?" One glance and I can tell he'll do anything I ask.

"It has been so long since I've seen her. And now, I . . . I don't know if I will again."

Zandria would be better at this, I know. She is the one with the flair for melodrama. But I think if she were here, she would be proud.

Understanding lights up Aro's face. "Now that is something I can help with. Take the next few days off, however long you need."

I wipe my eyes again and shake my head. "I can't. I am supposed to switch off and work at Leon's every other day now as well. He'll never give me the time off."

Aro squeezes my arm and smiles at me. "Oh yes he will. Trust me. I'll take care of everything. I'll tell him I need you here at the Palace for the next few days. I'll go to the shop right now and I won't take no for answer. He can't refuse me when I ask on behalf of the royals."

I widen my eyes. "You'd do that? I really do need this apprenticeship."

"And you'll keep it. I promise. Give me until lunchtime, and then that time is yours to spend with your aunt."

I give him a grateful, sad smile, letting his hand linger in mine longer than I ought to. He leaves with a purposeful step.

Zandria would be very proud.

My father paces the kitchen, the dim lights glancing off his dark hair like darts. "If anyone should go to the Chambers, it's your mother and me. But it's too dangerous now, and we have been strictly instructed to maintain our post at the shop in case anything of interest passes through. Besides, the Technocrats will be watching the pathways in and out of Palinor closely." He stops and throws up his hands. "What if one of the guards who took Zandria recognizes you? We can't risk both our daughters."

"They won't recognize me. I had a disguising spell on when they captured her, remember? And Remy and I have not been personally forbidden from leaving Palinor, just you two. I've secured the time away from my work at the mechanic shop, and since Remy is a guard, we shouldn't have any trouble leaving." I fold my arms across my chest. From what Aro told me at lunch, Leon was all too happy to have me out of his hair for a few days. Nothing Papa or Mama can say will stop me.

"I know when the guards change and how to get through the holes in their web around the city. I won't let Aissa out of my sight," Remy says.

My mother narrows her eyes. Outwardly, she doesn't seem half as upset as my father. But her hands worrying the hem of her shirt belie her true feelings.

Remy places a reassuring hand on her arm. My father won't stand still long enough for Remy to try the gesture on him. "Your daughter will be safe with me."

"Our other daughter wasn't safe anywhere!" Papa hisses.

The words cut me like a razor. She *should* have been safe with me, as we'd always been when together. Until that night.

I will do anything to get her back. Even if it means crawling on my knees to the Chambers and begging for the Council's help. The hollow spot in my chest burns with every breath. It won't go away until Zandria is safe again.

I halt my father's steps and grab his hands. The backs of my eyes sting. "Papa, I have to get her back. You didn't see what I saw. What they do to Magi they capture." The image of the baker and his son locked in a metal tomb flickers to the forefront of my brain. "I can't leave her like that for a second longer than necessary. I promise not to go back into the Palace to rescue her alone. The Magi are the only ones who can help Zandria."

I shoot a pleading glance at Mama. She nods her approval with glistening eyes. I turn back to Papa. His mouth is a hard line. I don't know what that means. I hold my breath, waiting for his response.

"You'd better keep her safe." He glares at Remy. "Or nothing will keep you safe from me." He drops my hands and storms out of the kitchen, heading for the training room in the basement. I can't blame him. I've run that room ragged ever since my sister was taken.

"When will you leave?" Mama asks.

I glance at Remy.

"First light. That's when they change the guard and so are less likely to pay attention to the two of us leaving."

"First light it is," I say.

I sleep fitfully until the threads of dawn weave across the sky. Our bedroom no longer offers the same warmth with only me in it. Instead, it feels desolate.

My bag is already packed with clothes and provisions. The patter of Remy's feet in the hall jolts me out of my light slumber.

Mama and Papa let him stay so we could slip out more easily. I'm through the door and walking next to him in seconds.

"You didn't sleep a wink, did you?" he asks. I shake my head in answer.

As we slip into the darkness, Remy looks at me and asks, "How are you doing?"

"As good as I can be, I suppose."

He snorts and takes my hand. I try to draw it back, but he holds it fast. His grip is rough and tight, nothing like Aro's tender one. "This gives us an alibi. We'll look like lovers sneaking off in the dawn. That may attract snickers, but not much undue attention."

I swallow my retort. He's right, even if I don't like it.

The steel city still slumbers around us; only the birds and other stray animals flit and skirt about. The sky is a foreboding gray, with a hint of light slipping in around the edges. Drizzle from the clouds dampens my braided hair in minutes.

I pull my cloak up over my head. "South gate?"

Remy nods. We make it past the square with only the wind and rain and crows to see us pass. Any guards remain safely ensconced inside their stations around the city.

It feels strange not to have a shielding spell in place, or one silencing our steps. But today we're playing the role of two Technocrats leaving the city to visit a sick relative at the seaport. The fact that Remy is a guard himself will shield us more than our spells.

The houses thin out and more shops line the streets as we approach the south gate. Shops geared toward travelers, like the cobbler and blacksmith. Or a food stall that always sells fruit and cheese and dried meats.

None are open at this hour. Not that it matters: we stocked up on those things before we even told my parents we were leaving.

Remy ducks his head, pulling me closer to his side. "Guards are changing," he whispers. Sure enough, stomping steel steps echo down the street followed closely by the guards themselves. I lower my eyes. Machines I can handle. After what happened to Zandria, these men are what really scare me.

I could take them apart piece by piece or stop their hearts where they stand with a simple spell. The thought makes me trembly and nauseous. With the machines, it's nothing; with a human, however horrible they may be, it's something else entirely.

"You're shaking," Remy whispers. I force myself to stop when I realize how close he's still walking next to me. His proximity is both comforting and disconcerting. It makes me miss Aro, and that sends my thoughts spiraling into a mix of guilt and desire.

New, sharp sounds bring me back to reality.

The second set of guards in steel boots tromp by with less gusto than the previous batch. They must be tired from keeping watch all night.

We hurry through the lingering darkness toward the south gate. Shadows of guards on the ramparts hover below near the entry to the towers. The fog and rain continue unabated, and when we approach the high wall, Remy hails the guard at the door.

The guard smiles with recognition. "Remy, what are you doing here at this hour?"

"Family emergency. We're headed to the seaport." The lie rolls so smoothly off Remy's tongue that I almost believe it.

Their small talk moves at a snail's pace, stretching each moment of clawing terror further than I can stand. I want to scream and run headlong through the gate, but I squash the urge down.

After what feels like an eternity, the guard opens the gate and lets us cross. The fog is thick like pieces of cotton and curls around our legs and arms. We head onto the main road that runs through the remains of a forest decimated by the Techno-Magi wars. Much of the standing wood is naked, petrified trunks, but here and there newer trees have begun to spring up over the last hundred years. Interspersed between them are mechanical trees made from green- and brown-tinted alloys like the ones in the square and the park. The Technocrats' attempt to remediate the destruction they wrought on the landscape with their terrible war machines.

Until we finally reach the cover of the woods, I can't shake the feeling of a thousand eyes boring into my back. The trek through the forest goes faster than I expect. Remy tries to keep up a conversation, but I'm not feeling very talkative.

A nagging feeling pricks me with doubt. I'll be prepared for whatever the Council decides. I already have a contingency plan worked out in the event they aren't interested in helping Zandria.

If they refuse, I'll use Aro for everything he's worth, my foolish heart be damned. Access. Information. I'll use him to find and free my sister.

I admit, his kindness to that Heartless child made me believe he was different. His devotion and passion lured me in. But at the same time, I hate him and everything he represents. That always must be the side that wins out.

"Watch out for that one," Remy says as we skirt around a bush with red berries and thorns hidden by its large green leaves. The horned holly bush. Once, when I was little, I scraped my arm on one while Zandria and I were playing in the woods near the Chambers. My arm began to swell almost immediately. But Mama knew what to do and we got to see firsthand the practical application of a transference spell. Zandria helped me home, and Mama used her magic to pull the poison out of me and into one of her other plants. It wilted almost instantly. I'll never forget the feeling—the burning poison like my arm was on fire, then the cool relief as Mama pulled it out of me.

I've given the thorned holly a wide berth ever since.

When night begins to fall over the forest and the sounds of wild animals rustle in the undergrowth, we look for a place to make camp. When my family used to summer at the Chambers, we took the main road and stayed at inns. But the direct route through the woods is faster, and there's nothing resembling covered shelter here. We have our bedrolls and food, and kindling for a fire if we dare.

It's cold enough and we're deep enough in the woods, we do.

We find a clearing with several large boulders. I start the fire while Remy sets out our bedrolls.

"You know, I have an idea in case it rains again."

I raise an eyebrow. "Will it keep us dry?"

He grins and my chest pinches. There he is. That's the boy I used to know. His grin slips away and he turns to the largest boulder. He whispers and gestures. Yet another spell I don't know. Isaiah must have a book or two he's held back from the rest of the Magi, the hypocrite.

I'll have to ask Remy to teach me later.

The boulder is part of the natural world and pristine—untouched by mankind—and with his magic Remy coaxes the boulder to reshape itself, forming a hollowed-out standing cave. We can sleep in relative comfort on our bedrolls and not worry about the weather.

It's brilliant. But I'm not about to tell Remy that.

"Not bad," I say.

"A compliment? Wonders never cease." Remy pulls out a piece of jerky.

"Don't get used to it," I say, and he laughs.

Then I remember my sister and my heart deadens yet again.

We eat in silence, the flames of the small blaze dancing before us and tossing shadows on the trees. Only one night, then we'll reach the Chambers. One night there, another on the way back, and we return to the city. So little time, yet all my hopes depend on what happens in these few days and nights.

The rain dribbles past every once in a while without bothering us, but the cave can't keep out the cold. The fire helps, but before long both of us shiver in our bedrolls.

"Come here," Remy says.

"Why?" I ask.

"We're freezing, and there's no reason for it. We're old friends, so come here. We need to keep each other warm."

"Not a chance."

I curl up more, but the cold still seeps under my cloak. I hold off as long as I can manage, but finally I give in.

"Fine," I say, and Remy wraps his cloak around us both. I stiffen at first with his arms around me, but after a few minutes I relax. It's not so bad, and it's definitely warmer. There is something rather comforting too about being in the arms of an old friend. Though mostly it just makes my wicked heart miss Aro.

"Have you considered what you'll do if they say no to your plea for help?" Remy asks so quietly, I almost think it's the sound of my own thoughts.

"What?" My face feels pale and drawn, but luckily my cloak is pulled close enough against the cold that he can't see.

"You heard me."

"A little."

He laughs quietly. "So that's what you've been doing all day instead of talking to me."

"Of course not." I adjust my cloak again and tuck my hands into my sleeves. My fingers are freezing.

"Why don't you trust me?" Remy moves his arm so he can cover my quivering hands in his.

"I do trust you." In a sense.

"No, you don't." His body heat seeps through my cloak,

warming me. Or it could be the heat of embarrassment coursing through me. I've been cold to him, it's true, but I didn't think my mistrust showed so clearly.

"What makes you say that?"

"You've changed. You used to be as warm as Zandria. Now . . ." He sighs, his breath tickling my ear. "You hold everyone at arm's length except her."

I swallow the lump that forms in my throat at the mention of her name.

"She lent you her warmth, you gave her your strength. You need each other."

My eyes burn, and I close them to keep the tears from falling. How can he know us so well when we haven't seen him in so long?

"I never forgot you and your sister, and I could never forget about Zandria, trapped somewhere beneath the Palace."

His words are a punch in the gut. Our cloak-blanket is stifling yet comforting at the same time. But I have no words to respond.

"I'll help you, even if my father won't. But to do that, I need you to trust me. Even if I say and do things in the Chambers that seem at odds with this. Sometimes I may need to keep up a pretense."

"You don't think they'll agree, do you?"

He doesn't answer, and that tells me all I need to know.

"Then why did you suggest we come out here?"

"Hope. If there's the slightest chance they'll help, it's far better than the alternative of you going in alone and getting yourself killed."

For one long moment, I hold my breath. I want to believe him. But I'm scared. I want to know what Zandria would think, but she isn't here to offer her opinion.

"I'll try."

"That's all I ask."

Remy doesn't say anything more, but I can sense something hides beneath the words left unsaid. The question is—what? And how bad can it be?

I squash those thoughts down and settle in to sleep. Remy's arms and the steady rise and fall of his chest against my back lull me into fitful dreams.

CHAPTER

25

I WAKE WITH A START. THE FIRE DIED HOURS

ago and the cold creeps over us, slinking into our bones despite how tightly we're wrapped together. I take a deep breath and allow myself a moment to relish the feeling of comfort that comes with being in Remy's arms. It's fleeting.

Because I'm not safe. Not here, not anywhere or with anyone.

Though after last night, I've decided to give Remy the benefit of the doubt. For now. He's right; he may have to play a role to win over his father.

Especially as I hate politics. I prefer action.

The instant I can take action, I won't hesitate.

Frustration spurs me from our makeshift cavern and the warmth of Remy's arms, and I begin to rebuild the fire. He sleeps so peacefully, with his dark hair falling across his eyes and warding off the sunlight. I wonder if he is cold now that I've left him.

Aro's face dances before my eyes in the flickering firelight.

No, no feelings for anyone. Especially him.

I toast some bread and cheese, and it isn't long before the aroma wakes Remy from his sleep. He stretches and grunts, then takes a seat next to me by the fire. "One of those for me?" He yawns sleepily. I hand him a piece of my breakfast.

I finish my toast in a few bites, but my stomach still rumbles. I ignore it; there is no time to waste making more, and we will eat just fine tonight when we reach the Chambers.

"We should go." I scrub out the fire and begin to pack up my bedroll.

Remy yawns again but rises to do the same. "We should get there by midafternoon if we don't meet any trouble," he says.

207

Hope fills me in just the way I shouldn't allow. "Then let's get moving."

Not long after midday the woods thicken, signaling that we near the Chambers. We walk for miles through the winding hills, the way growing ever tighter. This far from the capitol city, more trees survived or have regrown, and they form an uninterrupted canopy above our heads, blocking out all but the faintest trickles of light. Vine moss hangs down like locks of hair on a noble woman. And like those Technocrat nobles, the vines reach and grab and hold on to us longer than they should. I have to slice them from my arms more than once. It's no accident the moss and vines and trees are thickest here—the Magi help them along. These were seedlings when the Chambers was created one hundred years ago. Now the trunks are several feet thick and vines cling to every living thing. They wait for the Magi to step into the daylight again.

We round a tree, and there it is.

A deep ravine cuts the forest in half. Rocky crags line the edge and the downward view is crippling to even the bravest of men. Unless you know the secret route to get below.

Fortunately, we do.

We step out of the forest onto the cliff's edge. We join our magic as one, our hands weaving and lips chanting words. I have only ever done this with Zandria. So while Remy and I make it work, it doesn't feel quite right, not natural and seamless like it is with my sister. Rocks in the ravine tremble and shift in answer to our call. One by one they rearrange themselves into a familiar formation. In minutes, a stone stairway leads into the ravine.

"After you," Remy says. He guards the rear just in case.

I take the steep steps carefully. They're made more for giants than human feet. When my parents took me and Zandria here, we made a game of it, hopping down each step like it was a cliff. We never feared the ravine.

And never worried about being followed.

In hindsight, I'm sure it was all my parents thought about, and yet they still allowed us to play and have our games. So much weighed them down yet they managed to pretend all was well.

They were far better and more practiced spies than I'll ever be.

When we reach the bottom of the ravine, we use our combined magic to place the rocks in their original locations. It's like the stairs never existed.

Now the cloying quiet surrounds us, amplified by the steep, sloping sides rising a hundred yards above us. It feels like the world holds its breath.

A deceptive slit in the rock wall provides the opening we need. From above it looks like a mere shadow. Or a small indent.

But up close it's wide enough for me to slide right through.

The Magi's secret world never fails to astound me every time I venture into this cave. I know all about our magic and our tricks, but what they've done here is truly amazing.

Beyond the darkness of the outer tunnel, a new world of light and life begins. First, it's a glimmer of Magi-made sunlight around a corner. Then the rustling of branches from the gentle breeze blowing through the tunnel. The trickle of water that quickly turns into a steady stream.

Around the next bend is the world we once had topside across the entire continent. Everywhere is green. Plants grow out of the walls, climbing up everything. Thick trees and branches tower overhead. A river meanders over the rocks, forming waterfalls and new caverns, while fish leap within its currents. The heat of an unseen sun beats down on my skin.

It's the most beautiful thing I've ever seen and a jarring reminder of all we have lost.

We step onto the wooden bridge running through the vibrant gorge. I can't help staring at the ferns and trees and moss around us as we make our way to the central caverns. Every twenty feet or so, an entrance to another cavern pops up—homes where families hide. If the Technocrats ever find this place, they'll still have to ferret our people out from underground.

But that won't happen. We have too many safeguards in place. And I don't intend to fail the Armory any more than my sister.

Remy knows the way to the Council headquarters best, and I let him lead the way, content with enjoying my surroundings. This is the only place where Magi are safe.

When we reach a larger cave opening toward the upper end of the underground gorge, Remy ducks inside. He looks at me sheepishly as I follow. "Sorry. We need to see my father first, then we can get an audience in front of the Armory Council."

"We can't go directly to the Council?"

"Not when my own father is the head of it. It would look terrible if I tried to circumvent him, and it would do nothing to serve our cause."

I understand better why he was so adamant that I trust him. Who knows what he may need to tell his father.

"So you've decided to join us here," a deep voice says from the darkness. Suddenly light fills the cavern. We're in a sitting room and I can see beyond to what must be the kitchen. The walls are polished stone and light dances off them, mingling with the plant life that permeates the Chambers.

"Yes, Father," Remy answers. "We need your help."

Isaiah motions for us to sit at the table at one end of the room. "Shouldn't it be the other way around? Aren't you two supposed to be helping us?" He frowns. "Aissa, where's your sister?"

My heart drops into my feet.

"That's why we're here," Remy says before I can find the presence of mind to answer. "We wanted to tell you in person." Isaiah's face clouds over, and he turns his stormy eyes to me.

"Where is your sister?" His voice is soft, but an undercurrent of . . . something . . . runs beneath that sends spiders skittering over my shoulders.

"She was captured by the Technocrats."

The stillness I felt earlier in the ravine outside grabs ahold of this room. None of us move for several breaths. Isaiah's face doesn't reveal his emotions, so unlike his son's in that respect. It's impossible to tell what he thinks.

"Then you've been compromised." That would be his first thought. Cold and calculating. How did I ever think Remy was like him?

Worse, how could Zandria compare me to him?

"I have not been compromised," I say.

"You share a face. Of course you've been compromised. You want asylum here, is that it?"

Remy remains perfectly still, letting me decide what to tell of the story and what to hold back.

"We were experimenting with a spell that night. One that altered our appearances dramatically. We transformed before we went out on a mission." I pause to take the spell book from my satchel. "Here—we wanted to ensure it wasn't a fake before we turned it over."

"Where did you get this book?" Isaiah glowers as he takes the book from me, but the hint of interest in his voice gives me hope . . . and fear.

"Zandria found it while performing her messenger duties." The half-truth comes out more easily than it should.

"That's a dangerous and complicated spell."

"We're very good with our magic," I say.

Beneath the table, my hands twist in my cloak. It occurs to me that he never offered to take our cloaks, as though he doesn't expect us to stay long.

"What mission were you on when she was captured?" His face darkens again, but the interest in his voice increases.

"We went back to the tunnels to look for the library. We did it often. Every night that we could sneak away."

Isaiah's frown deepens. "The Armory Council will not be pleased to hear this."

"I'm sorry we disobeyed you, but we found things you should know about. The Technocrats are looking for something down there too. Maybe even our library. They have machines pulling down the walls. We destroyed the first set of them. But more will be back soon."

"Did you find out more about that door?" Isaiah asks.

"No, only that it's still there and still frustratingly difficult to open."

"I see. What was different about this night, then?"

I swallow the sand coating my throat. It doesn't help. The memory of Zandria's shocked scream will never fade from my ears.

"Guards aren't usually in the tunnels. This time they were. Zandria had run ahead . . ." My face burns with tears begging to be released, but there's no way I will cry in front of Isaiah. It won't help my case.

"So you disobeyed a direct order, endangered our mission, and your sister got caught in the process?"

"They didn't endanger the mission," Remy objects. "They continued in their given directive to seek out the Heartless heir during the day. These ventures were in addition to that."

Isaiah turns his inscrutable eyes on his son. "And by doing so, increased the risk of being caught. Which is precisely what happened. Don't you think we had a reason to change your mission? It was clearly more dangerous than we'd anticipated. We didn't wish to lose such promising operatives so early."

Heat colors my cheeks, searing all the way down to my toes. We should've listened. But both of us were lured by that strange door and the idea of being the ones to unearth our lost library.

"We were fools." I look Isaiah straight in the eyes. "I know that now. It's not a mistake we'll repeat."

"No, I don't think you will. In fact, if you want an audience with the Armory Council, you must swear to me that you will never enter those tunnels again unless directed."

I take a deep breath. "I swear it." Hope again kindles in my stuttering heart. "So you'll help us free Zandria?"

"We shall have to see what the Council says. They may not wish to help reunite a pair of headstrong girls."

His words are a slap in the face.

"They're key players in our network now, Father," Remy says. "They've done very well infiltrating the Palace and the Technocrats' networks."

"Maybe so." Isaiah turns the full force of his keen gray eyes to me. "But everyone can be replaced."

I can't help shivering.

Isaiah stands. "You can stay in the back rooms tonight. Tomorrow you can plead your case, and we'll see what the Council says."

WHEN I WAS A CHILD, THE CHAMBERS WAS

a place of freedom and comfort. But without my sister it's stifling to think how far underground we are. So much rides on the decision of the Council. We were caught while disobeying a direct order—how can I hope to convince them to aid us?

I toss and turn half the night running over what I will say, what might sway them the most, until I finally drift into a light sleep full of horrible dreams just before dawn. In them, I'm the one trapped beneath Palinor, locked away in a suit of steel. Crushed fingers, unable to move my hands for a spell. No way to move my mouth or form words with my ruined tongue. Cold broth poured down my throat at regular intervals is the only means to tell how much time passes. And tears—constant, stinging tears I can't wipe from my face. Until my tear ducts go dry and only pain and heaving sobs remain.

I wake, thrashing in tangled sheets, with someone standing over me. I get in a good punch before he grabs my hands and I realize it's Remy. A welt forms on his cheekbone.

"Aissa, it was only a nightmare. It isn't real."

I curl my legs up to my chest and bury my face in my knees. It *is* real. It's what Zandria is experiencing. That nightmare is her world now. It's all she knows.

When the sobs begin, Remy places a tentative hand on my back. Zandria doesn't deserve such treatment. None of them do.

The tears come harder and Remy puts his arms around me, holding me tightly. I bury my face in his neck. With Zandria's capture I lost a piece of myself. I need something, someone to hold on to. Someone who doesn't confuse me like Aro does. In a few minutes, my sobs subside to mere sniffles. I pull back and Remy places a hand on my cheek. His eyes shine.

Was he crying too?

"No matter what they decide, Aissa, I promise I will help you get Zandria out of there," he whispers. "I won't abandon her, even if they do. Even if I have to say something condemning today, know it's only a lie I must tell to protect both of you."

Emotions choke my throat and I can't find the words to speak. I nod in understanding.

I can trust Remy. But everything hinges on the Armory Council's decision.

An hour later, I'm dressed and ready to plead for assistance in freeing my sister from the clutches of the Technocrats. Isaiah doesn't join us for our silent breakfast. He appears precisely when it's time to take us to the Council meeting. He doesn't say much either.

I haven't the slightest idea what Isaiah thinks of my case. Wouldn't he want to save one of his twin daggers, as he once called us? Surely we're worth far more together than torn apart.

I cling to that thought with all my might as we cross the wooden bridges with the river running beneath. Every step takes us closer to their verdict. My hands have been sweating since I woke. The beauty of the place is lost on me today. The foliage and the light are as pretty as before, but my ability to enjoy anything is gone.

My nightmare returns full force and I stumble on the bridge. Remy catches me and helps me up. Forges, the thought of being imprisoned in darkness forever is enough to bring me to my knees.

We weren't warned in our training of what they do to the Magi they capture, and my parents were certainly surprised. Perhaps the realities will sway the Council.

It's early, but a few children play in the pools left by the falls and scamper over the bridges. A handful of Magi chat outside their homes. Life goes on as normal here and it cuts me like a torn sheet of metal. I want that normal feeling again.

Isaiah leads us to a cave at the bottom of the falls. Twenty men and women already sit in a circle within the room. Light fills the cave, as do pieces of furniture molded from the natural landscape—boulder chairs and footstools, even a gigantic petrified tree stump serves as a table.

I only recognize a couple faces, but that's not surprising. I never did have access to the higher-ups when I was a child. It's a miracle I have access now. The woman in a long blue robe is Masia Harkness, who Zandria and I aspired to be when we were children. She has long been revered for her dexterity with her powers. Magic flows from her to the earth with more ease than any other Magi known. Callum Porter, our historian, slumps in his chair, wiping the sleep from his eyes. Another man, younger than the others, looks very familiar to me, but I can't decide why. I don't think I know him from my childhood, but I'm certain I have seen him before. Recently.

"Remy," I whisper while Isaiah explains to the group they're here to hear my plea for the help of Armory resources. "Who is the man in the middle there, with the green cloak?"

He considers for a moment and frowns. "Darian Azul. He is not here at the Chambers often. He is usually off collecting intelligence."

"Do you work with him? I swear I have seen him before, but I can't place him."

"I don't. I can't imagine where you would've seen him. He spends more time away than here."

It niggles at me, but I don't have time to consider it further because the Council is ready to hear me out. Isaiah introduces me to each member, all of them nodding in turn. "Now, Aissa, what is it you ask of us?"

My first attempt at speech fails. My throat is too dry to make a single sound. I swallow and try again.

"My twin sister, Zandria, was captured a few nights ago by the Technocrats. They took her and they locked her in a steel suit. They broke her fingers and maimed her tongue. They do this to all Magi they capture so that they can't cast a spell, escape, or even move. They put them in sealed-off steel dungeon cells where no light or organic material can enter. The prisoners see nothing but endless darkness." I blink back the tears that threaten. "I need your help to rescue her. She is an integral part of our mission to find the Heartless Technocrat heir. I need her to complete our mission successfully."

Murmurs rumble throughout the room. The councilors glance from one to another.

A man in a red cloak speaks up first. "What do you expect us to do? Waltz into Palinor and open the Palace dungeon? How do you propose we accomplish that?" He practically spits the name of the Technocrat city.

"A team from the Armory, perhaps a half dozen, would be all the resources and knowledge we would need to get in and out safely," I say.

"What about the other prisoners? Your sister is hardly the first Magi we have lost to the Technocrats," Masia says.

"We can free them too. At the same time if possible."

Masia shrugs. "Why is your sister so special?"

Frustration burns inside my chest. *Because she's my other half,* I want to scream, but that would do me no good. Nor can I tell them it's because she's the only other one who can magick the machines. It is clear that this Council, like all Magi, cannot see technology as anything other than black and white. Unfortunately for my sister and me, we're gray.

Though knowledge of our unique talents might make them understand my pleas, it would ensure they'd never help us. So instead, I lie.

"We're twins. We're more powerful together. Our powers magnify each other's." Hopefully they never ask us to prove it.

Masia sits up straighter. "Fascinating. You shall have to tell me more about that sometime."

The man in the red cloak speaks up again. "You're basing her importance off your own personal sense of value. We have many other spies who are just as good as you two, and more experienced."

"But do you have any others who are so well-positioned? She's in the messenger service and I'm apprenticed to the master mechanic who serves the king and queen."

Many on the Council flinch and draw their cloaks closer. I realize too late I probably shouldn't have mentioned my apprenticeship. It's the job I was assigned, but my proximity to machines isn't going to help me win them over.

The green cloaked man, Darian Azul, strokes his chin as he considers me. "Yes, we do have others as well-placed. But not those who can magnify each other's powers."

Red cloak laughs. "Well, she could hardly go back to work once she is free. Nor can you, since you look just like her."

This is the part I dreaded. The part where I have to publicly admit to ignoring a direct order. "That won't be a problem. We were . . . we were practicing a spell to change our features when she was taken. She didn't look like herself at the time they put the steel hood on her. They had no way to identify her or connect her to me."

That awful hood will haunt my nightmares for the rest of my life.

"What were you doing when Zandria was taken?" Isaiah asks

pointedly. In that moment I know, with utter certainty, he has already made up his mind to deny my request. There'll be a vote of course, but Isaiah won't cast his in my favor.

He knew Zandria. He held us both when we were babies. He watched us grow up.

He will turn his back on us with hardly a second thought.

Zandria was right. He's cold. The coldest person in the country. Just as cold as the Technocrats.

The scariest thing is that I can't entirely blame him. That clinical part of my brain reminds me of how I didn't even try to stop the other Magi from being taken or help Vivienne when I saw her being tortured. But the sister in me is incapable of letting her other half waste away underground.

"We were in the tunnels beneath Palinor's Palace complex. We were looking for the lost library." My cheeks redden.

"Why? Isn't your mission to find the heir?" Isaiah says.

"We wanted to locate a magic door we stumbled upon a few weeks ago to see if we could figure out how to open it."

"That doesn't sound like it will lead to the heir."

I shake my head.

"You were told specifically to abandon the search for the library, were you not?"

"Yes."

Isaiah gives me a disapproving look. He isn't alone.

"Do you have anything more to say?" Isaiah asks me.

"Only this: my sister is important, more than you can understand. I need your help to free her and the other Magi. Once she is out of their clutches, the rest will be that much easier to free with Zandria on our side."

"Thank you, Aissa. We will deliberate and let you know our decision shortly." Isaiah ushers Remy and me toward the door and the waiting room beyond.

Remy squeezes my hand in support but otherwise we're silent. I try to be patient, but I can't seem to get comfortable in my chair. I pace instead, my thoughts boiling over with worry. Even the slightest noise sends my eyes darting to the chamber door. They did not seem inclined to grant my request, but I have to hope that through some miracle they will.

It doesn't take them long to come to a decision. When we return to the chamber where the Council waits, their faces are passive and serious.

That can't mean anything good.

Isaiah stands at the head of the room and speaks for the group. "We have decided against sending our spies on a rescue mission for your sister. I'm sorry. I'm afraid it's too risky and there's too high a chance of exposing our entire operation. Your sister made a noble sacrifice." He folds his hands together, tent-style, just as he did when he gave Zandria and me our new assignment. "Given your circumstances, we won't censure you for disobeying the order not to return to the tunnels. You are already paying the price of your foolishness and we wouldn't have you suffer any further."

My body goes numb from head to toe. All the faces of the Council watch me. To see what I will do, how I will respond. Fury twists inside me, swirling and rising until it swallows me up and cracks the ice covering me from head to toe.

They won't help me. They see the loss of my sister as a fitting punishment for disobeying them. Only that man I can't place looks sad.

The heat of anger consumes me, and I hear someone wailing, the wrenching sound filling up my ears. Remy's arms wrap around my waist and he forcibly drags me from the room.

"Let go of me!" I finally manage to shove him off when we're outside the chamber. I can hear them inside arguing even now.

We should have helped her——

What an outburst! She's spent too long in the city—
We can't succeed, not yet. We need our magic back first—
What is this door she spoke of?

"We have to leave now, Aissa," Remy says. "For your safety, we need to leave now."

All the fight slips out of me. Remy isn't the one I need to rail against. "My safety is the least of my concerns."

He grabs my shoulders and shakes me. "Snap out of it, Aissa! If you die or are detained, you can't help your sister. I know it seems futile now, but as long as you are on the outside, there's hope."

Hope is a funny thing. I don't think I'll have a use for it anymore.

WHEN WE REACH ISAIAH'S HOME, WE PACK

our things at lightning speed. We don't want them to change their minds about letting me return to Palinor. I still intend to complete my mission for the Armory, but not for them. It's for the good of my people, whoever may happen to lead them.

Steps echo in the hallway of the house-cave. Remy packs in his room and I hear his father open his bedroom door, then close it softly behind him. Curious, I sling my bag over my shoulder and put my ear to my door, humming the spell to amplify sounds.

"What have you found?" Isaiah says, his tone stern.

"Nothing you don't already know," Remy says. "They pursued the library even though you told them not to. And they paid the price for it."

"What of their magic? Anything to indicate they are doing something to increase it? What of Aissa's claim their magic amplifies each other's?"

My head throbs. Remy wasn't sent to Palinor to help us in our mission. He was sent there to *spy* on us.

It is all I can do not to tear down Remy's door and throttle him right this second.

"I've never heard that claim until today, and nothing I've seen supports it. When they practice magic, they do it just like any other Magi. There is nothing special about it, other than that they are very talented."

"Are you certain? Their range is farther than most Magi, and my reports say they've already learned spells many Magi have trouble mastering, like the shield spell. Where did they find that spell book?"

"I don't know exactly. Only that Zandria found it through her messenger work somehow, just as Aissa said."

"What of their parents? Could they have discovered something during their cover as antiquities traders and kept it for themselves? Could they be hiding more books?"

"No," Remy says. "They'd never do that. There's nothing suspicious about any of them."

I can practically hear Isaiah's skeptical look. "Don't let that girl's wiles entangle you. While her affinity for the machines is useful, it's a slippery slope. It could lead her astray. Focus on your mission."

"Yes, Father," Remy says.

The door closes, and Isaiah's steps echo down the hall, pounding into my brain.

Remy betrayed my family. That's why he was stationed at the Palace. That's why I kept running into him. Why he followed us to the tunnels that night. I clench my hands at my sides, willing my body to stop shaking with rage. I must get out of here now.

"Aissa? Are you ready?" Remy's voice almost startles me.

I open the door, then yank him inside my room. I have him pinned against the wall and my knife at his throat before he realizes what happened.

"When were you going to tell me?" I hiss. His face crumbles. "Aissa, I—"

"I heard *everything*, so if the next word you speak is a lie, rest assured it will be your last." I've managed to stop shaking and instead channel my anger into a violent calm.

"I've wanted to tell you since I first ran into you in the streets of Palinor. I—I hated having to report on you to my father."

My grip on the blade tightens. "Then why did you do it?"

"Do you really think I had a choice?" He shrugs helplessly.

"What did you tell him?"

"Only what you heard. I told him about the spells you and Zandria could do, and that you were going into the tunnels. That's it, I swear."

"Then why is he so convinced there's something different about our magic?" This is the part that terrifies me.

Remy eyes the knife warily. "Honestly, I don't know. He was surprised by how fast you learned spells, maybe? Nothing I've told him should have been cause for suspicion."

"Why should I trust you?"

"Because I warned you about this on the way here, remember? That I may say something you don't like. That, and I'm not going to report on you anymore. Not really. I'll just tell him there's no news until he decides to give me another mission."

I narrow my eyes at him.

"I swear it, Aissa. I'm done with my father's game." His face twists with misery. "I should have been there to help you and Zandria. I want to help you now. Please trust me."

I lower my dagger and put it back in my belt. Remy relaxes, just before I clock him across the face with my fist. He spins and braces himself on the wall. That's definitely going to leave a bruise.

Fire floods my veins, but I hold my magic back. "I'll never trust you again."

His shoulders droop. "I can't say I don't deserve that. I'll earn your trust back, I promise."

I snort. "Good luck." I pick my pack up from the floor. "I'm leaving now. Are you coming back to Palinor or are you going stay here to be your daddy's lapdog?"

Remy straightens. "You know I'm going back. We have a mission to complete."

"Then let's get out of here." I head out the door without looking back. I can't stand the sight of him.

I can't believe Remy, of all people, would do this to us.

"We need to be careful," Remy says, catching up to me. "One of my friends here told me they've seen Technocrats on the road recently. No one's found this place, but we must cover our tracks."

"Of course I'll be cautious. I'm not new at this." We emerge into the magic-made daylight and I take a deep breath, burying the sick feeling of betrayal that threatens to choke me. I don't trust Remy for a second, but I have to put up with him until we're back in the city. Many more people are out at this time of day, and they stare as we climb down to the bottom of the gorge.

"Does everyone know what I asked for? And that I was denied?"

Remy sighs. "Probably. They're a gossipy lot, not surprising since there are so few of us. There are barely five hundred Magi living here. Another couple hundred at least are spread out throughout the country as part of the Armory network."

I always try not to consider the numbers against us. The Technocrats have thousands of soldiers at their disposal. Once, we had thousands too. Now, we don't even have one thousand warm spell-casting bodies to the Magi name.

Steadying myself near the cave opening, I breathe in deeply. Yes, the Council denied my request, and someone I regarded as a friend has been spying on me. But these people are why I'll keep fighting alongside the Magi and the Armory and the Council.

Every single one of us plays an important role in our survival. I won't abandon them the way they've abandoned Zandria.

When we emerge into real daylight at the bottom of the ravine, Remy immediately tenses. "What's wrong?" I ask.

"I'm not sure," he says, his eyes roving over the edges.

"Is there a less conspicuous way out of the ravine?" I feel it too. Something with eyes, watching and waiting.

He groans. "No. It isn't the sort of place people leave often, and even less often in a hurry as we are."

We keep our backs close to the wall of the ravine, hoping whatever is watching will show itself. Nothing does.

"Which side is nearest the forest?" My sense of direction is turned around from the time spent in the Chambers.

"That way." Remy nods to his left.

"Good. I have an idea." He raises an eyebrow at me but follows anyway. We move stealthily, and it is frustratingly slow. When we finally reach the far end of the ravine, I place my hands on the dirt wall, trying to get a sense for the life inside. I close my eyes, feeling the pulse of the earth. The Technocrats don't understand that the earth itself is alive; they believe it's as dead and lifeless as the steel they wield. But there's so much vibrancy in it. Until people like the Technos kill it, char it, and turn it to steel and brick.

"What are you doing?" Remy asks, a tinge of worry in his voice. He keeps an eye on the edge of the ravine.

I hum, very softly. Not enough for anyone spying to hear, but the earth listens. The wall begins to split apart with a soft rumble.

Remy's eyes widen. "Aissa, no, it's too dangerous."

I pause in my spellcasting to glare at him. "What other choice do we have? Give away the remaining Magi and die too?"

"Fine. But we must be quiet as possible."

"Then cast a silencing spell while I do this."

We return to our tasks. The crevice expands inch by inch until it opens wide enough for us both to crawl inside.

That's when we hear the voices, bits and pieces of words and tones slipping down the sides of the ravine to reach our ears.

They don't sound friendly. They sound like soldiers. Something else mixes with them, something creaking and metallic.

Horror rolls over me. Did the Technos follow us all the way from Palinor? Or are they here for some other reason?

They could hardly have stumbled upon the entrance to the Magi world by chance.

"We must move faster. Help me mold the earth and rock into a passage up. We should head for the tree break."

Remy nods appreciatively. "Good plan. But first, I'm hiding our tracks."

While I ply the stone and dirt in front of us into stairs, condensing it, making it more compact, Remy undoes my prior work and rebuilds the wall behind us so it resembles its almost normal state—with one exception. A six-inch hole to let the air flow in. From the outside, it would look like any other crevice.

We make steady progress. I can tell we move higher—the veins in the rock change and shift, showing their age—but how much farther we have to go, I can't hazard to guess. We stop to rest for a few minutes an hour into our upward trek and share our lunch of bread and cheese in the dark. I hadn't planned on dining underground today. I squash the panic that threatens to break free. We'll find the surface again.

Hopefully it will be nowhere near those soldiers at the ravine.

Remy's face is drawn and serious as he chews his piece of bread, a soft flame burning in his free hand.

"What's wrong with you?" I ask. He isn't his normal self. But that could be from anything—his father, his uncovered deception, the Technos so close to the Chambers, being stuck gods know how many feet underground . . .

"It would appear I'm not keen on tight spaces." He takes the last bite, then wipes his hand on his cloak. "I didn't realize how much the idea of being buried alive bothered me until today."

I groan. "Did you have to mention that now?"

Remy manages a half smile. "You did ask."

"And now I wish I hadn't." I shake my head and run my hand over the floor, checking to see if I dropped anything edible. I'm still starving. All this magic use is exhausting. What I wouldn't give for a nice leg of chicken right about now—

Wait.

On the floor of our tunnel is a vein of marble. But marble doesn't usually appear in the same area as the granite and dirt we've plowed through.

And it feels exactly like the magic-enhanced marble we found under the Palace.

My fingers tingle. It's not as strong in magic as the one in the tunnels, but that must have been refined by Magi hands. This is the raw, living material. That's the strange thing about stone. In the earth, it lives and breathes and Magi can manipulate it. But once it's been severed from the whole, reshaped into something else, it dies. Magi power cannot touch it. I'm not sure yet what finding the source of the material means, but my brain reels with the potential implications.

"What are you doing?" Remy whispers. I suppose I must seem foolish, all crouched down and gasping over a bit of rock. Not that I care what he thinks now.

"Put your hand here." I gesture to the vein of rock, and he places his hand on it. He lets out a small gasp.

"What is that? I can feel the magic in it."

"That door I mentioned at the Council? It was made of this. Under Palinor and still alive with magic."

"This is why you and Zandria returned to the tunnels?"

"We thought it was crafted by Magi, but it appears to be natural."

"Not necessarily. This magic energy may only have occurred here because of the proximity to the Chambers. I'd be willing to bet the end of this vein of rock is somewhere in the gorge itself."

"Fascinating," I murmur. The rock may have taken on magic properties by osmosis. I wonder what else we could infuse if we tried? Perhaps the Magi accomplished it when they made that hallway and door and somehow kept the power alive long enough for the magic to stick. If so, this is a practice long lost to modern Magi.

"We should get moving. We must be hitting daylight soon," I say.

We continue our upward movement, and I take it at a steeper pace. Soon the rock gives way to heavy black dirt and thick white roots cut across our path.

We must be near the top now, or at least close. I feel lighter already.

Now we just have to hope we don't end up breaking ground in the middle of a Technocrat encampment.

The dirt begins to dry out, signaling we are close to the surface. I send an exploratory tunnel a couple inches wide straight up, just to see how long it takes to create a shaft of light. When the beam hits my face, I can see it's only a few more feet. Almost there.

"We should hold off for a few minutes, just to see if we can hear anyone or anything," I say.

Remy nods and murmurs the spell that increases sounds to our ears.

We wait a full ten minutes, but all we hear are animals skittering in the underbrush and metallic leaves rustling. Just like the forest proper. We push through the last few feet to the top and help each other out of the hole, then collapse onto the forest floor and take in the sunlight.

I'm relieved we're aboveground again, but the fury and the disappointment that spurred us to leave the Magi returns full force, along with the weight of Remy's betrayal.

My parents were right. I can't trust anyone. It all falls on me now.

With heavy shoulders we edge toward the road, alert for any sign of Technocrats. My magic fizzes in my fingertips, but I must be careful.

I have so much to hide.

Remy would undoubtedly tell his father if he knew my secret.

He'd probably throw me back into the ravine—without a staircase. He'd think I'm tainted, a traitor, but I know better—I'm gifted. I may hate the machines, but the ability to use the Technocrats' greatest creation against them is what could turn the tide of our secret war.

I squash down the tingling in my hands and the unpleasant feeling in my stomach and keep moving.

The moss on the trees tugs at our clothes, chiding us to remain in the forest. Perhaps it's trying to tell us something.

We forge onward anyway.

The road breaks through the trees ahead. From our current vantage point, it's impossible to tell whether there are people on it. It would be faster to return to Palinor using that road, but only if people we meet on the journey can't tell where we came from. Here, it would be as if we appeared out of nowhere—which is essentially what we did—and create suspicion.

We approach the light streaming into the forest while traveling with a sound-smothering spell. When we reach a point where we can remain hidden, but still see onto the road, we freeze.

Camped down below is a large squadron of Technocrat soldiers. Steel helmets and ranging animal-like machines. Huge copper horses bray and nicker, while leonine and lupine steel beasts prowl around the perimeter.

They've set up camp right on the ravine.

MY HANDS SHAKE. THEY'RE FAR TOO CLOSE

to the Chambers.

"Could they know?" I whisper to Remy.

"Definitely not."

"How can you be sure?"

He pauses. "Only Magi know about it. One can never be certain, but a Magi would have to betray the location. Betraying our kind would mean one's own death. It just doesn't make sense."

"The prisoners," I say, horror welling in my veins. "They might have betrayed it for a little freedom from their steel prisons. Or to prevent the Technos from maiming their tongues."

Remy is adamant. "They'd never."

"You didn't see what the Technos do." I shudder. "It could break even the most well-trained spy." I grab Remy's arm. "We need to warn them. We need to go back."

Remy's face contorts. "We can't. It's too risky. Even if we did tunnel back, the soldiers might see us in the ravine. The best way to keep everyone safe is to leave them alone."

I swallow the cutting retort on my tongue. He may be right, but I still hate it.

"Fine. We'll have to take the longer route through the forest. The road is no use to us now."

With the day as long spent as it is, we just make it to the clearing and hollowed-out rock we camped at a couple nights ago when darkness begins to fall. We decide to rest here, then head out again early in the morning. Hopefully we'll get past the guards at nightfall tomorrow.

We don't huddle together for warmth this time, and we don't

make small talk. The expression on my face keeps Remy's mouth closed. After what feels like hours, I finally manage to fall asleep.

When I wake, it's because I'm certain someone is staring at me. The horrible feeling crawls all over my skin.

Sitting in front of our now blazing fire is the man I thought looked so familiar at the Council meeting, now dressed in a black cloak with a silver stripe. I jab Remy with my elbow, then leap to my feet, magic at the ready.

"Why are you following us?" I hiss.

The man smiles, but the lines never touch his eyes. "I'm not following you at all. I'm merely returning to Palinor and I happened upon your camp. You really should be more careful. You and Remy there look ripe for the picking by thieves."

I bristle, but since I don't know this man nor what he wants, I'm not ready to reveal a thing about myself.

Remy rubs the sleep from his eyes and squints. "What on earth are you doing here, Darian?" Remy asks.

Darian. *Darian.* Why is that name familiar? It resonated with me when Remy told me in the Chambers, and it chafes that I can't remember.

The man gets to his feet, then bows in greeting. "As I told the lady, I'm on my way to Palinor and I happened upon you. Nothing nefarious in my appearance, I assure you. You might find my presence useful, actually."

I fold my arms over my chest. "How so?"

"I have friends in high places. The Technos trust me and let me move freely in and out of the city. I have access to one of the hidden entrances."

Remy's eyes widen in understanding. "Because they think you're their spy," he says.

Surprise stutters through me as I finally realize why I know his name. "You're the spymaster?" Of course, Darian Azul, the Magi spymaster. People rarely talk about him. They say he is like a ghost. Indeed, I did not hear his approach at all.

He could be either very useful or very dangerous.

"If you'll help us into the city again, by all means share our food and fire," I say to Darian.

"Thank you." The side of his lips twitch. "How did you get away from the Technocrats undetected?"

I smile, even though I try not to. "We made our own exit, then covered our tracks."

Darian raises an eyebrow.

"I tunneled into the far wall while Remy closed it behind us. When we hit roots, we came up in the forest."

Darian laughs, a hearty sound. I thought the spymaster would be morose and serious like Isaiah, but I find him warm and oddly likable.

Still, I know better than to trust him. He of all people would report my extra abilities to the authorities—namely, Isaiah. And that just won't do.

"That's brilliant," he says. "Let's eat, then get moving. I've already scouted the woods for a mile in each direction. We should be able to reach Palinor by nightfall."

Remy takes a seat next to Darian and passes him part of the bread in our packs. "I've been counting the seconds until I can return to the glorious barracks."

Darian laughs again. "I'm sure you have. The food must be delightful."

"Only the best for Palinor's finest."

We eat quickly, then break camp. Soon we march through the woods toward the city of the Technocrats. Remy and Darian chat quietly as they walk ahead, which is a welcome relief. The less I have to be near Remy right now, the better. I bring up the rear, always keeping an eye out for anything following us.

I can't help wondering if Darian is here to watch us. He is on the Council after all.

His appearance is too convenient for my taste. That makes me yet more suspicious—and watchful of our backs.

But our luck holds and only swaying moss and drooping limbs follow our path.

When we stop to rest briefly while we finish off our provisions, Remy scouts ahead to ensure no one catches us unaware. Darian leans against the tree next to me as he bites into some bread.

"Aissa, I know you're unhappy about the Council's decision."

I frown, then shrug. This might be a test, and I'm not sure of the right answer. Better to wait and see what else he says first.

He sighs. "Look, I don't think the Council is wrong to insist on waiting and I won't defy their decision. But I will be on alert for any intel that might help us find her. If I learn anything useful, you'll be the first to know."

Surprise throws me into confusion. "Why? Why would you help me?"

Darian swallows the last of his meal. "I've lost loved ones too. I understand the desperation you're feeling. I know it's hard to wait, even though we must."

I consider the spymaster for a long moment. This could be just another trap. A trick of Isaiah's, trying to learn my secrets. Or Darian could be sincere. I have no way of knowing for certain.

"Thank you," I say carefully.

Once Remy returns, we resume our trek in the same formation as before. Snippets of Darian and Remy's conversation flit back to reach my ears, but I mostly tune it out, lost in my own thoughts. When the light begins to fade, my anxiety deepens.

"How close are we?" I ask Darian.

"We shall be there very soon."

"How will you get us through the gates?" Remy asks.

"Don't worry, this will be easier than you think. Trust me."

Trust him. It's laughable. Trouble is, we don't have much of a choice.

"You won't turn us in?" I ask warily.

"I swear on the lines of power running through the earth, I will get you into Palinor safe and unharmed." Darian's face is serious now. "Follow my lead and we'll all be perfectly fine."

The dark deepens and the pinpoints of light between the trees signal our approach to civilization like sideways stars. Darian shows no signs of slowing. Remy doesn't appear at ease either, but we keep following the spymaster.

"You both stay directly behind me. If anyone sees us approaching from the main gates, you must appear to be my servants. Keep your heads down."

He strides forward without waiting for an answer. Magic itches at my fingertips with every step we take toward the road, but I keep it at bay. Darian stops at one particularly large metal tree not far from the edge of the forest. He twists a root poking out from the soil, and a panel in the tree slides open, revealing a staircase headed down.

Fear pounds behind my eyes, but I follow him into the darkness. When the panel closes behind us, Darian pulls a mechanical torch from the wall and it sparks to life. The shiny walls and steps lead us down into the earth. It must take us under the city walls.

The space between us and Palinor grows shorter by the second. I feel as though I might catch on fire, given how much the magic aches to burst free. How are Remy and Darian holding up without so much as flinching?

We turn a corner in the tunnel and a guard steps out to greet us. He recognizes Darian—and grins. "Lord Azul. You've returned from your journey early."

I don't recognize this guard from the Palace, but Remy pulls his cloak closer to hide his face.

"Yes, the southern territories are not as amusing for me as they used to be." Darian yawns. "I was bored."

The guard laughs, then gives Remy and me the once-over. I keep my head down as instructed, terrified he will know, somehow.

"These two have been with you the whole time?" He squints. "They look different than the ones you took with you."

"Perhaps they got too much sun. It is the south."

The guard laughs again. "Good point, sir."

He steps aside, and behind him is a staircase that rises up. At the top of the stairs, Darian hits a button, and another panel slips open, letting us out into an alley somewhere in the city. Darian strides right onto the street without so much as a backward glance and Remy and I emulate his posture.

He is a master, after all.

THE NEXT MORNING I RETURN TO THE

Palace. Remy's betrayal still haunts every
breath I take. Each word the Council said about
Zandria's sacrifice rings in my ears as a steady rhythm
that propels my work onward. Magic is funny like that.
It answers to my moods and obeys the feverish pace of
my mind. I finished testing the latest round of possible power
sources Aro gave me this morning in record time. One or two
were actually promising, which pleased him immensely. For my
part, I was happy to find he is as true as his word; he covered for
me with Leon while I was away, and the Master Mechanic does
not suspect anything was amiss. But working with Aro, being near
him, is harder and more confusing than ever.

When we return from our lunch in the hidden garden, Aro
lingers in the doorway and gently places a hand on my arm. It gets
a little harder to breathe when I step closer to him.

"I just wanted to say, I'm glad that you're back." The tips of
his ears have turned red.

Unexpected warmth floods over my skin. "It's good to
be home."

"How is your aunt?"

"A little better, thank you."

His fingers slide down my arm to squeeze my hand. My
insides shiver, but I return the squeeze.

He clears his throat. "I should let you get back to work."

I laugh. "Probably."

When he leaves I close the door behind him with my pulse
pounding in my throat. A tiny part of me genuinely missed Aro,
and it threatens to rip my heart in two.

But he is right about one thing: I must get back to work. Just not quite the work he was thinking of.

When I first began working at the Palace, I'd search for the heir under the cover of a cloaking spell when I'd finished my work for the day. It was risky, but I didn't know how long the opportunity would last. Now, my reputation as an excellent worker is growing at the Palace, so it shouldn't be too suspicious if someone happens upon my room while I sneak away and explore. Perhaps I'm getting reckless, but I no longer care. Without the aid of the Armory, I'm the only chance Zandria has for escape.

But first, I must find her.

She's somewhere beneath Palinor. We thought the drainage tunnels were tricky to navigate; these halls are even worse. Palinor has more passages than Zandria and I have secrets.

I leave my tools strewn about the workshop. If someone does poke their head in, they'll think I wandered off to the lavatory midproject. I throw my satchel over my shoulder, then slip into the hallway, heading confidently in one direction until I'm out of sight of the nearby guards. Caden has been a little too interested in what I've been doing ever since he heard that explosion, and to my relief he is not at the post nearby. When Remy and I were on speaking terms, he once told me that Caden spends more time in the kitchens than at his post. Given the fact the kitchens are preparing for a masked ball this week, I'm banking on him being there for a while.

I hum softly, hands in my pockets moving imperceptibly. Then the air around me shifts and shimmers until my presence is concealed. When I turn the corner and walk by a servant, he looks right through me.

Perfect.

Adrenaline and magic mix in my veins. No one can stop me from finding my sister. Not the Technos, not the Magi Council, not Remy or my parents. Every second she's locked away is one too many.

I make my way to the southern wing of the Palace. It's always more heavily guarded, and I already ruled out the north and east wings. A flash of a memory of the queen torturing Vivienne strikes me, and I feel myself pale. I don't wish to revisit those wings either.

The higher concentration of researchers is promising. I stop when I recognize a face in a group of gray-clad men and women heading toward one of the guarded doors in the hall.

So this is where Aro goes while I fix his machines and test his minerals. I have a feeling I'm on the right path this time.

I shadow them, passing the guards, and tiptoe down the winding stairs. Five flights later, we reach a researcher hall. Sterile white-and-steel walls greet me, the same as any other place in the Palace. But something's different here. It *feels* different this deep. We're well below the drainage tunnels Zandria and I snuck into. I let the researchers continue without me while I close my eyes and absorb the strangeness. The place hums, trilling in my veins.

Somewhere, not far, lies powerful magic.

The library? A critical mass of so many Magi prisoners? How many spies have been caught and tortured, locked away like my sister?

Someday, I'll free them all.

I follow the feel of magic, letting it tug me through the halls. None of the rooms have windows. I can't get a glimpse into them without stopping and it pains me to think of leaving all that mystery unexplored.

But the magic beckons.

The passage winds deeper into the earth. I continue humming as quietly as possible, growing paranoid that my power will fail me this far down. The magic draws me to one of the doors. I listen before working a spell to unlock it. When it clicks, I slip inside. No one waits in the sterile space, luckily, but then neither does anything particularly interesting.

Metal objects rest on tables, but nothing that strikes me as unusual for a Technocrat lab. They look a lot like the clockwork hearts Leon had me make for the Heartless hospital.

So where's the magic that drew me here?

Power crawls up my spine, tingling similar to a finger tracing a path. I swear I'm being watched, yet I'm alone. I circle the room, hugging the walls and cabinets, but no one else is here.

The cabinets.

I throw one open, but only metal parts greet me. The next is locked, though it opens to my spell. A stash of havani vials rests in there. Also useless.

The third cabinet's contents freeze me to the spot.

Books.

Books with worn, red leather covers and Magi runes on the spines. They look ancient. That strange feeling runs over my skin again.

Have the Technocrats found our lost library? Is this all that's left?

The shelves are packed with stacks of the books and I gingerly pull one down. I'm almost afraid to touch it, but my fingers buzz when my hand grips the faded leather.

I lay it flat on a table and gently open the pages. I don't understand all the words, but it's clear this is a spell book. I can make out some of the steps but the results are foggy. This dialect is far older than what we use nowadays. I'll have to show it to my parents. The ancient Magi language was powerful—and much of that tongue was lost along with our library.

It takes me a few minutes, but I eventually decide that, from what I can make out, the first book is a book of love spells. The next book I pull down is thicker and has drawings as well. It doesn't take me long to determine this one contains spells for Magi warfare. Definitely a keeper. It appears to be part of a set that looks familiar. For a moment I assume that it—or one like it—must have passed through my parents' shop at some point, but then it hits me.

The book Zandria's Magi friend gave her looks exactly like this. I turn to the spine, out of curiosity—yes, this one even has the same initials at the very bottom: *AA*.

How did he get ahold of something that's been hidden here, several stories belowground in the Technocrat Palace, for who knows how long?

It could be that her friend was caught and locked up too, and this is a holding area for captured Magi possessions. That would explain why his townhouse was empty, though this room looks to me like it's used for research, which makes no sense.

Puzzled, I take another book down, but I can't figure out the point of the spells. They don't look like any castings I've seen before. The language is too difficult to decipher and the drawings too strange.

It almost looks like the spells are to be used on nonorganic matter, but that's impossible. Until Zandria and me, no Magi was ever able to affect things with no life in them.

I put the three books in my satchel, silently promising to return for the rest. One or two a day and I'll have them all home in a few weeks. It kills me to leave any of them, but I won't be able to hide more than the three when I leave the Palace this afternoon. Even that will be tricky.

Getting caught with these would be very bad for my health and longevity.

Footsteps echo in the hallway and my pulse skyrockets.

My fingers go numb, but I force them to move through the

spell to make the air shield me again. I scramble under the nearest table for good measure.

The steps grow closer, closer, closer . . . and continue past the door.

My lungs empty. I wait a moment before I creep out from under the table, legs shaking. I hold on to the edge to steady myself. And attempt to clear a horrid vision of my poor sister trapped inside a metal hood, no sound or sight to comfort her. No twin to soothe her.

Endless nothing, endless night.

I tremble, then stop short.

This table has different devices than some of the others. They're made of odd materials and shapes that have no meaning for me—with one exception.

A couple of the objects are made from the same material as that door we found. The Technocrats know about it, and they're testing it. What in the flames could they be using it for?

Isaiah made me swear never to enter the tunnels again unless the Magi sent me, but I know I will have to break that vow. The only question is when.

I CAUTIOUSLY MAKE MY WAY BACK TO THE
room where Aro left me, weaving the air
around me like an invisible cloak. I stop the
spell just before I turn the corner of the last hall, and
quickly slip into my room. I set my bag, filled with the
stolen books, on a chair in the corner and get back to work,
eager to make up for the hour of snooping. Since I finished the
testing so quickly this morning, Aro also has me repairing a few
older, larger machines. Patrol mechanimals once shaped like giant
cats, now dented and dull and twisted.

I must finish at least one before I leave or Aro will wonder
why my pace has slowed. The bent metal straightens under my
magic, the wires in the empty sockets reach for their appendages,
and the feline body begins to take shape again.

I hear something behind me. It is definitely not Aro's usual
soft steps and knock.

I stop singing, pretending I'm examining the steel body. But
really, I'm letting all my magic pool in the palms of my hands.

I've been training for this for years.

Then I whirl around. Before I can take a breath, a metal sword
swings at my head. I duck, knocking my attacker's legs out from
under him.

Caden. That fool guard.

"I knew there was something wrong about you," he growls.
"Magi filth."

Fear fills his eyes. He's been raised to see people like me as
terrifyingly dangerous. I take a deep breath, getting ready to strike
with my magic, but he barrels into me again. I leap out of the way,

but I don't have much space to maneuver with three mechanimals taking up so much room.

He must have seen the parts of the one I was repairing go back together. If he stops and thinks about it, he'll realize my true secret. I can't risk that leaking out.

I lunge, but he's faster with his sword than I am at getting out of the way, and it slices into my shoulder. I grimace, but before I can get my bearings he's pinned my wrists against the wall.

"What are you after? You just appeared out of nowhere in the hall earlier. What do you know?"

"That the only filth here is you." I kick him in the legs, which makes him release one wrist but ends with his sword pointed at my neck.

He's going to kill me if I don't do something. I don't have enough use of my hands to do what my training calls for. If he kills me, he may as well be killing Zandria too.

I whisper a word to send my magic into his blade, then I do the unexpected and punch him in the face. He grunts, and I yowl as he yanks my hair, then digs his fingers into the wound on my shoulder. But I don't let go of the magic threads manipulating his sword. If I can't get a grip on him, at least I can control this.

I focus my magic on the blade. It begins to turn toward Caden. At first, he struggles for control of his weapon. He almost succeeds, but then I grab hold of it with my hands to use my magic and muscle combined. He doesn't understand what's happening until the sword is pointed at his own chest. Then it slides under his rib cage.

He falls to the floor, a gurgle on his lips and a stricken expression on his face.

My hands open and close of their own accord as I lean against the corner of the wall and slide to the floor. Each flick of my fingers casts another drop of murky red blood to the floor.

So much blood. It wasn't supposed to be like this. It was supposed to be easy, just a cast of the spell and a closing of my fist and his heart would squeeze in on itself. They'd think he had a heart attack. No poison, no trace.

Not this.

I curl into a ball and clasp my hands over my knees so they stop moving. Blood still flows from his wound, the pool crawling toward me like an accusation.

He shouldn't have been able to overpower me. I shouldn't have allowed myself to be caught by surprise.

I shouldn't have had to kill him like that.

The sickening suck of his own blade entering his body and the gasp that followed sounds over and over in my head. I clamp my hands over my eyes, my entire body shaking.

I don't know how long I remain that way, but eventually Aro comes for me. When he knocks on the door I try to speak, to find a way to explain this, to bring up a spell to hide the mess that remains.

My voice doesn't work. I can't speak, I can't breathe, I'm choking and gasping like a fish thrown onto the bank of a river. But he lifts me up, cradles me to him, and carries me far away from the blood and the gore and the awful thing I've done.

I may not have liked Caden, but other people did. He has—had—a wife and baby daughter. I'd seen him with them in the park. I stole him from them. Just like they stole Zandria from me.

But Caden isn't the one who took her. There is no vengeance here.

The hall is blessedly empty, but the steel walls turn my reflection back to me. Wide, panicked eyes, blood on my face, my ears, and clothes, blending into my hair. I look monstrous.

I squeeze my eyes shut to drown it out.

I'm vaguely aware of the fact Aro opens a door and sets me

down on a chair. The room is white, but that is all the detail that registers.

Shock, I realize, this is what shock feels like. Numb, hollow. Like you aren't quite in control of your own body.

Aro disappears for a moment, then sets something down on the table in front of me. A small metal bowl filled with water. He gently takes my hand. His eyes lift to mine as he washes my bloody hands with a warm, wet cloth.

"What happened?" Aro asks.

I try to answer, but again nothing comes out.

"Did Caden attack you?"

Unspoken words clog my throat. I'm frozen in place, my mind unable to form the lies I need to tell.

He rinses the cloth in the bowl, then dabs at the blood on my cheek. "It's all right. You're safe now. I'll take care of the mess."

Warmth trills through me, nudging away some of the numbness. Aro's helping me. He isn't going to turn me in as a murderer. But why? I killed one of his own, someone he knew.

The truth is, I already know the answer, but it is a truth I wish I didn't have to face.

Aro pushes my hair back behind my ear and wipes a streak of blood at the top.

"Why?" I finally croak out. "Why are you helping me?" If he can forgive me for this, could he see past the fact of my Magi blood? A terrible glimmer of something resembling hope sparks in my chest.

He takes my hands again and submerges them in the bowl to soak the blood out. "I can't lose my favorite mechanic, now can I?" he says softly.

I laugh. I can't help it, even though it's the last thing I want to do. I clap a wet hand over my mouth, then immediately spit it away.

"Thank you," I say. This is what I've been waiting for. To know he is devoted to me. But I don't feel the glee I should. All I feel is lost.

"Do you know why he attacked you? Did he say anything?"

My mind races, then finally latches onto the best lie I can think of at this moment. The truth.

"He burst in. Something about the Magi?"

"The Magi?" Aro frowns. "What would make him think that?"

I shrug helplessly. "I can't understand it. I was just fixing the machines. Everyone knows Magi can only use magic on natural things, and there weren't even any in the room. He took me completely by surprise."

Aro sits back on his heels and I hold my breath, praying he believes me.

"I can't imagine where he'd get an idea like that, especially about you." Aro sets the bowl aside on the table and his face falls. "Maybe I shouldn't have been so secretive about your work. If he had any idea what you were really working on, he'd know you're one of the most dedicated Technocrats in the city."

My heart squeezes. "Aro, this isn't your fault. Not in any way."

He holds me in his gaze for a long moment, stripping away every defense I have left against him. I may have succeeded in capturing his heart, but my own is tangled in the same net. "I'm so sorry this happened to you, Aissa. But I'm glad you were able to defend yourself."

"What should we do about the room?" I ask. My chest constricts the thought of it.

"I'll handle it. I know who can be discreet about these sorts of things."

I blink at him, unable to help wondering how often he's had to handle this particular sort of thing. There's still so much about him I don't know.

I want to. I want to know everything. And not just in service to my mission.

"You asked why I'm helping you. I . . ." Aro sighs and dries my hands on a clean cloth. "I trust you. You've kept my projects secret, and you seem to feel as deeply about the Heartless as I do. I can see it in your eyes when I speak of them. That's why. You've helped me, and now I can do something in return. And—" Aro pauses to press his lips to my fingers. "I care about you quite a bit."

My breath has vanished from my lungs, and my skin alternately flares hot and cold. I can't look away, can't even blink, under the intensity of his gaze. What would it be like if we were not on opposite sides of this war?

He is kind, intelligent, and relentless in pursuit of his goals. And there's just something about the way his features work together. Not overly handsome, but when he talks passionately it's like he glows.

I don't want to love Aro. I *can't* love Aro.

Yet I do.

"Thank you." I squeeze his hands and lean forward to press my lips to his cheek. It is full of promises I cannot hope to keep.

He holds my hands for a few beats too long before standing to clean up the bowl and rags, but I don't object. This was my goal. Make him trust me, confide in me . . . fall for me.

I feel awful.

I HAVE YET TO QUASH THE TWITCHING IN MY

hands since I killed Caden yesterday. I've
trained my whole life to be a spy, to do what's
necessary; I always knew I'd have to kill someday.

I never dreamed killing the people I hate would
affect me like this.

My mother healed my shoulder and hands a little—but not
too much—so physically I hurt less. My parents assure me this
is normal for a first kill, but the Technos took my sister; they're
holding her captive. I should feel nothing for them.

Knowing that doesn't stop the image of Caden playing with
his small daughter on the green from haunting my waking hours.

It is Aro's fault. My feelings for him are getting in the way
of my mission and tainting how I view all Technocrats. It was so
much simpler when I could see everything in black and white, the
way the rest of the Magi do.

I approach the Palace this morning with more trepidation than
ever before. But no guards have come to take me away.

I walk down the steel halls toward my workroom filled with
trepidation. In mere minutes I'll return there, to the research room
where I killed a man. The bloody floor took over my nightmares
last night. When I turn the corner, I spy Aro talking with one of
the guards. He sees me and his eyes brighten. He meets me before
I reach the workroom door.

"I've arranged a new room for you today," he says, leading
me down another hall and another spiral of stairs into the lower
levels. Some of the tension in me releases. I don't have to go back
to that place and be reminded of what I've done.

He opens a door and leads me inside. The room looks nearly

identical to the one I worked in before, and the same stack of remaining mechanimal parts awaits me. Someone has even washed the blood spatter off them.

"You really do think of everything, don't you?" I say. Fighting my feelings for Aro is even more difficult in the face of his kindness.

Aro takes my hand, his fingers wrapping around mine. A quiver runs through my belly. "I told you I would. I brought you into the Palace. The least I can do is keep you safe."

"Will I be punished?" I know just how much Queen Cyrene loves to dole out punishments.

Aro shakes his head. "No. I took care of it."

"How?"

He looks away. "I told my superior it was me. That Caden attacked me out of nowhere and he died accidentally in the struggle. He's picked fights with others before, and I'm—I'm a more valuable employee to the crown than a simple guard. No one questioned my story."

His pale gaze burns into mine and the full weight of what Aro has done hits me. It is suddenly harder to breathe than it was a moment ago.

"I don't know how to repay you." Strange new emotions swell in my chest. Try as I might, I can't quite hide my astonishment at all this Technocrat boy has done for me.

Aro shakes his head. "You don't have to. But you could join me for lunch in the garden today?" His blue eyes glitter with a charming sort of hope.

I squeeze his hand. "Of course."

"Good," he says. "Good." He runs a hand through his hair, a small grin teasing his lips. "I'll see you then."

The morning passes in a blurred mix of guilt and confused emotions. Aro has done something to me. Changed me somehow. I should curse him for it. But without him, I'd probably be sitting in a cell next to my sister right now.

I wish we were not from two warring factions. That he was on my side, or I on his. That my love and my loyalty were not at odds with each other.

When Aro knocks on the workroom door, I set my things aside and he leads me up into the tower where the garden hides. He must have already stopped by the kitchens because he carries a couple of sandwiches for us. Once we're on the stairs he takes my hand.

I can't decide whether it's worse for me to encourage him as I have been or stop him. It may better serve my mission for him to fall completely in love, but I'm not sure it's best for me.

Like it or not, his hand steadies my tilted world for a few minutes. I don't let go.

He opens the door to the garden, and fresh air brightens my heart. All the green—real, natural green—surrounds us. I close my eyes and breathe in the scent of the flowers. Violets, roses, lilies, and several others I can't pinpoint. They almost remove the stench of blood that has followed me since yesterday.

Aro laughs. "Are you all right?"

I open my eyes and sit next to him on one of the benches. "Sorry. I don't think I realized how much I love this place until just now."

He takes a bite of his sandwich and nudges me with his shoulder. "Sometimes I think I'd go crazy here if I didn't have this to escape to once in a while."

"I believe it."

Aro sets his sandwich down and reaches into his pocket. He pulls out a gold envelope and hands it to me.

"What is this?"

"Open it."

I frown, and soon find a piece of parchment with silver script inside. It's an invitation to the masquerade ball the Technocrats have been preparing for all week.

It's also the perfect excuse to come here at night and search those areas I haven't been able to risk during the day.

"I hate these things, but it might not be so bad if you were there," he says.

I stare at the invitation, then smile. "I think I can make it. But if it's a masked ball, how will I find you?"

Aro grins and holds out a tiny purple flower—a violet. "A hint."

"That's it?"

"It's enough, I promise." He tucks the flower behind my ear, his fingers brushing over my skin. I can feel the tips of my ears reddening.

I pocket the invitation, and we finish our lunch. The hour is already half over.

Too soon, we leave the garden behind. The violet is still nestled behind my ear, and when we reach the stairs, he claims my hand again. The tingling glow between our palms keeps the garden close for a little while longer.

But our steps are too quick, and he opens the door to my workroom too soon.

"Thank you," I say for what feels like the thousandth time, but still not enough. "For everything."

He closes the door softly behind him. "You're welcome."

He turns my hand over in his, then gently presses his lips to my palm, sending my head spinning all over again. Then he's gone, and I'm left with the cold machines and my brightly burning heart.

The rest of my day passed in a blur. Our quiet lunch in the garden was a welcome relief, especially after the horror repeating in my brain. The lies Aro used to cover Caden's death have removed me entirely from the scenario. He was true to his word and cleaned up my mess with absolute discretion, but nothing he does can remove the stain it's left on me.

I'm at home in the training room, punching away my frustrations, when I hear the door knocker. My parents answer and I race upstairs at the sound of Remy's voice. If he's here, he must have news. My parents are as furious with him as I am, though I know they won't refuse him entry if he's here about our mission. That trumps everything else. And today I need something—anything—to take my mind off this choking guilt.

A tall man whose face is hidden by a cloak stands next to him. The door closes behind them and the man lowers his hood.

Darian Azul, spymaster, stands in our hallway. He tilts his head in greeting.

This visit must be serious indeed.

"Please, sit down." Mama gestures toward the kitchen table.

We settle, and Mama and Papa exchange a concerned look. We know Isaiah well, so while his visits are rare and unexpected, they're not wholly shocking. Having the Armory's spymaster drop by is another story entirely.

"I have word of your mission," Remy says to me, then turns to my parents. "And Darian Azul has a message for you." Their faces are pale and drawn, but not surprised.

They were expecting this. They probably already know what the message is.

"The Armory Council requires your presence in the Chambers immediately," Darian says to my parents. "I'm afraid they didn't give me any more than that, simply asked me to deliver the message personally to ensure the weight of the request is taken seriously." He pauses. "I trust that won't be a problem?"

"We'll have to make some arrangements, but we can leave at dawn the day after tomorrow," Mama says, taking Papa's hand in hers.

The thought of them leaving me, now of all times, is unbearable.

"But why? They gave you no hint?" I ask.

He shakes his head. "A good spy knows better than to ask." His rebuke, though kindly spoken, hits me like a slap across the face. "If I had more to give I would."

I sit up straighter in my chair. Despite his offer on the road to Palinor, I'll be damned before I fully trust him. I'm sure he knows more. Isaiah might have sent him to spy on me too if Remy really is refusing to report back, like he claims. I can't have Darian figure out that I plan to go after my sister on my own.

Before the silence lasts too long, Remy clears his throat and turns to me. "Have you made any progress?"

Until tonight, I've refused to speak to him since we returned from the Chambers. He looks nervous.

"I believe I've uncovered where they're hiding the child," I whisper in a low tone. Even in our kitchen, I feel uneasy saying the words aloud. "There's a part of the Palace that's too well-guarded, in a highly trafficked area that leads down into the depths of the building. I've seen the children, doctors, and the king and queen go through that door, but never the servants or outsiders. I haven't been able to get nearer to it even with the shield spell during the day. There are just too many people. But the Technocrats are preparing for a masquerade ball this week. And I may have scored an invitation. It's the perfect opportunity to check it out."

What I don't tell them is that at night I've been reading the spell books I found in the Palace lab, hungrily searching for new spells that might help me find and free Zandria. Which is exactly what I aim to do at the ball. I haven't even told my parents I have the books; instead they're hidden away between the cushions of my bed.

"Excellent," Papa says. He glances at Remy, mistrust in his eyes. "You got orders from your father this morning, didn't you?"

Remy looks uncomfortable. As though something is very wrong. He shifts in his seat, then folds his hands before speaking. "Yes. Darian brought word to me too."

"Well?" I say.

Remy stares at the dull metal table for a long moment. A hard knot begins to form in my gut.

"When you find the princess, you'll take her and hold her for ransom. Then you'll tell me, and the Armory will demand the Technocrats release all of the Magi prisoners in exchange for their child."

"I already know that. Do you really think they'll give in to those demands?" I clench my fists, nails digging into my palms. "What's changed?"

"One way or another, you must kill her. Either after they release the prisoners or when they refuse. Father says that's why he named you and Zandria our Twin Daggers—he always intended for you to kill the heir." Remy's voice cracks on the last word, but he looks me straight in the eyes. "The Technocrats' reign must end. But it's best if we can save our fellow Magi in the process."

My heart shoots into my throat, making it impossible to speak. If the ransom idea works, this would save my sister. But if it fails and we have to kill the heir before the prisoners are freed, we're sacrificing them all.

And I'll be sacrificing a child in the process.

My mouth runs dry and I can't seem to find the words to speak. Mama beats me to the punch. "You want Aissa to kill the heir? Most in the Armory aren't given their first kill until twenty at least." She takes my hand and squeezes. My parents were the first people I told as soon as I got home that awful day. We have not yet reported my real first kill, though Remy must have heard by now that one of his fellow guards has vanished.

Remy gives Mama the most miserable look I've ever seen. "My father insists. She's the only one who can get close without raising suspicion. Only a handful of people at the Palace know who she is. It has to be her."

The truth slips between his words. Isaiah has been watching me, setting me up to expose the secret of why my and my sister's magic is stronger than most. He wants me to do this because I'm more talented than Remy and more expendable than Darian. I don't like this any more than Mama, but I've long suspected it would be my true task. And I can't deny an order directly from the Armory without repercussions. I'm dying to know why the Armory demands this, but I know better than to ask. Darian's rebuke from moments ago still echoes between my ears.

"I'll do it." I grimace at my parents. "I've prepared myself for it."

Or so I'd once thought. If I can barely handle killing a guard who attacked me, can I really kill a child? Let alone one Aro might be close to? What if it goes wrong again? My stomach heaves, but I choke it down. If they give in to our demands, perhaps Isaiah can be persuaded to be lenient. I'll be praying to every god there is that they give us what we want.

Mama pulls me to her and kisses my forehead. "You've always been the brave one, Aissa." The words she doesn't say press down on my chest. *Braver than Zandria.* But if I'm so brave, why couldn't I save my sister that night?

"I'll expect the Armory to help me find Zandria in return for what they need me to do. Especially if I have to kill a little girl." I glare at Remy. He should've told me this the second he found out, especially if he's sincere about wanting to make amends.

"I can make no promises on behalf of the Armory, you know that," Remy says.

Darian speaks up. "I will put in a good word for you with the Council, but I won't make a promise I'm not certain I can keep either."

"Fair enough," I say, unfolding my arms and letting my shaking fingers fall into my lap. "Then I suppose I have no choice."

I take a deep breath to steady myself. The Technocrats' masquerade ball is tomorrow night. Now that I have an invitation, I can sneak in and investigate while they're otherwise occupied. I'll look for the girl too.

"I will do what is expected of me."

PALINOR'S PALACE IS ABLAZE WITH LIGHT

and activity tonight. Many flock to the ball,
costumed and pretending to be someone else.
No one pays attention to me, the girl in the black-
plumed, iridescent dress and mask. Mama bought us fine
dresses for special occasions when we turned sixteen, but
this is the first time I've worn mine. One just like it, but in green
instead of black, sits in Zandria's closet. It almost feels wrong to
wear it without my sister, but then again I'm doing this all for her.

I sneak down alleyways connecting my home to the central
square, then join the throng of people making their way toward
the Palace. We walk together in a flood of bodies to the main
entrance.

The best place for me to hide is in plain sight.

I've told my parents that I'm only going in the hope of finding
the Heartless child unguarded. Tonight the whole Palace will be
swarming with people creeping about the grounds and halls.

Despite what I may have promised, I have every intention of
looking for Zandria at any opportunity too.

The night air whispers against my cheeks and rustles the feath-
ers in my dress and mask. Its energy fuels me, making me feel
braver than I am. I wrap myself in the darkness, the ability to hide
in a mass of people without even using magic. A grin spreads over
my face.

Tonight, I'll find something. I feel it in my bones. I refuse to
go home empty-handed.

The crowd tugs me along, across the grounds of the Palace and
up the stone-and-steel steps. The guards give us a cursory glance.
Everyone who was invited was given a steel pin to wear on the

shoulder of their costume that consists of three concentric circles intersected by a diagonal line. The Technocrat emblem. Aro gave me mine, and I pass the guards' inspection easily.

The crowd jostles me onward, and we proceed down the polished metal hallways. The reflections off the mirrored walls make it appear as though thousands walk with us. An endless sea of people in costume and disguise. Who could possibly pick me out in this?

I note every hallway and guard posted near each. Some are already nodding off, others remain at attention. By the time we reach the doors of the ballroom, I have my escape route planned turn by turn.

The ballroom itself is a glittering, gleaming masterpiece. Long tables with stark white damask cloths line the walls, heaped with piles of food—buttery pastries, skewers of meat and vegetables, plates of noodles and potatoes, and bowls of punch. Just looking at them makes me hungry. I settle into a corner, far away enough not to be too tempted, and examine the crowd instead.

It's a parade of monstrous elegance and excess. Women flounce across the floor, some in dresses made from leather like mine and others in steel skirts and bodices adorned with jewels, gold, and silver. One woman nearby is dressed in a white gown with platinum filigree lining the hem of her skirts. Her partner is in all black, with similar platinum designs edging the bottom of his jacket that meet to form a sharp point at the back. Across the room, another woman is decked out in a ruby steel skirt that clangs like a bell with every step she takes. I almost feel underdressed with the few steel adornments on my own gown.

Music plays in the corner, automatons pumping out tinny yet beautiful sounds in a way that feels false and strange though I have heard their music many times. There is an undercurrent of wrongness to them that always pricks against my ears. I prefer the timbre of the human voice or the strings and woodwinds the Magi play. Natural sounds; that's what I love.

I swallow my discomfort and move around the huge room, on the lookout for anyone familiar. I worry Remy might have followed me. He isn't scheduled for duty, but he's still trying to prove he's on my side. We don't currently see eye to eye on what that means.

Thankfully, I have seen no sign of him. I do spy others I recognize. Darian Azul, with his strange, pale, almost clear gray eyes, winks at me as he parades by with a woman dressed in a blue-tinted steel frock, embellished with matching silk and silver lace. I nod my head in return, then quickly walk in the other direction.

I wonder if any of these attendees are Magi too. Perhaps one of the more infamous code names, like the Dart, the Mace, or the Spear will be spinning (or be spun) nearby once the festivities begin. I could walk right by them and never know. Maybe even the Hidden Knife is here, preparing for some daring scheme. The real, older one, not the young man who tried to convince Zandria just to make himself look good. Somehow, he must have figured out she was Magi and faked those letters in our code language to pique her interest. It worked.

Suddenly the crowd goes still and silent. King Damon and Queen Cyrene, dressed head to toe in gold garments embellished with sparkling white and black diamonds, enter the ballroom. Hand in hand, they march down the center of the room, and the crowd parts to let them through. They climb the steps to the platinum-coated thrones as though they own the place.

Which, of course, they do.

Once the king and queen reach the top of the stairs, they face the crowd. Their masks move as they smile. My head begins to buzz. I hate them with every ounce of magic in my blood.

"Welcome," King Damon says over the hushed crowd. He

smiles, and his metal-tipped teeth flash sharply. All eyes are trained on them. It would be the perfect opportunity for me to slip out. But before I can make my exit, a hand grabs my elbow and I freeze. The face gazing down at me is hidden by a dazzling violet-tinted steel mask, cut at angles to make it sparkle as it catches the candlelight. But it doesn't hide the pale blue half-moons of the boy's eyes.

"We are delighted you could all join us here this evening," the Technocrat king continues. "This is a special night. One where we celebrate our final triumph in the war with the magic makers in spite of their last curse. This is our night to celebrate our victory."

"Make merry," Queen Cyrene says, her eyes sparkling like ice in the sun as she surveys the crowd. "Eat and drink your fill!"

The crowd erupts in applause and parts yet again as the king and queen take the floor to begin the first dance of the evening. The boy at my elbow pulls me toward the dancers, and though I want to resist, something in his eyes makes me weak in the knees.

I know who this Technocrat boy is. And though I shouldn't waste much time on him tonight, I can't help myself. I'm lost to my own weaknesses. And that weakness is right here in the flesh.

He leads me into the mass of revelers. His eyes never leave my masked face and I'm drawn into them like bottomless pools.

The boy floats me across the floor, amid the little buglike machines that follow their masters. One in particular is all too familiar. The pressure of the boy's fingertips through my dress makes my skin tingle.

It's Aro. I'm certain of it. The violet colors were my clue. Sparky's presence confirms it.

And I'm certain Aro knows exactly who he dances with too.

The way his hands guide me over the polished steel floor. The way his eyes gaze into mine in a manner that's both affectionate and possessive. I haven't been able to forget the gentle touch of his hands since he cleaned Caden's blood off my fingers. I'd recognize him anywhere.

He pulls me close, but I don't fight. I don't want to. My breath can't catch up to the steps of the dance and my skin feels as though I've fallen into a metal forge.

All I want right now is to be closer to Aro. And for this dance to never end. I don't want to return to my grim reality.

For these few moments, I'll pretend that it's true. That it's possible for this Technocrat boy to feel any positive emotion for this Magi girl. That we are not mortal enemies trapped in a centuries-old feud.

That he wouldn't slit my throat if he knew what I could do.

The music twines around us, moving us across the room. I swear my heart whispers his name with every beat, and his pulse under my fingertips perfectly matches my own. In some ways we're so very much alike.

The dagger strapped to my thigh beneath my skirts digs into my skin. A sharp reminder to be cautious, but it's much too late for that.

Those pale eyes. The kindness there. The determination. Aro is as driven as I am and knows what he wants—we just happen to be at cross purposes.

He brushes a wayward strand of hair from my cheek, his thumb lingering longer than it should. My breath catches in my throat as he pulls my face closer. Our feet no longer move and the crowd is far behind us. The cool night air of the patio curls around our bodies as our lips finally meet. Tentatively at first, then fiercely searching for something tangible to hold on to, some connection between us, stronger than the fragile threads that have connected our hearts thus far.

The spark between us bursts into lightning, and everything but the kiss disappears.

But like all things with us, this too can't last.

We break apart breathless, his hands now planted at my waist. I push up his mask. Aro grins in a way I haven't seen before. Like we're sharing a secret no one else knows. All the tension and drive that usually fill him have dropped away, leaving only the teenage boy behind.

Something inside me cracks. My whole purpose is to undermine everything Aro holds dear. And I'll do it too, without so much as a backward glance.

My hands shake and I let his mask slip back down.

He pulls mine off next. I can't stand to see my face reflected in his eyes. I kiss him instead. That way I can pretend he isn't the boy whose life I must destroy. He's someone else.

But, oh, those kisses. Aro is wild inside, and the pull is magnetic.

My light cloak falls from my shoulders and I shiver, though his hands are hot against my skin.

The echo of voices around the corner is the only thing that can separate us.

We hurry behind the mech-rosebushes, huddling together in the dark while other partygoers wander by. He wraps his arms around me and I lean into his shoulder.

For one last moment I close my eyes and pretend we're just two people desperate to be as close as possible to the other.

"Aissa," he whispers. "You know I'm yours. Don't you?"

My eyes sting. I do, but I also know I'm a player in a dangerous game.

"I—" My throat closes unexpectedly. How have I gone so far astray? "I must go."

I rise before he can speak, walking away from the bushes and the startled look on his face as quickly as I can without attracting attention. I keep my head high, but inside I dissolve into tiny pieces.

He is not for me. And if I stay any longer, I will forget my mission entirely.

By the time I round the bushes, I'm already humming the shield spell. I can't have Aro follow and further distract me. I wind my way through the crowd, doing my best to dodge and weave so as to not touch a soul. I stop for no one now.

What a fool I've been, playing at love with Aro. I brought myself into this mess and I don't see it ending well. Love is not some tender thing; it is cruel and sharp and cuts far deeper than I ever dreamed.

I finally navigate through the ballroom and back into the corridor. Only a handful of guards remain, and they've clearly sampled a bit too much of the punch, judging by how they sway at their posts. With my shield up, I easily breeze by them. Now to find that heavily guarded corridor again.

I slip down the hall, taking turns left and right from memory. The door should be somewhere just beyond here. In minutes I enter the hallway, but I'm disappointed to find several guards convened in front of the door. My earlier confidence flails in my chest. I can't open it without attracting attention. I may need to try another door tonight, but I know I will eventually find out what hides behind it. It must be important to be so well guarded, especially tonight of all nights.

I wait patiently in the hall for a time, hoping the guards will move on. If it was only one or two, I might be able to distract them. But five? Not a chance. Instead, I turn my attention to finding the dungeon and my sister.

Part of me wonders if the guarded door could be the one that leads to the dungeon, but my instincts tell me otherwise and I trust them over anything else.

I head for the lower levels, where I've been helping Aro work on finding a new power source. Only one guard stands at this door and I slip by him with a simple distraction.

I use more caution than usual tonight and remove my shoes, then tiptoe down the stairs two at a time. I'm intrigued by the other rooms and halls I have yet to explore, but I'll investigate these other places later. I'm convinced they keep their prisoners somewhere deep below. Even Remy hasn't been able to find where our people are held for certain yet.

For now, I must know more about the deep recesses of the Palace. The walls start as steel and whitewashed panel, but once I reach the level just below the deepest I've gone with Aro, they change. Much metal remains, but more stonework is mixed in. The air is danker here too.

Something about entering this new lower level gives me the creeps. I step onto the landing and whisper the spell to unlock the first door. But when I peek into the room, I'm disappointed. Cold storage. In fact this whole level is cold storage. I return to the stairs and try the next level down.

At first glance, it appears to be more of the same. But something doesn't feel right. My gut insists there's something hidden. I study the doors and walls. What nags at me so much?

There are six doors, four on one side and two on the other. Initially, I assumed that meant the rooms on the left are bigger and so need fewer entrances, but when I open them I see that's not the case at all. They're the same size and shape as the four on the right side.

Which means there are two rooms' worth of space unaccounted for and apparently inaccessible by this hallway. Curious.

I enter the second of the two doors on the left and give the walls on all four sides a thorough examination. Nothing untoward presents itself. I frown, then try the first door on the left and repeat the same process. Still nothing out of the ordinary.

I'm missing something.

I return to the second room, then run my hands over the wall that should connect to whatever is between the spaces. I poke, I prod, and I pick at every possible seam.

Nothing.

I summon my magic and, holding my hands to the wall, hum and focus on finding any hidden doors. The wall shakes and a tiny notch near the base of the floor recedes inward. A seam appears, then another across the top, then the bottom and other side. It swings open, revealing a landing and staircase leading down at a steep angle. I grin, preparing myself with the shield spell. If Zandria were here she could work the sound-dampening spell too; I'll have to go on bare feet instead.

I creep down the stairs, then pause halfway down. Something in the air is wrong. It's too quiet. I hold my breath, listening for any sounds. Breathing. I hear someone—or several someones—breathing in the room below the stairs. Almost like they're waiting for me.

Ice spreads over my back, slow and deadly. I brush off my fears. They're foolish; why would anyone be waiting for me? No one knows I'm on my way down here.

Unless . . . unless Remy or my parents told someone I was planning to explore the Palace. But they would only tell another Magi, not a Technocrat. My imagination is running away with me. Aro has me all discombobulated.

But I check my shield spell, just in case.

When I reach the last step I take a silent, deep breath and scan the room. There are at least twenty elite guards. Each of them watching a door or stairwell like mine. There appear to be several possible means of entry to this hidden room.

So many guards, even with the masquerade dancing above our heads? It doesn't make sense. I note every entrance and exit, mentally extrapolating where those doors and stairs might lead. All the while, I do my best to keep my heart from galloping out of my chest. My shield holds and I sneak back up the stairs, praying I make it to the top and into the other room without making a sound. The last thing I need to do is draw more suspicion.

However crazy it may seem, someone must have told them. The question is: who?

When I reach the upper levels I pause before the door to recast my shield spell. If the guards not at the ball are all downstairs, there probably won't be anyone in the halls, but after what I just saw I'm not taking any chances.

I crack open the door and peer into the hallway, then slip out once I determine it's empty. I may have run out of luck while trying to find the dungeon tonight, but I can still return to look for the heir. A hint of nausea creeps through my gut, but I know what I have to do. Cautiously, I make my way through the halls until I reach the point where I've seen the Technocrat children go with their nannies.

There are no guards at the door now. I realize I did see some children at the ball, but they were clearly healthy. The king and queen wouldn't allow their sickly daughter to parade in front of the masses anyway. I keep the shield spell up, then step into the hall.

I halt when the door opens and out steps Aro, still dressed in his costume. I swallow my gasp and remain perfectly still.

He looks both ways, then takes off down the hallway opposite me. For once his pet machine isn't with him.

What could he have been doing behind that door?

Perhaps it doesn't hold the key to the Heartless princess, but to what the Technocrats are doing so secretly in the tunnels beneath their Palace. As a researcher, Aro is very much involved in that. Or maybe I was wrong about the dungeon's location.

The ache that never leaves me slices through my chest. Zandria's here somewhere. Out of reach. She's depending on me.

I creep across the empty hallway and with a quick, whispered spell open the door that swallows the children every day.

It's another hallway, long and brightly lit. This disconcerts me. I'd hoped for more cloaking shadows. Even though I know my shield will hold, I find the darkness reassuring.

Because I know the only thing that hides in the darkness here is me.

I sneak across the steel floor. The walls are white and sterile, but no doors appear until I reach a crossway. A hall stretches in both directions, but a door lies immediately on the left and that's what I choose.

I can't quite escape the feeling that I'm a mouse in a trap about to close. Finding those waiting guards earlier has made me paranoid. I need to get out of this exposed area, and fast. Panic wriggles in my chest. I can't be taken unawares again, like I was with Caden.

With an ear to the door, I close my eyes to listen. No sound whatsoever.

The doorknob doesn't budge. Locked.

"*Apere,*" I whisper, and hear the satisfying click as my magic takes hold and turns the tumblers. I open the door with shaking hands and peer inside.

It's empty. The room is lined floor to ceiling with steel. That and a small bed are all that's inside.

I leave it behind and return to the hall. The next two doors reveal rooms identical to the one I just left.

But what can these spaces be used for? There are no toys or anything indicating children. Each is sterile, clinical, almost . . . like a cell.

Is this how they treat their courtiers' children? Maybe what I've seen in the afternoon is the children being trotted off for forced naptime. I shudder.

I'm about to leave the fourth strange steel room when angry voices blast down the hall and the original door I entered slams.

Someone's coming.

And they're not happy.

"What do you think you're doing?" hisses a woman. The voice is familiar, but I can't place it right away. "Taking off like that? Without your watcher?"

"I'm sorry, I—" Aro's voice freezes the very blood in my veins.

"Don't even try to explain. There is no excuse! Do you have a death wish?"

"No, I swear, I— Ow!"

I slide the door open a crack, whispering my shield spell again for good measure.

The Technocrat Queen drags Aro down the hallway by his elbow. She has a frighteningly strong grip on his arm due to the metal reinforcements in her sleeves and fingers. He winces as she drags him right by my hiding spot. I flatten my body against the wall—if there were ever a time to test the strength of my magic, this is it.

Why would it matter to the queen if Aro wanders the Palace? He does it every day. I ought to make my escape now, but my curiosity won't allow it. I know the queen has a listening room; perhaps she really was the one listening in through Aro's mechpet, Sparky.

I start to tiptoe after them, but when she pauses her tirade to frown at the hall behind her, my pulse stutters so loud, I'm certain she'll hear it. They say the king and queen have been augmented with certain technical enhancements. I can see none aside from the metal grafts on her arms and hands from where I stand, but that doesn't mean they don't exist.

The frown mars her lovely heart-shaped face for only a fleeting moment.

"What is it, Mother?" Aro says.

Shock seeps into me like oil creeping through my veins.

Mother?

I place my hand on the wall to steady myself.

"Nothing. I thought I heard footsteps, but it was the echo. Now come. You are not to leave your room. You do not appreciate the repercussions of what might happen should the wrong people discover who you are tonight." Her grip on his arm is so tight it leaves the skin red.

I'm still frozen when the last door in the hall slides open and lets them inside. All I can hear is the banging of my heart against my ribs.

Aro's mother is the queen.

That means Aro is a prince.

The king and queen only have one child—one they refuse to own publicly because it was born deformed. It was born Heartless.

Aro is Heartless.

Oh Forges, Aro is *Heartless*.

He's the one I've been searching for. The one I've been ordered to kill.

I stumble into the nearest open room just before my legs give out. I slide down the wall to the floor. The faint voices of Aro and Queen Cyrene arguing still reach me, but my world has reversed on its axis.

Our intel was bad.

The royals don't have a daughter. Did they spread that misinformation? Do they know about the Armory's spy network? If so, how much do they know about our operations?

Do they know about me? If they do, then they know about Zandria—and that means whatever torture they're putting her through will be one hundred times worse than normal.

I try to stand, but my legs and arms quake so badly I can't get a grip on the walls. Before I regain my footing, the door to Aro's room slams shut. I listen as Queen Cyrene locks it behind her and strides down the hallway. I curl into a ball, making myself as small as possible and praying she doesn't decide to look in this room.

A flutter of skirts breezes by the door and I catch my breath. No hand reaches down to drag me up. Only the click-clack of the queen's footsteps and the opening and closing of a door echo back to me.

I breathe out a sob.

Oh, Aro.

This is what I've been raised to do. It's what Zandria and I have worked toward our whole lives. Refusing to do my duty would make it all for nothing. Make her capture and torture for nothing. I'd be letting down the scattered remnants of my people.

But it's Aro.

My chest aches and I double over. I've always known nothing could ever come of the feelings I've kept hidden in my heart, a tiny firefly hovering in the darkness. I've always known the plan was to destroy his king and queen and the stranglehold of power his people have.

I never once thought I'd have to kill him myself.

I'm such a fool. Harboring feelings for Aro is the worst sort of betrayal. I let myself fall in love with the Technocrat heir. And tonight at the ball—I wished so badly to pretend, just for a little while, that we weren't Technocrat and Magi, divided by an impassable gulf.

It was pretend. A mask, like the ones we wore. Now the harsh reality settles in.

I must kill the boy I love.

The ghost of his hands roves over me, a whisper of his words caresses my lips, leaving me quivering while crouched by the wall.

How can I kill him?

Finally, I struggle to my feet, wipe my eyes, and stumble for the door.

Do I betray my people or my heart?

AFTER ALL I'VE SEEN TONIGHT, I DON'T LIN-
ger in the Technocrat Palace for fear of other
traps or running into Aro again. I don't know
what to say to him now that I know his secret.
Instead, I work my way home as quickly as I can. My
dark thoughts trail behind me.

It is the wee hours of the morning when I finally enter my
own home, but the light is on in the kitchen and Mama sits at the
table over a cup of tea. Her face seems to have aged lately, the fine
lines more prominent than I ever remember them being before.
The loss of my sister takes a toll on her too.

Mama nods her head at me as I sit next to her. "How did it
go?" she asks.

I frown. "I'm not sure." My hands twist in my lap. I can't
admit to my feelings for Aro, to kissing him, but the rest of my
adventures give me pause. "I was able to explore some of the
deeper levels of the Palace, but I didn't find what I expected."

I immediately should tell Mama that Aro is the heir, but something holds me back. My head still whirls, wondering if somehow
I might be mistaken.

Mama pats my hand. "At least you ruled some of it out. The
Palace is huge. It's all progress." She examines her tea. "Did you
see any sign of the dungeon or your sister?"

My face flashes hot. "I have been instructed to wait."

Mama sighs. "I know my daughters. Neither of you could
ever leave the other behind for long. So, tell me, did you find
anything?"

I wonder if she stays up late like this every night since Zandria
went missing. The dark circles under her eyes imply she does.

I drop my hands into my lap. "I didn't find her. But there was something strange. I may have found an entrance to the dungeon, but I'm not sure."

"What was so strange about it?"

"All but a handful of the guards should have been in the ball-room with the guests. But when I reached the lowest level yet, the room was filled with guards armed to the teeth. They were completely silent. It was . . . It was almost like they were waiting for something." Waiting for me. I shudder.

Mama frowns. "That is very strange. Have you spoken to Remy about this?"

I shake my head. "But earlier today he confirmed the guards were supposed to be stationed at the ball."

"So Remy knew you'd be trying the lower levels." Mama narrows her eyes. "Who else knew? Did you tell anyone else?"

"No, of course not. Only you and Papa and Remy." I remember our visitor from the night before. "And Darian Azul, the spymaster."

Mama leans back in her chair, a faraway look in her eyes. Someone knocks on our front door and I nearly leap out of my chair. Mama puts a firm hand on my arm.

"Aissa, go into the training room. Now."

"But we get visits sometimes from—"

"Now, Aissa. After what you just told me, I'm not taking any chances. I fear we've been compromised."

"Compromised? What do you mean? By who?"

"We don't know how many Magi prisoners they have, or what they might know. Or how much torture they might be able to stand." She points to the living room. "Now go."

Heat rushes through my veins, but I do as I'm told. Mama is thinking of my sister. She's the only one in the dungeon who'd be able to give us up. My chest feels tight and itchy.

As soon as the training room door closes behind me, ghostly fingers force me into a nearby chair and I cannot help but obey. Mama casts a spell on me even as she answers the door. She must know more than she's telling me.

I hear voices, but not enough to make out what they say. I may not be able to use my hands right now, but I can still hum.

"*Ampleo*," I mutter, but I can't hear everything like I should. One of my parents must be casting a silencing spell.

"Why are you here?"

If whoever it is responds, it is too low for me to hear.

"What is going on? Get your hands off me!" My father's voice rings in my ears. I hear his feet being dragged across our floor. There must be several men up there.

I gasp. The Technocrats have found us out.

I have dreaded this day my whole life.

"I don't care about the oaths we swore or how you figured it out—you cannot have her. I won't let you," Papa says.

My mind whirls. An oath? What did my parents swear to the Technocrats? Every muscle screams against Mama's spell, begging for me to help my parents. But her magic holds me still.

I hear the bass thrum of a man's voice but not the words. It is quickly followed by the marching beat of boots systematically moving throughout our house. Several minutes pass, the seconds punctuated by the sounds of men searching our home and turning everything— tables, chairs, you name it—upside down in the process.

The search finally stops, and I hear the hum of the stranger's voice again but still no words.

"Some things are more important than oaths," Mama says in response.

Then she shrieks. A sound I've never heard from her lips, but the pain in it is unmistakable. Something thuds on the floor, then another thud follows shortly.

Tears stream over my face and I struggle against Mama's spell. Please, please let my parents be all right. I've already lost Zandria. It is too much to even consider.

Maybe they got the drop on our visitors instead. Maybe—

I hear the sound of boots on wood, then a door closing. A long, excruciating moment passes before the spell holding me tight to the chair suddenly releases.

I leap to my feet. With numb fingers, I scramble to unlatch the lock on the secret door. I hardly remember throwing it open, running into the living room, and sliding through the hall.

Two bodies lie by the door. Twin pools of blood creep toward me, jarringly reminding me of Caden's death.

I can't breathe. I can't even wail. Shock seizes my chest, forcing all air from my lungs. This is a hundred times worse.

I fall to my knees between Mama and Papa, their images blurring.

"No," I whisper over and over. I grab their hands. Both are unconscious, eyes closed, a scant rise and fall of their chests. Their pulses get thinner with every second.

In the same rhythm. Their hearts slow and then stop at the very same time. Not an instant between them.

I freeze.

My parents' wounds are the same—not similar. *Exactly* the same.

Mama has a cut across her cheek, the fingers of her left hand are broken, and a knife sticks out of her chest.

Papa has the very same cut and broken fingers. And the same wound, but no weapon to make it.

There is only one explanation for how two Magi could die in the same way at the same time from a single wound.

My parents loved each other too much to live without each other. They must have performed the forbidden Binding ritual some time long ago.

And now they're both gone because of it.

For the second time that night, my world teeters on its axis.

I've just lost my entire family.

I double over, the grief slicing me in two. This can't be happening. I need them. My temple throbs, blurring my vision. I close my burning eyes, wishing with all my might that when I open them everything will go back to normal.

But nothing does. My parents' bodies are sickeningly still. Minutes ago, I was chatting with Mama like we usually do. She was full of spark and courage. Her tea is probably even still warm.

Now they've been snuffed out. I never got to say goodbye. Not to them, not to Zandria.

A sob cracks my chest, and for a few moments the macabre sight before me disappears again.

I wipe my eyes with my sleeve and take several deep breaths. With a start, I realize they each drew a rune next them in their own blood. Mama wrote *letter* and Papa wrote *floor*. To a Technocrat, they'd be meaningless, but not so for me.

My chest aches. One last instruction.

From my place on the floor, I let my simmering magic flow into my hands and weave a spell that tosses up the floorboards in the room like kindling. Power courses through me, fueled by rage and grief. I see no hidden letter, and repeat the process in the kitchen, then the den.

There, under the floor in front of the fireplace that hides the training room door, is a box. I grab the box, then throw the floorboards back together in a rush.

The lock is useless against me. Inside the box is a folded letter, written in Mama's neat hand. Tears slop against the backs of my hands as I read, slack-jawed.

If you are reading this, we have been discovered and have not survived.

There is so much we had planned to explain when you were older and had completed a few more missions. When you were ready to hear what we have to tell you. We only hope that you are ready now.

We have told you before that your powers must remain secret from all people, the Magi as much as the Technocrats. But we knew more about your magic than we could admit to you. At least until you had proven yourselves.

During the last few generations the Magi Empire ruled these lands, our kings began to hoard power, and kept some of the most powerful spells out of the hands of the general populace. They took the best and brightest Magi and trained them in the Great Academy you have heard of. Only the most promising were allowed to learn the strongest, most complex spells.

Unknown to the crown, a secret coalition of Magi and Technocrats formed the Alchemist Alliance and began to run experiments with an eye to regain the power legends claimed the people of these lands once had over everything—organic matter and inorganic matter. Dedicated members in this alliance volunteered for these experiments, hoping to bear children who had been altered by magic. But Magi relations with Technocrats began to fray. Attacks on intermarried couples increased, and the Alliance grew more and more desperate as the Technocrats in the north became an increasing threat.

You see, the Technocrats were not a separate people from us. They were us. Magi born powerless who long ago left our cities and built their own settlements in the north. According to the history that's been passed down to us, these powerless Magi appeared around the same time the other Magi lost the ability to affect more than the natural, living world. We don't know why this schism happened, but it was the Alchemist Alliance's mission to reverse it. To give us all—Magi and Technocrats alike—our powers back.

But it occurred over generations, and eventually the Magi came to believe their magic was pure because of this defect, and the Technocrats buried all memories of prior times except their hatred and resentment of us.

That resentment festered in the north, as you know, and spurred them to create the machines that were our undoing.

The Alliance was more convinced than before that restoring our powers was the only way to prevent a war and so redoubled their efforts. But they were betrayed, and all but a handful were executed. Your family on both sides traces back to the few remaining members of this hidden sect, and the knowledge of the Alliance's experiments and our altered bloodline has been passed down to each generation.

In order to maintain our bloodline, certain spells must be cast and materials injected during pregnancy. It's necessary for the parents to be bonded to ensure the spells work and the mother lives through it, as the connection doubles the mother's strength. We had to perform the Binding rite. We both saw the wisdom of the Alliance's plan, though not in quite the way they did.

The Technocrats are too far gone, too twisted by evil and machines, for them to be worthy of magic. They must be destroyed. You, our own twin daggers, are the first to be born a success. Our families have been working toward your creation for almost two hundred years, and now the mutation cycle is complete.

This is the real reason the other Magi would punish you for your magic—it marks you as part of the Alliance, however unwitting. Your very existence poses a threat to a belief the rest of the Magi hold dear: that we have never had a connection to the machines. That we're the pure, rightful leaders of this country. Most Magi don't even know about the Alchemist Alliance, but those on the Council do. And they will see anything that challenges these beliefs as treason. They can't control the machines and they wouldn't be able to control you. They would undoubtedly execute you.

Aissa and Zandria, you alone have the power to destroy the

Technocrats. You will be stronger than any Magi we have ever seen. You will do great things. We are so proud.

But be careful. Isaiah is suspicious. You must not let him, or any other Magi, discover what you can do.

You will have to train and rely on each other, and when the time is right you will strike the Technocrats at their heart. To do that, you must find our lost library. All the Alchemist Alliance's work is contained there within a hidden chamber, and the spells and the knowledge will keep you safe and give you everything you need.

Our spirits are ever with you,

Mama and Papa

The full weight of my parents' confession bears down on me. My twin and I are not some happy accident. Our parents, our entire family line, did this to us.

We're the fruition of an experiment two hundred years in the making.

I SPEND THE REST OF THE NIGHT WEEPING IN
the hidden training room, unable to wrap
my mind around what I've learned. Though grief
tears through every muscle, I bring my parents' bodies into the basement to say a final goodbye.

They've given me back my first mission: find the lost
library. I need answers, I need to know how I'm supposed to do
what I was created for.

But I can't do it alone.

I surround my parents with bricks on the earthen floor, then
sit just outside the circle. I thought I was all done with tears, but
more pour down my cheeks. The empty ache in my gut that's been
there since Zandria was taken expands and threatens to swallow
me whole. It feels bottomless.

I will make their murderer pay.

"*Fiero*," I say, and a flame appears in my hand. I place it on my
father's chest and his shirt catches fire. In my free hand I weave
a spell to dissipate the smoke as soon as it appears. Then I close
his eyes and kiss his forehead, dousing it with tears. I repeat the
action with my mother, then I pull my knees up to my chest to
watch them burn.

Hours later, I cover my parents' ashes with dirt from the floor and
finally get to my feet. My body is sore, but it is nothing compared
to the pain and panic ever tightening in my chest. Someone murdered them. Somehow the Technocrats found us out. This was not
your average raid. This was different.

This was personal.

I'm willing to bet the king and queen don't know about it yet. They would never pass up an opportunity for a spectacle or to make an example. No, this was someone else.

I'm going to find out who. And I know just who will help me.

Though I hate Leon's mechanic shop, I must keep up appearances. Aro and Leon worked out an agreement that I'd work three days at the Palace and three more in the shop each week. Today, I return to Leon's with fear quietly nestled under my heart, and my escape bag under my arm. I must be ready in case I need to run. Before I snuck out the back of my home this morning, I packed it full of provisions, the spell books I stole, some daggers, and that strange piece of key-shaped marble I found in the townhouse. I must behave normally for now, but my magic is primed and ready to use as defense at a moment's notice.

If I want to find out who killed my parents, I have to remain among them, pretending nothing is wrong in order to draw the killer out. If it all goes sideways, I'll use the spell to change my appearance and find another way inside.

It'll mean giving up Aro and whatever foolhardy thing has blossomed between us, but it's something I never should have started. With all that's happened, my mind keeps dancing around the fact he's the heir. No wonder he's so secretive.

I'm going to have to betray him. Capture him. Kill him.

Bells on the door jingle as I enter Leon's shop. I hear his customary greeting grunt from the back. He never even gets up from his table now, and only gives me a brief look when I take my seat at my worktable. A broken mechpet waits for me, and I start working in silence.

I need to find a way to get to the Palace today. Any errand will do.

I finish fixing the small mechanimal quickly and bring it out to wait for its owner at the front desk. When I return I close the door behind me louder than usual. Leon looks up.

"All done with that one. Do you have any errands for me?" I ask.

"You're getting faster. That's good. Just be sure the quality of work doesn't suffer."

"It hasn't."

He nods and turns back to his work, a mess of parts I can't puzzle out. "Go to the miners' shop. We need more havani." He looks up again. "Be careful with it."

"I will."

I head out before he can change his mind. Being trapped alone with my thoughts in the mechanic shop with Leon Salter is unbearable. I need to talk to someone who can understand. There's only one who is capable right now, though I still guard my trust.

At first, I go in the direction of the miners' shop, but once I'm out of Leon's range of vision, I circle back and head for the Palace.

Remy sees me when I arrive on the Palace grounds, but no one else bats an eye at me because I'm here so often. I give Remy a meaningful glance and duck into the gardens.

A few minutes later, he follows, glancing behind as we weave among the mechtrees. I find a spot deep between two large trees and move my hands discreetly in a sound-dampening spell just in case anyone passes by our hiding spot.

"You shouldn't be here today," Remy says. "This is your day to work at the shop, isn't it?"

"Yes, but it was urgent that we speak." I scratch at my arm for the hundredth time today before realizing it is already raw.

"So you're speaking to me again?"

I swallow, my retort dying in my throat. I have no one left to talk to but Remy.

Concern creases his brow. "Is it Zandria?"

My face turns hot and I bite back the tears welling in my eyes. I must not cry. I must complete the mission and rescue Zandria. Mama and Papa would want that.

"What's going on, Aissa?"

I can't look at Remy. If I do, I'll fall apart. I must be strong and steel-hearted like they taught me. Feelings have only ever gotten me into trouble.

"When I got home from the masquerade last night, Mama was awake. We were debriefing when we were interrupted by someone at the door. She insisted I hide in the training room." I pick at the hem of my cloak. Mama made it for me years ago. "Whoever it was had Technocrat guards with him. They . . . they killed my parents."

Remy gasps. "What? Both your parents? How is that possible?"

A tear escapes one of my eyes. "He only had to kill my mother. I had no idea until last night, but my parents performed the Binding ritual when they married. Killing my mother killed my father too. The very same wounds, even the same pulse flagging under my fingertips. I—"

Remy cuts me off by putting his arms around me and pulling me close. I can't hold it in any longer, and the tears break loose on his shoulder.

"Do you know who it was? The man at your door?"

"No," I say between sobs. "My parents cast a dampening spell, so my amplify didn't do anything but cancel it out."

A somber silence passes between us like a chill on the evening air.

I pull back and clutch one of Remy's arms. "We have to get Zandria out. They were talking about a girl. I think they meant me or Zandria. We need to get out of Palinor."

"Have you determined where they keep the prisoners?" Remy asks.

I shake my head, as frustrated as he is. "No, not yet. But I have narrowed it down to somewhere below the fourth level under the Palace." I twist my fingers nervously. "At the masquerade, I snuck down, but I didn't get as far as I'd like," I say. "I think we've been compromised."

Something bright and tense burns in Remy's eyes. "What happened?"

"I tried one of the lower levels, but when I got to the bottom of the stairs, a whole slew of guards was waiting around the corner. It was like they knew."

Remy strokes his chin. "Do you think that's where they hold the prisoners?"

"Why else would it be so well guarded during the ball? Everyone else was either upstairs or half into their cups, or both. Something's down there that they don't want anyone to find," I say.

"Or they just don't want anyone to get out." Remy frowns.

"I believe we can reach the dungeon through another route, but it might be even more dangerous."

"How so?"

"We'd have to go through the drainage tunnels." I wrap my arms around my middle. "The place where they caught Zandria." And almost caught me.

"You aren't keen on doing that, are you?" Remy says.

"I'll do what needs to be done."

Remy places his hand over mine. "I know you will, Aissa. You always do."

My face warms, but I shove those feelings down into a deep, hidden place. One day I might allow myself the freedom of emotions, but for now I must retract them all to guard those I love who are left.

"When will you be ready to put our plan in motion?" Remy asks.

"The day after tomorrow. I need to make a few more preparations," I say. "I'll be at the servants' entrance at dusk. And I'll be in disguise."

"I'll be ready and waiting," Remy responds.

"Thank you," I say, "I knew I could depend on you."

"I swore to you that you could, and I meant it."

I bite my lip. "What about Darian Azul? Do you think he might help if we tell him about . . . about my parents?" I swallow the hard lump in my throat.

Surely the Magi Council member and spymaster would want to know that two of his spies embedded in Palinor have been murdered. He might have an idea who did it. Maybe he'd even help me get revenge.

Or he might tell me to wait and be patient like the Council did when Zandria was taken.

Still, he could have some answers.

Remy considers. "Possibly. He does know where every spy in the Armory is stationed and the details of their missions. But I doubt he'll share much information with us."

"How do I find him?"

He shakes his head. "You don't find Darian Azul. He finds you."

Disappointment fills me. It's just me and Remy then. We'll have to do this on our own.

Remy clears his throat. "Now what of your mission from the

Armory? Have you found out where they hide the Heartless heir? My father will be furious when he hears you've freed Zandria from Palinor's dungeon and devastated about your parents, but positive news about the heir might dull the sting a bit."

I can't lie to Remy about this, no matter how much I wish to, not when I know the truth. It's my mission; these are my people. I cannot allow my feelings for Aro to betray everything else I hold dear.

"I've made progress," I say vaguely, hoping he will let it slide. To my chagrin, he doesn't. "And? What have you found out?"

"Everyone's wrong about the heir," I say. My throat closes to a pinhole.

"What are you talking about?" Remy says.

I can barely breathe as I whisper the words. "It's not a child. It's Aro."

Remy's features darken, yet I detect a hint of pleasure mixed with the shock.

He has never liked Aro and now I've handed over an excuse to kill him.

"The researcher you've been working for? How do you know?" Remy asks hoarsely. We were so close to the Heartless heir so many times with no idea. Standing next to him, chatting with him, pretending to be nice and civil to him.

And me, flustered by his attentions, foolishly trying to use him to lead me to the child.

He was right there all along.

"I was searching one of the hallways in the upper levels where the courtiers' children go. I thought that might be a good place for them to hide their child." I pause, frowning. "The queen burst in with Aro, dragging him back from the ball. I peered through a crack in the door and saw them go by. He called her Mother. There can be no mistaking it."

"We see him around the Palace all the time." He runs his hands through his hair. "They really are hiding him in plain sight."

"Exactly. So you see, we have a problem. I don't see the kidnapping plan working out so well anymore," I say.

Remy groans. "That will be considerably more difficult. A mere child would've been easy to capture and keep hidden. Aro is another challenge entirely. He's more likely to be on his guard, especially if he knows why his parents keep him a secret."

I nod, not yet willing to admit to Remy how close I've gotten to Aro. He trusts me. Capturing him would be easy.

"I'll have to tell my father about this." Remy gives me the most miserable look. "He won't be happy."

"What I want to know is, why we didn't know about this sooner? How did we get such bad intelligence? Do you know who gave the Council that information?" I ask.

"I wish I did," Remy says, "but my father didn't share that with me."

"Whoever it was, they were fed that bad intelligence by the Technocrats. The king and queen may know more than we suspect. I think we should wait to hear from your father before proceeding any further with the mission."

Anything to delay this terrible charge and focus on Zandria.

Remy stares at me for a few moments, then nods. He doesn't look me in the eyes when he says, "I'll wait for his response, but I already know what he'll want you to do."

I hold my breath, terrified of what Remy is about to say.

"He'll want you to kill him."

My entire body turns to ice, and Remy places a hand on my arm. "Look, if it's any consolation, Father shared something with me that you've been wanting to know."

My eyes snap up to his. "He told you the endgame?"

Remy nods. "He did. And he made me swear not to tell you.

But I'm done keeping secrets from you, especially if we might have been fed bad intel."

"Why? Why does Isaiah want us to kidnap and murder the Heartless heir so badly?"

Remy swallows hard and paces between the mechtrees. "One of our spies has successfully infiltrated the upper echelons of the Technocracy. They are very close to the king and queen. So close, they have named this person their successor in the event their heir does not survive. Our source says they still hope for a cure to be found in time. But if the heir dies, our spy is next in line for the throne."

Something electric courses through my blood. It all makes sense now, and I can't deny the plan is the perfect revenge. But the price is Aro's life.

Remy stops his pacing. "Can you imagine it? A Magi sitting on the Technocrat throne? Decreeing laws, pardoning prisoners as they see fit. Full control over the operations of the regime. Of the army. Our freedom would be ensured. This plan has been in motion for a decade, and it's coming to fruition now. My father insists the timing is right, and that means they need the heir out of the way. I'm sorry, Aissa. If you refuse to kill Aro, my father will send someone else. He is far too committed to this path to turn back now."

A sick feeling wells up inside me. "Remy, this Magi who's close to the Technocrat royals—could they be the source of the heir intelligence?"

Remy frowns. "Yes, I think that's very likely. They're in a position to know."

"And yet they gave us incorrect information."

An uncomfortable silence settles between us.

Remy clears his throat and speaks first. "There could be many reasons for that, I'm sure."

"I can think of only two, and neither means anything good for us and our mission."

He tilts his head, waiting for me to continue.

"Either this Magi spy isn't as trusted by the Technocrats as they believe, or they lied."

The question is: why?

THE NEXT DAY I RETURN TO THE PALACE TO

toil away in my workroom on the new power
sources Aro left out for me. I've been here all day,
and he still has not shown up, not even for lunch.

My nerves are on edge. No guards have come knocking at my door to arrest me this morning, nor did anyone
else appear at my empty house last night. Sleeping on the training
room floor was nowhere near as comfortable as my bed, though
it is safer. Now I'm taking a huge risk returning to the Palace, but
this is for my mission and my sister.

That's the real reason I'm here. Why I'm doing everything I
can to pretend nothing has changed for me. My insides are broken
shards, held together only by my resolve, and that's fraying at the
edges.

Remy received a message from his father this morning. Isaiah
was surprised to learn that the heir is male and older than we
thought. If we can't capture Aro, my instructions are to simply kill
him, just as Remy predicted.

Kill Aro because he stands in the way of making our move
on the Technocrats. If they find a cure for his condition before he
dies from the repeated surgeries to replace his mechanical heart,
it could ruin years of work and planning and sacrifice. Including
my own family's.

I'll do it, find my sister, and leave this awful city forever. I
don't see how I can fulfill my parents' dying wish to find the
library now, and the weight of that failure is slowly crushing me.

I didn't ask to be given the gift and curse of my magic. I just
want it all to be over.

I'll do anything to make that happen.

The last time I saw Aro, he told me he loved me. That is a thing I can use, however much it pains me.

Every sound from the hallway makes my pulse spike. The afternoon is turning into evening now; it's unusual for Aro to wait this long to check on my progress. Maybe he regrets what he said at the ball.

But then I hear steps followed by a familiar thump of a little mechanimal. They stop outside my door. My heart takes a seat in my throat.

Aro steps inside. His expression is strange—hopeful and fearful at the same time. I smile at him, and he relaxes.

"How is it going today?"

I look at the pile of minerals before me. "Not well. None of these produced much. Maybe we'll have better luck tomorrow."

He looks disappointed but only for a moment. "Aissa," he says, stepping closer. "I'm sorry I—"

"I know what you're going to say. Don't apologize. I'm not sorry." I close the distance between us and slip my hand in his. His pale eyes light up like steel in firelight.

"You're not? I thought—you left so suddenly."

"I . . . was surprised. But I'm definitely not sorry."

"Not even a little?" One side of his lips quirks up.

"If anything, I wish you told me sooner. I feel the same. I'm sorry I left so abruptly." I squeeze his hand. "You should try being more open. Especially with me."

He looks down. "My family is very strict. Openness . . . isn't something I'm used to."

I bite down the retort that comes to mind. The king and queen are well-known for their secrecy.

"What about honesty?"

"Honesty? Of course. I may not always be as honest with my parents as they'd like, but I've always been honest with you."

"No, you haven't been entirely honest with me," I say. Hello pot, meet kettle, I know.

He frowns, but when I place my palm on his chest, right over where his heart should be, understanding washes over his face. Sad, brutal understanding.

The hard weight of the steel ticks beneath my fingers. When we've embraced before, he's never held me close enough to feel it. Now I understand why.

"How did you figure it out?" he asks, taking my hand off his chest and pressing it to his lips instead.

"Why did I have to figure it out? Why didn't you tell me?" It's strange, but I can't help feeling a little betrayed by this fact. Even though I'm the one charged with killing him.

"Come with me." He cracks the door and glances down the hall, then tugs me into the nearest room after him. It's a storage room, filled with odd parts of old machines saved for scrap metal. I can't help feeling as though eyes watch us here, but he seems to think it's safe enough.

I position myself near the door and my dagger presses into my thigh, a constant reminder of what I must do. Eventually.

"It's safer to talk here," he says, regret etched into the lines of his face. "They never bother to bug the storage rooms." I realize his mechanimal is still outside in the hall. He must have realized the queen—his mother—was listening to him.

"Well, what do you have to say?" I fold my arms over my chest, but he takes my hand. My fingers warm instantly, but I remain unmoved.

"I'm sorry." He kisses my palm and I wrench my hand back. I can't handle his caresses right now. Not like that. I've let things go much farther than they ever should have.

He sighs. And proceeds to remove his shirt.

"What on earth are you doing?" I snap. He doesn't answer. He doesn't have to.

His skin is fair and lean-muscled, just as I pictured in my stolen daydreams. Except for the area where his heart should be; instead there's a round patch of skin that looks like a purple bruise. Thin, dark tendrils weave over his chest where the battery's poison seeps into his veins. But nothing creeps up his neck or down his arms, and his skin isn't graying yet. I remember what the nurse at the Heartless hospital said about symptoms appearing at the six-month mark. His next replacement operation is probably four or five months away.

After a couple more transplants, he'll die anyway. The thought steals my breath. My resolve frays a little more. Must I really kill him? Surely the Technocrats can't be that close to a cure, can they? If what I've been working on here is any indication, they're nowhere near finding an alternate power source.

"Give me your hand," he whispers. I don't fight him when he takes it and places it over his false heart. We stand inches apart, only the sound of our breath breaking the silence. Aro's eyes burn toward mine. This time I meet them.

"Have you seen how they treat the other Heartless?"

I shake my head. He doesn't need to know I saw him at the hospital visiting the other Heartless children.

"Like pariahs. Like they might be contagious." His face twists. "I don't want to be treated differently. I just want to live."

Anger at everything—my stolen sister, my murdered parents, and now this dying boy—floods me. "But how could you kiss me, tell me you're mine, when you're just going to die?"

He places his hands on my shoulders. "Would you have even gotten to know me if I had told you sooner?"

He's right, of course, but I can't squash this anger. I'm furious with Aro and his secrets, with the Armory for charging me with ferreting them out and now with killing him. And with myself for not having the resolve to do it when this would be the perfect time. He's vulnerable and he has no idea I'm Magi. I could stop the ticking inside his chest. He'd die in seconds and it would be chalked up to a malfunction.

I'm the worst sort of assassin. I'm a liar, I'm deadly. And I'm afraid.

"I don't know," I whisper.

It's too much. I'm surrounded by death, and I've fallen for a boy who may as well be dead. Love has violently upended my life, defying all reason, sense, and loyalty. It is the most powerful force I've ever encountered, and for the first time in my life I don't feel confident I can defeat it.

My head spins, leaving me weightless and dizzy. I've never felt more alone in my life.

"I'm sorry, I know it's . . . inconvenient." He backs away and begins to pull his shirt back on.

"Wait."

He stops and stares at me. I trace the lines of poison with my index finger. If I didn't know what they meant, I'd think the way they curl is oddly pretty. "Does it hurt?" The steady ticking thrums under my fingertips.

"Sometimes."

"I'm sorry this happened to you." I mean it too. More than he knows.

"Now do you understand why I hide it? Aside from my parents and Leon, the only one who knows is the Head Scientist. His wife was Heartless. She died less than a year after they married. He understands." He grasps my hands tightly and I squeeze back. "That's why we're trying to find a better power source. Something that will last longer and won't poison us. I know my life will be short, but if I can do that, be a part of that, it means something."

"I do understand." I'm doing the very same thing—working toward a world that will be safe for people like me. Unfortunately, that means keeping the world as dangerous as possible for people like Aro.

I've made such a mess of things. I don't think I'll ever untangle these threads.

"You won't tell anyone about this?"

"I'll keep your secret," I lie. Nausea creeps up my sides. I thought I was used to lying, but this feels so much different. So much *worse*.

He exhales in relief and rests his forehead on mine. "I knew I could trust you."

The knife in my heart twists further, but I still have to play the game.

"Of course you can."

Aro again pulls one of my hands to his chest and presses it to the dark circle. His voice is a hoarse whisper, his breath tickling my face and sending shivers over my entire body.

"I don't know how much time I have left. Two surgeries, maybe three. I don't expect to live more than three more years at most, probably less." He shudders and I shudder with him. The thought of his life being snuffed out troubles me in a way I should be immune to. I'm failing at that as well.

"Don't talk like that. You'll find your power source and you'll be fine." If I don't stop him first.

"The odds of the power source panning out before my time comes is slim." He wraps his arms around me and I don't want him to let go. His embrace chases the dizziness away. He tilts my head up so I'm gazing into his eyes. "It's all right." He seems oddly peaceful. "I'll hang on as long as possible. But this is no great shock for me."

I want to speak, but the words lodge in my throat. He's gone through his whole life, knowing it will end when it's only in full bloom. I cannot fathom it.

"I'm sorry," I whisper.

He kisses my nose in response, making my entire body hum. I need to leave. Soon. Or I'll be lost completely.

"Don't be. Every second the clock in my heart ticks off is one I wish to spend with you."

A blush washes over me from my head to the tips of my toes. I don't want to leave. I don't want to be the one to kill him. I don't want him to die. I've seen enough of death these past few days. I'd do anything for a tiny taste of light.

"It's late. I should be getting home. My parents will worry." Another lie. Another stab in my heart.

"Stay a little longer?"

"Here? In a closet?"

He laughs, then kisses me whisper soft on the lips. "No. But we did miss our usual lunch. The least I can do is make sure you're fed dinner before you leave."

"You're serious?" The idea fills me with excitement and dread.

He nods, hope lighting his eyes.

Perhaps, just for a little while longer, I can forget I have to murder this boy. Just one more night. Then my heart will go back to being invincible. If it can.

I grin, and Aro tugs me out of the room and down the hall. His watcher, left outside the storage room, trails after us. He takes me along the same path we've traveled many times to the kitchens. The cook smiles knowingly at our entwined hands when she gives us our food. It isn't long before we reach our secret place, the garden hidden in the maze of Palace rooms. When Aro opens the door, I gasp. I've seen this room many times now, but never before at night.

A new array of flowers blooms, and many of the ones I know well are tightly closed up now that the sun has gone down. I've loved the chaos of colors that's usually here during the day, but now every flower seems to be dripping in white and silver and gold. The moon and stars shine down, bathing everything in soft light. It smells different too—sweeter than usual. I might actually love this more than the daytime.

Aro puts his hands on my waist and I lean into him. He guides me to a corner of the room next to a tree with huge silver blossoms like bells that sway as we near. Usually we sit on one of the benches in the middle, by the gurgling fountain, but this time we curl up together with our sandwiches on one of the cushions placed in each corner of the room.

"This is incredible," I say breathlessly.

"I thought you'd like it. It's so peaceful here at night, even more than during the day." He runs a hand through his hair and gives me that lopsided grin. "I have to admit, I've wanted to share this with you for a while."

I catch his hand in mine. "I'm glad you did. Do you often stay late at the Palace?"

"Oh yes, they have an entire wing of extra rooms for sleeping set aside for research staff to use when they want to work late. The king and queen believe that letting them stay onsite is more efficient."

I play along; he doesn't need to know just how many of his secrets I've uncovered yet. "And I imagine they are nicer than the ones you have at home?"

He laughs, then presses his lips to mine, setting my soul on fire. Lush flora surrounds us, but I only have eyes for Aro. Stupid or not, this is what I want. This is the light I need.

When he kisses me again, I curl into him and feel the weight of my dagger. I quickly unsheathe it and shove it under the cushions. I can't have Aro seeing my weapon. The runes along the handle alone would give me away.

Then I lose myself in the sweet kiss, letting the night sounds and our soft, whispering voices soothe the pain and grief simmering in my veins.

Sunlight trickles in through the greenhouse windows, waking me and setting my skin on fire.

What have I done?

Panic tears over me, but I keep myself together as I untangle myself from Aro's arms. For one moment, I stop to stare at Aro, still sleeping on the cushions in his rumpled uniform. The morning sun toys with his hair and makes it look like it's made of gold. He is so still and pale that one might mistake him for a corpse, a sharp reminder of my unfulfilled mission.

That is what I should have been doing last night instead of cuddling up to my enemy.

But the memory turns my insides fizzy. I know better.

And yet I don't regret falling asleep next to Aro like I should.

I find my satchel, then hunt for my dagger. The empty strap is still pinned to my leg, but the dagger remains stubbornly missing. I can't lose it for so many reasons. I thought it was under the cushions, but it's not on my side anymore. It must have slid away. Or perhaps I just wasn't paying very good attention to where I put it.

I turn my back to the sleeping boy. I hum softly, weaving my hands in front of me, all my focus on the dagger and calling the runes to me. A soft shuffling comes from behind the silver-blooming tree.

This can never happen again. Next time I have the opportunity to be alone with him like this, I must kill him. Tears brim in my eyes, but I remain focused on my spell. Moments later, the dagger jolts loose and flies into my hand.

A soft gasp comes from behind me and I whirl, every fiber of my body turning to ice.

"What . . ."

I brandish the dagger. "Don't say a word."

I've ruined everything. How could I be so careless as to toss aside my weapon? It was a foolish mistake. One I know better than to make.

I can't come back to work at the Palace. From the look of betrayal and shock in his eyes, I can tell Aro knows. He's the prince. Of course he'll tell his parents. That's what I would do if I were in his position.

I have to kill him now.

The memory of Caden's sword piercing his flesh shoves to the forefront of my mind. I freeze.

"You're Magi," he whispers.

"Shut up," I say. "You know nothing."

He doesn't even move from the cushion. I could do it. Right now. I could slit his throat. Or use my magic to stop his clockwork heart.

I could do it.

But I don't. Instead, I run.

WHEN REMY MEETS ME AT THE SERVANTS'
entrance of the Palace, he startles. I warned
him I'd be in disguise, but I don't think he
expected a different face.

"It's me, Remy." At least my voice is still my own.

"Aissa?" I nod, and he hurries me inside. "How . . .
That spell you and Zandria found. Incredible." His amazement
is short-lived. "I searched half the city for you last night. Where
did you go?"

I pull my cloak closer and prepare to hum the shield spell as
we near the main halls. He grabs my arm and pulls me into an
empty room, spinning me around to face him.

"Look, I've trusted you without hesitation all along. I need
to know I can rely on you now, especially when I'm about to put
my life in danger and potentially jeopardize our entire mission."

"You're one to talk about trust." I shake his arm loose. "Fine."
I say, biting my lip. "I was in the Palace all night."

"You what?" Remy echoes.

My face heats with embarrassment, but fortunately my cloak
hides it well enough when I turn away. "I was trying to relocate
that passage we found into the Palace from the tunnels."

"You were there alone?" Remy says with disbelief. "Why
didn't you take me with you? Aissa, you've got to stop taking
foolish risks. I know you're upset that my father wanted me to
report on you, but you have to believe I didn't tell him anything
of importance then or now."

Better to have him admonish me for some imagined slight
and untaken risks than the real reason. My stomach tingles when
I think of Aro.

I remind myself of what Aro would do if he saw me again and I shove those feelings away. His words in the early morning light haunt me.

Magi . . .

Aro may not be quite like the other Technocrats, but he has more reason than most to hate the Magi. Especially if it really was a Magi curse that caused the Heartless to be born that way.

I've been hiding all day, unable to return to Leon's workshop for fear Aro will hunt me down, even with a new face. A faint hope flickers in the back of my mind that he will dismiss it as morning grogginess.

"I won't do it again. I just needed some time alone."

His expression softens and we head back into the halls. "I know; just be careful. Please. I'm worried after what happened to your parents."

My eyes sting. What would my parents say if they knew I'd spent last night with a Technocrat? I just needed to feel something— anything—that wasn't all this grief and pain.

But nothing can hold that at bay for long.

We skirt a group of guards and their mechanimals but they barely notice us. By the time we're clear of them, I'm humming the cloaking spell to cover myself. Remy can wander the Palace because the other guards know him, but I can't now, not even wearing a new skin. I will be his shadow tonight, and if we get into trouble, I'll cloak him too.

We reach one of the few doors I haven't tried yet. The guard nods at Remy when he opens it and strides inside, careful not to hold it open too long to let me pass through unnoticed. We don't meet a soul down here tonight; it's deathly quiet. The Magi library we hunted for is hidden in the depths below, secret and unreachable.

It was hard knowing that before, but after reading my parents' letter, being so close and unable to reach it is almost physically painful. I need to get there again and soon. There's a reason I packed certain items from my home before I left. Just in case.

Remy squeezes my arm, the same disquiet reflected in his eyes. This place, the entire Palace, is troubling. "Yesterday, I saw them take some prisoners down here," he whispers. "That's why I was looking for you last night. I wanted to tell you."

The hallway winds downward without the usual stairs, in a way that is dizzying. We listen for voices to ensure we don't run into any guards. I may be able to hide myself, but I still have mass.

Everything about this place makes me uneasy tonight. I clutch my dagger close to my body, ready to strike with magic or murder. I fight off visions of Caden's blood and Aro's kindness, telling myself I will do what is needed.

We reach a landing with more stairs leading down and a hallway adjacent to it. The heat of Remy's body close behind me is comforting as we tiptoe down the hall as fast as possible. At the far end is another set of stairs, with no other doors in sight. The steel here doesn't gleam like it does upstairs; this must not be a well-traveled area.

We tread carefully, and our luck holds. We make it to the next hallway—this one with many intriguing doors—without incident.

"Do you have any inkling which one we want?" Remy whispers.

I shake my head. "No, but I want to know what they're doing behind all of them. They don't look like cells."

We each take a side of the hall and listen at the doors before opening and investigating each room. The first few are storage areas; nothing of particular interest there. Just piles of bolts and screws in one, and panels upon panels of steel in another.

"I don't think this level will hold much interest for us," Remy says, and I can't help but agree. "How many levels does this place have?" he asks.

"I don't know. I haven't explored them all." We head back down the hall and take the stairs to the next level. As we reach that floor, one of the doors slams open and two men in long robes hurry down the stairs. We hold our breath behind our shield until they pass.

We hurry toward the door they just left, catching it before it closes all the way. I peek inside.

It's empty now. Remy and I exchange a look, then duck into the room.

It appears to be a lab, similar to the one where I worked on the potential power sources. Machine bits are strewn over the tables, and diagrams and charts line the walls. Some of them look like the Magi's runic symbols. I'm reminded of that other room I found almost a week ago with Magi books and trinkets.

What are the Technocrats trying to do down here?

We examine the parts, but they don't give up any answers, much to our dismay. They could be pieces of the hearts as easily as they could be for Sparky, Aro's pet machine.

Remy eyes the runes with a frown. "I don't like the looks of that at all."

"Neither do I."

We go through each of the next two floors in the same manner, sneaking, listening, peeking. Most of the labs are empty, yet in complete disarray, as though the people working there were summoned away suddenly. Either that or their clean-up etiquette is far slacker than mine.

The question of who summoned them and why eats away at me as we move from room to room and floor to floor. It's not until the fifth floor down that we again see signs of life.

Even as we start down the stairs, we hear people abuzz about something. We recast our spells, then proceed with caution. Thirty or more men and women in gray researcher uniforms swarm the hallway, milling around and babbling. Snippets reach our ears from our hiding place on the stairs. The hall is too full to risk going farther. It would be too easy for any one of them to bump into us.

"Do you think they really did it?" one says.

"It's going to work this time, I'm sure of it," says the woman next to him.

"I hope they don't blow up the lab," remarks another girl, who rolls her eyes.

"Can you imagine the implications?"

The thrill in the air is palpable, thick enough I could almost reach out and grab ahold of it. Remy's brow furrows into the bridge of his nose.

"I don't like how happy they are," he whispers.

"It makes me suspicious," I say.

A few minutes more of waiting, then the crowd thins as they file through a door in the middle of the hallway.

When they're out of sight, we hide in the room next door. We can listen through the wall to find out what has them all so excited. If it were Zandria and me, we could make a tiny hole in the steel wall and peek through as well. But I can't risk it with Remy standing next to me. Not being able to use the full extent of my power is frustrating. But as I look at Remy now, with his hands moving in the spell for amplification, my resentment fades a little. He misses Zandria too. Regardless of what he may have done in the past, he's the only one willing to help now.

Remy's spell takes hold and the noises are amplified for us to hear. For now, the only sounds are a lot of muttering like we heard in the hall. I pace the floor of the dark room. "*Fiero*," I whisper, and light flares in my palm. When I hold up my hand, I gasp.

Against the back wall are three glass-and-steel cases. Wires and tubes stretch from them through the wall of the other room, but they give no sign of activity.

Something about them chills me straight to the marrow. My

hand shakes, the light in front of me quivering. I take a deep breath and draw closer to the cases.

"What's that?" Remy asks.

"I don't know," I say. "But I don't think it's anything good."

Remy stands beside me, his own light revealing more about them. The glass cases are an outer shell that hold steel cases inside. Tension worms over my back.

I *really* don't like the look of these.

We can't see much else other than the steel and shadow inside them, even when we hold our lights right up to the glass. But the three of them stand there, solemn, silent, and creepy.

"I can't make heads nor tails of them. Can you?" I ask.

He shakes his head, then returns to the wall and his amplification spell. "Not a clue. Though I suspect we're about to find out."

The Technocrats in the next room grow quiet. Every nerve in my body feels as though it's strung as tight as a wire.

We both put our ears to the wall, desperate to hear as much as possible.

A man with a deep voice speaks to the gathered workers. "We called you here for a demonstration. We have been working on locating a new sustainable power source for some time. Now we have finally made some progress."

Though we can't see the man, the smile in his voice is clear as day. Shock works its way over my body.

Remy stiffens. "It can't be," he whispers, disbelief written on his face.

I recognize that voice too. It's Darian Azul, Magi spymaster.

"We have devised a means of infusing power into certain minerals receptive to it." Something clinks from the room and I imagine Darian picking an object off a table and holding it up for the room to see. "This sliver of rock can now power a machine heart, but only after the infusion process. Watch and learn."

A whirring sound echoes from the next room, resonating into ours and making the floor tremble. We steady ourselves against the wall.

The glass cases light up. The air is sucked from my lungs. One glance at Remy, and I can tell he feels the same.

Wires run through steel-reinforced holes in the glass and connect to the steel cases nested inside. The wires and tubes hum with energy as though a switch has been flipped in the other room. I'm sure it has. Because now we can see into the shadowed steel.

There is a square glass section we couldn't see before, just about eye level.

And inside each is a face.

I can't look away from the nearest one. Its mouth is drawn into an O, screaming with no hint of sound, pain etched in the creases around the wide, unseeing eyes. It's Paul, the baker's son.

I stagger back. Understanding races through every inch of my body, jolting me with horror.

They're using the captured Magi as a power source.

Somehow the Technocrats devised a way of siphoning off the magic and drawing it into pieces of minerals.

And I *helped* them.

And so did Darian Azul.

Remy places a hand on my shoulder, his face as drawn and horrified as my own must be.

"We have to save them."

"We have to *leave* them, Aissa. You know it's too risky. We don't have the resources to save them all tonight."

I gape. "That's unconscionable. We can't."

Grief steals over his face. "We *must*. There's no way we can escape unnoticed with them all. Not while the Technocrats are actively pulling magic from them. They're in the middle of a demonstration. Besides, we don't know what Darian is up to. We have to trust him. He's the spymaster and he must have to do things in order to stay in the royals' good graces. There may be a bigger picture here that we can't see. We can't blow his cover now."

I whimper. I don't want Remy to be right. He can't be right. And then I realize he isn't.

"It's him, Remy, it has to be. That well-placed spy who's been named the successor? Remember, that guard called him Lord Azul when he snuck us back into Palinor." Horror fills every bit of my lungs and I have to fight not to scream. "I can't fathom what he's playing at, but he's been feeding the Armory misinformation. We can't trust him."

Remy lowers his voice. "I don't know. Maybe you're right. Do you want to rescue your sister or not? We can only save one and still hope to get out of here alive."

His words hit me like a stone. However much I hate him for it, he's right this time. We must find Zandria. That's all that matters in this excursion. I'm not leaving without her.

But still . . . I can't abandon them here like this. I imagine Zandria's face caught behind the steel and glass, mouth set in a permanent scream. I can't bear it.

"We'll find Zandria," I say, rising to my feet. "But we'll give them a chance to get out."

Remy shakes his head. "You're signing our own death warrant if you do."

I stare him down, the sounds of the demonstration still ongoing. Someone asks a question—how it all works, where the power comes from—and I recognize the new voice too.

Aro.

My heart leaps in a mix of desire and despair. There he is in the next room, discussing how to sap the life out of a Magi.

I brace myself on a nearby table. Remy can't know how much Aro has affected me. I take another step, then pause as I hear the answer to Aro's question, clinging to the faint chance he doesn't really know what's going on.

"We're utilizing geothermal energy from the earth deep beneath the Palace. We draw it up, then harness it in these minerals," Darian says. *He's lying.* He's lying to the entire room. Aro doesn't know what they're really doing. He might still be as innocent in all this horror as I'd like to believe.

Though I'm not as convinced as Remy that Darian is too.

"But where are these geothermal vents?" Aro asks, and I can hear the frown penetrating his voice. "We have no reports of them or of anyone guarding them, to the best of my knowledge."

"They're kept hidden. And for good reason," Darian says, with a hint of irritation. "We don't want anyone poking around and ruining the entire operation."

Oh, Darian is very good. He has the whole room convinced he is telling the truth. Even Aro doesn't pipe up again.

But why lie? They all hate the Magi—wouldn't they be happy to see them tortured in such a manner?

I wonder . . . Perhaps more Technocrats are like Aro than I realized.

The demonstration appears to be over, as the light from the cases dims to nothing. But before it's gone, I can see that the Magi are now unconscious and listless in their cases. The only one I recognize is Paul. Darian continues to answer questions about the technical applications of the new power source. He claims that they're still perfecting it but expect to have a fully functioning prototype energy core within a few months.

They're closer to a solution for the Heartless than I realized. That's why I've been ordered to take out the heir now. Aro has to die before the prototype is complete for the plan to succeed.

Nausea lurks in my gut as I think about Zandria and how this could easily be her. In fact, the demonstration would go far better if it was. With our special breed of magic, who knows what we could do.

How can Darian let this happen to his own kind?

I scramble over the wires and examine the connection they have to the glass chambers. I tug them, but they refuse to give. If I can unlock these three Magi, they might have a fighting chance at escape, even if we can't lead them out ourselves. I hate to admit it, but Remy isn't wrong. They're dead weight now, and trying to carry them out in this state would be too risky. We need to get out of here before anyone comes into this room; hopefully when they wake, they'll be able to make their own getaway.

I glance at Remy; he's listening to the other room and not looking my way. I position myself so I'm out of sight behind the cases, and then begin a handspell. The wires dance at my command and relinquish their hold, slipping neatly onto the floor. A few more motions coax the locks on the back to unwind and release. Remy notices the hissing sound the cases make when they slip ajar.

"What are you doing?" he asks, wide-eyed.

"Giving them a chance." I march forward and grab his arm. "We should go before they begin to leave."

I'm rattled by what we've uncovered. Desperation to get out of this hallway and move on to another level that might hide my sister consumes me.

When we flee into the hall, we run into Aro leaving the other room. But I'm still cloaked. Remy nods at Aro and stations himself outside the door as though he was sent here to guard it. I silently pray Aro turns away soon so we can run down the stairs.

Instead he paces the hall, agitated, until another man steps out of the room to cries of "Head Scientist! Head Scientist!" from those still hoping to ask more questions. He tilts his head down to speak to Aro and I see his face clear as day.

All doubt vanishes. It really is Darian.

He suddenly stops talking to Aro and notices Remy. The smile that crosses his face is terrible. He makes a quick gesture with his hands, half hidden by his sleeves, and I can feel his magic crackling over me.

My magic halts, and without it, my shield fails. Pain ricochets over me as the bones in my face rearrange themselves into their original shape. I double over.

That traitor cast a reveal spell on me.

Remy gasps. Aro's face turns several shades and contrary expressions in a matter of seconds. Joy to red embarrassment, then confusion, and finally an ashen shade of understanding.

In that moment, Aro knows exactly what I am. If he had any remaining doubts, they're gone.

We have no reason to be here, to be leaving that room, except for being spies. And the only people with a reason to spy on the Technocrats are the Magi.

The shock and disappointment on his face gut me worse than any dagger. Remy drags me down the hall, but we run into guards coming up the stairwell. We flee up but there are more.

The hall swarms with Technocrats, some of them familiar, others not.

Every avenue of escape is blocked. There's too many for us to take down with our magic. We're trapped.

I've failed my sister for the second time.

THE GUARDS DRAG US DIRECTLY TO THE DUN-
geon; not even an audience with the king and
queen.

Worst of all, no opportunity to plead our case
before they separate me and Remy and lock us both in
steel suits. At least I assume they do the same to Remy. I have
no chance to see.

Keeping their distance, they bind my hands into the steel-
shackled cuffs and gloves, so tight I can't even wiggle my fingers.
My jaw is strapped shut with a steel band before I can sing a single
word. Panic thrums up and down my body, stringing my magic
as tight as a bowstring, but without an avenue for release. I fight
them every step of the way, but every move I make is meaningless,
futile, foolish.

I am completely at their mercy. And I know just how merciful
Technocrats can be.

The only saving grace is that they haven't smashed my fingers
or burned my tongue yet. I assume that means they plan to interrogate me first.

The guards are mute. They don't look me in the eye as they
place the awful steel hood over my face and buckle it onto the
steel torso cage.

Raw panic slides over my skin, but I couldn't even thrash if
I tried.

I wonder if they avoid Magi prisoners on purpose. If they have
to pretend we're not human, that we don't feel, in order to carry
out the orders they're given.

Rage and terror seethe inside me, spinning my magic in a
whirlwind desperate for release.

Now I know how Zandria has felt since her capture.

Cold. Alone. Constant darkness, enough to drive even the sanest of people crazy.

My nostrils flare and my breath rasps in the hood, echoing back to me. My lungs can't get enough air. The steel enclosure is suffocating. Even burrowing underground to escape the Chambers wasn't this terrifying. In a burst of desperation, I try once more to thrash my way out of this prison. I barely budge it, and my attempt to scream only comes out as a squeak.

I sob as dizziness overtakes me. Like I'm falling and can't seem to stop.

When my breathing finally calms enough, my mind kicks into overdrive, whirling with the implications of how I got here. Darian intentionally revealed me. He put us here.

He wanted to capture us. My stomach lurches. Whatever Darian is up to, it isn't in service of the Magi; I am certain it's in service to himself.

My thoughts halt, homing in on one point. The other Technocrats called him Head Scientist. What was it that Aro told me the other day about the Head Scientist?

He had a wife who was Heartless and died much too soon. His grief impelled his work, which helped him understand Aro's plight.

The image of the blackened metal heart hidden in a drawer rushes forward. Bile rises in my throat.

Zandria's mystery man is Darian Azul. He's the Hidden Knife.

I reel, stuck in the metal suit, unable to move, to scream. I was so wrong, about so many things.

The unknown man I'd begun to feel a kinship with, a fellow Magi who had the bad luck to fall in love with a Technocrat, is the one who betrayed us all.

And while I didn't believe Zandria at the time, I don't doubt for a second that our spymaster is the real Hidden Knife. Our legendary, most well-placed spy is a traitor.

How did I not see this earlier? Who else would have access to secret books of powerful magic knowledge and a little-used townhouse? I found Darian's questioning gray eyes unnerving, but to my sister they would be full of mystery—one she'd need to puzzle out. He's younger than he first appears too, and handsome in a dark, mysterious sort of way.

Zandria would've fallen for him in a heartbeat. And when he shared his knowledge of spells, it would've sealed her affections.

But Darian is not the intriguing, romantic figure Zandria believed he was. He's harvesting power from his own people. Magic trickles in my veins, sending electric shocks into my arms as the full weight of understanding threatens to crush me.

Darian Azul is the reason my sister was captured.

I have no doubt my sister happily showed off her magic to impress him. If he's doing something so advanced as infusing magic into objects, he of all people might have known her magic was different. At the very least, he would have realized how powerful she is. If Zandria told him about the door, she would've admitted to our regular trips to the tunnels too. He knew exactly where we'd be; he only needed the guards to lie in wait.

He met with the Council at the Chambers. He convinced them not to help us, I'm certain of it now. Then he pretended he was our friend, on our side. He pretended to care for my sister.

That's the worst part, because I trusted him too.

He's a traitor. My skin, cold from the metal crushing my body into place, quivers like a leaf.

He knows where the Chambers is located. That party of Technocrats camped so close to the edge—they couldn't have been there by accident. Just how much do the Technocrats know about us and our last surviving members?

How far has Darian's betrayal gone?

Fire burns in my veins. There is no worse torture than being trapped like this when all I want to do is claw Darian's eyes out.

The Technocrats can't fathom what they've done. They've only made me more determined to get Zandria out of here and away from that disgusting traitor.

My heart twists in my chest as I think of one particular Technocrat. How ridiculous is it that now, of all times, my thoughts of Aro are not of hatred. Instead I wonder what he must think of me.

That I'm not the sweet mechanic he thought I was. That I lied and deceived him with every breath I took.

He has every reason to be furious with me. I should be angry with him, but I only feel the dull, aching certainty of our inevitable doom, like a poison seeping through my marrow. There is no scenario in which our star-crossed love can survive.

He's the Heartless heir. I was ordered to kill him, to demonstrate to the Technocrats they're not safe. Not in their steel city or their Palace. And neither is anything they hold precious.

My people will dig up every secret they have and use it against them. That's the message Aro's spilt blood will send.

Because one way or another, the Magi will kill him—and had I escaped, I would have found a way to do it myself. And the king and queen's line will die with him, leaving the road to the throne open for Darian.

But I failed. The Technos will kill me instead. Or the other scientists will siphon off my magic to use as a power source and give life to hundreds of Heartless children. Darian will find another spy in the Armory to do his dirty work.

What I don't understand is why Darian hasn't used Zandria yet. With the way our magic can affect the machines, I have a sneaking suspicion it could easily power one of those hearts with very little help from the Technocrats. And if he knows the truth about us, wouldn't he want to use us?

The darkness creeps over my skin, raising prickles I can't brush away. He was there at the Armory Council when I lied and told them that we can magnify our powers when we're together. To have both me and Zandria under Technocrat control is a prize that could power their machines for as long as we live. Darian hasn't used her yet . . . because he's been waiting for me.

Forges, he killed our parents. He came for me, and when they wouldn't give me up, he killed them.

Panic returns twentyfold, electrifying every nerve. I need to get out of this. Now.

Despite the difficulty of moving my face and mouth, I find a way to hum in the back of my throat. It's faint and only releases the tiniest stream of magic, but it's enough to make the bolts holding the hood on my steel suit quiver. Poor Zandria; if they ruined her tongue, she wouldn't be able to manage even this.

They can kill me if they must, but I won't let them use me. Not like that. And I won't let them touch Zandria either.

My throat is dry, but I keep humming. Not so loud as to attract a guard, but enough that I can feel the pressure of the magic releasing little by little in a satisfying flow.

The bolts continue to quiver. Hope springs in my heart.

The melody in my head rises higher, then cadences to a lower note. One of the bolts wriggles out of its hole and pings on the floor. I hold my breath, praying no one heard it fall.

One minute passes. Then five. Then ten. No one responds to the singular noise in the darkness.

I try again, humming and focusing my thoughts on where I believe the bolts and buckles to be. A few minutes later, another bolt drops to the steel floor. Another ping and waiting period to be sure I'm not found out.

My determination solidifies.

Footsteps ring down the hall, followed closely by a familiar thump-thump-thud.

Aro is coming to me.

Bile rises in my throat, but I choke it down. I can't stand the thought of facing him now. I can't afford love. But love doesn't wait for permission. It swoops in and drags you off without waiting for your reply.

At least my sister fell for another Magi spy. Though love wasn't kind to her either. Love is only madness.

My racing thoughts are interrupted by Aro's voice arguing with someone. A guard perhaps. I can't understand what they say, only that Aro is very unhappy. The lock clicks and the footsteps enter my room.

He doesn't say a word as he unbinds my prison from the low ceiling. Chains clink together, then the tautness in them goes slack. I'm guided, more gently than I'd expected. My knees hit something hard. A chair, perhaps. Then I'm pushed down into it and my hands rest on a table of some sort.

Pressure on my shoulder and a small vibration on my neck startle me as I realize Aro is unscrewing the hood.

I don't dare to breathe for fear of breaking my own heart.

He removes the last screw and lifts the helmet off my head. Cool air rushes in, and I blink at the bright lights as he removes the steel band around my jaw as well.

"Aissa," Aro says. The crushing sadness on his face smashes into me like a brick wall.

There are a million things I want to say. I'm sorry for hurting him. I'm sorry we can't be together. I'm so, so sorry he had to find out. Especially like this.

But I can't speak. My throat has closed up, choking off any apology I might make. While part of me loves him, another part of me is furious he had anything to do with the people who took my sister. Who would plug her into a machine and siphon off her life.

I hold on to that rage so not to get swept away.

"Aissa," he repeats, his eyes like pale blue flames. "What are you doing here? And with that guard? They say that you're both Magi." He leans forward, his voice reduced to a whisper. "They say they're going to keep you here in this"—he waves to the suit I'm trapped in—"forever."

I remain silent, staring back at him, trying not to shake. I can't show weakness. Not now. No matter how much I wish to put my arms around him or touch his face.

It's far too late for that.

"Please." His voice cracks. "Tell me they're wrong."

Somehow I manage to find my voice. "They're holding my sister. I came to get her out." I won't give him the satisfaction of an answer to his Magi question. Not yet.

His face turns slack with surprise. "Your sister? Why?"

"They found her where she didn't belong. They suspect her of being a Magi too."

His expression turns grim. "Your twin must be down here as well, then."

"She is." I take a deep breath, I have my own questions for Aro. "Do you know what they're doing to the Magi prisoners?"

His eyes narrow. "They're confining them so they can't damage the outside world anymore."

"That's not all they do."

"What are you talking about?"

"What do you know about that new power source they demonstrated tonight?"

"Not a lot. One of the other scientists found a mineral that can be recharged and holds power for an extended period of time."

I laugh bitterly. "What do you think they're powering it with?"

His jaw goes slack. "They said it was powered with the geo-thermal generators."

"That's a lie." I lean over the table, though it's difficult wearing these chains. "Look in the room next to the demonstration room. It has three steel cases. Each one contains a Magi. They've found a means of transferring magic to the mineral. It's a very different sort of power altogether."

Aro looks queasy. If he's as oblivious to the truth as I suspect he is, I can understand. He wants to believe his people are good and righteous.

They're not.

But I'm no longer certain that the Magi are either. Our tactics—spying, lying, plotting to kidnap and kill defenseless children—are no better.

Suddenly Aro's face twists. "You're lying. That's all this is. Darian warned me you'd lie to confuse me." He stands up from the table, shaking. "That's why they keep Magi like you locked in steel. You're too dangerous. If Darian didn't want to interrogate you first, they would've maimed your tongue already."

Horror crawls over me like fire ants. They really did burn Zandria's tongue then. No wonder she hasn't been able to get out on her own. I hate Darian more than I ever imagined possible right now, but I can't bring myself to out another Magi. Though perhaps I can still do something.

"I wouldn't trust Darian. He wants you dead."

Confusion, then disgust flashes over Aro's face. "You're grasp-ing at straws. He's my friend."

I shake my head. Despite all this, I can't bear the idea of Aro dying because of Darian's duplicity. "I know who you are, Aro. And so does Darian. Did you know he's next in line for the throne . . . after you?"

Aro turns a terrible ashen shade as the weight behind my

words hits. He sits back down in shock. "How—how did you figure it out?"

"That you're the prince?" I scoff. "Please, no mere researcher would know all the hidden spots in the Palace so well."

He swallows hard. "How can I believe a word you say?"

I have no words to defend myself to Aro. I am dangerous. I am a liar. I came to the Palace looking for him, to kill him, even though I didn't realize it at the time. Until this morning, I hadn't decided if I would actually do it.

I failed this mission because I let my emotions get in the way. I won't make that mistake again.

"Have you nothing to say for yourself?" Aro asks with disbelief.

I pause for a moment before responding. The night we spent in the greenhouse repeats in my mind's eye, making my pulse spike. A mix of fond remembrance and despair.

"I meant every word," I say.

"What?" he says, face pale and drawn. "What do you mean?"

I keep my voice as steady as possible. "I meant every word I said to you last night."

"Another lie," he says, but his face as he turns to leave looks even more crushed than when he came in.

"Look in that room. You'll see I'm not lying. Not about anything."

He stands with his back to me for a full ten seconds before opening the door. A guard returns and locks me back up in my metal suit. I'm so exhausted, I don't even think of trying to over-power him with my magic.

I pray Aro takes my advice. And that his heart is as good as I believe.

I DON'T KNOW HOW MUCH TIME PASSES, OR

how long I'm suspended in a steel prison. All I
know is that it's too much. I could be murdered or
maimed at any moment with no means of defending
myself. Visions of the queen's interrogation of Vivienne
drift through my brain. I tremble, but only slightly shake the
metal suit. I'd rather die than have to endure this endless waiting.
It's a torture of its own. I can't help but wonder whether my sister
has tried ending it all.

I only hope that if she has, she failed. I need her alive.

She's all I have left.

I doze, fading in and out of consciousness, memories of my
parents and my sister haunting me. Hands shaking my suit startle
me awake. My eyes fly open to see my nightmares made flesh:
Darian Azul stands before me, the metal helmet in his hands. Fear
slithers over my skin.

"There you are, Aissa," he says, loosening the band around my
chin and setting the helmet on a table in the corner of the room.

"Traitor." The word slips out before I can stop it.

He smiles. "I see you're smarter than your sister. But I am not
a traitor. In fact, I'm dedicated to the same cause as your parents."

I go still. "I doubt that."

"Ah, so you do know about the Alchemist Alliance, then.
Zandria did not pick up on a single hint I dropped."

My skin bristles at the thought of this man being anywhere
near my sister. "You trapped her. You tricked her."

Darian tilts his head in concession. "I did. But not for the
reasons you might think. We're on the same side, and I can offer

you and your sister everything you desire if you'll help me. In fact, if you agree to help me, you and Zandria will walk out of here free as birds and with more power than you can imagine. Allow me to explain." He pulls up a chair and sits in front of me while I'm still strung up in my suit. "Tell me, Aissa, what do you know about the Alchemists?"

My mouth is a hard line. While I can't deny part of me is intrigued by his promise to free Zandy and me, I don't trust him for a second.

"This is your tactic?" He folds his hands in his lap. "Do you know how the Heartless came to be?"

I frown. "Everyone does. It was the great Magis' final curse before the Technocrats bombed them."

Darian shakes his head. "And here I thought you were smart enough not to believe everything you read in the Technocrat history books."

"It's in the Magi history books too."

"Because it's a convenient lie. Only a few know the truth, and they're not the ones in power at the Armory. But people like your parents and me, we know the truth."

I bite my tongue. I hate how much I want to ask what really happened.

"If you know about the Alliance, you must know about their experiments?"

I risk a nod.

"They wanted to regain our lost powers, and to find a way to merge our two peoples back together and maintain peace. During one of those experiments the alliance of Magi and Technocrats released alchemicals into the country's water supply. It was supposed to reignite the Technocrats' dormant magical gene; instead it planted the seed of mutation in the populace, and with each generation it grows more prominent."

My mouth drops open and ice slides over my back. I'd always been told it was the Magi's fault, but this was not what I'd expected.

"Shocking, isn't it? Queen Cyrene and King Damon were equally shocked when I told them. They tasked me with finding a way to reverse the mutation. But it also provides an opportunity to finish the Alliance's work and create a perfect hybrid of magic and technology. This is what I am trying to do. With the power you and your sister hold, that goal is within reach."

"That's why you needed the Magi prisoners," I say. Horror spins in my head.

"But with you and your sister willingly using your magic to help me meet my goals—our goals—I might not need them anymore."

Shock shivers over me. Darian really does believe the lie that we can augment each other's powers since we're twins. If I only do what he asks, I could set all those prisoners free . . . but I already know at least a portion of the price: Aro's life. I have no doubt that is only the beginning of what Darian will require.

"But why are you trying to use the Magi to power the hearts?"

Darian sighs. "Aissa, you already know the answer to that."

Confusion fills me, then clears, leaving the answer. "Your wife. She must have started as a cover, but you fell in love with her. But how did you—" My words choke off. "You were there," I whisper.

His smile widens. "Yes. Hidden under a shield spell."

"So the spell books Zandria told me you kept in your house, you must have moved them yourself to the labs . . . But why?"

"I had my reasons. My family has been protecting them from the other Magi for a long time. Some are very, very old. They belong to the Alchemist Alliance. As does that key you stole." He leans closer, a wicked look in his eyes. "You may have discovered my secret, but in the process, you revealed your own."

My pulse skyrockets. I'm an idiot. I should've known better. I was so desperate for an ally that I didn't even think.

"I was sitting at my kitchen table when I heard you picking the lock on my back door. I concealed myself, but I was curious to see what you'd do. Imagine my surprise when I watched you open my locked drawer without using your hands."

The bottom drops out of my stomach.

He knows.

"That's why you killed my parents. You wanted to capture me too."

He raises an eyebrow. "I didn't *want* to kill them. They neglected their duties to the Alliance. They kept you two secret instead of telling me about your unique powers as they should have years ago. But I knew there was something special about Zandria after I saw her use her magic. She is more powerful than any other Magi her age I've encountered. After I heard you tell the Council how you and your sister's magic magnifies each other's, I knew I needed to have you both before I began any experiments."

A very, very tiny piece of me is relieved that he hasn't hurt Zandria. Yet.

He sits back. "Your parents were fools. They should have simply handed you over. That's why you and Zandria were created—to be the tools of our salvation. They had no right to keep you hidden away, especially from other members of the Alliance. Once I realized who Zandria's parents were and that you were her twin, I could have taken you at any time. But I chose not to. I'd rather have you willingly help me, and as the fruit of the Alliance, that request should not have been met with resistance. Especially once I already had Zandria as collateral."

I swallow hard, desperate to bury the overwhelming grief that rears its head.

"But," Darian continues, "since I was left with no choice but to take you by force, I had to make it look official. You can thank your parents for that."

"What exactly are you trying to do that requires our help?" I ask. "You've already succeeded in getting yourself named the successor to the throne."

He laughs. "Very clever indeed. Remy must have told you why you were instructed to kill Aro. Isaiah will be so disappointed. I, on the other hand, appreciate that cleverness."

"You've been lying to us. Feeding us misinformation about the heir. You're playing both sides, aren't you?"

He smiles and holds out his hands. "I am playing the role I was born to as a descendant of the Alchemist Alliance, the same as you and your sister. Damon and Cyrene believe I am their spy. After I made myself invaluable to them as a scientist, I told them I had been approached by someone who tried to convert me to the Magi cause. They insisted I pretend to be a convert. Over the years, they have asked me to spread many lies to the Armory. In return, they gave me more and more power and placed more and more trust in me. That power and trust is exactly what I will use to destroy them."

"But why have you turned against the Magi too? You're supposed to be our most trusted spy."

Darian's face clouds over. "The current Council is made up of fools. I went into this believing what you and all other Magi are trained to accept: that the Technocrats are evil. And many, many of them are, especially the royals and the rich. But there are those who could be turned against their king and queen, like those who've known the Heartless and lost them."

"Like you did," I whisper. "You fell deeply in love with her. Your marriage was never an act."

He nods. "And the Council would have punished me for it if they knew. It's a treasonous offense. So I hid it, I hid her from them.

It wasn't hard to do. I had already earned the title of spymaster and I ensured any Magi sent to Palinor only knew about one or two others stationed here. There was nothing I could do to save her, but together you and I can save so many others."

I swallow hard. "What do you think the Council would do if they found out?" I'm trying to show concern for him, but truly I ask only for myself.

Darian looks me straight in the eyes. "They would almost certainly make an example of me. I would be executed."

My breath halts in my chest. "But you're so well-placed. Surely your punishment wouldn't be so severe." Mine, however, if they discovered my true feelings for Aro. . .

"I'm too well-placed. That's the problem. All they'd need to hear is that I loved a Technocrat and that would be it. They'd assume I'm compromised and too dangerous to leave in such a sensitive position." Darian leans closer. "And what about you? I know about the time you've been spending with Aro. He's told me what he feels for you. Even asked advice once or twice, since I'm his mentor. What do you feel for him?"

My mouth is suddenly lined with needles and my face flushes with heat. It is all the answer Darian needs.

He leans back. "Then they would make an example of you as well."

I can't help but stare at him for a long moment, terror clutching my throat. I don't know if he's trying to scare me or if he's right, but I fear it's the latter.

Finally, I find my voice again. "Why kill Aro? Why do you need the throne now? He'll be dead in a couple years."

"Not if I am successful in my work, and with your help, I will be very soon." He sits up straighter. "Now we come to the crux of the matter. I don't believe the Heartless are a mistake at all. They're exactly what we need. There's a vein of ore steeped in magic near the Chambers, and I've been able to use that as a conduit to infuse Magi power into the hearts and keep them beating for a brief time. But with your ability to actually use magic on technology, there is no telling how many pieces of ore we could infuse and for how long. If we can find a way to harness your powers, we could make the Heartless virtually indestructible." He shrugs. "I can't let that happen to the one person standing in the way of my ascent to the throne. Aro was useful for a time, a very eager and brilliant helper, but now he must go."

I cringe, thinking of what he really means by harnessing our powers. Those awful steel-and-glass cases. "So that is why troops are gathered by the Chambers. You're harvesting the ore."

Darian smiles. "I stationed them there to set up a camp and staging area to begin mining. They don't yet know how close they are to the Magi stronghold . . . but they might if there ever comes a time when I need to keep Isaiah—or anyone else—in line." The threat underscoring his words is perfectly clear. He took Zandria to ensure my cooperation; I have no doubt he'll follow through on the threat to the rest of the Magi too if he deems it necessary.

"Your wife is gone. It is too late to save her. What do you get out of helping the Heartless now?" There's something broken and unhinged inside Darian, but I can't completely shake that strange sympathy, that connection I'd felt when I'd only known him as Zandria's mysterious friend. We share the experience of loving not only a Technocrat, but one born Heartless. And the fear and guilt that comes with it.

Darian laughs. "They will be devoted, indebted, to me. As they grow older and stronger, they will become my army, which is where you and your sister come in. You will supply them with a steady stream of magic so the army can grow in strength. And just imagine the new weaponry we could create—like nothing ever seen before! I've already begun the process by adding more alchemicals to the water supply. When I take the throne, no one will be able to compete with my subjects. And if you agree to help me, you and Zandria will have all the freedom and power you ever wanted. You can name your position in the new regime."

This man's feelings for a doomed woman led him into similar circumstances as me, yet somehow his love resulted in a demented plan. This is what years of living with the Technocrats has done to him. I'm willing to bet losing his wife broke him. I wonder if that was the same time he came up with the plan to take the throne.

"What about walking out of here today, like you said earlier?"

A terrible light gleams in Darian's eyes. "You and your sister will help me kill the king and queen and their heir. We'll blame it on an unnamed Magi who escaped the dungeon. A faceless scapegoat we can pretend to chase. Then my reign can begin."

"And if I don't agree to help you?"

He scoffs. "Then the Council will learn what you and your sister really are. And of your love for Aro, of course. I, personally affronted by your grave transgressions, will ask to dole out the punishment myself, but in secret so the other Magi don't learn of what you can do. Then I'll bring you back to Palinor. I don't need you and your twin for your minds, just your magic and your genes. I'd rather have the pair of you willingly become my personal trusted spies and spellcasters, my own Twin Daggers. But I will drain you dry if I have to, until you both agree to help me start a new line of Magi with restored powers. We can squash any Technocrats—or Magi for that matter—who object to our rule. Between our Heartless army and our new all-powerful bloodline, we'll be like gods."

His eyes are fervent and flamed. And it is the most terrifying thing I've ever seen.

I jump when a knock sounds at the door behind us. "Sir?" a voice calls.

Darian opens the door and a guard pokes his head inside.

"Apologies, sir, but we've just received word that the queen has sent for you."

He closes the door and picks up the helmet from the table. "Consider my offer, Aissa. Because you will help me. You *and* your sister. Whether you like it or not." Then the steel band is tightened and the helmet descends, locking me in darkness once again. My breath comes in short, stuttered bursts. I have to find a way out of here—fast.

I can't let Darian do this, however great the temptation of freedom. It's one thing to recruit willing participants to topple a regime; it's another to experiment on your own kind to get there. And the idea of Darian being king . . . I shudder.

The worst part is I can see how he got to this place. His grief combined with the knowledge that both the Magi and Technocrats would kill him if they knew the truth resulted in a twisted scheme to take over by force to solve things his own way.

Suddenly, something heavy thuds against my cell door, and I jolt in my metal cage. The thing that thudded grunts then hits the floor.

Every nerve in my body tenses. Darian couldn't be back already. Is someone here to kill me? Why else would they disable the guard?

The key ring jangles. Whoever they are, they're coming for me.

My breath quickens, and I rail against the steel holding me in place.

I'd hoped to get out of here alive.

The door opens, and soft footsteps enter my chamber. Real fear ripples over my skin. I can't recall ever being so vulnerable, so exposed. They could stick a knife into my gut and I couldn't do a thing, not even move my hands to stem the flow of blood from my body. I'm completely at the mercy of this intruder.

And no matter what Queen Cyrene may say, Technocrats are not known for their mercy.

The intruder stops in front of me. I no longer hear them move, but I feel the prickly presence of eyes lingering on me and hear the whisper of a breath.

My mind races to discern the identity of the intruder and what he or she could possibly intend to do.

He breaks the silence first. "I'm sorry, Aissa."

My racing heart nearly stops. Aro stands in front of me. Aro, who took out the guard in front of my cell. Aro, who left here so furious earlier.

"I'm sorry I didn't believe you. I'm sorry for what they're doing. I'm sorry they took your sister," he says, the crack in his voice severing me to the core. "I'll help you get her out of here. I'll make this right. I'd even swear off my family name and heritage if it would help."

I choke down the lump in my throat as the key he stole turns in the suit's lock. He slides open the mouth plate in my helmet and releases the metal strap holding my jaw in place. Relief floods over me like cool water.

"Aro. They're right about one thing," I say.

He sighs. "You're Magi. And your friend and sister too."

"Yes." That one word is all I can manage. My ancestors' magic experiments caused his birth defect. The thing that caused his parents to hide him away. The same thing that has condemned so many innocent children.

None of us are truly innocent.

The key resumes turning in the other parts of the suit and I let out my breath.

"I'll help all of you. I'll help free the rest of the Magi we hold down here." His voice lowers. "What you are surprised me. Shocked me, really. But I fell in love with who you are. The faction you belong to doesn't change that. If I were in your position, how can I say I wouldn't have done the very same?" He pulls the hood off my head, and light and air pour over my face. Aro stands there, steel helmet in one hand, key in the other, pale hair glimmering in the half light. The pack the guards took from me is slung over his shoulder. His eyes ignite with tender ferocity and it's all I can do not to kiss him right then and there.

My emotions betray me at every turn. Loving Aro is madness, and that love saved my life.

He's turned everything I have ever learned about Technocrats on its head.

Soon the last manacle has been cast aside and Aro hands me my pack. He runs his fingers through his hair, then reaches out to take my hand.

"Did you really mean every word?" he asks, looking at me with eyes full of fear and hope, mirroring my own feelings exactly.

"I knew how different we were from the start. I knew how impossible this would be, but I couldn't help falling for you." I squeeze his hand, then run my thumb over his knuckles. I'm out of that awful suit, free from it, free to breathe the air, free to touch someone else's skin. *Free.* All because of Aro.

"I have to know. What were you using me for?"

My face falls and my gut twists.

"Look, I know you're a spy. You had to be on a mission of some kind. I'm sure you used me; I just want to know what it was for."

This is the part I have feared. It's haunted my dreams for days. The part where I tell Aro I was sent to find, kidnap, and kill him.

He squeezes my hand reassuringly. "I've braced myself for it. I doubt it's pleasant."

I take a deep breath, then straighten my back. "We received intelligence that the king and queen had a child who was born Heartless. My mission was to find their heir. You provided an opportunity to access the Palace."

He blinks. "But why? The king and queen have never acknowledged any children."

"We believed it was a girl who was being kept hidden in the Palace. It wasn't until recently that I discovered it was you." I wince. "I overheard you call the queen Mother." My fingers reach out toward his chest of their own accord and I have to fight to draw them back. "I knew you were the one I was looking for."

"What did you intend to do once you found me?" He catches my fingers and places them over his heart. It ticks beneath my palm in a disconcerting manner. It's the epitome of unfairness that this good-hearted person doesn't have a heart at all.

"Zandria and I were supposed to kidnap you and hold you for ransom. We were told we were looking for a girl of about ten or eleven. We had no clue you were grown, let alone a man."

He draws me in, one hand on my hip, the other holding my palm firmly to his chest. My head spins.

"What was the price of my ransom? Money, or something else?" He frowns but doesn't relinquish his grip.

"The freedom of our prisoners beneath Palinor."

"And if my parents refused to acknowledge me as their son and pay that price?"

"Don't make me say it."

"You were told to kill me if that happened, weren't you?" I can only nod. "Would you have done it?"

I wince. Would I have killed Aro? "At first, yes. But then I got to know you. By the time they told me the plan had always been to kill the Heartless heir, I was too far gone to carry out those orders. That's why you must be careful of Darian Azul. He's one of us—he wants you dead. You cannot trust him."

He places his hand on my cheek and I lean into it.

"Thank you for the truth."

Before I can take another breath, his lips urgently press against mine as though we should be running for our lives.

And really, we ought to be.

I wrap my arms around his neck and curl my fingers in his hair. But we must get my sister and Remy first. I can't allow Darian to touch her.

I break away.

Aro takes one look at my face and it's clear he understands. "Right. Your sister and your friend. We need to get you out of here." He takes my hand again. "I've known Head Scientist Darian for years. I trusted him. I don't know what his plans for me might be, but when I saw the room you mentioned and realized what he was doing to the Magi, using them to power the mineral, it was sickening. He has a terrible sense of irony using magic to power a machine that would keep those afflicted by a Magi curse alive. But that doesn't make it right. Treating them as less than human is wrong, no matter what may have happened in the past." He kisses me softly on the nose. "I think it's time we stop punishing the Magi for the deeds of their ancestors. Starting with you and your friends."

For the first time in days, pleasant warmth fills me from my head to my toes. This is the first glimmer of light I've found since my sister was taken away, and since the Armory Council refused to help me find her. My people may not want to stand by me, but I have found others who will. With Aro on my side, I can't help but succeed. "We must stop Darian from using my sister in one of those cases."

"I know where your sister and your friend are. They're not far from here. But we should hurry. The queen doesn't really need Darian, and we must leave before he returns."

We slip out of the room hand in hand. Something strange and new wriggles in my belly, something I didn't expect to ever feel again: real hope.

ONCE WE'RE PAST THE UNCONSCIOUS GUARD,

Aro whispers, "Can you conceal us with your magic? Does it work like that?"

Without hesitation I hum the shield spell. Aro gasps as magic tingles over him for the first time. "It does that sometimes," I say.

"Amazing. I could've used this when I was trying to sneak out of my chambers."

Aro leads the way down corridor after corridor, taking turns with hardly a backward glance. Finally he stops outside one of the cells and fiddles with his keys. "This is where they're holding your friend. Your sister is farther down. We can get him first and he can help with her."

She's been stuck here in her own private hell with enough time and solitude to drive a person completely mad. Have her muscles already begun to atrophy from lack of use? Moving in those suits is impossible.

"Yes, Remy will help us." I frown. "Though he may not understand why *you're* helping us. He'll be suspicious."

Aro shrugs. "I can't blame him."

He opens the door and strides over to the silent, motionless suit suspended from the center of the room, then begins to unscrew the bolts and remove the panels. I help while whispering reassurances to Remy.

"It's me, Remy. And a friend. We're getting you out, as well as Zandria. It will be all right." He grunts in return, until we get the mask and band off and then he mumbles, "Thanks."

When he sees Aro, he flinches. "What is he doing here?"

"He just saved our lives, so whatever doubts you're having, forget them. He's on our side and helps us at great risk to himself."

Remy opens his mouth to object, but I cut him off. "Unless, of course, you'd like to continue your stay in this lovely steel suit?"

He gives Aro a sidelong glance. "I suppose if he betrays us, I can't be any worse off than I was a few minutes ago."

Aro laughs. "That's the spirit."

We finish freeing Remy from the suit, then Aro leads us into the hallway again. Remy starts the sound-dampening spell, leaving me free to concentrate on the shield. Aro's eyes widen as he realizes our steps are now soundless. He even taps one of the walls with his knuckle as we pass to see if it makes a noise. He grins when it doesn't.

He slows his pace as we venture deeper into the dungeon. Several times he signals us to stop and wait while a guard roams past. All three of us flatten ourselves against the walls, just in case any of them get too close. Aro's face furrows with fear with each encounter, followed by surprise and wonder when they pass by without a second glance.

When we stop in front of Zandria's door, he seems more nervous than before. "What's wrong, Aro?" I ask.

He bites his lip. "It's probably nothing. But there are more guards here tonight than usual."

My hands tremble though I will them to stop. Remy shakes his head behind me.

"What do you mean?"

"It's probably nothing. Just be extra careful not to let that shield down, all right? They might realize you're missing sooner than I'd hoped."

He fumbles with the key though manages to get the door open. It squeaks and we all freeze, horrified by the sound echoing in the hall. While Remy could cover the people in our little group with the dampening spell, he couldn't cover the door. But no stomping feet or shouts follow. Only silence echoes back.

We open the door and find Zandria in her cage suit. My chest expands with lightness and my eyes begin to water. I've found her at last. I can even hear her breathing inside the helmet. She's alive.

I remind myself I don't have time to celebrate now. I blink back my tears of relief, and Aro and I immediately get to work disassembling Zandria's prison while Remy stands watch by the door.

We make quick work of it, and when the last bolt pops off the hood I tug it off to see my sister's face. Her eyes are closed, and she lolls in the suit. Dried blood rings her lips, and my stomach turns with the understanding of what they must have done.

"Help me get the rest of this off," Aro says. I'm jolted back into action. She doesn't look like herself at all. She looks half dead.

When Aro pulls the final piece of metal off her body, she slumps into my arms. I pat her cheek, trying to wake her up. "Zandria! Zandria!" I say in a choked whisper. My hands begin to quake. I've risked so much to get to this moment. My sister has to make it through this. Failure isn't an option. "Why isn't she waking up?"

"I've heard this happens sometimes," Aro says. "They get sick from the metal being so close to their skin."

I can see why that would bother other Magi, but it shouldn't bother Zandria too much.

"What can we do to make her better?" Remy growls.

I stare at my sister, my hand pressed to her cheek. I'd feel ill too if I hadn't had any contact with the natural world and my magic in days. She's running hot with a fever and her mouth is swollen. Her tongue must have gotten an infection after they burned it with the poker. Her hands are swollen and discolored too.

"I know." Before my parents were killed, I spent every night up reading through those books I found in the palace's lab. One of those spells is exactly what I need. I hope.

I sing, so softly no one in the hall could possibly hear, praying this actually works. If it doesn't . . . well, I can't bear to think about that right now. "*Recreo, recreo.*" I call on her to heal herself, to quell the festering infection, and for her burned flesh and broken bones to become new again. My power mingles with hers, warming it, teasing it upward into life and action. Little by little, the healthy color returns to her cheeks and the gray pallor begins to fade. Her jaw moves as her tongue heals. Her fingers flex as her hands return to their normal shape and color. Relief lightens fear's grip on my chest.

Soon she breathes more easily and her cheeks are warm. "Zandria," I say. She moans and turns on her side, coughing. I rub her back. "You're safe now."

Her eyes squint, hunting for mine. "Aissa?" she whispers. "Am I dreaming?"

Tears singe the edges of my vision. "You're not dreaming, I promise. It's really me. And Remy, and Aro. He's a friend. He's here to help us escape." Zandria curls into me, wrapping her arms around my middle. "I missed you so much," I murmur into her hair.

"I thought I'd never see you again," she says.

"I'd never leave you behind." I squeeze her tighter, not wanting to let go.

"I'm sorry to break this up, but we must hurry," Aro says. "Can you stand? Do you think you can walk or run if necessary?"

"If she can't, I'll carry her," Remy says. Zandria flickers a smile at him.

"Ready to try?" I ask, and she nods. I put my arms beneath hers to lift my sister to her feet. She sways unsteadily, gripping my shoulder. I keep my arm firmly around her waist as she takes a few shaking steps. With each one she puts more weight on her feet and her steps get stronger. She eases her grip.

"I'll be all right," she says.

Aro checks the hallway to confirm no guards are in sight. When he gives us the all clear, we proceed down the hall, Aro leading. Remy follows next, again weaving the sound-dampening spell, and Zandria and I bring up the rear. I continue to hum the shield spell in spite of the distraction of helping Zandria along the hallway. Soon she hardly needs to lean on me at all. But not once does she release her grip on my hand.

Aro takes us down several twisting and confusing corridors. From the expression on his face, Remy doesn't look half so pleased at Aro's company. If I didn't know better, I'd suspect Remy was plotting to stick his dagger into Aro's back the very first opportunity he gets. That's the mission his father has given us, and I don't entirely trust him not to.

I'll do whatever is necessary to ensure that doesn't happen. Aro isn't our enemy. And as tempting as it might be to see a Magi on the Technocrat throne, I have no doubt Darian would be far more dangerous than King Damon and Queen Cyrene.

"There's an exit in the lowest levels," Aro says. "It leads to the drainage tunnels beneath Palinor." He meets my eyes. "I trust you can find your way out from there?"

"We can. We know those tunnels well."

Zandria stiffens next to me. "It's fine," I whisper. "I'll explain later, but for now, know that we can trust him."

She relaxes, but only a little. A hint of nervousness pinches the back of my brain. There's no telling how my sister will react to all the things I must tell her.

How the Council refused to help us. How the man she fell for betrayed us. How I betrayed everyone by falling in love with the enemy and our target.

That our parents were murdered by Darian, and we're part of a secret alliance dedicated to creating Magi just like us. My stomach lurches. I've been so focused on saving my sister, I haven't fully processed much of this yet. I keep tucking these awful truths away, and I do it again now. When we're out of Palinor, we'll have the freedom to grieve, to come to terms with what we are. But not now.

"Good," Aro says. "We'll just have to slip by the guard posted there."

"Is it just one guard?" Remy asks.

"Usually, yes," Aro says, then frowns. "On occasion there are more, but hopefully that won't be the case today."

"You should've taken them out first," Remy grumbles.

Aro gives him a withering look. "Sorry, I don't normally sneak people in and out of the Palace. You'll have to forgive me if I didn't think of everything."

"It's fine," I say, glaring at Remy. "We appreciate all you've done and all you're risking by helping us."

His pale eyes glint in my direction. "I wouldn't do it for just anyone."

My face burns hot, and I can feel the weight of Zandria's gaze on me.

"It's up ahead," Aro says. "Stay quiet."

The inches between us and one last guard creep by at an interminably slow pace. When we reach the corner, Aro peeks around it, trusting us to keep him hidden with our magic, then reports back.

"There are three men. Two guards and the Head Scientist."

"Darian's here?" I'd hoped we'd escape without running into him again.

"Darian?" Zandria asks with a tremor in her voice.

I put my arm around my sister. "I'm so sorry. He betrayed us. He's the reason you were caught. I'll explain it all once we're free." For one moment, I fear she will crumple into my arms, but she only sags, then straightens her spine. There's the sister I know.

"I can't believe he'd do that . . . but it makes sense," she whispers, then cringes. "I never should have told him we were exploring the tunnels."

I squeeze my sister close. "There was no way for you to have known."

"He does present a challenge." Aro sighs. "Can you conceal me if we need to fight them? I understand you think he's after me, but I know him. He convinced my parents to allow me to work toward finding a cure for myself. And then he took my work and twisted it." His hands turn to fists. "I can't leave here with you; I have to stay and continue my work and put a stop to his."

"Darian will kill you if you get in his way. And you're in his way simply by existing. Your choice is to leave and live or remain and die." It kills me to say the harsh words, but he needs to understand the real stakes before he makes a rash decision.

"If I leave, I'm letting him win. I'd rather stay and do what I can to fight."

I have no other argument to give. If I were in his position, I'd say exactly the same thing.

"So, can you conceal me while you take them out?" Aro asks again.

I exchange a look with Zandria. "Yes," I say, "we can do it."

"Good, because we can't get around them and get to the door. One guard is practically sitting on it. We'll have to go through them to get out of here. We go on my count."

Aro looks around the corner, cloaked in our magic, and holds up his hand. He ticks off the fingers for one, two, three, GO.

We rush around the corner in an invisible mass. The first guard falls to Remy's dagger in seconds, while Aro grapples with the other.

Zandria freezes beside me. She doesn't breathe either. It's one thing to hear Darian betrayed us, but it's another entirely to see the proof with her own eyes.

His gaze is trained directly on me and Zandria. "Your shield can't hide you from me," he says, subtly moving his fingers in a spell.

Of course it doesn't. He removed my shield easily when he caught Remy and me in the hall. Just a few flicks of his fingers was all it took to cast his reveal spell and ensure no one would notice what he had done. When an odd fizziness trills over us, I know he's done the same thing now, leaving Aro exposed as well.

He turns to Zandria. "I'm so glad you tried my spells. It led me right to you that night in the tunnels. Did you know that the more practiced Magi can detect magic and track it?"

She curls into me, like a hand is crushing her rib cage. She had no clue what he is. Her misery is thick and palpable, coloring the air around us. I pull her up straighter. He won't get the better of us. Not this time.

"Run," I hiss.

I PUSH ZANDRIA TOWARD REMY AND ARO

and the exit, positioning myself between
them and Darian. The door opens behind me,
but Aro still struggles with the guard. "Remy, help
him, please!" I cry.

I can't take my eyes off Darian for a second. I want to
kill him where he stands so badly, it hurts to breathe. With the
remaining guard too distracted to notice, his mouth begins to
form the words of a spell.

My magic is at my fingertips before I've even finished saying
the words of my own spell: "*Fermito!*" Darian's mouth snaps shut.
At first he's shocked, but then I swear he smiles. He must not have
expected us to know that one. Dueling spells are not exactly part
of the Armory's standard training. My eyes stray to the sword at
the side of the fallen guard. It would be so easy to send it flying through Darian's heart . . . but then I'd expose our secret to
everyone.

My parents wouldn't want me to take my revenge at such
a risk.

Before I can consider that any further, metal grinds against
metal with a horrible screech, and I turn to see the guard drive his
dagger into the spot where Aro's heart should be. The guard's face
goes white when he realizes he's just stabbed one of the Heartless.

Magic rages inside my chest and I drag the others to the door,
shoving them through. Darian grabs my arm, but it's Zandria who
shocks him with a bolt of electricity. He's thrown back.

I leap through the doorway, tugging my sister after me. I slam
the door shut, then turn to Remy.

"Get Aro down the corridor! Go!" Remy gives me a strange

look, but for once doesn't question me. He holds Aro up and practically carries him down the tunnel. The second they're out of view, I place my palms on the door Zandria's holding closed against Darian and the guard.

"You know what we need to do." Zandria nods. Together we weave the spell—her with her hands, me with my humming. The metal door heats and begins to melt where we focus our magic, warping and sealing itself to the wall and doorframe. Darian and his guards will have a hard time getting through that.

We run after Remy, and I stop short when we catch up. Aro lies prone on the ground of the passage, with Remy standing helpless over him. I drop to my knees by his side. When I yank the dagger from his chest, he yelps with the pain.

Aro's life pours through my fingers, along with the poisonous sludge of the perforated power source. His clockwork heart is damaged beyond repair, even for me. I'm not sure where all the missing pieces are and there's no time for another surgery to replace it.

If his parents would even allow it after he betrayed them.

"Aissa," his whispers and winces. "Go."

"No."

"What are you doing, Aissa? He's one of them, we have to leave him," Zandria hisses behind me. She has no inkling of the extent of my real feelings for Aro, nor what I've done, how selfish I've been.

My pleading eyes make her draw back. I've never been one to show an excess of emotion. The tears glittering in the corners of my eyes are enough to convince her this means everything to me.

Aro sputters and reaches up to touch my face. "I'm sorry."

"Hush," I say, trying not to flinch at the blood on his fingers. I hum the incantation that will help heal his wounds and staunch the flow of blood. The trouble is, the blood isn't flowing much because his clockwork heart limps through each turn. Smoke curls out of the top.

I must do something.

"Go," he says again. The pain in his eyes makes me want to clutch him to my chest and never let go. I want to tell him everything will be fine.

But it won't. Nothing will ever be fine again if Aro dies. Not for me.

"Aissa, come on. He's a Techno," Remy says. I look at him with baleful eyes. He takes the hint and shuts up.

Aro is no mere Technocrat. He's the reason my heart beats. He's the only thing that could make me consider betraying the Magi. Just like Darian did. But I won't make his mistakes.

"Take Zandria and follow the passage until you hit the drainage tunnels. If I'm not there in ten minutes, leave without me."

"Aissa!" Zandria says. "I'm not going anywhere without you—"

"Please." My sister gapes at me, then squares her shoulders.

"You better be there soon."

"I will, I promise. Now go. I need—I need to say goodbye."

Zandria's curiosity at my behavior is quickly transforming to frustration, but she and Remy hurry away nonetheless. There is so much I must explain to her.

Aro's pulse is thready and weak, but he tries to wave me away. "Go, Aissa."

"I'm not going anywhere. I can't." My whispered words crack. I need him to be all right. The skin on his chest begins to knit together from my spells, but the smoke still billows from his heart.

I can't help thinking of my parents, the two of them lying on our floor, bleeding from identical wounds. And me, stuck in the basement, unable to do anything to stop it. They loved each other too much to live without the other. My chest aches as if my own heart is breaking right along with Aro's.

And then, I know exactly what to do.

I whisper into Aro's ear. "You know what I am now. But you

don't know all of it. I'm more special than you think. I won't let you die."

He tries to shake his head, but he only manages to grimace in pain.

"I'm going to try something. If it doesn't work, know how much I love you. I'm sorry for the lies I told. I'll do anything in my power to make it up to you." Tears blur my vision, but the hint of a sad smile crosses his face as I straighten up and place my hands over the remains of his clockwork heart.

Ever since we were young, my parents trained Zandria and me to destroy machines. Over the past couple months toiling with machines in Leon's workshop and the lower levels of the Palace, I've learned I can use my power to make them work again even if I can't repair them fully. But they'll only last as long as I cast the spell.

Yet there is one spell that will tie his mechanical heart to my own, and ensure it turns as long as mine beats.

The Binding ritual was in one of Darian's books I found in the Palace labs. Permanent spells are rare and are supposed to be difficult to master. This spell transfers a piece of a Magi's life force to another person, but surely I can do the same to a machine when it's bound to a human body.

At least I hope I can. I'm already feeling the fatigue from melting the door to keep Darian at bay.

It will mean that as long as I live, Aro's heart will tick. I will be forever bound to him, and he to me. The ramifications of that make me dizzy, but there's no time to ponder them now.

I close my eyes and mutter the words of the spell over and over, all the while focusing inward on that part of me where the magic lives. It coils inside my abdomen, slowly trickling upward. The spell calls the magic up, words and power combining in a tangible way. Even with my eyes closed, I feel it coalescing in my palms. Light flares and forces my eyes open.

My skin illuminates as magic flows through my frame. Aro gapes at me.

"Incredible," he whispers. "Your power is beautiful."

With every word I speak, the power pooling in my hands swells. How much is enough? What is the right amount to keep his heart working indefinitely? Just the thought of him needing another operation terrifies me. He wouldn't make it through, not in this state. Magic seeps into his body and his eyes widen.

"What are you doing?"

"The only thing I can."

I focus all my thoughts on Aro—his kindness, his loyalty. We may have been at cross-purposes, but there's so much in him to admire. All that goodness must stay alive and in this world. With all my heart, I pour my magic and love for Aro into the machine in his chest. The steel parts glow under my palms, and Aro cries out, though whether it's from pain or surprise, I can't tell. And it's too late for me to stop.

The smoke fades to nothing and my own heart races as the magic begins to take hold in me too, but I continue the incantation. Every cog in Aro's heart must be thoroughly imbued with my magic so it keeps working and moving. Magic will grease the space between. No more need for havani. In fact, I'll need to get rid of what's left in this one. I can't fix Aro's heart only to have him die of poisoning soon after.

The hole in his chest exposes the top where the power cell rests. It has turned a frightening greasy black. I coax it out with magic, the piece turning in place until the latch holding it in clicks and lifts. I drop it to the side, but the swirls of poison still infect Aro's chest and limbs. Never stopping the incantation for a second, I concentrate on pulling out the poison and pushing my magic into the space left by the power cell.

Everything Aro was searching for has been right here, with me, the entire time.

My hands begin to ache as the poison seeps into them. The dark material stains my fingers and creeps up my arms. I double over with the pain, but never let go of Aro's chest.

The spell finally ends. His clockwork heart continues to glow and moves at a regular clip. His skin has almost healed around it. Pain from the poison ratchets through me, but I calm my quivering hands long enough to place the cap back on the power cell. The clockwork exudes a faint reddish tinge as his regenerating skin closes over it. I hope it never fades.

I don't recall when Aro lost consciousness, but the rise and fall of his chest and the ticking of his heart reassures me he is indeed alive. He groans.

"Aissa," Aro says hoarsely. "What—what did you do?" He sits up, rubbing the spot on his chest where the mechanical heart beats.

"It was a spell, a powerful one. The short version is that I took a piece of my life force and magicked it into your heart. It won't stop turning as long as I'm alive."

Amazement colors his face. "Magic can do that?" He frowns. "But how can you be sure it will last that long? I don't know what my parents will do after what happened with Darian, but if they're angry, they may not be in a mood to schedule a surgery for me . . ."

"It will last forever. You won't need any more surgeries. The spell is a Binding rite. We are bound together. As long as my heart beats, so will yours, and vice versa."

"Aissa, that's such a risk . . ."

"And I take it willingly." I give him a wry smile. "Don't worry, I'm very good at staying alive."

"Thank you," he whispers. He reaches for my hand then grimaces as he holds it up. I can't hide my wince or the gasp that slips out. I try to pull my hand back, but he holds it fast.

"This is from the havani, isn't it?" he asks, examining the bruiselike color now tinting my skin.

I nod, gritting my teeth against the pain radiating through my arms. "I had to get it out of you quickly. Since I was performing the Binding spell, it transferred to me."

He pulls me closer and rests his forehead against mine. "You didn't have to do that. I always knew I was going to die soon. I was prepared for it."

"I wasn't." I kiss him softly, then sit back on my heels. He gazes at me with a strange look in his eyes.

"Am I really going to live as long as you do? Honestly?"

"Yes," I say firmly. "I have seen the spell work before. You're safe."

He swallows hard and tears glint in the corners of his eyes. "I have spent my whole life being told I was going to die young." A strangled laugh escapes his throat. "I never really prepared to live."

He pulls me close again, wrapping his arms around me and burying his face in my neck.

"Run away with us," I say, though I already know the answer.

He releases me and shakes his head. "You know I can't. I belong here. I have to work against Darian. We can't let him win."

I help him to his feet and kiss him one last time, terrified I might never see him again. It is bittersweet.

"Where will you go?" he asks.

"It is probably better if you don't know. Just in case."

"Of course, you're right." He takes a step back, still holding on to my hand. "Will you come back?"

"I don't know," I lie. If I return to Palinor, I have no doubt the Technocrats will hunt me down. I am effectively banished from my home of the last several years. Death would be kinder, but there are other things just as important as our love. "I will find a way to get in touch. I promise."

"Be safe, Aissa." He puts my stained hand to his lips, then retreats down the other side of the corridor, giving me one last watery smile before I lose sight of him.

I stumble down the tunnel in the direction Remy and Zandria fled while the poison works its way toward my chest, searing my veins and crawling up my neck. I reach the entrance to the drainage tunnels and shove through. Then I tumble to the floor, landing at my sister's feet.

"Aissa!" Zandria cries. Remy isn't here. He must be scouting ahead. She turns me over in spite of my efforts to curl into a ball.

"The poison from the power cell," I spit through clenched teeth. "It was leaking into his chest. I had to pull what was left out to fix his heart. I need your help with a transference spell." One of the first spells every Magi spy learns is how to transfer poison from one's body into something else, usually a plant or the earth. Normally I could do this on my own, but I fear I'm too weak right now. And if I don't do something soon, the havani might kill me.

"Why would you do that? Why would you risk *anything* for a Techno?" Her hot tears sting my cheeks. After what she's been through, she'll never understand. I can't blame her.

"I love him," I whisper.

Something deep in her eyes hardens. "Here," she says, handing me my dagger and glancing behind her. "Take this."

I wrap my twitching fingers around the hilt. I did my best to hide it while I was with Aro, but it feels as though fire runs through my veins. Is this what the Heartless go through every day? If so, I have to wonder who the true heartless people are—the Technos or the ones who created the cursed experiment that led to it?

Zandria waves her hands over me, but all I can feel or hear or see is this pain. I'm being burned from the inside out by the awful black ooze. Dying by this dagger would be a kinder way to go.

Then it begins to subside as my sister guides the poison from my body. It slides back down through my arms and trickles into the dagger. I grip the hilt tighter as the pain lessens. Soon I can sit up again on my own and Zandria ceases weaving her hands, wrapping her arms around me instead. I clutch my sister, grateful to have her back at last. She's changed, but she'll always be my other half. Without her, I'm incomplete. And now another part of me is tied to Aro too.

"Look," Zandria breathes.

The blade of my dagger is black as shadows. And just as poisonous as the horrid stuff that taints it.

Remy marches around the corner, relief and frustration on his face when he sees me.

"Get up," he orders. "I'm not waiting around here for the entire Technocrat army to gather their arsenal."

"What about the heir?" Zandria asks. "Aren't we supposed to find her?"

The way she says those words—so clinical, so like me only a few weeks ago—stops me cold. Remy stays silent.

"No," I say. "I won't do it."

Zandria's face turns pale and Remy looks as though he wants to strangle me.

"Why not? Those are our orders," Zandria asks.

"Aro is the heir," I say, pointing back down the tunnel. "I'll fight anyone who tries to kill him." I keep my hand on my now poisonous dagger in case Remy gets any ideas. Zandria's mouth hangs open, moving up and down as if she's a fish gasping for breath. "But Remy's right. We do need to leave now."

I usher Zandria forward, ignoring the glare Remy shoots at me.

I'm not sure anyone—Technocrat or Magi—will forgive me for what I've just done.

WE FLEE DOWN THESE TUNNELS, THOUGH IT
kills me to leave Aro behind. Hopefully he
can convince them he was only a victim and not a
party to our escape. And he'll keep his distance from
Darian.

I hate not knowing whether I'll see him again, the owner
of my literal and figurative heart.

We run headlong until Zandria tugs at my hand, and I slow
my breakneck pace. Our surroundings are suddenly familiar to
us both.

The hall we've stumbled into is made of the same glittering
black marble as the tunnel we found so many weeks ago. Magic
fizzes around us, raising the hair on my arms. My energy begins
to return, and we move faster. Remy can hardly keep up.

The hall grows thinner and branches off into other passages,
but they don't share the mysterious substance in the walls. We
stick to our path and soon we're rewarded. This is the hallway
we were in before. The one with the very intriguing yet highly
frustrating door.

I turn to Remy. "This will take us to the door we found weeks
ago. The one we're certain has magic. Can't you feel it? Touch the
walls, here." I place his hand on the vein of magic. "Can you feel
that buzzing?"

Remy laughs. "Yes . . . yes, I can. But how is that possible?"

"We don't know," I say.

"We just know it resists our magic," Zandria says before I can
stop her.

"What do you mean? Of course your magic wouldn't affect it."
Remy looks back and forth between us.

"Zandria, no, he can't be trusted!" I plead with her, but she shakes me off. The look in her eyes is one I haven't seen before.

"Right now I trust his judgment over yours. You just revealed our secret to a Heartless Technocrat of all people." Her rebuke smarts. I ball my hands into fists, unable to decide if I'm angrier with her for her stupidity or at myself for taking risks I never dreamed would be necessary.

"You did what, Aissa?" Remy's face has gone pale.

"Our magic can affect machines as well organic matter and the elements," Zandria says. I groan. There is no turning back now.

Remy's eyes widen.

"You must keep it secret from everyone, especially your father," I say. "Swear you won't tell."

"Do you really think I'd rat you out?" he says.

"Yes. I do."

"Aissa!" Zandria says.

"He's been reporting on us to Isaiah."

"No, he ordered me to report on you, but I told him as little as possible."

"So you claim." I fold my arms over my chest. "If Isaiah finds out, I will kill you myself."

Zandria snorts. "What happened to you? You refuse to kill a Technocrat, and then turn around and threaten an ally?"

"So much has happened. I will explain it all. Trust me." I take my sister's hands. "You know me as well as yourself."

Remy is still grappling with Zandria's confession and runs a hand over his face. "I can't believe you hid that from me all this time."

"If anyone found out, they'd ban us from the Chambers if not outright kill us for being tainted. You know how your father is. How the Council is." Bitterness flavors the last words as I recall the way they shot down my plea for help. Thankfully we didn't need them after all.

"How long have you been like this?" Remy asks.

"Since we came into our magic," I say, taking him by the elbow. "Look, just come and see the door. Maybe this time we can open it."

It's farther than I expected, but when we reach it, Remy grows quiet and serious. The door glitters darkly.

Zandria squeezes my hand. She may be hurt and confused by my recent behavior, but this door calls to her as much as it calls to me. And I'm still her twin.

"I never thought I'd see this again," she says. I put my arm around her waist and she hugs me back.

"I'll always come for you." I risk a small smile. "I have an idea."

Her eyes gleam. "Do you have a new spell?"

I shake my head, still smiling.

Remy frowns. "Then what are you so happy about?"

I laugh. The Technocrats didn't remove my clothes or check for hidden pockets in their rush to bind me up in that awful suit. I reach for my hidden pocket and pull out the small key-shaped piece of black, glittering marble and hold it up. It warms at my touch and the magic inside it thrums beneath my fingers.

I may have puzzled over it before, but now the connection is so obvious that I'm grateful I've kept it with me since I found it, just in case.

Zandria gasps; Remy stares it down.

"It's a key for this door," I say.

"Where did you get that?" Zandria asks.

"After you disappeared, I went looking for help. I'd seen you go into a townhouse not far from the square one day, and I'd hoped your new friend would help. I had no idea at the time that it was Darian, but I found this when I searched his house."

"How do you know it will work?" Remy asks.

"You saw what they were doing. They've been working to find

a material that will hold the charge of our magic. Once while I was investigating the lab levels, I found a room with several bits and pieces of this strange marble, and wires were connected to some of them." I frown.

"You think this is what Darian is using to power the hearts?" Zandria says.

I close my eyes for a moment as the truth hits me. "That must be why Aro was down here in the tunnels in the first place. They just want the rock; they don't care what's inside it. Except for Darian. He would've known it was special in a heartbeat. He's probably the one who sent Aro down here looking for it in the first place." Zandria's face shifts from happiness to horror. "And remember that vein of marble we found as we escaped the Chambers, Remy? That was why Technocrats were so close to where the Magi live. They know it has powerful properties and they want to use it for their own ends."

"We have to stop them," Zandria says.

"We'll stop them from using the other Magi to power these unwillingly, but not today. We must find the library and then leave as fast as possible." The words scratched in blood and our parents' letter haunt my dreams. Finding the library is the only thing that will banish them. The only thing that will give me any sense of peace.

"Maybe we should just leave," Remy says.

"No. I didn't tell you this before. My parents . . . they . . . they charged me with finding the library. I can't leave Palinor without obeying their last wish."

Zandria recoils. "What?"

I grab her arm. "I'm so sorry. Once we're free, I will tell you everything, but we need to do this first."

Zandria absorbs this, her face contorting with grief. At first I'm afraid she's going to fall apart, have a classic Zandria fit and immediately demand answers. But she pushes down her pain. Just like I do.

My sister has changed so much. We both have.

I advance on the door that once frustrated us so thoroughly. What's behind it will change all our lives for the better. Or worse, depending on the answers we find.

I'm willing to bet Darian is planning to take the library for himself. He's appropriated the Armory's mission—and the Alchemist Alliance's—and twisted it. He's convinced himself his work is for the betterment of both our people, but really it's in the service of building his own power. He would take the spoils of our broken magic and lost lands for himself.

The spells and amulets and who knows what else hidden here are for all of the Magi to share. We're more powerful as a group than as a single person. Nearly losing Zandria taught me that beyond all doubt.

I tremble to think what could happen if that power fell into Darian's hands.

My breath catches when I try the key in the lock and it fits perfectly. I twist, half expecting it not to budge. But it turns smoothly, and the door opens with a satisfying click. The inside is all darkness.

"*Fiero*," I whisper, and Remy and Zandria follow suit. I step through the door first, holding up my palm.

What I find makes me want to burst into tears.

Not from the joy of finding our long-lost treasures, but from the sudden, unexpected horror of all my hopes crumbling to dust and ash. It takes several moments before I can find words.

"What happened? The outside of the room is perfect and untouched," Remy says.

I fall to my knees, the sharp sting driving home that this is real. I wish it were only a nightmare.

Debris surrounds us. Everything is a sickening gray, dust-coated color. Once-lovely marble pillars lay broken at odd angles on the floor. Shelves that must've been made from fine mahogany are burnt to a crisp or splintered into pieces. Cases and caskets that may have contained precious scrolls are shattered and strewn around the floor. Everywhere we look is destruction, destruction, destruction.

My chest aches.

We thought what was behind this door had been protected from the wars. That precious treasures lay safely behind it. There were nights when Zandy and I would stay up trying to guess what might be there, if it really was the library and what it might look like.

We never, ever dreamed of this.

I get back to my feet, trembling. Something terrible happened here. Then the survivors must have sealed it in. But why bother? My head spins as my heart pounds in my chest as though it is too much to keep beating anymore.

This can't be all that's left. We fought so hard to find this. "It isn't fair!" Zandria whispers hoarsely.

She kicks a stone tile on the floor. As she does, an idea sparks. The Alchemist Alliance was embedded deep in the Magi power structure. According to our parents' letter, they had access to the library. And a hidden room. "Zandria, remember how we first found the entrance to this section from the drainage tunnels?"

She brightens. "Of course," she says. "Aissa, you're a genius."

"What are you talking about?" Remy glances between the two of us.

"There's more here than meets the eye at first glance. Hidden complexities and layers."

Remy puzzles at every shadow and corner. "What are you seeing that I'm not?"

"There may be a hidden room," Zandria says.

"One that only we can find," I add. "Using our magic."

Remy's eyes widen. "So that's how you two excelled so quickly."

"It didn't hurt that we're naturally talented too," I say. "Now, let's see what we can find. Remy, look for any hint of a seam or doorway while we test the walls."

"But we could be here all night," Remy says.

"I was locked up because I was looking for this," Zandria says. "You expect us to leave it behind when we're so close to figuring it all out?" Her face turns red and blotchy.

Remy holds his hands up in front of him. "I'm not looking for a fight, you know that, Zandria. I just don't want to see all of us get caught again. We can't depend on Aissa's friend being able to save us a second time. Not after all the risks he took."

The thought of Aro stings. I have to leave him and Palinor behind if we want to live beyond sunrise.

"With three of us, we can cover more ground. If you find anything promising, let us know." I send Remy to the other side of the room. Then Zandria and I call up our magic and turn it on the walls.

The first time we did this in the drainage tunnels, we began by poking holes in the walls, then refilling as we went. Later on, we figured out how to probe the walls for hollow spaces without making a mess. Now we work together, starting in the middle and working outward, hoping to reveal a space beyond the bricks and stone. Remy scours the opposite walls for any hint of a doorway. We make it halfway through with no success before another idea lights under me.

"Hold on," I say. "What if we're going about this the wrong way?"

"What do you mean?" Zandria asks.

"We're looking to the side, but that's not how the entire complex above was built. The Technocrats built down—what if they got that from the ancient Magi?"

"How would they have done that? They hate the Magi."

I shake my head. "This is another thing I will explain later, but trust me when I tell you—the Technocrats come from the Magi. They *were* us, long ago."

"So you think there might be something below us?" Remy says as he approaches.

"Exactly."

We move to the very center of the room and examine it more thoroughly. There is a broken statue toppled over, leaving a dusty, charred panel behind. I place my hands on the panel, singing a spell to move it, when a soft click echoes in the chamber. Zandria and I exchange an eager look. The panel depresses into the stonework, revealing stairs leading down and a small chamber beneath. Hope sings in my chest as we tentatively walk down the narrow staircase and reach a landing.

No debris or wreckage here. It's untouched. A table lies in the center of the small room and on it are a couple books and a rolled sheet of parchment.

My heart races. Runes cover the walls, though I'm not sure what they mean. That's one of many reasons we need the library. We've lost so much of what makes us Magi that we don't even understand half of what our ancestors used to communicate and perform magic. And now I must find out more about the Alchemist Alliance. About the people who created us. What they did.

We walk over to the table and open the books. The first contains spells more powerful than any I have seen before, even more so than the ones I found in the books in the Palinor lab or the one Zandria got from Darian. Controlling the ocean and the moon, the path of the sun—any one of these things would be very dangerous in the wrong hands. It would be far too easy to use them for ill than for good.

The second book is an enigma. It's written in ancient runes—which we can't read very well—and is filled with loose pages and strange markings and notations.

We unroll the parchment next and a slip of paper falls out of it. I pick it up and read:

FOLLOW THE PAST TO THE FUTURE.

"It's a map. This must lead us to the real library. No wonder there are not many books here—they hid them somewhere else before the attack."

"Then it's not as lost as we suspected," Zandria says, eyes shining.

"No," Remy says, "only hidden away from all living memory."

I pocket the map and the smaller notebook, and Zandria clutches the book of spells to her chest.

"We need to get out of Palinor," I say.

"Then we'll find the real library," Zandria agrees.

We will follow these clues and find our lost magic spells and treasures if it's the last thing we do. Someday, we will be free and won't have to lie to everyone we love.

Someday, we will walk in the light and live a life crafted by our own hands.

But first we need to tear this place apart.

Above us, stones and debris move, the telltale sounds of guards on our trail. Zandria and I exchange a look. We stand back to back and pull Remy to our side so he stays safe. Zandria weaves her hands and I hum the spell. Our magic fizzes in the air around us, churning and rumbling. The walls vibrate with our combined powers and the foundation over our heads begins to move and reshape. The spell reaches a fever pitch. Stone and metal scrape together, screaming like a wounded animal, but we don't stop. We rebuild a portion of the structure over our heads, floor by floor, into one giant staircase, until we see daylight reaching through the street above us.

Then we let go. Zandria falls to her knees, but Remy and I help her up. We have a path to the topside. A crack in the city. We cover ourselves with the shield spell and climb our way to the top. It's the middle of the night, but a small crowd begins to gather in stunned silence, punctuated by the occasional wail.

Our secret is out; now everyone will know someone has the power to use magic on metal. But, safe in our shield, we ascend unnoticed. Then we walk among them, headed for freedom.

ACKNOWLEDGMENTS

TWIN DAGGERS HAS BEEN A LONG TIME IN THE MAKING. I BEGAN writing this book back in 2012, and it's been that book of my heart, the between-contracts-guilty-writing-pleasure ever since. In short, I adore this story, these characters, this fantasy world very much, and it's lived in my head for a very long time. I'm so grateful that this book will finally be out on bookshelves, and to all those who've had a hand in bringing it there.

First and foremost, thank you to my ever-patient super agent, Suzie Townsend, for waiting literally years for me to send her this manuscript that was "almost done, I swear" for far longer than I expected. And, of course, for loving it as much as I do and finding just the right home for it.

I'm so glad this book landed with Blink and my fantastic editor Hannah VanVels, under whose guidance Aissa and Zandria's journey took flight. You are an absolute delight to work with! And a big thank you to the entire team at Blink for making me and my weird little book feel so welcome, but especially Jacque Alberta, Annette Bourland, and Jennifer Hoff.

I must also thank the many critique partners who kindly read this manuscript in its early stages over the years and provided excellent feedback, including Sakura Eries, Michelle Hauck, Chris S., Eric J., Suja, Tracy Smith, Christina Busby, Amy Trueblood, and Amanda Panitch. Your insight and encouragement was, as always, invaluable.

And finally, my husband, Jason—thank you for helping me making this whole crazy writing gig work and bearing with me when deadlines are tight. You're the absolute best!

CONNECT WITH MARCYKATE CONNOLLY!

WEBSITE: www.marcykate.com

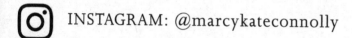 INSTAGRAM: @marcykateconnolly

TWITTER: @marcykate

FACEBOOK: @MarcyKateConnolly

GOODREADS: www.goodreads.com/marcykate

MARCYKATE CONNOLLY is a *New York Times* bestselling children's book author and nonprofit marketing professional living in New England with her family and a grumble of pugs. She can be lured out from her writing cave with the promise of caffeine and new books. *Twin Daggers* is her debut young adult novel, and she's also the author of several middle grade fantasy novels including *Monstrous* and *Ravenous*, and the Shadow Weaver series. You can visit her online at www.marcykate.com.